CHARITY

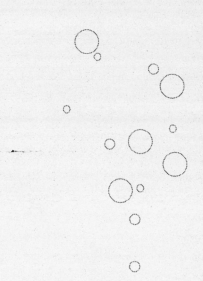

Fiona O'Brien lives in Dublin where she works as a freelance copywriter. *Charity* is her first novel and is in no way based on Dublin's hob-nobbing, fund-raising, designer-clad D4 set, of which she is not a part. She is currently writing her second novel.

CHARITY

FIONA O'BRIEN

**NEW
ISLAND**

Copyright © 2002 Fiona O'Brien

CHARITY
First published September 2002
by New Island Books
2 Brookside
Dundrum Road
Dublin 14

www.newisland.ie

This edition published 2003

The moral right of the author has been asserted.

isbn 1 904301 28 2

British Library Cataloguing in Publication Data.
A CIP catalogue record for this book is available
from the British Library.

Typeset by New Island
Cover design by Glen Saville
Printed in the UK by Cox & Wyman

10 9 8 7 6 5 4 3 2 1

For my late parents, Brian and Mary O'Brien,
a relentlessly stylish pair who weathered the vicissitudes
of Dublin 4, a challenging marriage, and not a
little tragedy, with elegance, fortitude, and bursts
of startling good humour. The show goes on!

Lornagh

The drive across town was taking forever. So much for bus lanes, Lornagh fumed. If she didn't make it home in the next 20 minutes she'd be in trouble. Even then she was cutting it fine.

Lawrence had promised to get back from the site early today, so with a bit of luck she might get him to listen to her do a final run-through of the speech. Thinking about the night ahead, it was hard to believe that it had all finally come together. No going back now. All the months of endless committee meetings, fundraising and frantic organisation were poised to culminate in what the press had promised would be the most glamorous ball of the year. They'd all be at the Anglesea tonight: the Beautiful People; the It girls;

the movers and shakers that made up Dublin's ever-glittering 'charity set'. 7.30 prompt for the champagne reception. And Lornagh would be there to greet them. That's if the godamn traffic would unsnarl itself. The balmy weather that Dublin had been enjoying was reflected in the leisurely, unhurried demeanour of its citizens, who were becoming so laid back as to be positively Mediterranean. Although it was nice to get a chance to put the roof down on her ancient little MGB and feel the wind in her hair and the flies in her teeth, it was bloody irritating if you were in a hurry. Craning her neck to peer as far as she could along the line of cars, Lornagh put her hand on the horn.

'What's your problem, babe? Relax.' The sweaty driver of a convertible BMW in the next lane leered across, giving her the benefit of a well-practised smile and revealing yellow teeth beneath fleshy lips.

'I'm in a hurry,' Lornagh said, smiling sweetly. 'Some of us have a life.'

The Leer wasn't impressed. 'Can't be much of a life, love, judging by that banger you're driving.'

Lornagh looked at him pityingly. 'The MGB is a classic and, speaking of cars, you might want to check your oil.'

'Nothin' wrong with this machine, babe,' he winked, patting his stomach.

'I was referring to your face. There are some very good

products on the market these days to deal with over-active sebaceous glands.' Lornagh knew she was on borrowed time. To her right, The Leer was working up to a slagging match. To her left, the bus lane beckoned. There was only one way forward.

Feeling a guilty rush of adrenaline as she pulled out and surged ahead, Lornagh reflected on her lamentable sense of timing. All her life, it seemed, she had either been too early or too late. Take her hair for starters. Only she could have screwed up the courage to go for a shaggy crop when only minutes later the sleek, straight-as-a-poker-to-your-shoulders look was the only style for any self-respecting tresses. Months of determined growing out now yielded a choppy, chin-length bob which, she told herself, was very 'Meg Ryan'. Her mother cheerily assured her she looked just like an Afghan hound. 'I do wish you would wear your hair *off* your face, Lornagh.' The constant refrain was uttered with exasperation. 'You've got my wonderful cheekbones: the least you could do is show them off.'

She was nearly there. Just a hundred yards or so and she'd be able to hang a left and head for Ballsbridge; maybe bus lanes weren't such a bad idea after all. Her timing didn't fail her. With just 20 yards to go, he stepped out. Appearing from nowhere from behind a parked car. Lornagh braked hard and pulled in.

'Do you realise you are in a bus lane?'

'Yes, guard. I'm very sorry, guard.'

Grovelling wasn't Lornagh's strong point, but she put on a hell of a show.

'Licence and insurance certificate please.'

Old Leery passed by and honked loudly in approval as Lornagh collected an on-the-spot fine and a lengthy caution.

After what seemed like an eternity, she pulled up outside Lawrence's house in Sandymount. To her relief, his bike was leaning nonchalantly against the red brick wall. Lornagh closed the roof of her car wearily and got out. She was greeted by a delicious aroma wafting from the general direction of the garden. Pushing open the side gate, she made her way round to the deck, where Lawrence was concentrated intently on the barbecue. He looked ridiculously handsome in faded jeans, his carefully cultivated six-pack covered only by his favourite cooking apron. He looked up as she joined him. 'Darling, you're looking frazzled. What on earth are they making you do in that place? I thought it was a charitable institution.'

'Don't ask.' Lornagh sat down and grabbed a breadstick to nibble.

'Bad day?' Lawrence raised an immaculately groomed brow.

'Let's just say, eventful. And I'm late for the ball.'

'Then upstairs with you immediately, Cinders,' Lawrence ordered. 'Your fairy godfather has taken care of everything. There's tons of hot water.'

'Brilliant. Oh shit, look at the time. And I need to perform serious surgery.'

'Nonsense. A quick hair wash, a slick of lipgloss and you'll be the proverbial belle. The natural look is in, so I'm reliably informed. Get a move on.'

Upstairs, Lornagh quickly shed her clothes and headed straight for the bathroom.

The steaming water from the power shower almost pinned her against the wall, but it was just what she needed. Bit by bit she could feel the day washing away and the knot of tension between her shoulders unwinding.

Feeling considerably more human, she pulled on her favourite towel robe and began to comb her wet hair.

Lawrence stuck his head around the door, depositing a welcome glass of bubbly on the dressing table. 'You looked like you could do with a bit of fizz. By the way, some man rang earlier, didn't catch the name, something about the painting?'

'Oh thanks,' Lornagh took a gulp of the champagne gratefully. 'That's a relief. It must have been one of the committee, they promised to let me know the painting had arrived safely at the hotel in time for the charity auction tonight.'

'Shame,' Lawrence remarked despondently, lounging against the wall. 'I was looking forward to having a rugged workman about the place for a few days!'

Lornagh grinned. She could always rely on Lawrence

to make her feel better. He was gay, much to the dismay of her female friends, and very definitely 'out of the closet'.

She had known him practically all her life and he was her dearest friend and confidant. He had whooped for joy when Lornagh had told him she was returning from New York and insisted she stay with him while her newly acquired apartment was being worked on. Lornagh was more than happy to avail of the offer which, she guessed correctly, had more to do with Lawrence's intuitive shrewdness than a need for company.

More to the point, it also meant she didn't have to stay with her mother. Lornagh found Angela's movie-star antics or histrionics, depending on the mood, unsettling at the best of times. Lawrence, more than anyone, was aware of that and, astonishingly, the only person on the planet who got consistently rave reviews from the revered, if eccentric, Mrs Lemass.

After years of hard work, Lawrence's career as an interior designer had finally taken off, and when he learned last week that he'd landed his own TV show, Lornagh – and a hundred or so of Lawrence's other close friends – had celebrated for a very liquid weekend. She still wasn't the better of it.

Grabbing her hairdryer, she flipped her hair over her head and let the hot air do its stuff. God knows, she'd been listening to enough of it for the last few weeks.

Forget her degree in social science: what Lornagh needed, she thought wryly, was a first-class degree in bullshit.

She tossed back her freshly dried hair and thought about the speech she had to make tonight at the ball on behalf of the charity. She'd written and rewritten it until every word reverberated in her head. It was short and to the point, interjecting just the right amount of levity without detracting from the seriousness of the cause that St Rita's Refuge for Women and Children represented.

Just then, the insistent ringing of the doorbell interrupted her thoughts.

Bloody hell! The taxi was here already. She hurriedly stepped into her dress and, grabbing her bag, ran for the door, almost spraining her ankle as she crashed into a startled Lawrence. 'Steady on, Cinderella!' Lawrence inspected her approvingly from top to toe. 'Absolutely divine. Now, remember! Deep breaths, meaningful pauses, and *project!* You'll knock their socks off!'

Lornagh hugged him. 'I wish you were coming with me.'

'I'd only upstage you! Anyhow Mauricio and I are escorting your mother and Lady Sheldon, or had you forgotten? I'll be there to cheer you on, don't worry. Just give the crowd a flash of that megawatt smile of yours and they'll be too dazed to notice anything else.'

Stooping to tighten her wayward evening sandal before it went the way of her teetering confidence, Lornagh missed the taxi driver's open-mouthed look of admiration as five feet ten inches of drop-dead gorgeousness planted itself precariously on his back seat.

'The Anglesea Hotel, please.'

'Er, righto.' The driver blinked disbelievingly in his mirror at the vision who was a dead ringer for that Cameron whassername in the movies.

'And could you hurry, please?' Lornagh was apologetic. 'I'm already late.'

He'd quite happily have driven to hell and back.

Simon

Simon was savouring the anticipation of the triumphant night ahead. It had all gone perfectly according to plan. In just a few hours, his life would be transformed. He would have Lornagh panting for him. Then, after she had grovelled for an acceptable amount of time, he would graciously take her back. She would, of course, be pathetically grateful. They always were. And, flush with the proceeds from the painting (he estimated a minimum of £500,000), he would finally have cash to flash. He would refer to it of course as his 'trust fund' and that would finally make that exclusive set she mixed with sit up and take notice.

They would marry after a whirlwind engagement (the ring had already cost him a bloody fortune, but Simon had been determined to get the biggest and the best; after all, it would reflect well on *him*). Anyway, it was an investment in his future, he reminded himself. Good PR. He had to appear to have sufficient funds. And that would shut up those bloody interfering busybodies who dared suggest he might have ulterior motives. His boss,

Michael Moriarty, had arranged a substantial loan, and more importantly directed him to a suitable society jeweller – or rather, *gemologist*, Simon mentally corrected himself.

The wedding, of course, would feature heavily in the society magazines. Simon knew Lornagh wasn't keen on publicity, but he'd talk her round. He had already planned the engagement photo spread. He would lounge nonchalantly, exuding gentrified style, on various antique sofas in Lornagh's mother's home in Grovesbury Road.

Then, he thought gratifyingly, he would finally live in the style he had always wanted to become accustomed to, thanks of course to Lornagh's inevitable inheritance.

He checked his reflection carefully in the mirror: it was imperative he looked the part. Running his hands confidently through meticulously maintained dark waves, he noted, with satisfaction, not a single grey in sight. Thank God he still had it. Having just turned 40 (35 if he was asked), he was grateful to have any hair at all. Plenty of his contemporaries hadn't been so lucky.

A pair of heavily lidded, big brown eyes peered back at him. They were his pride and joy. Mind you, he'd have to watch the drinking, it was beginning to take its toll. His eyes looked distinctly bleary and the broken veins on his face were definitely becoming more pronounced. He reached for the concealer and eye-drops he kept hidden behind his mirror. Not that there was anything *wrong* with men wearing make-up, it was really quite acceptable these days, but all the same, it wouldn't do for people to get the wrong impression. And impressions mattered *a lot* to Simon.

He reached under the bed to retrieve his well-thumbed copy of *Etiquette for Gentlemen* and turned quickly to the appropriate chapter. He could recite it backwards at this stage, but a quick brush up wouldn't go amiss. 'Gala Balls', 'Dinner Dances', 'How to Make an Entrance', 'Valet Parking', 'Addressing the Attendants', 'An Appropriate Tip', etc. Simon read intently, devouring every word. He despised people who didn't know *how to behave* . There was no social situation, no gathering for which he hadn't studiously prepared. He'd made a career of advancing himself socially from the moment he knew he was attractive to women. But tonight was important. Tonight the eyes of Dublin's *beau monde* would be upon him. Not to mention Lornagh Lemass. It was the perfect opportunity.

He took out his carefully pressed dinner jacket and trousers for inspection. They were perfect. His shirt was pristine, and would be set off marvellously by the beautiful onyx studs (a birthday gift from Lornagh).

It was time to get dressed.

He opened the chest of drawers, drew back the meticulously folded tissue paper, and inhaled the intoxicating aroma of expensive silk. Stroking the sensuous fabric, goose bumps appeared unbidden as he reverently pulled the underwear slowly up his legs. He sighed in ecstasy. There was nothing like it.

On went the black silk socks. The winged shirt and bow tie, expertly tied. Trousers next, and finally the dinner jacket.

He took a long, slow look in his full-length mirror, carefully assessing every detail. He looked good. Very good. It had all been worthwhile. He would never have to work again. His mother would be very proud. She was always saying there was no woman worthy of him. Anyway, women married for money all the time, and no one so much as raised an eyebrow.

Lornagh was different though. She wasn't just a looker. She had what was referred to as class. Breeding. There was an elusive elegance about her that he had never seen in any other woman.

He almost found it a turn on. *If only*. She really wasn't his type at all. Usually he went for the more obvious types. Preferably married, they were always bored and willing. No strings attached. And if they got too clingy, he just found another, single and hopeful. It always worked. Anyway, sooner or later they all turned out to be the same.

He immediately dismissed any troublesome thoughts from his mind. He had to remain focused, confident. The underwear did it for him every time. Made him feel comforted, in control. And since he had no intention of bringing anyone home tonight, his secret would be safe.

He strode out the door and into his leased Jaguar, a

tall, dark handsome figure in evening dress. And a pair of pink silk La Perla panties.

Melissa

The white Hiace van thundered down the N7 heading for Dublin.

Melissa hadn't had her suspension rattled so much since her courting days in Pascal's caravan.

Any minute now they'd be stopped for speeding, and that would be an interesting conversation, she mused, given the contents of the van.

She still wasn't the better of her ordeal. And it was far from over yet. In fact, she thought grimly, the best was yet to come.

She looked around to check on Dolce and Gabbana, her two highly strung pug dogs (named after her favourite designers). Both of them, to her horror, were blissfully asleep, curled up with Eddie's grisly pitbull in the back of the van.

Somehow, throughout the nightmare, they had become inseparable. The whole ghastly episode, Melissa thought, must have unhinged them. They had probably retreated to a past life. She would have to take them straight to her psychic animal healer the minute she got home.

That's if she ever did get home. It seemed quite a remote possibility at the moment. But she had to remain positive.

She sneaked a look at Eddie, mouth set as he sat behind the wheel, humming to himself. He still had it, damn him! Still exuded that dangerous sexuality. Unlike his bloody ogres of henchmen in the back. Melissa didn't know which was worse, their overpowering body odour, or the overpowering memories they brought back.

Sensing her scrutiny, the infamous crooked smile spread across Eddie's face as he turned towards her. 'Nearly there, pet, 20 minutes, at the most.'

'I've told you not to call me pet,' Melissa snapped, her nerves beginning to jangle. He always had that effect on her.

'Sorry. *Mrs* Sheehan.' Laughter was barely contained in the gravelly tones.

Melissa was about to reply but clamped her mouth shut. It was no use; it only encouraged him. And no matter what scathing remark she came up with, he always made her feel stupid. He knew too much. Anyway, it was nearly over. And then she'd never have to see him again.

She wondered how Pascal was coping. He never was very good under pressure.

She wouldn't think about it now. God knows, she'd find out soon enough.

And as for that bollix Michael Moriarty! He would

find out just who he was dealing with. To think he had thought he could toy with her *and* deceive her. Well, they had a little surprise planned for him that he wouldn't be counting on.

The sophisticated suburbs of Dublin 4 finally loomed ahead and Melissa nearly fainted with relief. As they passed the turn to Grovesbury Road and its imperious Tudor mansions, she thought longingly of her gorgeous designer dress, hanging unworn in her walk-in wardrobe. She almost laughed out loud. To think she'd been plucked, pummelled and pampered to within an inch of her life for the last six months in preparation for this ball tonight. What a joke! She rubbed her wrists tenderly – they were still smarting from the ropes – and inspected her manicured nails idly, as if they came from another world. And in a way they did. Amazingly they hadn't so much as chipped. And neither, she thought triumphantly, had she. Yet.

Forget designer ballgowns and blow-drys. The entrance she was going to make tonight would go down in ballroom history.

She checked her Cartier Tank Francaise. Bang on time. The Anglesea Hotel rose majestically in front of them.

'Right,' said Eddie grinning as they screeched to a stop before a startled doorman.

'Just tell us what way you want to play this.'

Melissa got out of the van mustering as much dignity

as she could, considering she was accompanied by four armed thugs.

She looked at Eddie and smiled. Some things never changed. He still found trouble as much of a turn on as ever.

She, on the other hand, had waited three mind-numbing, unending, terrifying days for this moment, and she was going to get her money's worth.

'Play, Eddie,' Melissa said firmly, 'wasn't quite what I had in mind.' She paused searching for the right words. 'I want you to frighten the shite out of him.'

Eddie smiled. He patted her super-suctioned bottom approvingly. 'Right then, lads! You heard the lady. Let's go!'

The lads duly lumbered into action.

As Melissa tottered close behind in her six-inch Manolos, a vice-like grip found her elbow. Eddie's smile never reached his eyes. 'Just remember, pet, you're not out of this yet, right? One false move an' we take things into our own hands.'

Melissa knew she should have been paralysed with fear. But for some strange reason her mind was playing tricks on her. She just kept praying that no society photographers would be hovering in the lobby.

She'd never live it down.

That's if she, and hers, ever got out of this alive.

Pascal

Pascal sat in his study, head in hands, the drained bottle of Paddy beside him a testimony to his wretchedness. He hadn't left the house since the first phone call.

For two nights now he had waited, tense and alert for any news. Silence echoed all around him. The vast house seeming to sense his anguish. Even the staff tiptoed around like mice. It was strange how empty it was without Melissa. He even missed those wretchedly spoilt dogs of hers. Pascal rubbed his weary eyes and paced the floor. If anything had happened to her he'd never forgive himself. It was all his fault. He had no one to blame but himself. If only he'd been there when it happened instead of her. He clenched his fists in anger just thinking about it. If they so much as laid a hand on her, they'd regret it. Regret the day they were bloody born.

Their wedding photo stared down at him from the marble overmantel. Melissa had wanted it retouched. After yearly cosmetic reconstruction, her appearance had evolved considerably; in fact she was barely recognisable. Their wedding photo, she felt, was unfavourable documentary evidence. But Pascal for once had put his foot down. He smiled ruefully, thinking of the early days. When they had been happy. They hadn't had much. But at least they'd had each other. But that was before everything had changed. Before he began to make serious money. Before Melissa had become more interested in climbing ladders that in Pascal's opinion would only lead to unhappiness and discontent. And the more money he made, the worse it got. No matter what he bought her, or where they lived, it was never good enough. They'd moved house so often on Melissa's whims that his head spun even thinking about it. Then they'd have to add the conservatory. The swimming pool. The gym. And then somewhere else would take her fancy. And it would start all over again.

He should have put a stop to it long ago, he knew he should, but somehow it had just seemed easier to keep her happy. Only it never seemed to last for long. They had finally ended up here in Grovesbury Road. And look where it had got them.

Pascal jumped as the door opened. Maria, their South American live-in housekeeper, tentatively popped her head around it. 'Meester Sheehan,' she was reproachful, 'you must eat sometheeng. Eet's not good for you to be like this.'

'It's all right, Maria, I couldn't eat a thing. I'm not hungry.'

'I leave this soup for you. It will keep you estrong in your troubles.'

Pascal smiled weakly. 'Thank you, Maria, that's very

kind.' She slipped quietly out of the room, shaking her head.

Pascal sipped the soup. It was warm and tasty. Maria was right. He couldn't afford to weaken now. Not when everything counted on him remaining calm and clearheaded.

He caught sight of his diary, sitting open on the antique leather desk. It was July 8th. The date of that wretched ball Melissa had got so wrapped up in. Well, they wouldn't be going now. That was for sure. He wondered bleakly if he would ever see her again. *Stop it, he warned himself. Be positive. It'll be all right. It has to be.*

The sound of the phone made him jump out of his skin. He took a deep breath and picked it up.

'Sheehan?' The rasping tones had Pascal's full attention.

'Yes,' he replied steadily. 'This is Pascal Sheehan.'

'I hope you haven't tried anything stupid. No tapping? No police? 'Cos you know what'll happen.'

'No.' Pascal's steady voice belied his intense anger. 'There are no other parties involved in this conversation, just as you instructed.'

'Good. Now listen carefully, Sheehan.' The voice continued. 'There's a certain gathering you and Melissa were planning to attend this evening. Am I correct?'

'The charity ball?' Pascal was flummoxed. 'What the hell has that got to do with anything?'

'Leave the questions to me.' The low tone was threatening. 'D'you want to deal or not?'

'Yes, yes, of course.'

'Good. Now there's a nice little designer number hanging in Melissa's wardrobe, you know the one?'

'Yes, I know.' Pascal grimaced. *It only cost £3,500 – how could I forget?*

'Right, then get yourself togged out in your monkey suit and bring Melissa's dress with you. We'll meet in Room 303 at the Anglesea at precisely 7 p.m. Got it? And Sheehan …' The voice was smiling, he could tell. The bastard was enjoying every minute of it.

'I'm listening.' Pascal's grip tightened on the phone.

'Don't try any funny stuff, you won't be doing Melissa any favours.' And with that the phone went dead.

Jesus! Pascal thought as the blood drained from his face. This was much worse than he had thought. They were obviously dealing with a raving lunatic. But there was *something*, yes definitely something familiar about that voice. It just didn't make sense. None of it did. Pascal was baffled.

He checked his watch. One hour. Just one hour to deliver the goods.

He got up to head for the bedroom and Melissa's vast wardrobe. Suddenly the flicker of a smile began to spread across his face. This was Pascal Sheehan these guys were dealing with. Not some mincing, mealy mouthed Southsider. He hadn't got to where he was without

21

picking up a few tips along the way. He hurried to his secret safe and, opening it, took out a small book. Flicking quickly through the pages he found the number he wanted. Better still, it was ringing. The voice on the end of the line was weak and rattly.

'Jacko?' Pascal waited, holding his breath.

Cackles of laughter rang down the line. 'Pascal Sheehan! Well, well! I didn't think I'd be hearing from you again in this lifetime!'

'Jacko,' Pascal spoke urgently. 'Look, there's no time to explain. I need a favour.'

'Name it, my good man!'

Carol

Carol dipped a perfectly pedicured toe into the froth of Chanel No 5 and shivered appreciatively. Perfect. The water was hot enough to be almost unendurable for five minutes; then it would be delicious. Baths, she thought to herself, were a bit like men: the really good ones made you suffer for a while. It was inevitable.

But hey, that was life for you. No pain, no gain. As far as Carol was concerned, you got the life you deserved. Or – in the case of most people – settled for. And now, after years of hard slog, she was finally claiming her reward.

No siree, suffering was not for her, much more fun to watch other people flounder.

And watch she did. The highs, the lows, the triumphs and the disasters which comprised the lives of the people from whom she made a living. And a very nice living it was, thank you very much! *Carol Calls* was the most avidly watched entertainment show in the country. A perfect example of an idea whose time has come. It was a lighthearted magazine-type slot launched by the nation's new television station, TV 2000, and it covered the latest social events and 'in' venues for the It girls to see and be seen at. It was Carol's brainchild, and she was justifiably proud of it, but presenting it was the real icing on the cake. It finally gave her the recognition and clout she knew she had always deserved. It had been hard-won success, but worth every grovelling, gruelling moment. She'd come a long way since her lowly start in trade journals. Now, she was Somebody. A woman to be reckoned with. The thought gave her an almost unnatural amount of pleasure. Not alone did she get to every hot event in the country but, more importantly for Carol, she had power. Real power. A feature in her programme could make or break a person's social standing, wreak havoc in marriages and ruin careers overnight.

'Serve them right,' she thought impatiently, soaping her voluptuous breasts. Most of the fawning little busybodies made her sick to her stomach. Tonight would be no different. 'Carol darling, over here! You look divine, Cari, come and sit here for a minute, I simply must tell you …'

And so it would continue, the beseeching glances, the veiled bribes, the ill-concealed longing for a mention, and sometimes she would oblige and sometimes not.

Carol sighed with pleasure and gave her imagination free rein, gleefully reliving her favourite fantasy. Oh yes, it involved flesh all right, just an ounce or two. In fact,

Carol's much indulged fantasy featured Ireland's most sought-after, high-profile gynaecologist. The one man who had ruined her life, or tried to. It may have been 18 years ago, but she felt the abandonment and rejection as acutely as if it were yesterday. And she was going to make him pay – if it was the last thing she ever did.

He might be riding on the crest of the wave now, fresh back from America with his list of degrees and his heiress fiancée with big teeth and bigger silicone boobs, but Carol had a revelation that would throw a spanner or two in *that* particular set of works. And it would be well worth the slow agonising wait she had been forced to endure.

It had taken a lot of work, a lot of research and a lot of patience. But then, Carol had learned to wait, to bide her time, to seize her moment. That's how she had gotten to where she was today. Timing was everything. And she had learnt a long time ago to rely on nobody but herself.

She wondered would he recognize her; after all, she'd changed completely from the mousy, timid young girl he'd left behind. She'd worked hard at that too. The nose job she'd treated herself to five years ago had more than paid its dividends, and the braces she'd resolutely worn in her twenties had provided her with a perfectly aligned smile. Even her personal trainer was impressed with her dedication. She'd never be stick-thin, but then, who wanted to be? Men preferred something to hold onto. But she'd lost two stone, toned up and shaped up, and developed a style that flattered her shape. That and the six-weekly strawberry-blonde highlights had done the trick. She was a regular little bombshell! She was witty too; men enjoyed her company, and she enjoyed toying with them, leading them on. It made her feel in control, paying them back for the years they had ignored her.

Stepping out of her sunken bath, she swathed her curvaceous figure in a plush towel, admiring her prettily feminine reflection in the mirror. Her mouth curved in a slow smile. Oh yes, Mr 'Goldfinger' Stevens was going to pay, and tonight's charity ball provided the perfect opportunity.

After all, Carol reflected, reaching for her tweezers, charity *does* begin at home.

Michael

Michael was packed.

The elegant Louis Vuitton case stood obediently by the front door. Funny to think it contained his life, or rather, his *new* life. Still, Michael mused, it was all he needed. That and the tickets. He patted his inside pocket confidently. Everything was in order.

Originally he hadn't planned on showing at the wretched charity ball, even though he was the chairperson. 'Supervisor of Funds', no less. What was it in aid of anyway? He could never remember. Something to do with single mothers or suchlike. What did it matter? As far as he was concerned they were all the same. Same faces, same venues, same auctions, same boring cardboard cut-out excuses of people. No wonder he was bored to death. No wonder he'd needed some excitement in his life.

He'd tried doing it all the right way. In fact, he had been exemplary. He'd made his parents proud. He'd justified the expensive education, done brilliantly at University College Dublin and gone on to become one of the country's top accountants. Not to mention man-about-town. Michael Moriarty was a name people recognised. As was his company, Romany Investments, which had been singularly successful.

He'd married the perfect girl, who'd gone on to become the perfect wife. They lived in a perfect house with four perfectly lovely children. Two boys and two girls. They were perfectly happy. And Michael was so bored he had to pinch himself to stay awake. He was only 42, for Christ's sake! At first he had put his restlessness down to the usual mid-life crisis. Except his had started at 29. Felicity, his beautiful and understanding wife, had no idea. He kept his thoughts on that score *very* much to himself. No point in rocking the boat. He'd tried everything to distract himself, even golf (that had made him feel about a hundred), but it was all too easy. Michael excelled at sports as much as he did in his career. He'd even gone to a therapist for a while, but that had been a bore as well. He didn't need to *talk* about himself. He needed to *live*. Feel the blood coursing through his veins again. Remember what an adrenaline rush felt like. And that's how it had all started.

Other women had always found him attractive. That was nothing new. And for a while the flings had, he acknowledged, added a *frisson* or two to his day. But eventually, they all became tedious. And that's when he'd move on. To something a little bit more exciting. A little closer to home. It wasn't enough to have an affair with a stranger, or an attractive colleague. Michael began to work his way slowly through his wife's friends, and then his friends' wives, the ever-decreasing circles finally tweaking his jaded sense of humour. Oh, if only they knew! The private phone numbers, the tantalising snippets of gossip, the *absolutely confidential* morsels. The so-called friends. Hah! Pay them a nanosecond of attention and flattery and they'd betray it all in a heartbeat. They were all idiots. Vain, egotistical, self-absorbed bores.

Except Melissa, he had to admit. She was something else altogether. Michael didn't know whether to be appalled by her or laugh at her. But he had to admit she amused him. The fact that she was the wife of his biggest client and business partner, not to mention next-door neighbour, only added to the attraction.

The trouble was, they had all turned out to be expensive. Melissa in particular. Sure he had done well for himself. You didn't do much better than Grovesbury Road, the most expensive address in Dublin's exclusive 'embassy belt', he thought wryly. But his outgoings had increased accordingly. And the kids! Hell! Did everything have to have a label on it these days? Whatever had happened to originality? And Felicity! It wasn't that she was demanding or anything, but he had to keep her in the style she was accustomed to. In fact, sometimes he wished she *would* be difficult. Keep him on his toes. But she just remained unnervingly efficient and smiling. He

29

shouldn't moan, he supposed, at least she kept herself busy with her successful au pair agency and those interminable courses of hers. She wasn't always under his feet and whining, like some wives he could think of.

Dipping into the client accounts had begun as a temporary solution to a temporary problem. After all, it was only *borrowing*. Moving things round for a bit until interest rates went up again and he could recoup on the investments. Only they weren't going up. They were going down. Steadily. Michael refused to panic. He did what he always did when things didn't turn out quite as he had expected (like the time he'd been caught cogging in his exams): he blithely carried on and put the annoying little incident right out of his mind. His therapist would no doubt have called it 'denial' or some such tidy term, Michael mused. But that was the trouble. Life wasn't tidy. It was unpredictable. Like him. And that's why he got on so well. He rolled with the punches. He understood 'the rules'. Heck! He *wrote* them!

He checked his watch. Simon would be coming by any minute with the papers. He'd better get the suitcase out of sight. Not that Simon would ask any questions. He was far too respectful. Not, as they say, a lateral thinker. In fact, Michael doubted he had any thoughts at all of his own. Which made him the perfect assistant. Simon was so impressed with Michael and his lifestyle, he followed any course of action he suggested without the merest glimmer of concern. Just as well, Michael thought as he checked his e-mail. If he had even the faintest idea of what was about to unfold he'd probably have a heart attack on the spot. Well, they were all in for a bit of a shock. It would do them good. Wake them all up from their self-induced comas of complacency. And he wouldn't be here to pick up the pieces. For once in their lives, they'd have to think for themselves, and fast. He took a last look around his plush office. The gas fire burned effusively under the elegant marble mantelpiece. Richly coloured walls were littered with various framed certificates and photographs of Michael with his celebrity clients. Most of them would be at the ball tonight. He smiled. He was glad he had decided to go along after all. He needed the distraction. And more to the point, the cheque for the charity funds would have final signature – and he would put it to much better use. £50,000 wasn't much in the scheme of things, but it would tide him over for the next few weeks until he could safely access his lovingly nurtured Swiss bank account.

Things had got a little out of hand this time, he had to admit.

The net was closing in.

But he, Michael Moriarty, was getting out.

CHAPTER ONE

'So, Lornagh, what do you think?' Sister Kay asked, as she swooped triumphantly into Lornagh's tiny office.

'It sounds too good to be true. Where's the catch?' Lornagh was as gobsmacked as everyone else on hearing the news.

'Of course it's not too good to be true!' Sister Kay's nostrils flared in disapproval. 'It's an answer to prayer. A miracle. That's what it is. They do still happen, you know. The trouble with you young people is you're all so sceptical.'

'I know, it takes years of practice, Sister Kay. Well, I have to admit it does provide the perfect solution to our problems; it's just, well, so unexpected.'

'That's what's so wonderful.' Sister Kay was beaming. 'An extremely generous offer for this dilapidated old place, relocation to a building designed to our own specifications, complete with new purpose-built housing for our mothers and children, not to mention a *leisure* centre, and the rest of the site developed for beautiful offices and apartments. Why, that nice Mr Sheehan is a saint.'

'Hmm.' Lornagh was noncommittal. 'He certainly does have to put up with a lot from *Mrs* Sheehan.' Lornagh was privy to regular updates from her mother who lived next door to the Sheehans.

'I don't know anything about that.' Sister Kay sniffed. 'As far as I'm aware she's a very charitable, hardworking woman. Isn't she the driving force on the committee for this wonderful ball they're organising on our behalf? And that reminds me, Lornagh, you'll have to put together a video and speech that reflects the work of the charity. You know, so everyone understands the importance and relevance of what they're contributing to.'

Lornagh had been waiting for that. As head of PR for St Rita's Refuge for Women and Children, it fell to her to organise the charity's involvement and representation in the fund-raising event, and she was dreading it.

'You know lots of people in the communications world, don't you?' Sister Kay was warming to her theme. 'Some of our mothers would do very well on video, you know, and I could talk for a bit, and we could even have a song or two ...'

Lornagh cut in hurriedly. 'It's all right, Sister Kay. I'll organise things – you needn't worry.' The last thing she needed, Lornagh thought, was Sister Kay pouring her effusive energies into orchestrating a well-meaning pop video of the charity. The very thought was enough to bring her out in a rash.

'Well, if you need any help, you know where I am ...'

Lornagh hid a smile. The coming months, she thought to herself, were going to call for a lot of diplomacy, starting tonight at the first meeting of the committee. Whether she liked it or not, Lornagh was involved, and heavily.

Coincidentally, Simon, her boyfriend, was also on the committee. His boss, Michael Moriarty, was the charity's financial advisor. As his 'right-hand man', Simon was involved in the raising and supervision of funds, and seemed only too glad of a chance to shine before his 'mentor', as he referred to Michael; but also, Lornagh suspected, to show off and ingratiate himself with the rest of the committee.

She surprised herself by this unexpected display of disloyalty. So what if Simon went overboard about things occasionally? He was kind, attentive, good-looking; and, she reassured herself, he bore no resemblance whatsoever to the philandering cads she had been attracted to in the past. That was all behind her now. Simon treated her well, and that was what mattered, wasn't it? She would just have to get used to it. She immediately silenced the little voice that had been niggling her lately and resolved to forge ahead with her new, sensible life, back home in Dublin.

'Hi, Simon! Good workout?' The receptionist at the health club threw a flirtatious look in his direction as he was leaving.

'Yeah! Great!' Simon smiled, giving her an appreciative

once-over. Small, brunette, good little body and way too much make-up. She'd be a right little raver, he'd bet. He must take her for a drink one of these days; it was always good to keep up to date on who was playing at what and with whom.

Are you married or do you workout at Bayside? went the well-known quip. The upmarket fitness centre was a notorious hot spot for extra-curricular fitness programmes. The membership cost was not for the weak of wallet, but the rewards were well worth it. Anyone worth his or her salt in the city was a member. Simon prided himself on being a member of as many clubs in Dublin as he could manage to join. After all, he was a gentleman; and it had cost his parents a lot of money. The minor public school they had sent him to in England had eaten up most of their life's savings, and they very much expected a return on their investment. Particularly his domineering Spanish mother, Louisa, who had married his mild-mannered Anglo-Irish father assuming he would inherit the family estate in Meath. Discovering it was already owned by the bank by the time of Simon's grandfather's demise, they had immediately moved to Dublin, where Louisa vowed that her beloved only son would restore the family to its rightful honour, no expense spared. Simon had been packed off to school in England with strict instructions to 'do well' and forge connections with as many suitable friends as possible. He had excelled at the former, and failed miserably at the latter. Considered 'not quite one of us' by his English classmates, he was made pitiful fun of, and promptly nick-named Paddy Dago. Back home in Dublin, he didn't fare much better. In the all-too-long summer holidays, he took refuge in his mother's cooking and her reassurance that he was from 'too good a family' to mix with the local crowd. As a result, Simon's weight ballooned, as did his overwhelming sense of resentment. By the time he hit Trinity, the only thing that kept him warm at night was his surplus flesh. It was only when his finals were rapidly approaching – accompanied by vivid premonitions of his mother's predictably contemptuous reaction to anything less than a first-class honours degree – that Simon managed to stay at his studies long enough to forgo the guilty trips to Bewley's, where he used to regularly stave off his hunger pangs. That, and meagre funds dictating a healthy walk to and from college rather than taking up two seats on the 46A, resulted in a most gratifying, if unexpected, weight loss. Simon didn't need much encouragement. He immediately joined the local gym and became addicted to working on the emerging body beautiful. By the time of his conferring, nobody recognized the tall, dark, Antonio Banderas lookalike. From then on, the women flocked around him in droves. But no relationship lasted longer than a few months. It was more than just the simple matter of making up for lost time: Simon Sullivan discovered that, just as he'd always suspected, sooner or later all women were controlling bitches, just like his darling mother. No wonder he felt at home in his club; at least you only had to pay to belong.

It was, in fact, at one of these, the Royal Irish Yacht Club, that he had met Lornagh.

He had spotted her having dinner with a group of people and had immediately recognised the tall, slender blonde with the bewitching smile. Luckily, he had known one of the guys at the table, and, when dinner was finished, he had wandered over to say hello and wangle an introduction. After loitering meaningfully, he had been asked to join them for a drink, and his flawlessly thought-out pick-up plan had been put into action, without so much as a chat-up line being uttered.

Simon had been attentive and chatty, and Lornagh reserved. Having just returned after five years in New York, she was reassuringly out of touch with the Dublin scene, which suited Simon perfectly. He had done his research meticulously, and it had paid off. Not suspecting for one moment that Simon knew almost more about her than she did herself, Lornagh found him charming, and they had been an item for the last three months. And Lornagh, he thought to himself, had been quite a revelation.

Tall and blonde, with a lively intellect, she posed an intimidating prospect for most men. But then Simon was definitely *not* most men.

Closer inspection, had he cared to employ it, would

have revealed a healthy disrespect for convention which, along with her offbeat sense of humour, was what her friends loved most. This escaped Simon altogether. And he certainly hadn't counted on her surprisingly passionate nature. Simon was rather disappointed about that. He had presumed the physical side of their relationship would be brisk and perfunctory. And he was having to put on a suitably convincing performance. It was becoming a drag. He hoped desperately his 'little problem' wouldn't resurface. It would ruin everything.

The last girl he'd been involved with had ended up with severe depression and a hefty bill for counselling. Of course he had encouraged her to think it was all her fault. And it was, really, Simon rationalised to himself. If 'society' kept expecting him to have an attractive woman on his arm, it wasn't his fault.

He thought instead about what he would wear tonight to the first meeting of the committee. It was a marvellous opportunity to impress Michael Moriarty and of course to make connections with the *right* sort of people. They were all movers and shakers, and most of them were loaded. Lornagh had said she'd meet him there, which was intensely irritating. He'd relished the thought of them arriving together and making a grand entrance. It would have enhanced his credibility no end. Oh well, it was only a matter of time. And things, Simon thought smugly, were running perfectly according to schedule. If he hurried, he'd just make his sun-bed appointment.

Shit! Shit! Shit! She'd put on a whole pound! Bleedin' diets! They were all a load of ... what was that new expression she'd been taught recently... codology? Or was it poppycock? She could never remember. Her elocution teacher had been desperately trying to expand Melissa's vocabulary without any great success. It took all Melissa's steely determination to persist with the silly old bat. But she'd read recently that a well-rounded voice was an integral part of the sexual weaponry of the true seductress. And Melissa collected weapons the way other women collected accessories. Besides, she was sure she had noticed Felicity Moriarty and her snooty friend sniggering at her the other day at lunch when she'd botched the menu pronunciation. She'd bloody show them. If she could extend her nails, she could extend her vowels and finish her consonants, whatever *they* were. By the time Melissa was through, she'd be braying with the best of them, stupid asses that they were!

She may have started her life in Dublin's inner city, but Melissa was determined to eradicate any lingering evidence of her background, and what Melissa wanted, Melissa went after. She'd even got rid of her horrible cellulite! And everyone had told her *that* was impossible. Financially, it had taken what most people would regard

39

as a substantial mortgage. Physically, it had required practically a whole body transplant. But she had done it.

Anyway, Pascal had more money than the lot of them put together. The thought never failed to generate a warm glow in the mercenary depths of her being. The Felicitys of this world might have their airs and graces, and their carefully cultured tones, but money was the only language that spoke in the Dublin of the 21st century – *everyone* knew that. Theirs might be 'newer' than most, but it worked just as efficiently. And anyway, Melissa didn't see the point in being subtle. What was the good in having tons of money if you couldn't flaunt it?

'Mareeeya!' Melissa shrieked into the intercom system for her housekeeper.

'Yes, Mrs Sheehan?'

'Where's the hairdresser? Wasn't she supposed to be here at 9.30?' Melissa's 'every other day' home hair appointment was the crucial start to her morning.

'She's stuck in traffic, Mrs Sheehan. She just rang to say she's running about ten minutes late.'

'Humph.' Melissa was not impressed. 'Bring Dolce and Gabbana up to me will you? Then you can take them for a little walk. And tell Matt I want the car outside at 11.'

Running late! Who did she think she was? When hairdressers started talking like feckin' surgeons things were going too far. She was probably hung over. Well, she'd better not be. Melissa needed her blow-dry to be particularly effective today. The first meeting of the committee was this evening, and she was going to give her extremely attractive next-door neighbour Michael Moriarty a full blast of her newly acquired sophisticated sex appeal.

Any sign of trembling hands from her hairdresser would not be appreciated. The only trembling Melissa tolerated was when she herself was the direct cause of it.

Pascal was not having a good day. It had started badly and was deteriorating by the hour. For starters, Melissa had discovered the secret stash of *Caravan Connoisseur* magazines he had so carefully hidden in his study, and he duly had to listen to half an hour of hysterical ranting about how 'common' they were. Pascal could never understand her aversion to them. He had made his fortune from caravans in the early days and Melissa had been only too happy to show an interest in them *then*. In fact, he recalled, she had been positively enthusiastic. Now the only touring she did was in her Mercedes Sports. Pascal bought her a new one every year. He sighed, scratching his head wearily. Those were the days when life had been simple, or so it seemed at any rate. How on earth had things gotten so out of hand?

And now, to make things worse, she was dragging him along to this diabolical committee meeting of hers tonight. No wonder he felt miserable. A room full of toffee-nosed socialites who only tolerated Pascal for his immense wealth. Melissa, of course, was too stupid to see it. Having remorselessly clawed her way up the social ladder for the twenty-odd years since she had married Pascal, she really thought they had 'arrived' at last. Pascal knew better. He scratched his head mournfully – the new hair transplant Melissa had insisted he get earlier in the year had never settled down and his scalp itched unbearably. It was too bad.

The only glimmer of hope left was the slim chance that he could get away early this evening and slip off to meet Eva. The very thought of it made him feel better already.

Suddenly the patter of tiny feet and familiar snuffling noises rudely interrupted his reverie. Pascal and Melissa did not have any children, much to his regret. Melissa, instead, focused all her affection on her two overbred and neurotic pugs who were, according to her, 'the only really *aristocratic* dogs', and whom she fondly referred to as 'my babies'. They followed her everywhere she went, announcing themselves as they did now with much snuffling and sneezing, due undoubtedly in this instance to the unmistakably overpowering scent of Melissa's current perfume. She rounded on Pascal with a shriek.

'For feck's sake! You're not seriously wearing *that?*' Melissa's high-pitched tone was heavy with contempt.

Pascal sighed. Try as he might, with all his money and access to the best tailors in London's Saville Row – and despite Melissa's most rigorous attempts with personal shoppers – he always managed to look unkempt and uncomfortable. He had come to accept it long ago. Melissa never had.

'I thought this was the one you liked,' he said lamely, stroking the expensive navy-blue silk suit nervously.

'Oh, it'll have to do,' snapped Melissa, tossing poker-straight tresses impatiently.

'Come on, will you, we'll be late.' Her spiky heels clacked menacingly on the Italian marble floor as she swept ahead through the hall and towards the waiting Bentley.

'Good evening, Mrs Sheehan.' Matt, their chauffeur, was as solicitous as ever, holding the door.

'Don't you think we should drive ourselves, pet?' Pascal attempted faintly.

'Are you *determined* to be a gobshite?' Melissa hissed at him under her breath. 'Don't you know *anything* about making an entrance? And Pascal,' she added meaningfully, 'do not, I mean don't even *think* of mentioning caravans to *anyone* here tonight, do you hear me? We've come a long way since feckin' caravans.'

Pascal nodded miserably. His head was starting to pound and itch at the same time. How was he ever going to get through the night?

Carol was deeply immersed in research for her upcoming TV slot when the phone call came. There was nothing unusual to be observed in her demeanour as she took the call, not a flinch, not a smile, not one flicker of her face betrayed her intense emotions as she listened quietly, replied in non-specific monosyllables and, with only the slightest of tremors, replaced the handset. So he was finally home.

The rest of the afternoon passed in a surreal daze. She perused scripts, dictated sound-bites, and to all intents and purposes was her usual, relentlessly efficient self. The only vaguely uncharacteristic action she took was to send her PA. home early at five o'clock so she could have the office to herself. She had to think, had to keep calm. It had been a long wait, but now the real work could begin.

She quickly closed the door and sat down at her computer. Tapping in the appropriate information, she leaned back in her chair and waited. In a matter of seconds, the face that invaded her nights and possessed her days for the last 18 years appeared in bold, glorious technicolour before her very eyes. It almost took her breath away. So the bastard had his own web site, did he? Mistake number one, thought Carol as she hungrily began to devour every word in every sentence that described in gushing terms the great Dr Gerald Stevens, gynaecologist to the stars.

'Now Carol, don't be silly, there's nothing to worry about.' Carol's mother had been brusque and tight-lipped about the trip to the doctor. She came from a long line of women who believed discussions and explanations about 'women's troubles' should be reserved for the surgery. Anything else was

simply too awful to contemplate. The GP had been quite definite that Carol's 'problem' was not in his territory, and had referred mother and daughter to a gynaecologist. Carol, being a particularly sheltered 16-year-old country girl, had no idea what was in store for her. And her mother was not about to offer enlightenment. She marched her daughter into the consulting rooms a few days later, and relinquished all responsibility for the impending examination along with her GP's referral letter.

'Dr Stevens will see you now, he's our locum for the week while Dr Murphy's away.' The doctor's secretary smiled primly.

Carol would never forget the first moment she saw him. He was quite simply the most gorgeous man her impressionable eyes had ever beheld. He had been kind too, and reassuring, putting her gently at ease when she comprehended the mortifying horror that the peculiar stirrups and chair had in store for her. Afterwards, she had been so consumed with embarrassment she was unable to raise her eyes from the floor. Nothing in her wildest dreams had prepared her for the ordeal.

'Now, there we are, young lady! That wasn't so terrible, was it?' He had smiled, his warm eyes twinkling. 'Come back and see me in a week or so, and we'll make sure everything's back to normal.'

And so began the interlude in Carol's life that would colour her opinion of all men in the years to come and which she would refer to in her journal as the Ultimate Betrayal.

The invidious bleeping of her e-mail facility brought her back to the present and the ever-darkening evening. Quickly closing down the web site she checked her message. It was from Jimmy, an old colleague from her newspaper days.

'C U 4 a drink (or 3!) at the Anglesea. Press reception to announce details of the charity ball to end all charity balls. U will be there I assume???'

Carol groaned; she had clean forgotten all about it. Rooting out the invitation from the pile on her desk she looked over it quickly, double-checking if showing up was worth her valuable time. Suddenly her eye caught a name on the committee list and she gasped. New committee member and medical consultant to St Rita's Refuge for Women and Children was no other than Dr Gerald R Stevens.

Michael Moriarty arrived at the Anglesea Hotel a respectable ten minutes ahead of time and was directed by the attractive receptionist to one of the many private function rooms.

Simon, his assistant, was predictably there ahead of him, shuffling papers and setting out pencils and notepads for twelve committee members. By seven o'clock, almost everyone was there and a lively murmur of conversation filled the room. A discreet waiter filled glasses with red or white wine as people chatted amiably about the miserable weather and swapped Christmas horror stories.

Michael cleared his throat and tapped the wineglass on the table in front of him to call the room to silence. With a bit of luck, he'd get the committee meeting over with reasonably quickly and then escape, leaving Simon to tidy up the loose ends. The thought of staying on for the drinks reception following the meeting, to announce details of the ball to the press, definitely did not appeal. Besides, he had a pressing engagement with an extremely attractive Polish accountant who had been brought in to help with the overload in the office for the last three weeks, and she gave a new meaning to the term 'reappraising one's assets'.

'Ladies and gentlemen! Fellow committee members! Your attention please!' Michael's resonant tones cut through the idle chatter. People eagerly took their seats and settled down, looking forward to what they hoped would be a quick briefing before they got down to the *real* business at hand: seeing, being seen, engaging in crucial conversation with the right people and throwing back a few glasses of free wine.

Most of the people there only knew the 'public' Michael Moriarty, and so were unprepared for the subtle change that occurred as the easy pleasantries he exchanged gave way to a brisk, business-like approach, and his legendary charisma began to spread through the room until it became an almost tangible energy.

One by one Michael astutely sized up the committee members. And before long, even the most indolent and ineffectual among them were volunteering to tasks that just a few moments earlier would have had them fleeing the room.

Pascal Sheehan hid a smile as his eyes met Michael's briefly across the table. Pascal was well aware of the effect Michael had on people. Men, women and children alike found him irresistibly charming, dogs crossed the street to be patted by him, and Pascal never tired of watching him in action. In fact, it was because of Pascal that Michael had agreed to be involved in the charity at all. Pascal's pushy wife Melissa had been pestering him for a suitable chairperson; Pascal had, in turn, pleaded with Michael; and, although Michael had sworn he would never again get dragged into the thankless task that was 'charity fund raising', he couldn't afford to refuse Pascal. After all, Pascal was his biggest client and, more recently, his business partner in Tiger Investments. And, of course, Pascal had been right. Nobody did it like Michael.

Only he could persuade you to give up precious time, donate a family heirloom or raise buttock-clenching amounts of money and make you feel as if a rare honour had been bestowed upon you. It was that very ability that had made him such a barracuda in the boardroom. Michael could fleece people in one fell swoop and leave them smiling indulgently behind him.

'Now, about this auction ...' Michael was interrupted as the door of the room opened and a stunning blonde girl hurried in, followed by a strikingly handsome man with shoulder-length dark hair, sporting a rather flamboyant outfit of leather trousers and fashionable sheepskin coat. What was remarkable, Michael noticed, was that he managed to carry it off. Anyone else would have looked ridiculous.

'I'm so sorry we're late,' the girl apologised profusely as she took her place at the table beside Simon who, Michael noticed, had neglected to rise from his seat as he usually did when a woman entered the room. In fact, Simon had a face like thunder and was pretending to be absorbed in his notes, surreptitiously snapping his braces. Michael immediately recognised the familiar indication that Simon's stress levels were shooting through the roof; it was always a bad sign when the brace-snapping started.

'Lornagh!' Melissa, who had been staring at Michael with ill-disguised lust, was momentarily distracted by the arrival of the glamorous couple and greeted the girl excitedly in her newly acquired Dublin 4 accent. 'How nayce to see you, Lornagh dear! Ay hardly recognized you! Everyone, this is Lornagh Lemass!'

Lornagh smiled back at the unabashedly curious faces around the table and introduced her companion. 'Hello, Melissa. Sorry we're late, everyone. This is my friend, Lawrence Fitzgerald, who has kindly agreed to join us.'

'And a very great honour it is!' added Lawrence, bowing theatrically as he pulled up a chair on Lornagh's other side.

Lawrence, it was obvious to Michael, was extremely camp.

But that didn't stop Simon looking as if he could happily stick an axe in the man's head at that very moment, Michael noted with interest.

So this was Lornagh Lemass, the famous prodigal daughter of Grovesbury Road! What on earth was she doing going out with Simon? Michael wondered. And for how long would she remain unaware of his conflicted personality? Not to mention his past. Neither of which bothered Michael in the least. When someone had something to hide he could be enormously helpful, if just a little bit of pressure were applied. And Michael knew better than most where and when to apply it. But clearly this girl was bright, and definitely sexy. No, Simon, despite his best attempts, couldn't hope to last for long. But it would be terrific fun watching him tying himself in knots while he did.

He would stay for a quick drink or two after all, thought Michael, as he wrapped the meeting up swiftly.

CHAPTER TWO

After a long day at St Rita's, Lornagh was pulling up outside her mother's house in Grovesbury Road. It was Angela's birthday, and Lornagh was taking her out to dinner. Thinking about it, Lornagh wasn't even sure what age Angela was this year, and her mother certainly wasn't telling. 'Age is only a number, Lornagh, and birthdays serve only to celebrate how wonderful one looks.'

Standing on the steps of the large, decaying house that had been her home, Lornagh took a deep breath and rang the doorbell. Having a gin-loving, chain-smoking, retired movie star for a mother wasn't always what it was cracked up to be.

Mary, the old housekeeper who had spent most of her adult life with Lornagh's mother, answered the door and peered out suspiciously. Because of the extra inches it afforded her, the high, elaborately back-combed beehive she had graduated to in the '60s, and stuck to ever since, threatened to topple her over at any minute.

'Hi, Mary!' Lornagh bent to kiss the little woman, who chirped with pleasure to see her. 'We're inside.' Mary nodded conspiratorially towards the little room off the magnificent but faded drawing room, where her mother alternately watched TV and speculated on the general state of modern Dublin, comparing it most unfavourably to her heyday in the '50s.

'Hi, Mum.' Lornagh walked through the once tastefully furnished room where magnificent antiques slumbered peacefully under deep layers of dust. Angela, used to relying on 'staff' all her life, refused to acknowledge that the large house was now well beyond Mary's erratic attempts at housekeeping. Instead, she preferred to live in decaying grandeur with her adoring former seamstress from her modelling and acting days, who was equally happy to indulge in remembering the good old days through a haze of alcohol.

She was struck, as always, by her mother's astounding beauty. In repose, Angela Lemass's face retained the extraordinary serenity that was still spoken of with awe throughout Ireland, where red-blooded men wistfully recounted a brief meeting or chance encounter that remained forever engraved on their memories.

Angela reclined gracefully on her favourite chaise-longue and proffered a smooth cheek for her daughter to kiss. 'Darling! You're just in time. We're having a little drink to get us in the mood. Mary!'

'Yes, Mrs L?'

'Fix Lornagh a gin and tonic, would you?'

'Coming right up!' Angela and Mary regularly slipped

into American parlance – a hangover from the 'Hollywood Years'.

'Mum,' Lornagh protested, 'the table's booked for half past, we really should get going.'

'Relax, Lornagh. We've plenty of time for another teensy one, haven't we, Mary?'

'Oh yes, indeed, Mrs L – just the one, mind.'

Lornagh knew when she was outnumbered. 'Fine, I'll go and ring for the taxi.'

'We're so looking forward to a nice evening out, aren't we, Mary?' Angela said, looking fondly at Lornagh as she came back into the room.

Lornagh smiled, taking in the flamboyant Balenciaga kaftan in which Angela somehow managed to look elegant even though it had been considered over the top in 1963 when it had first seen the light of day.

'Wow! Those flowers are amazing.' Lornagh had just noticed the magnificent arrangement of at least three dozen white roses. 'Who are they from?'

'Aren't they something! Kirk sent them all the way from Los Angeles. Isn't he a sweetie? All these years and he still remembers.' Angela sighed. 'All those movies we did together, why it seems like only yesterday.' At sixty-odd years of age, Angela had lost none of the renowned sense of drama that had, in another lifetime, brought her fame and adulation. 'Where's Lawrence? Isn't he joining us?'

'He's on a job in London. He sends his love and says he'll report to you post-haste upon return.'

Angela adored Lawrence who, when he visited, was more than happy to engage in ardent discussions about fashion, gossip and, more importantly, to listen to Angela reminisce about her halcyon modelling days when she had been one of Balenciaga's revered muses.

Angela lit a cigarette and inhaled deeply. 'What was I saying? Oh yes, Lawrence! How is the darling boy? I do wish you two would stop the pussyfooting and get it together.' Angela was determined to launch into her romantic fantasy of the moment.

'Mum, Lawrence is gay.' Lornagh yawned. 'I've told you a thousand times.'

'Piffle.' Angela exhaled emphatically. 'It's only a matter of meeting the right girl, and you know he adores you.'

'Not in that way!' Lornagh was worn out with the recent alarming train of thought her mother was pursuing. 'Mum, Lawrence may be between partners at the moment, but he is very definitely gay.'

'Oh, for heaven's sake, Lornagh, don't be so dramatic! Lots of men go through a phase when they're … they're experimenting.' Angela waved dismissively. 'It doesn't *mean* anything. And you make such an adorable couple. So … so *sophisticated!*'

'Mum.' Lornagh was firm. 'Lawrence is gay, and I happen to be seeing somebody anyway.'

'Seeing somebody.' Angela made a face. 'Why can't you young people do what young people are *meant* to do

– instead of sitting around watching each other, *so* boring. In my day, at least we had fun! Who is he anyway, this man?' Just then the taxi arrived. Saved by the bell, thought Lornagh with relief.

'Come on, Mum, Mary, we'll be late.'

'Don't be silly, Lornagh – they'll never give away a reservation if they know I'm coming. You did *say*, I assume?'

'Naturally. I imagine they're on full alert. Now come *on*.'

'I do wish you'd stop rushing everybody, Lornagh. No wonder you're looking haggard.'

Fifteen minutes later, Lornagh paid the taxi driver and followed Angela and Mary into the Shelbourne Hotel on St Stephen's Green. Angela favoured the elegant main dining room, preferring it to any of the of the trendy new restaurants that abounded in the city. 'There's nowhere *left* to go anymore, is there, Mary?' she would sigh. 'Jammet's, the Russell, even the Hibernian.' She fondly recounted all her favourite '50s haunts. 'They're all gone.'

They made an arresting trio: Lornagh with her tall, blonde good looks; Angela in full 'Hollywood' mode, complete with ankle-length mink and cigarette holder; and Mary, all of four feet eleven, including her beehive, in an artfully altered couture cast-off of Angela's.

'What about a little peek into the Horseshoe?' Angela

said, hearing the lively noise level emanating from the hotel's famous bar.

'No way, Mum, our table's ready and we're already late.' Lornagh knew that it would be the end of dinner if Angela made it into the Horseshoe Bar.

'Oh all right, all right. You're such a bossy boots, Lornagh. It is *my* birthday after all.'

Seated at last at her favourite window table, Angela finally settled. Lornagh breathed a sigh of relief. Champagne was ordered immediately and Angela preened as a few elderly diners recognised her and looked suitably awestruck.

'So, Lornagh, this new man of yours, do I know him? Or his family?' Angela asked brightly.

'I doubt it.'

'Well, don't keep us in suspense. Who is he? What does he do?'

'His name's Simon Sullivan and he's an accountant.' Lornagh immediately regretted relinquishing the information.

Angela looked at Mary with raised eyebrows. 'Well, surprise, surprise! A Mr Boring to join the ranks of Mr Stingy, Mr Unavailable and Mr Married. Really, Lornagh, you'll have to develop more imagination than that. You must have *some* of my blood. You need a Real Man. At least that married chap in New York sounded vaguely interesting, even if he was a weakling.' Angela was warming to one of her favourite themes: Lornagh's hopeless choice in men.

'Mum, please! Not tonight. We're having fun.'

'I'm beginning to think *you've* forgotten how. You need to lighten up, Lornagh, flirt a bit, and meet some entertaining people. Lawrence thinks so, too.'

'Mum, you haven't looked at the wine list. What do you fancy?' Lornagh changed the subject deftly, making a mental note to talk to Lawrence upon his return.

'I don't need to. I'll have the lamb, accompanied by my favourite Chateau La Fite Rothschild 1967. What a year that was! Remember, Mary?'

'Oh, indeed I do, Mrs L.'

'That was the year *you* were conceived, Lornagh.'

'As if I could forget.' Lornagh could feel herself blushing.

'Where are they all now, Mary? So many dead and gone,' Angela said, misty-eyed.

Dinner proved to be a great success. The food was wonderful, and Angela was made a suitable fuss of by the waiters, as she eagerly engaged in trips down memory lane with the few elderly members of staff who remembered her.

Afterwards, Lornagh dropped Angela and Mary off, declining the nightcap that was enthusiastically offered.

Alone in the taxi on her way back to Lawrence's, Lornagh wondered fleetingly if maybe her mother was right. Was she really turning into a head prefect? Well, someone in this family has to be responsible, she thought. She'd had her flings, done all the 'single girl' bit, and look where it had got her.

Initially, New York had been a blissful escape for Lornagh. Growing up in Dublin the daughter of a famous movie star had its drawbacks.

Angela Delacey, as she was then, had been a highly successful model in the '50s, so much so that London, then Europe, had clamoured for her.

It wasn't long before the inevitable screen test followed, then the move to Hollywood, where Angela's distinctive looks and colouring resulted in her becoming the darling of the studios. Famous for her beautifully pale skin, burnished copper-coloured hair, slanting green eyes and an air of natural reserve, she was a breath of fresh air compared to the usual jaded Hollywood starlets. Many publicly acclaimed movies later, along with multitudinous affairs with her leading men – 'they all fell for me, darling' – she gave it all up, as was the fashion in those days, to marry the most persistent of her many suitors, the immensely wealthy and aristocratic Maxwell Lemass, and returned home to settle in her native Dublin.

Lornagh often wondered whether Angela had married Maxwell because he adored her small daughter Lornagh as much as he did Lornagh's mother. At the time, being a single mother was still frowned upon; although Angela, surprised and delighted to find herself pregnant in her mid-thirties, flouted convention at every opportunity, proudly introducing the young Lornagh as 'my love child'. She never revealed who Lornagh's father was, simply because she claimed she didn't know: 'Much more fun to speculate, darling! Anyhow they were all gorgeous …'

Maxwell's choice of bride had not been popular with his aristocratic family, but he had worshipped Angela, and the marriage had been happy; and Lornagh had gained a doting and indulgent father figure. When Maxwell Lemass died suddenly thirteen years later, any hope of stability for Lornagh died with him. She was just fifteen.

Lornagh spent the following years throwing herself into her studies, and was rewarded by a first-class honours degree in Social Science and English from University College Dublin and a congratulatory phone call from her mother who missed her conferring because she was 'visiting an old friend' in Switzerland. Lornagh was privately relieved.

After a two-year stint in a Dublin advertising agency, Lornagh decided to make the break and headed to New York. Hooking up with some friends from home, it wasn't long before she had secured a job with an international ad agency in Madison Avenue, the epicentre of the advertising world, and a cosy apartment in Greenwich Village. Lornagh blossomed in New York. Away from the claustrophobic notoriety of her mother, and surrounded by the relentless buzz of the city, she was finally able to live.

Although she was never at a loss for a date, Lornagh was relatively uninterested in the various men she came across until, at a dinner party that her flatmate organised, she was introduced to William Bartlett Jr. It was mutual lust at first sight and Lornagh had never felt anything like it. It wasn't until three months into the relationship, when she was madly and utterly in love with him, that she discovered there existed a Mrs Bartlett Jr. And, indeed, a six-month-old William Bartlett the Third.

Lornagh was devastated. She embarked on the relentless seesaw of agonising despair and elation for a further six months (expertly manipulated by her lover) before finally extricating herself from the whole sorry mess. Worse was to follow. William Bartlett's wife had taken it upon herself to employ a private detective to keep tabs on her husband's extramarital exploits. It came as somewhat of a surprise, then, when Lornagh's mother received a transatlantic phone call from Willam Bartlett's wife. In threatening tones, Mrs Bartlett suggested that Angela tell Lornagh in no uncertain terms to stay away from *her* husband.

Angela rose to the challenge magnificently. Buoyed up by six G&Ts, she announced in her famously dulcet tones that she had never in her life stooped to hobnobbing with a common American tart who couldn't hold on to her husband's affections and she wasn't going to start now. She further informed the astounded Mrs Bartlett Jr that Lornagh was an innocent abroad from an impeccable background who 'must have been seduced by the sleazeball you are unfortunate enough to call your husband'. She hung up before the speechless American woman could muster a reply.

Angela immediately seized the opportunity to pop over to New York to offer strategic advice – 'You must ditch him *instantly*, darling, if he won't leave his wife for you; countless men left their wives for *me*' – and catch up with a few old friends. The result, for Lornagh, was catastrophic. In the space of a few hours, ageing movie stars were calling to her apartment, and her friends and the media were having a field day: 'How come you never told us you were Angela Lemass's daughter?'

After a week, the stress proved too much. At an important work presentation, where Lornagh was pitching the latest in a never-ending line of concepts to the agency's most unpleasant, if vitally important, client, she finally snapped. When Mr Lewis Shine of 'Dayglo' Hair Products Inc, America's bestselling hair-care range, rejected, yet again, another brilliant idea for a TV spot, Lornagh calmly suggested that maybe it was time he shoved his precious shampoo where the fruit acids would make his eyes water. She was fired on the spot.

Lornagh decided she had had enough of New York, and packed her bags for Dublin. Back home, the position of public relations director at St Rita's offered her a chance to combine her media experience with her first real interest: social work. She bought an apartment in

Sandymount and set about building a new, sensible life for herself.

As far as she was concerned, she had had a close brush with disaster.

Losing her cool at the presentation in New York had been most unlike her, very out of character. And she didn't intend to ignore the warning signal. Lornagh Lemass didn't scare easily, but she was utterly terrified of turning into her mother.

'Lot number 315, a pair of George III crystal decanters,' the auctioneer's smooth voice continued briskly.

Simon stood at the back of the room, studying his programme intently. Immaculately turned out in a velvet-collared navy Crombie overcoat, he peered over the rims of his newly purchased half-moon glasses and nodded confidently in the direction of the auctioneer to start the bidding. The crystal decanters were just what he needed to complete his carefully collected set of antique tableware, and he reckoned with a bit of luck he could get them cheaply. He looked around the room surreptitiously. At 4.30 p.m., most of the crowd had thinned out. Simon had had his eye on the pair of decanters for a while, and the fact that they were near the end of the day's lots meant there shouldn't be much competition.

One or two dealers made a few half-hearted bids and the bidding hovered at £500 for the pair. A snip, Simon thought confidently. He nodded again and the deal was done.

'All done then, at £600 to the gentleman at the back.'

Simon swelled with pleasure. He patted his hair, and gave his details to the clerk and left. He was almost ready to give his first dinner party to introduce Lornagh to a few carefully chosen acquaintances and to show off his sophisticated taste for the finer things in life. She was bound to be impressed. Simon had been studying fine art assiduously for the last two years at evening classes and had to admit he was becoming quite a connoisseur. He may not have been able to afford a course at Christie's or Sotheby's, but Simon knew that antiques were second nature to him; they were in his blood. The fact that he had, until very recently, only seen them on the pages of the journals that he pored over was something he preferred not to dwell on.

He strolled down Grafton Street and towards the car park, pausing to peer into the window of a jeweller whose wares glittered invitingly. A ring would have to be the next serious purchase and he reckoned it was going to set him back quite a bit. Still, it had taken him a long time to find a girl as suitable as Lornagh Lemass and he had every intention of ensuring that the relationship became a permanent one. He opened the door of his newly leased Jaguar carefully and slipped behind the wheel. It was costing him a fortune but it created the right impression and that was what mattered. Reaching for his mobile phone, he dialled the number of the restaurant that his boss, Michael, had recommended. He was taking Lornagh to dinner tonight and nothing but the best would do.

Engineering the luxurious car carefully out of the car park, he headed home, narrowly avoiding the rush-hour traffic. Having reached his apartment in the exclusive Sweepstakes development in the heart of Ballsbridge, he let himself in, poured himself a drink, and sat down at his desk to study the ten-year-old fine art catalogue for the umpteenth time. There was absolutely no doubt about it. The painting was a genuine Le Souquet. It was staring out at him in all its gloriously faded abandon. Simon took a deep breath. He would have to be careful and move with the utmost caution lest he draw attention to the masterpiece. He could hardly believe it! Lady Sheldon herself hadn't even spotted it! So much for the aristocracy, Simon thought disparagingly. Imagine living with a genuine work of art worth hundreds of thousands hanging on your wall and not even recognising it!

He had seen the painting for the first time when Lornagh brought it from Lady Sheldon's house to Lornagh's mother's for safe-keeping, after the silly old bat had donated the painting to be auctioned for charity at the forthcoming ball in aid of St Rita's. Simon had admired it, and on closer inspection he recognized a certain quality about it. After careful research, he had unearthed an old catalogue from a past exhibition in

London and identified the painting correctly. He was especially careful not to alert Lornagh to his discovery. She would have run straight to the National Gallery to have it valued and that would have been that. Simon was damned if a bunch of women and their snivelling brats were going to benefit from *his* astuteness! Now all he had to do was make sure that no one else spotted its value, and so far things were looking good. The committee had put a reserve of £2,000 on the painting. Simon could barely conceal his glee. He was prepared to bid generously, up to three, maybe even five thousand at the auction, and the painting would be his. Then … Simon smiled, finishing the remains of his drink … it would be plain sailing. Very plain sailing indeed.

He took a quick shower and, admiring his reflection in the mirror, headed out to pick up Lornagh for dinner.

As he pulled into Lawrence's house, he grimaced. He hated the fact that Lornagh was sharing a house with him. He didn't like Lawrence one little bit. And he was pretty sure the feeling was mutual. He exerted far too much influence over Lornagh, in Simon's opinion. The sooner her apartment was finished the better. Simon couldn't understand why Lornagh didn't live with her famous mother in Grovesbury Road. Simon hadn't met Angela Lemass yet, much to his disappointment, despite dropping several heavy hints. Oh well, it was only a matter of time.

Lornagh, thankfully, was ready when he called at the

door. He had no intention of going in and having a drink while Lawrence considered him with that vaguely dismissive air that Simon always felt so acutely. Well, he had better watch out. When Lornagh was married to *him*, things would be very different.

'Good evening, Mr Sullivan, always a pleasure to see you!' Louis, the *mâitre d'* at the stylish restaurant on Stephen's Green, was suitably effusive as he beamed at Simon and Lornagh. The hefty tip Simon had slipped him when he called in to make the booking earlier had been well spent. It was most important that Lornagh assume he was a regular in the exclusive establishment. It had nearly killed Simon to part with the money but he had no choice. Michael had warned him that he hadn't a hope of setting his foot across the threshold otherwise.

He had dressed to the nines for the occasion and was pleased to see that Lornagh looked ravishing in a simple black shift dress. Simon also noted the admiring glances that followed them as they made their way towards their table. It was true, he thought, stealing a glimpse at his reflection in the mirrored wall beside them: they made a very handsome couple.

The food was as delicious as the exotic menu had promised, and the evening was progressing well. Simon chatted happily about the in-depth nature of his work while Lornagh listened dutifully. It was time to pick his moment.

'I was, ah, mulling over the possibility of a little getaway,' Simon said ponderously in his affected English accent. 'It would do us good to get out of town for a night or two. What about going away for a weekend *a deux*?' He flashed Lornagh a meaningful look as his full lips curved in a smile. 'We could leave on Friday at lunchtime.' Simon was keenly aware he hadn't taken Lornagh away yet and he was anxious to move the relationship on a notch or two. In truth, he dreaded the thought of being alone with a woman for two whole days and nights. But it had to be done.

Lornagh seemed rather startled, he thought. Well, she was bound to be, really. It wasn't every day a girl was invited away for a weekend with the most eligible accountant in Dublin, Simon reminded himself. He smiled indulgently as her fork poised midway on its journey. 'Well, Simon, I'd love to, but I can't do this weekend. Friday's our busiest day at St Rita's, and I promised to spend some time going over details of the plans for the new building with the management this weekend. It's the only time we can all get together.'

'That's ridiculous, Lornagh.' Simon poked angrily at his plate of oysters. 'You're never away from the place as it is! Can't you just say you've got some important social event you have to go to – you know, a friend of your mother's or something – that you can't possibly get out of?' Simon was fed up to his pearly crowned back teeth with St Rita's. It simply wasn't the right image for

Lornagh to be cultivating. He would much rather she was still in advertising; that would be much more glamorous to drop into conversation. And if she had to leave that behind, surely she could have found herself a PR job with a high profile? With all her experience and her mother's connections, she could have landed something really tasty. Simon sighed crossly; he really didn't understand her at all sometimes.

'Simon!' Lornagh's face was incredulous. 'My work is important to me. Can you understand that? If I say I'll do something, or be somewhere, then I will. I can't believe you'd expect me to make up some stupid lie. If I want to go away for the weekend, then I'll say just that to them!' Lornagh was becoming angry.

Beads of sweat began to break out on Simon's forehead. 'Look, I didn't realise your charity work was so important to you. We can go away another weekend.' He was doing his best to look magnanimous.

'It's not *charity* work,' Lornagh thought she was going to burst a blood vessel with frustration. 'I've told you a thousand times, Simon, I am *employed* by St Rita's. That means they pay me a salary!'

'Whatever.' Simon was bored by this idealistic outburst; he was determined to steer the conversation back to safer ground. 'We'll go back to my place after dinner; we can have a nightcap and ...'

'I don't think so, Simon.' Lornagh really wasn't in the mood: as far as she was concerned the evening had been ruined. 'Dinner was lovely, thank you very much, but I have an early meeting and I'd really like you to take me home now.'

'Of course.' Simon was so angry he could hardly speak. First to have his weekend away turned down, and now to be treated like a bloody chauffeur. But that wasn't all that was making him angry. He had gone to exceptional trouble to find a sympathetic doctor who would procure a plentiful supply of Viagra for him. In anticipation of what he expected would be a romantic night spent with Lornagh attending to his every need, he had taken a double dose of the little blue pills. He now had the most ferocious hard-on of his entire life. He was going to have to walk very, very carefully if he was to leave the restaurant with any shred of dignity at all.

Melissa was having outrageously good sex and was enjoying every second of it. She locked liposuctioned legs around Michael Moriarty's back and squeezed hard.

'Bloody hell, Melissa!' Michael gasped for breath. 'You'll crack my ribs!'

'Whatever it takes, babe!' Melissa had no intention of relaxing the momentum until she had reached a satisfactorily pleasurable conclusion. When she finally released her vice-like grip, she rolled over and gave an appreciative whistle. 'Where'd a nice boy like you learn all those naughty tricks?"

Michael smiled. He had no intention of telling her,

although he reckoned, of all the women he had come across, Melissa would probably get a kick out of hearing about all his exploits, in and out of the boardroom. Still, much wiser to keep all of that to himself.

'I could tell you, of course, but then I'd have to kill you!' He smiled evilly and reached across to stroke the curve of her pouting mouth. Making love to Melissa was a bit like tangling with a tiger — you never knew quite what you were dealing with, or when an affectionate cuddle could be followed by a deadly strike. It was part of her attraction.

Heading for the shower, he felt pleasantly invigorated by their steamy encounter — just what he needed to revive his razor-sharp instincts before his meeting with Eddie McEntee: and he'd need to be sharp. He was dicing with danger on this deal — and it gave him an incredible rush. But he was ready. More ready than he had ever been.

What he wasn't ready for was what greeted him on his return to the bedroom.

'So, what's this?' Melissa was casual but her lazy drawl was laced with steel as Michael emerged, still damp from his shower, to see her holding up the small white packet.

Shit! That was all he needed. He kept his tone deliberately light. 'Going through my pockets, eh? I didn't think you were the suspicious type, Melissa.'

'I'm not.' Melissa smiled benignly. 'Just curious.' As she trailed a dangerously long scarlet fingernail down his spine, Michael felt himself shiver. 'Let's just say I like to know what I'm dealing with. I wouldn't have thought drugs were your style.'

Michael thought quickly, and decided to be straight. Melissa would never buy bullshit.

'We all need a little pick-me-up every now and then. My lifestyle is completely hectic these days, you know that … I have to be sharp. Don't tell me you've never tried them.'

Melissa studied his handsome reflection in the mirror and decided not to pursue the matter. Seductresses didn't nag. Nonetheless, she filed the discovery away with her many other titbits of vital information. She decided to be philosophical about it. For now.

'I used to do quite a bit as a kid, but I gave it up. I knew a few people who got into real trouble with them. It wasn't worth it. Anyway, they wreak havoc with the complexion.'

Michael chuckled. That's what he loved about her: she always saw the ruthlessly practical side of things.

'I've got to go.' Michael finished dressing with more speed than usual. 'I'll talk to you later. Be good.' He kissed her and left, not a little unnerved by the exchange. He'd have to be more careful; he couldn't afford to slip up, not now.

After he'd gone, Melissa was uncharacteristically pensive. She didn't want to admit it, but she was disappointed in him. She despised weakness in anyone and saw any kind of dependency as a distinct character flaw. Still, he was fun, witty and terrific in the sack. And he could be useful to her. And what made it all worthwhile was that that snooty wife of his, Felicity, would have to watch her step now. Or she'd be in for a few unpleasant surprises.

'Maria!' Melissa called sharply to her maid over the intercom. 'Flow me a bath!' (Melissa particularly liked this newly acquired verb, so much grander than 'run me a bath' or even 'draw me a bath'). 'And make sure Jesus,' (Melissa pronounced it correctly as 'Haysoos') 'has taken Dolce and Gabbana for their walk!' Melissa didn't trust Maria's husband, who worked as gardener-cum-handyman for them, as far as she'd throw him. He was as lazy as sin, in her opinion. And she was pretty sure he'd been at the booze. She would have to keep a much closer check on him and the bar. Still, Maria more than made up for his inadequacies.

A long, hot bath would revive her in time for her vitally important appointment. This afternoon, Carol Dalton and the producer/director of the *Carol Calls* programme were calling to 'recce' the house and run through the script of the interview they would be doing with her. Melissa couldn't wait. She would have a chance to show off the sumptuous interiors of her magnificent home. The whole road would be green with envy!

Melissa had been startled but thrilled when Carol of TV 2000 and the *Carol Calls* show had rung her and suggested the interview. Melissa never missed an episode herself. Being interviewed on the 'at home' slot was a dream come true. She hoped they could do at least part of the interview in her newly decorated drawing room, where she had installed a vast antique desk in a corner from where she conducted her 'charity' work: accepting and discarding invitations and making vital phone calls to important people. The room was more than large enough and, better still, it had a wonderful view of the landscaped gardens and Romanesque-style swimming pool. Such a pity it was winter, Melissa mused, but if it was at all clear on the day, she'd make sure they did a 'pan' around (she'd been brushing up on camera terms) to show the house off as much as possible.

Humming a cheerful tune, she headed for her wardrobe and looked critically through the racks of designer clothes before selecting her favourite leather trousers, teaming them with a sleek, leopard-skin jacket. Just because she was a charity queen, she reminded herself, it didn't mean she couldn't impress them with her avant-garde sense of fashion.

The big Mercedes pulled off the M50 and continued down increasingly narrow country back roads. Pascal was salivating at the thought of what lay ahead. A big greasy fry-up, with a bit of luck, and a pot or two of good strong tea. Eva, his long time mistress, was the only woman who had ever really understood him, he reflected. She had been there for him over the years with love, tea and sympathy whenever he had needed her, without one word of reproach ever passing her lips. He should have married her, of course, and he had fully intended to, until he had come across Melissa. Pascal smiled at the memory. He had been on his way back from a caravan show in the south of England, where he had been viewing and purchasing the latest models for his flourishing business, and was having a bite of dinner on the ferry before catching a bit of shut-eye.

Suddenly the sound of raised voices from a nearby table interrupted his meal. The volume increased steadily until it ended in a shriek of outrage. Pascal turned around in time to witness a whole plate of spaghetti bolognese, followed swiftly by a pint of Guinness, being thrown over a rough-looking fellow by his indignant blonde companion.

Fisticuffs followed. Pascal, horrified at the thought of anyone hitting a woman, went to her rescue. The couple were restrained, the young fellow taken away to be cleaned up. Pascal bought Melissa a drink and, in between sobs and expletives, listened to her tale of a miserable biking holiday ending in a miserable fight with her miserable sod of a boyfriend.

Pascal thought he had never seen anyone so gorgeous in his life. With her big blue eyes and teased and lacquered golden hair, he thought she was the epitome of '70s glamour. He was completely smitten. He also thought there was something distinctly familiar about her. As they stayed up all night talking, it suddenly hit

Pascal like a bolt. Melissa had lived in the same neighbourhood as him growing up. He could hardly believe it! The tough, chubby little kid he remembered couldn't possibly be this gorgeous creature!

A swift, passionate romance had ensued upon their return. Pascal was delighted to have a flashy blonde on his arm and Melissa was pleasantly surprised to find she enjoyed being treated well by a man for the first time in her life.

Eva, his steady girlfriend, had been dismayed when Pascal broke up with her, but they remained good friends. Pascal and she had kept in touch over the years, but it wasn't until his marriage had reached an unbearable low that they had taken things any further. Neither ever regretted it. Pascal often thought that without Eva's kind, almost motherly, loving he would never have gotten through the hard times, or indeed have reached the position he had today. She quite simply adored him, and gave him the time and consideration Melissa couldn't and wouldn't. More importantly, she allowed him to be himself. With Eva, Pascal didn't have to watch his pronunciation, or wear stupid designer suits, or hold his knife and fork a certain way, and he loved her for it.

He pulled up outside a large field and got out of the car. In the darkness, the light from the windows shone like a beacon of refuge. Pascal opened the rusty gate to the field and got back into his car, switching off the lights before driving down the little-used track. Pulling on the handbrake, he took a moment as he switched off the engine to admire, yet again, his favourite purchase. This, his rendezvous destination, was no bachelor pad, no cosy *pied-à-terre*: no, Pascal and Eva's secret love nest was a caravan. No ordinary caravan, mind you, the Majestic Tourer Continental was the state of the art 'king' of the caravan world, and had set Pascal back £45,000. But it had been worth every penny.

Caravans were the first great love of Pascal's life, but Melissa wouldn't dream of letting him own one – not now. Pascal, on the other hand, never forgot he owed his livelihood to them.

If it hadn't been for the fantastic success of his first business venture with them, he would never have progressed into the leisure industry and from there established his property empire, worth millions. Oh no, Pascal Sheehan was only too happy to stay in touch with his roots; he only wished desperately his wife was too.

As he got out of the car, Eva appeared at the door wearing her favourite apron over a tweed skirt, her face wreathed in smiles. She hugged Pascal warmly and pulled him inside.

'Goodness, look at the state of you – I thought you were lost!' She poured a generous helping of his favourite whiskey into a glass and settled her plump frame into the expertly engineered seating area.

'Sorry I'm late, love,' Pascal sat down beside her, feeling himself relax at the soothing sound of her voice.

It did him good just to be near her. 'I had that meeting with Michael Moriarty I was telling you about. It went on much longer than either of us anticipated.'

'How's it all going?' Eva smiled encouragingly. She was always interested in his work, although sometimes her mind reeled with all the wheeling and dealing he did.

Pascal smiled broadly. 'If I say so myself, I think this is the best thing I've ever been involved in. It's going to be great. The people at St Rita's accepted our offer for the building last week, and approved the plans for their new offices, and the planning permission's come through for the development of the rest of the site.' Pascal raised his glass. 'It's all systems go! I wanted you to be the first to know, I couldn't have done any of it without you, Eva.'

'Nonsense!' Eva refused to take any credit, but she was secretly thrilled that he still thought of her in that way. 'So what happens next?'

'The builders are ready to come in now. I've put up my share of the money, I'm just waiting for Michael's share to kick in.'

'You're sure you can count on him?' Eva was still protective of Pascal even though his business achievements had reached giddier heights than either of them had ever imagined.

Pascal sipped his drink thoughtfully. 'Michael's all right. We've done business together for too long now not to trust each other. Besides, without me, he's got no hope whatsoever of realising this deal.' Pascal smiled down at Eva's worried face. 'Look! Michael Moriarty's got more clients with money to invest than I've had hot dinners. It's just a matter of getting through all the red tape. I've seen the paper work, everything's ship-shape, so stop worrying!'

Eva smiled and snuggled up against him. 'I'm sure you know what you're doing, love – it's just that it's such a *huge* amount of money. I don't know how you can get a wink of sleep with all those millions of pounds changing hands.'

'It's my chance to put something back, Eva, to finally make a difference to the area I grew up in. And I'm fortunate to be in a position to do that.'

'Pascal Sheehan.' Eva was serious. 'You're too nice for your own good, do you know that?'

'No, but I do know I could eat a tinker's arse through a hedge, I'm so hungry! Where's that fry-up you promised me?'

'Okay, guys, let's go.' Carol was heading off to do the recce for her upcoming 'At Home' interview. It was her favourite part of the job.

This week she was interviewing Melissa Sheehan, aspiring socialite and wife of multimillionaire Pascal Sheehan; and today they were calling to the house to go over the format that the interview would take. Maura, the producer/director of the programme, accompanied her, and the cameraman followed behind in the TV 2000 jeep.

It would be the first time Carol had been inside a house on the much-documented 'Millionaires Row', aka Grovesbury Road, and she was looking forward to it immensely. It was amazing what people would reveal in what they perceived as the privacy of their own home.

With the cameras artfully set up, and Carol's carefully cultivated 'listening' interview technique, it was no time at all before her interviewees forgot they were being recorded for national television, and felt instead as if they were in the company of a good friend. Men, in particular, found her easy to confide in. Just the right amount of gushy, flattering remarks, a few sympathetically probing questions, not to mention her meticulous subject research, and it was not surprising that Carol found herself privy to some extraordinarily personal insights and revelations. It made her programme particularly riveting viewing.

And this one, she thought shrewdly, would be more interesting than most. When Carol researched a subject, no stone was left unturned. Her producer on the show had long since given up questioning budget increases for a sudden necessary ticket to some obscure location – inevitably to track down a crucial 'link' in a story. Carol was even known to have worn faultless disguises to observe her subjects unseen as they went about their business (or somebody else's), totally unaware of her relentless shadowing. She would, in fact, have made a perfect detective, and had seriously considered it as a career before she had fallen in love with journalism and the media.

Melissa had certainly turned out to be a 'meaty' subject. Initially, Carol knew little about her other than her relentless pursuit of appearing as regularly as possible in the social pages of various magazines.

But research had turned up a far more complex individual. Melissa, it turned out, had been born Mary Pat O'Malley, the youngest of 11 children in a family living in Dublin's inner city. It was here she met her future husband, Pascal Sheehan. Their families had lived across the street from each other. It was a rough start in life by all accounts, with alcohol abuse and wife beating rampant in the neighbourhood. Most of the kids she had grown up with had turned to a life of crime or become heavily involved in drugs. Melissa had nearly ended up going down that route herself. Rumour had it she had been involved with the local 'bad boy' of the neighbourhood, who had eventually ended up in prison; but, despite Carol's best attempts, the story became vague and insubstantial as the few remaining people who remembered Melissa became distinctly reluctant to divulge any further details on the subject.

Carol focused her thoughts as she waited to make a left-hand turn from Ailesbury into Grovesbury Road, then pulled up outside 'Sudbury', the Sheehans' house, and its imposing electric gates. She dialled Melissa's number from her mobile.

A woman's foreign accent answered. 'Good afternoon, the Sheehan residence.'

Carol gave her name and waited as the gates pulled slowly open. A sleek sports car pulled out from a neighbouring house and the woman driving it nearly fell out of the window trying to peer out when she saw the TV 2000 jeep. Carol smiled wryly as the gates closed behind them. This may be Grovesbury Road, the most expensive road in Dublin 4, but it suffered just the same from nosy-neighbour syndrome as anywhere else. Some things, she thought to herself, never change, no matter where you live in Dublin.

Michael was experiencing a feeling he hadn't had in a long time. His heartbeat was up; his palms were becoming moist and his breath quickened as he walked purposefully towards the site. He couldn't possibly be nervous, could he? He dismissed the thought as utter nonsense and concentrated his mind on the meeting in hand. He thrust his hands into the pockets of his coat and increased his pace. A slow mist was rising above the canal, seeming to hover eerily in the evening dusk. Around him, the sounds of the city receded as weary commuters edged home in the slow-moving traffic.

Try as he might, the vague feeling of unease refused to be shaken as he turned the corner and made his way under the dimly lit street lamps towards the old St Rita's building that was to provide vital access to the building site. He headed down the narrow path and stopped at a pair of run-down wrought-iron gates that had definitely seen better days. He shivered involuntarily and checked his watch. 5.55 exactly. He would wait for ten minutes and not a second more.

'Moriarty?' The gravelly voice cut through his thoughts and despite himself Michael jumped. He turned around to see the figure of a man emerge from the darkness. As he approached him, Michael made out a slim, well-built physique of about five feet ten. The man was dressed from head to toe in black, his long coat accentuating dark, brooding features. Dark hair, beginning to grey at the temples, reached his collar.

'McEntee?' Michael moved towards the man, extending his hand in what he hoped was a confident greeting.

'My friends call me Eddie.' The man smiled a slow, crooked smile, revealing surprisingly white, even teeth. He ignored the hand Michael proffered and lit a cigarette, his eyes never leaving Michael's face for a second.

'It's good to meet you finally, Eddie.' Michael gave Eddie the benefit of his most charming smile, thinking that never had the niceties of introduction seemed so superfluous. He felt as if this man somehow had instant access to every thought that had ever flickered through his mind and was perusing them at leisure. It made him feel distinctly uncomfortable.

'Let's have a look at this site of yours, we can talk money later.' Eddie inclined his head towards a car that crept slowly out of the shadows; at least one bulky figure sat in the back. A bodyguard, no doubt, Michael thought, apprehensively.

'Sure,' Michael said crisply, with more confidence than he felt. 'Follow me.'

As they made their way around the site, Michael gave Eddie the sales pitch of his life. He explained the detailed plans for the huge development of houses, apartments and office buildings which, in such a central city location, would transform the run-down area into an extremely sought-after location. He told Eddie of the difficulty they had first faced in gaining access to the site, blocked as it was by the old building of St Rita's, and how Pascal Sheehan had saved the deal by making them an offer they couldn't refuse: not only buying the building outright, but insisting that he build a brand new centre for St Rita's on the site with new housing for the mothers and families who sought refuge there, a counselling centre and a fantastic new leisure and sports centre – all of which he intended to finance himself. It was, as even Eddie agreed, a perfect and extremely generous solution to a tricky problem. Of course, the rest of the new residential development would pay for itself in profits without a doubt, but they wouldn't have been able to go ahead with any of it had it not been for Pascal's altruistic intentions winning access for them through the St Rita's deal.

Michael tried to be nonchalant as they headed back towards the waiting car. 'You can see for yourself how lucrative a deal this could be. What do you think?'

Eddie's eyes narrowed as he smiled at Michael. 'You need it more than me, pal! How much are we talking?'

'Fifty million. Pascal's putting up the other fifty. And I've plenty of eager investors who'll be only too happy to jump in if you're not up for it.' Michael thought it no harm to remind Eddie McEntee just whom he was dealing with. 'But we need to move quickly, planning came through last week.'

'What's in it for you?'

Michael's palms were beginning to sweat profusely, but this was the moment: he had to go for it. Ten million pounds would just about get him back on track. 'Twenty percent, take it or leave it …'

'Suits me.' Eddie smiled his slow, unnerving smile. 'I've got some funds sitting around that need investing – the sooner the better as far as I'm concerned. You've got yourself a deal, Moriarty.' Eddie extended a hand as cool as alabaster and Michael shook it heartily.

'Call me Michael, please.' Michael hated himself for sounding simultaneously sycophantic and relieved.

A huge man got out of the car and held the door open

for Eddie. From the car he held Michael's gaze with what felt uncannily like contempt. 'Oh, and Michael …'

'Yes?' Michael felt the hairs on the back of his neck stand up.

'I don't have to tell you I expect complete discretion in our business dealings.' Eddie's voice was as cold as the February air that clung around them, coating every word in great bursts of freezing breath. 'No paper trails, right?'

'Of course.' Michael swallowed.

'Okay,' Eddie smiled again. 'What is it you yuppies say? My people will talk to your people.' He laughed softly. 'You'll be hearing from me.' And with that the door closed, and the big car slid back into the darkness from which it had so suddenly emerged.

Feeling as if he had somehow managed to engineer a stay of execution instead of closing the biggest deal of his life, Michael headed back to his car and drove to the nearest pub where he ordered a large whiskey. Coming face to face with Eddie 'The Shark' McEntee had taken more out of him than he cared to admit. If only Pascal Sheehan had any idea who the other 'investors' were. Not to mention his own incredibly correct wife, Felicity. All hell would break loose! As it was, he wasn't too happy with the whole situation himself, but he hadn't had much choice in the matter as things had turned out. He took his whiskey to a quiet corner of the pub, ignoring the comehitherish glances of two attractive young career-women types, and sat deep in thought as he cast his mind over the recent events that had led to this: getting involved with the man who was widely regarded as the most dangerous in the country.

Bloody Celtic Tiger, Michael thought to himself bitterly. We were all getting along just fine the way we were. Now everybody wanted everything and they wanted it now. Not next week, not tomorrow: now. Who could have expected property to spiral the way it did? It was obscene! And interest rates ... well, he took a sip of his drink and smiled wryly, he'd got that one wrong, very wrong. He'd *had* to dip into client funds; he had no choice. What was he supposed to do? Tell Felicity, his aristocratic and perfectly groomed wife, the house would have to go? Or tell Pascal Sheehan, 'Sorry, old chap, you know that bit of company investment I was talking about? Well, it's all gone kaput now!' He almost laughed out loud at the very thought of it. And although Felicity loved him in her own way, he knew a lot of her crowd hadn't approved of the match at the time. Didn't think him good enough. He didn't come with a braying accent or title and a couple of thousand acres of land. But he'd shown them! All of them!

He'd had to borrow – for everyone who depended on him, not for *himself* ...

It was when he took a gamble on interest rates going up again and they hadn't, that the first cold little hands of fear had begun to clutch around his heart. He couldn't fail, not now, not when he was so close ... so tantalisingly close.

And that's when the cocaine had started. One of his extracurricular girlfriends had introduced him to it when she showed a genuine concern at his lack of enthusiasm for their usually lively, if intermittent, trysts. Even the bedroom had become lacklustre for Michael in the current circumstances. And the cocaine had done it. Made him feel like his old self. Better, even. He was invincible again. He could do no wrong. Everything was on the up again – literally!

From there he progressed to a quick toot before a heavy meeting, or dealing with a difficult client, and lately he had to have a constant supply of the stuff. Nobody had any idea, he was pretty sure about that. Sure, a couple of the girls he played around with did it now and again, but he made sure they knew nothing about his increasing habit.

It was his dealer, Joey, who had upped the ante in the end. They all got greedy, the bastards. It had happened one evening a few weeks ago. Michael was just getting ready to leave the office when his secretary said there were two men to see him on urgent business. The minute she mentioned Joey's name, Michael knew he was cornered. He let his secretary go for the evening and invited them into his office trying desperately to remain calm. Their business was quick and to the point. They were well aware of the extent his dependency had reached and said they wanted to help him. Michael's blood had run cold at the words. It was simple, they had said. *You help us and we'll help you.* Otherwise, they'd make sure the only line he'd need would be in the obituary column. They showed him a range of cleverly incriminating shots of Michael with his dealer, clearly exchanging money for drugs, and a few more of his meetings with various women for good measure. Their boss, they continued, was keen to conduct a little *business* with him. The simple matter of a little money being invested, with the utmost discretion and confidentiality. Michael would hear from them in due course as to where and when the meeting with Mr McEntee would be conducted. And then they had left.

Michael shuddered, remembering the chill he had felt in his bones despite the heat of the crackling office fire.

And that was how he, Michael Moriarty, King of the Deal, had found himself involved in a money-laundering operation with the biggest drug baron in the country breathing down his neck.

CHAPTER THREE

Lornagh tried to stifle a yawn. Early morning meetings never brought out the best in her, but today she had only herself to blame. Wendy and Avril, her best friends since school days, had dropped in last night armed with several bottles of white and the latest gossip. After disposing of the former and catching up on the latter, they had looked at their watches to discover it was 4.30 in the morning. At the time it had seemed hilarious. Now Lornagh was feeling the effects. Luckily for her, she didn't have an active role to play in this meeting so, as long as she listened, looked interested and made the appropriate noises at the appropriate times, no one should be any the wiser.

Around the table, Sister Kay and a few of the charity's board of trustees listened enthusiastically as Pascal Sheehan and Michael Moriarty took them through the proposed plans for the new St Rita's building. Although everyone had heard what was being planned for the site, it was another thing altogether to actually see the plans, and admire the brilliantly crafted miniature model that had been built for the meeting. Both exceeded everybody's expectations, and it was readily acknowledged around the table that the architect had done an incredible job.

'Who is the architect, by the way?' Even old Mrs Keating had been roused out of her usual stupor. 'Damned fine job!' she boomed, waggling two of her three chins.

Sister Kay, who was pink with delight, jumped in before Pascal or Michael could answer her question. 'It's Sean O'Rourke.' The name was uttered with uncharacteristic reverence.

'Isn't he the chap behind the whole Temple Bar thingy?' Lornagh had never seen Mrs Keating so alert in her life. Usually she dozed through every encounter lasting longer than ten minutes.

'That's him.' Sister Kay was thrilled that the major talent they had on their side was being fully acknowledged.

'But he must be costing us a bloody fortune!' Mr O'Dea, the local TD, looked horrified.

'Not a penny!' Sister Kay tried not to sound triumphant as she delivered her astonishing news. 'His mother is my best friend. We were at school together. Sure, I've known Sean since he was a twinkle in his father's eye. He wouldn't hear of taking a fee for the work. His own father died when he was only five years old, and his mother had a tough enough time bringing the five of them up. When we approached him, he said he'd be delighted to take on the project.'

'And I must say,' Pascal interrupted, 'he's been an absolute pleasure to work with, hasn't he, Michael?'

'Lovely guy,' Michael agreed heartily. 'And incredibly talented. He's put untold work into these plans. We had a good idea of what we wanted, but he's enhanced the whole project beyond belief. I'd say we have an award-winning building on our hands.'

Lornagh was only half-listening. She couldn't get the recent evening she had spent with Simon out of her mind. She rubbed her eyes wearily and tried to focus her attention.

'Well, that's it really, folks. We'll keep you all informed as the work progresses.' Lornagh could hardly hide her relief as Michael's crisp voice cut into her reverie, winding up the meeting.

Back in her little office, Lornagh stared glumly at the pile of research literature she had promised herself to go through and abandoned it in favour of a mid-morning cup of tea.

As she sat back down at her desk, she sipped her tea thoughtfully. What was wrong with her? Why was she feeling like this? Was she being too critical again, or was Simon really being a pain in the backside? She had talked the whole episode over with Avril and Wendy and they had covered it thoroughly from every angle.

'They're all bastards! The trick is to accept it. At least he's good-looking,' Wendy had said dismissively.

'Mm,' agreed Avril. 'He reminds me a bit of Antonio Banderas in *Zorro*.'

'Does he wear a mask to bed and tear your sheets to shreds with his large sword?' Avril had quipped, and they fell about laughing.

To be fair, Simon had rung her the very next morning to apologise if he had upset her in any way, and she had to admit he had been thoughtful and attentive to her all week, even giving her the space she so desperately needed. What was eating her? He was good-looking by any standards, and, as he kept reminding her, he had prospects. What they were, Lornagh was never too sure. Why did she keep holding back? Lornagh knew Simon was serious about her, but lately she just couldn't seem to respond. It had been lovely in the beginning, she reminded herself. All right, so he didn't make her laugh like Lawrence did, and he wasn't the most interesting man she had ever come across, but surely that didn't matter so much? He was kind and steady and he genuinely seemed to care about her. Wasn't that what mattered in a long-term relationship? *And he's bloody boring!* The little voice had risen to a scream lately …

Lornagh shut it out. She couldn't bear any more of these internal dialogues, they made her head spin. The voice was having none of it. It began to beat in her head like a drum …

And what about your sex life? it screamed. *That's bloody boring too – or haven't you noticed?* She had noticed, truth be told, but, like all the other niggling little worries, she had pushed the thought from her mind hoping it would eventually go away. She thought about it now and tried to pinpoint the exact moment it had begun, but she couldn't. And it wasn't that sex with Simon was *bad*, it just felt, well, sort of *reluctant* on his part. Maybe it was her fault? Maybe he didn't fancy her in that way? He did seem to drink rather a lot before taking her to bed. Maybe that had something to do with it? She thought about the time she spent with him in his apartment when she stayed over. He was always generous and went out of his way to make everything nice for her, but she felt an increasing sense of separateness when she was with him. As if there was a part of him that would always be locked away. Come to think of it, there were a lot of things that were locked away in Simon's apartment. She had discovered that when she was looking for some shampoo in the bathroom and had been trying one of the bathroom cabinets, only to find it locked. When she had asked Simon about this, he had said it was a precaution because he didn't trust the woman who came in weekly to clean for him. Lornagh had thought it rather excessive at the time and then forgotten about it. And from that moment on, Simon had religiously made sure there was a selection of all her favourite toiletries kept on view in the bathroom. She supposed she should have been flattered – some men had a fit if you wanted to leave your toothbrush overnight, never mind anything else. All the same, it seemed a little odd.

Just then Jayne, one of the volunteer workers, popped her head around the door. 'Well, aren't *you* the dark horse?' She dragged behind her what must have been the largest, most opulent bouquet of flowers Lornagh had ever seen.

'They're for me?' Lornagh asked doubtfully, searching in vain for her favourite freesias amongst the extravagant array of greenery.

'That's what the delivery man said!' Jane couldn't hide her curiosity. 'Well, go on, open the card, for heaven's sake.'

Lornagh opened the small card and read the neat, precise handwriting, which she recognised immediately as Simon's. *Have dinner with me tonight,* it read. *Longing to see you, love Simon.* Lornagh felt vaguely embarrassed at the note, although she had to admit the flowers were spectacular. 'They're from a friend,' she said, feeling Jayne's uncomfortably piercing gaze upon her.

'Some friend! They must have cost an absolute fortune. Let's hear more about this "friend" of yours.' Jayne had no intention of being fobbed off.

Lornagh didn't want to seem dismissive, but she really didn't want to talk about Simon right now. 'There's nothing to tell Jayne, really, it's just someone I've been seeing for a while.'

'Looks like you'll be seeing a lot more of him if he's this keen.'

'I'd better go and put these in water,' Lornagh said,

taking the vast arrangement out to the tiny kitchen where she tried as best she could to stand the flowers in a bucket of water until she could bring them home. Much as she appreciated the gesture, she wished Simon had sent the flowers to her at Lawrence's house; she hated attention being drawn to her private life when she was at work. She pushed any mean, petty thoughts firmly from her mind. Really! What on earth was the matter with her? She had just received the most wonderful bouquet of flowers in the world from her boyfriend and she was complaining? It was time for her to snap out of this weird mood.

Sitting back at her desk, she was about to pick up the phone to thank Simon for the flowers when she suddenly realised there was a man in her office.

Hunkered down on the floor, he appeared to be measuring the area where Lornagh had asked weeks ago for some extra shelving to be put up. Even though they would be moving to new offices, she badly needed the temporary storage space and was relieved to see that the handyman had eventually shown up. 'Is there any chance you could get those shelves up before the end of this week?' Lornagh asked him. 'I know it's hardly worth it since we'll be moving soon – but I was promised them weeks ago …' An accusing tone had crept into her voice, but frankly she couldn't give a damn. She was feeling tired and irritable due to lack of sleep, and fed up to the teeth with the amount of paperwork that was threatening to take over her tiny space.

There was no response so Lornagh tried again. 'Excuse me, I was just …'

'I heard you.' Drawing himself up to his full height of six foot four inches, he turned around slowly and regarded Lornagh with what she felt was unnecessary disdain.

Honestly, Lornagh thought impatiently, this day was going from bad to worse and it wasn't even lunchtime. She really wasn't in the mood to deal with surly workmen. 'Look, if it's too much trouble just forget it!' she snapped.

As he brushed past her in one stride, heading for the door, Lornagh felt a small stab of panic. You never really knew who or what you were dealing with these days. For all she knew, he could be an irate husband of one of their mothers – they were always warned to be on guard. Only last year one of the social workers had been held at knife-point by a vengeful husband.

This man's imposing presence was making her tiny office even more claustrophobic. He paused for a moment, studying Lornagh with amused curiosity. 'I'll see what I can do …' And before she could think of a suitably curt reply, he was gone.

Lornagh was furious. Bloody workmen! They were all the same. This one clearly had notions about himself. Granted, he was good-looking, in a sort of dishevelled, rugged way, but he could do with some serious work on his people skills. Feeling increasingly aggravated,

Lornagh rang Molly, the part-time secretary, determined to practise some of the assertiveness she had been reading about in her latest self-help book.

'Molly, would you try and grab the handyman who was in my office before he leaves the building? I'm desperate to get those shelves up, and he's just disappeared.'

Molly sounded surprised. 'What handyman, Lornagh? Ed's not coming in until next week – it's the soonest we can get hold of him.' Lornagh put the phone down feeling even more confused. What the hell was going on? She checked her watch. It was nearly lunchtime.

She would head out and grab a sandwich, go for a walk and try to clear her throbbing head. Maybe the afternoon would prove more productive.

Pulling on her coat, she ran into Jayne, flushed with excitement on the corridor.

'Did you see him, Lornagh? Isn't he divine?' Jayne was beginning to babble. 'He's going over the whole building before the old place is demolished …'

'I've no idea who you're talking about.' Lornagh was anxious to get some fresh air. 'The only person I've come into contact with is an arrogant workman who looked at me as if I'd asked him to build a time machine when all I wanted was some shelves put up!'

Jayne's mouth dropped open as she began to shake with laughter. 'Lornagh Lemass, you feckin' eejit! What planet are you on? That was no workman! That was Sean O'Rourke!'

Simon was humming a happy tune to himself as he sat in his office at Romany Investments. Everything was back on track. He had been seriously worried that his last dinner with Lornagh had damaged his carefully thought-out strategy, but a week of the classic 'slushy' treatment had eradicated any mistakes he might inadvertently have made. He had apologised profusely to her the next day, given her plenty of space (nothing like a bit of time on her *own* for a girl to properly appreciate a man) and sent the most extravagant bouquet of flowers to her office. When she had rung that evening to thank him, he knew she had been completely bowled over. Women! They were so predictable.

He glanced through the e-mails: nothing too taxing, and the sponsorship for the St Rita's ball was coming along nicely. He knew Michael was impressed by the way he was handling things. There was no doubt things were running more smoothly since he had joined the company. Michael and he made a good team, and Pascal Sheehan was so busy with his other property interests he was hardly ever in the office. It was only a matter of time, Simon felt sure, before he was made a partner. He had already been invited to Michael's incredible house for dinner on several occasions.

Simon had been particularly careful to be at his most

effusive and to behave impeccably. He found Michael's wife, Felicity, a little tricky, though. She was a very charming, elegant woman, but lacked *warmth*, Simon felt. He had caught her staring at him once or twice during dinner with a peculiar look on her face, especially when he had been regaling the table with his knowledge about antiques and how much they cost. As Michael and Felicity's house was immaculately furnished with generations of beautiful pieces from Felicity's family, Simon had had plenty of chances to show off his carefully cultivated skills. In fact, he had been so determined to impress, he had taken the opportunity of bringing a Polaroid camera with him on an earlier occasion when Michael had had to drop by the house to pick up some papers and had invited Simon in to wait. While Michael was out of the room, Simon had taken shots of three antique pieces and a particularly nice painting. He had then shown them to an acquaintance of his who was an expert in fine art, and had discovered their exact style, period and current value, so he could appear to be suitably knowledgeable whenever the opportunity presented itself. Simon didn't believe in leaving things to chance.

As Michael was out of the office at the moment, it was the perfect time to concentrate on more important business. The Dinner Party. Simon was determined to plan it to perfection down to the last tiny detail. He had been poring over foodie magazines for weeks just to be sure what particular table settings and cuisine would be suitable for the menu. He would hire a suitable caterer, of course, but he didn't believe in letting *them* advise him. He wondered about a Victorian theme for the evening.

Even though his three-bedroomed apartment was in a modern building, Simon had insisted his interior designer decorate it in classic nineteenth-century style. And, although the poor man had put up quite a battle to do the whole place in tasteful neutrals, Simon had put his foot down. It was a challenge, he admitted, but then that was what he had hired a decorator for. The result had been well worth the effort. Every time he walked in his front door, he felt as if he was entering another era. When people had behaved *properly*, and men had been treated with the respect they deserved.

He thought about whom he would invite. Michael and Felicity, of course. He'd probably have to invite Pascal Sheehan then too, although he couldn't stand that coarse wife of his, who was downright rude to him on occasion, and he'd noticed Pascal's table manners left a lot to be desired. Never mind, he'd make sure to seat them next to someone less important. That was four, and he and Lornagh (who would be guest of honour, of course) made six. His table could take ten comfortably, but with the especially elaborate table settings and array of cutlery he was planning on, eight would be a better number. Eventually he settled on Dr Gerald Stevens and his American fiancée, Candice, to make up the number. He had only met Gerald once or twice since he had arrived back in the country but, as he was medical consultant to St Rita's, he would no doubt be delighted to be included in such a select and influential gathering. It would be the perfect *entrée* to society for them. Better still, since Gerald's fiancée was American, Pascal Sheehan's table manners wouldn't be so obvious. Americans had *very* strange ideas about how to hold a knife and fork.

The Sheehan household was in a flurry of activity. From the moment the crew had arrived with Carol, the pace had been frantic. Angles were checked, lighting was tested and furniture was moved with lightning speed. Melissa had never seen anything like it. If this was television, she wanted more! She wasn't so keen on Maura, the producer/director, though; she was far too uppity for her liking. Especially when she said that half the furniture in her drawing room would have to go. Melissa was miffed. She had wanted it to be a special feature. It would reflect her good taste, she felt, and serve as an inspiration to the viewers, who would pick up hints on interior decoration. Not that any of them would be able to afford to replicate *her* innate style. 'We've been through this before, Melissa,' Maura said, brusquely. 'Everything was agreed at the recce, remember?'

At least she had managed to persuade them to keep her recently acquired antique desk in shot so she could sit behind it as she talked about her charity work. Carol had backed her up at the time, Melissa noted with satisfaction. She missed, however, the mischievous smile she had shared with Maura, when Melissa's back was turned.

Her make-up and hair had been done to perfection. The outfits presented more of a problem. Melissa couldn't make up her mind which of them to wear, so she decided she would appear in her three current favourites. She felt they would convey the very different aspects of her personality and the many situations she had to respond to throughout any one, hectic day.

Maria, her maid, had been treated to a blow dry and a new black dress with a white apron and hat for the occasion.

It was time to begin.

'Okay, everybody, we're ready to go!' Maura was brisk. 'Sound, Larry?'

'Yup.'

'Happy with the light, Roger?'

'Affirmative!'

'Continuity, Sarah?'

'Sure thing!'

'Okay. Let's go for a take!'

'Aaand … action!'

Carol smiled to camera. 'Hello there. Today it's my great pleasure to invite you into the home of Mrs Melissa Sheehan, tireless charity worker,' Carol gave an arch look to camera, 'and busy socialite. Melissa.' Carol turned to Melissa, who was beaming. '*May* I call you Melissa?'

'Of course you may, Carol.' Melissa inclined her head prettily.

'This is a wonderful room, Melissa. And I love this fabulous antique desk.' Carol's ironic tone was lost on Melissa. 'Do tell us about it.'

'This is what I call my *informal* drawing room, Carol. Ay'm very sensitive to colours, and Ay find the deep turquoise and powder pink scheme very relaxing, so it's where Ay conduct most of my charity work. The desk is Louis the Fifteenth, and Ay daren't tell you how much it cost!'

'Really? Louis Quinze, how interesting.'

'No, no, Louis the Fifteenth!' Melissa trilled, putting her foot in it unwittingly. She was only just mastering English: correct French terminology was as yet quite beyond her.

Carol quickly continued, trying hard to suppress a smile. This was going to be even better than she had hoped. 'When did you develop this interest in antiques, Melissa? Was it a taste you acquired early?'

'Er, not exactly Carol, but it's become a bit of a hobby of mine.' Melissa didn't like Carol's tone. She changed the subject deftly and began to chat about her involvement in various charities, taking particular advantage of the moment to mention St Rita's and the forthcoming ball. 'It's a wonderful cause you know, Carol,' she said earnestly. 'Those mothers and children have been through hell, and it is going to be the most *glamorous* ball of the year without doubt.'

'I'm sure it will, Melissa.' Carol smiled innocently. 'Speaking of good causes, and your own involvement with so many, was this prompted, do you think, by your experience of charity as a child?' Carol was fully aware that Melissa's family were on the receiving end of more than one charitable institution in her youth.

Melissa's eyes narrowed. This interview was not going the way she had envisaged at all. She deflected the question as best she could, but she was beginning to get flustered. 'Ay have always felt, Carol, that when one is fortunate to have so much,' she paused, 'that it is one's duty to give something back.'

'Okay, guys! Let's take a break!' Maura said, winding up the first stage of the interview.

'You're doing really well, Melissa,' Carol flattered her, 'you're a natural in front of the camera.' Melissa threw her a suspicious look before hurrying off to change into her casual outfit for the next take, which was to be filmed in her bedroom suite.

Just then Maria and two other girls came into the room carrying large silver trays of afternoon tea and refreshments, followed by Jesus who, Carol noticed, seemed to be a little unsteady on his feet.

'Crikey!' Larry, the sound man, was incredulous. 'Is this for us?'

'Don't get carried away, Larry,' Maura warned him. 'We're running tight on time here.'

'Ethcuse me,' Maria was apologetic as she whispered to Carol. 'Mrs Sheehan, she ask me to tell you she need 'alf an hour more with the hairdresser and make-up.'

Carol shot Larry and Roger a look as they started to snigger. 'Tell Mrs Sheehan ten minutes max, Maria. We simply don't have a minute to waste here.'

Maria rolled her eyes to heaven despairingly. 'Okay, but she won' leesen!'

'Just do your best,' Maura sighed. 'Come on, guys. Tea break's over. Let's get the equipment upstairs and crack on.'

Melissa's bedroom suite was something else. It was decorated throughout in an extraordinary combination of black and gold; heavy drapes framed a vast four-poster bed and the mirrored walls threw out an alarming array of reflections.

'I haven't seen myself from so many angles since I was in the Hall of Mirrors!' Larry did a twirl.

'Just get on with it, will you?' Maura hissed at him.

A strange squawking sound was coming from behind a closed door and Melissa was nowhere to be seen.

'Does anybody know where Mrs Sheehan is?' Maura shouted to be heard above the din as the crew struggled to get set up.

'I think she's in the bathroom,' said Mandi, the make-up girl, smiling conspiratorially.

Sure enough, Melissa emerged from behind the door looking pleased with herself. She was sporting a pair of skin-tight leather trousers and a jacket trimmed in what Carol vainly hoped was fake fur. 'Ay was just doing my voice exercises,' she said to nobody in particular. 'My voice coach warned me to warm up. She says Ay have a wonderful timbre.'

'Would that be in the leg department or the acting department?' Roger quipped to Larry, who snorted with laughter.

'Melissa, we really must hurry!' Maura could see things getting way out of hand here. 'Otherwise we'll have to forgo the segment where you take us through your renowned dinner parties, and that would be such a pity …'

That finally got Melissa moving. Everything was settled and they were just about to go for the second take, with Melissa reclining on her vast bed, when Larry, the sound operator, called a halt.

'Hold it! I'm picking up a sound here that's not quite right.' He looked puzzled. 'Is there a generator running?' As if on cue, a black nose poked out from underneath the bed valance, and Melissa shrieked with delight. 'Gabby darling! Come to Mummy!'

'Ah,' said Larry, 'a dog – I think. Mind you I've never heard one that makes a noise like that before.'

'She's not a dog,' said Melissa indignantly. 'She's a

pug. These are my adorable babies, everybody! Dolce and Gabbana, named after my favourite designers.' Melissa simpered as the dogs arranged themselves on the bed beside her, snuffling for all they were worth.

'This is great, Larry!' Maura whispered to him. 'Make sure you get it all, we can't afford to miss a trick!'

'Melissa,' Carol looked suitably awestruck as she started the second stage of the interview. 'Do tell us about the inspiration behind this *fabulously* decadent bedroom.'

'Well, Carol,' Melissa smiled indulgently. 'Ay'll let you into a little secret. Ay've always been fascinated by Cleopatra, so Ay chose an Egyptian theme for my boudoir suite. In fact, Ay was once told in a regression-therapy session, that Ay was an Egyptian princess in a past life.' Melissa paused for effect. 'It really doesn't surprise me. Ay also rule my little empire from the bedroom!'

Strangulated sounds were coming from behind the camera as Larry and Roger helplessly convulsed with laughter.

'Do go on, Melissa, this is fascinating.' Carol could hardly contain herself. 'I know you weren't born and bred in Grovesbury Road – but Egypt? How intriguing,' she continued probingly. 'Clearly your decorating taste has, er, evolved considerably.'

Melissa shot her a sharp look, but Carol seemed genuinely impressed.

'Of course Ay had help, Carol, but my decorator was

very much influenced by my suggestions.' Melissa began the tour of the vast *en suite* bathroom, also decorated in the Egyptian style. Three perfect miniature pyramids rose majestically from behind a huge sandstone bath. A bidet nestled in a miniature model of the Sphinx and an open sandstone shower and jacuzzi took up the entire opposite wall. At the flick of a switch, the overhead lighting changed the ceiling from rosy hues of dawn, to the darkest navy of night from which a million stars seemed to twinkle.

'The ancient Egyptians were brilliant astronomers, of course,' Melissa pronounced knowledgeably, as she fiddled with another switch, 'so my decorator reflected this in the lighting arrangements, see? Ay can vary the constellations on any given night.' She giggled as cleverly arranged spotlights came on in various combinations. 'That way Ay always make sure Ay have a favourable horoscope.'

'D'ya suppose she bathes in asses' milk?' Larry nudged Roger.

'The only ass around here is the poor eejit who's paying for all this crap.'

Eventually it was time for the third and final segment to be set up in the dining room. Jostling downstairs with the equipment, the crew swapped meaningful looks when, warming to her role, Melissa swept down in a startlingly revealing evening creation, to talk to the nation about her entertaining skills. Her freshly straightened hair had bronze extensions added to it to match her dress, and as she floated around the vast room in a shimmer of sequins, Roger immediately zoomed the camera in for a close up of her magnificent cleavage. Unawares, Melissa leaned forward into shot and smiled to camera as she began to talk about her lavish dinner parties. 'My husband knows a lot of very important people of course, Carol, and Ay have to be ready to entertain at a moment's notice.' She sat down on one of the dining-room chairs and patted the seat next to her for Carol to join her.

Carol steeled herself. It was now or never. Her timing had always been impeccable. She leaned towards Melissa, smiling warmly as she went in for the kill. 'It wasn't always like this though, Melissa, was it?'

Melissa blinked momentarily. 'Of course not, Carol!' she gave a tinkly laugh. 'We've done a *huge* amount of work on the house.'

'No, Melissa,' Carol wasn't going to be deterred. 'I mean your *life* wasn't always this …' Carol searched for the right word, 'this *luxurious*. You know the real meaning of having to struggle, don't you? Your early life was rather less *fortunate*, wasn't it? In fact, isn't it true that your real name was Mary Pat O'Malley, and you grew up in considerable poverty? You've reinvented yourself admirably, Melissa, but it must be hard to reconcile this vast wealth with your earlier upbringing?'

For an awful moment, Melissa thought she was going

to scream. Her eyes narrowed and a hundred voices shouted in her head to kill this bitch with her bare hands. But she was being recorded. They'd have it on tape for the whole of Ireland to sneer and laugh at. It had all been a set up! This sly, nasty little bitch of a reporter thought she could crack her. Well, Melissa Sheehan hadn't clawed and grovelled her way up for 20-odd years to screw it up now! Melissa thought like lightning, and suddenly it hit her. She remembered the famous Panorama interview with Princess Di and, like a true pro, she bit the bullet.

To everyone's amazement, the corners of the pouting mouth began to tremble, and a sad little smile hovered. 'Of course, Carol, Pascal and I weren't always this well off.' Melissa lowered her eyes and paused for a moment, before returning a fluttering sincerity to the camera. 'In fact, yes, as you say, we know the meaning of what it is to struggle. But we've both worked hard, and I think we can safely say we've made a success of our lives.' The crew held their breath as two big tears rolled down Melissa's cheeks. Overcome by emotion, she looked to the camera and sniffed, 'Ay'm so sorry, forgive me for becoming emotional, but that's why my charity work means so much to me.' Melissa dabbed her eyes and shook her head gently. 'You see, Ay *know* what it's really like to be on the outside. Ay *understand*. And the only thing that matters is love. In this life, if you don't have a solid, loving relationship, nothing else matters. The rest is, is ...'

Carol jumped in to create a memorable television moment. 'Just the hollow trappings of success?'

'Exactly. If Pascal and Ay were to lose all this,' Melissa waved theatrically at the vast room, 'we would still have each other.'

Maura drew a finger across her throat, making frantic signs at Carol to back off.

'Melissa,' Carol's voice was warm with emotion. 'Thank you *so* much for sharing your fascinating life with us.' She had just wrapped up one hell of an interview.

'Okay! Cut! That's a wrap!'

As the crew began to dismantle their gear, Melissa leaned in towards Carol and whispered to her: 'Think you're very fuckin' smart, don't you? Well, get this! Try anything like that again, an I'll fuckin' burst you. Now gerrourra my house! And you'd better hope you have a job to get back to when I've finished with you!'

'Pascal?'

'Mmm.'

'Are you listening to me?'

'Mmm.'

'I think we should go on a camping holiday around Ireland this summer.' Melissa's sarcasm failed to penetrate.

'That sounds nice.'

'In a tent!'

'Mmm, yes, whatever you like, love.'

'PASCAL!' The roar made whatever hair of his own he had left stand on end. 'You haven't been listening to a word I've said, have you?'

'Sorry, love.'

'Humph! I don't know what's got into you! I'm having lunch in town. Make sure Jesus takes Dolce and Gabbana for their walk.' Melissa raised her eyes to heaven. 'And for feck's sake, put on a decent pair of trousers! The landscape gardeners are coming round at 12; if they see you looking like that they'll think you're the hired help.'

Since the interview on 'Carol Calls', Melissa had been even more insufferable than usual. Not, as she had first presumed, because she had been humiliated before the nation, but because, as is the way of the insightful interview, the unimaginable had been achieved. Melissa Sheehan had become, overnight, a national celebrity. A star. The press was clamouring for her and she was loving every minute of it. It was another cross for poor Pascal to bear.

He waited until he heard the front door close with a resounding thud and let out a long-suffering sigh of relief. A few Melissa-free hours were too good to waste. He didn't feel like going into the office. Come to think of it, he hadn't played hookey for as long as he could remember. He would make a few calls, catch up on the latest issue of *Caravan World* and see if he couldn't track down Charlie for a pint or two.

The lunchtime crowds were beginning to gather as he made his way down Merrion Row. Pascal thrust his hands into the pockets of his favourite duffel coat and braced himself against the bitterly cold wind. It felt good to get out and walk again. And it was the perfect day for a pint. He pushed his way into Doheny & Nesbitt's and searched for the familiar face among the throng. Sure enough, his old friend Charlie was sitting hunched over a pint in his favourite corner, his beady eyes scanning the room. When he saw Pascal, his wizened little face lit up. 'How's the man?'

'Grand, grand! And yourself?' Pascal sat down, rubbing his frozen hands.

'Still here, despite myself,' Charlie wheezed. 'What'll you have?'

'Two more of these, my friend.' Pascal nodded at the half-finished pint of Guinness sitting in front of Charlie as he caught the barman's eye. 'And bring us a slab of your hairiest beef!'

'Spoken like a true carnivore,' said Charlie nodding happily.

'So, where've you been hiding out lately?'

'Oh, I keep myself busy.'

Pascal smiled. Even in retirement, Charlie liked to preserve an air of mystery. In all the long years he'd known him, Pascal could never remember getting a straight answer from the man.

'You're looking well.'

'I look like shite! And I feel worse!' Charlie smiled wryly.

'Still on the fags? Even after what the doctors said?'

'I won't go without a fight. And without the fags and my pint, there wouldn't be any fight. Now what about yourself? Still building for Ireland?'

Over roast beef and a few more pints, Pascal brought Charlie up to date on the general state of things. All the while, Charlie listened intently, scrutinising Pascal as carefully as if he was one of the criminals he had so often hunted to ground.

Pascal couldn't remember when Charlie first came into their lives: he was only grateful that he did. Pascal's father had been a violent alcoholic and took out his bitterness at the world's general shortcomings on his wife and nine young children. One or other of them was always getting into trouble growing up, and Charlie, being one of the local guards, used to drop in on a fairly regular basis.

As a young boy, Pascal grew to rely on him, and Charlie kept him fascinated with stories of old Dublin and its criminals. It wasn't until many years later, when his mother had died a premature and disillusioned death, that Pascal had found Charlie sobbing in his car long after everyone had left the graveside. It was only then it dawned on him that the constant visits had meant something much more to Charlie and Pascal's mother than keeping a vigilant eye on the young Sheehan boys. Later that night, they had got plastered together, and Pascal had asked him about it.

'I loved her,' Charlie had said simply. 'She loved me too, but she would never have left him.'

It was thanks to Charlie, Pascal often thought, that he had stayed on the straight and narrow at all.

'You haven't mentioned the lovely Melissa.' Charlie was as sharp as ever. 'Is she still giving you a hard time?'

Pascal's face tightened. 'What else would she do?'

'Melissa's all right, Pascal. I said it then, and I'll say it now. She's one of us. Don't forget that.'

'Try telling her that!'

'She needs a firm hand, that's all. I hope all this Dublin 4 living isn't turning you soft?'

'I don't know, Charlie. I don't bloody know any more, and that's the truth.'

'Ah, I see.'

And over another few pints, Pascal found himself telling the man who was the closest thing he ever had to a father the sorry tale of his floundering marriage.

It might have been in the Shelbourne, or possibly in O'Donogues, or maybe even in the Waterloo, that the conversation took the general drift of who had seen whom, doing what where. At the time, it hadn't meant much to Pascal. But he would remember the remark later with the blinding clarity of hindsight.

'Word is out Commiskys are having nothing more to do with Michael Moriarty,' Charlie had said. 'I saw Michael with Old Man Commisky the other day in the Berkeley Court and he didn't look like a happy man.'

Commisky & Son was one of Michael's biggest clients, so the remark caught Pascal's attention.

'He didn't say anything about it to me.'

'Ah, maybe it's just talk. How is Michael these days?'

'Same as ever. That reminds me, I must talk to him this week. That's if I can ever catch him between shaggin' meetings.' And then another pint had miraculously arrived in front of him, and the moment had drowned in a slow, sweet appreciation of the black stuff that was arguably Dublin's finest export.

It was half-past eleven that night before Pascal, tired but happy, discovered he had forgotten the remote-control gizmo for the electric gates that now denied him access to his fortress of a house. The sequence of numbers that he punched in repeatedly to release the code proved equally unsuccessful. Undaunted, he managed, with great aplomb, to clamber over the imposing red-brick wall from where he dropped and collapsed in a graceful heap. The security camera that captured this valiant effort would later reveal a small, shabbily dressed individual hurling himself with great intent towards the front door, where some malevolent forces had, in his absence, conspired to arrange an obstacle course. As Pascal entered into armed combat with the elaborate constructions created earlier that day by Melissa's landscape gardeners, the security lights flashed on, and the ominous wail of the burglar alarm sounded like a banshee. The front door opened to reveal a terrified

Maria wielding a carving knife and Jesus behind her brandishing a Big Bertha golf club still in its wrapper. As he fell across the threshold, Pascal Sheehan, one of the richest men in Ireland, reflected that it was not for the first time he felt like an intruder in his own home.

Carol sat tapping at her lap-top while her headful of tinfoil highlights cooked under the watchful eye of her colourist. Not for her the idle chitchat of the hair salon. If she had to indulge in two and a half hours of blonding every six weeks, then she made sure she put the time to good use. The special 7.30 a.m. regular appointment she held was a concession from the salon, but they more than benefitted from the generous publicity Carol generated for them. And she had no time to waste. Her interview with Melissa Sheehan had sent ratings soaring and she was riding the crest of the wave. A big day was ahead of her, chock-a-block with meetings, not least of which was her imminent encounter with her old friend Dr Gerald Stevens. It had been surprisingly easy to arrange in the end. She had simply appealed to his generously oversized ego. Of course he had no idea who she was; she had changed her surname from Doherty to Dalton when she had married her weak, ineffectual husband. The marriage had only lasted 18 months. As soon as she had got her foot in the door at RTE she had dumped him.

Organising the meeting with 'Gerald' had been a walkover. She had contacted his office, spoken with his secretary and asked her to inform Dr Stevens that TV 2000 was interested in doing a profile on him, his successful career and his return to Ireland. She hadn't had to wait long for a reply. His secretary had got back to Carol's office saying that Dr Stevens would be delighted to accommodate her. *I'll bet,* thought Carol savagely. And today was the day. She was seeing him for a preliminary chat in his office so that she could draft the outline of the eventual TV interview.

She quickly scanned her research again and made a few more notes on the important angles through which she would approach this first meeting. Scrolling through the pages, she checked each fact, rehearsing every meticulously thought-out question in her head.

'You're nearly done now, just a few more minutes,' smiled Zach, colourist to Dublin's gliteratti, checking Carol's colour carefully.

After duly being shampooed and rinsed, Carol sat back to enjoy her blow dry and admire the rapidly emerging benefits of bleach. Three quarters of an hour later, the transformation was complete. She paid the bill, tipped her colourist and stylist generously, and made her way into the nearby ladies' room to survey the result. Smiling, she silently thanked God for the miracle of modern science. She was a walking advertisement for it! This was thanks to some smartass she had worked with in her journalist days laughing at her when she had confided to him her ambition to break into television one day. 'Hey Carol,' he had laughed, 'don't get your hopes up – you've got a great face for radio!' Well, she had shown him!

There was no way he or Gerald Stevens would recognize this slim, strawberry-blonde, power-suited executive! She checked her watch and shivered in anticipation. Time for a wake-up call, Dr Goldfinger Stevens, she said to herself. You've got an appointment with your past.

The first instalment caught Michael unawares.

'A Mr Owens to see you.' Michael's immaculate secretary looked distinctly disapproving as she ushered Joey into the office.

'Thank you, Katy, that will be all.' Michael's face was impassive as he rose from behind his desk. He waited until Katy had closed the door behind her. 'I've told you never to come to the office.' Michael was white with anger. What if Simon or, God forbid, Pascal were to see him?

'Oh, too late for that now!' Joey said cheerfully. 'Strict instructions from the boss! Personal delivery, he said. Make sure it goes straight to the man himself, he said. It's all there. You can count it if ya like.' Joey looked hopeful.

'That won't be necessary,' Michael said coldly.

'Oh, yeah, and this,' Joey produced a small package from his inside pocket and held it out to Michael, 'is on the house. A token of Mr McEntee's appreciation.' Joey put the package on Michael's desk. 'Nice place you've got here,' he remarked, nodding appreciatively as he looked around.

'Thank you.' Michael willed him to go. 'Well,' he smiled dismissively. 'If there's nothing else, tell Mr McEntee I'll be in touch.'

Joey looked incredulous. 'No one gets in touch with the boss. He'll get in touch with you, when he's good an' ready. Think about it, Mickey.' Michael flinched at the insolence. 'Did I ever give you a number for Mr McEntee? Well, did I?'

Michael cursed himself for his stupidity. 'Er, no, no I don't believe you did, come to think of it.'

'Exactly.' Joey jabbed a finger under Michael's chin. 'An' I won't be, neither.' Smirking as Michael shrank back into his chair, Joey made for the door. 'Like I said, you'll be hearing from us. Righ'?' And that was his parting shot.

Michael sat down wearily. The black Adidas holdall Joey had deposited sat invitingly on his desk. He may as well take a look. It was all there – and then some. At a quick calculation Michael reckoned on at least £250,000, flicking through one pack of grubby notes. There was no going back now. He shifted uneasily in his chair. Well, so what? This would get him back on track. He should be pleased; instead he found he was feeling rather weak. With a rush of relief he remembered his 'free' gift. Pressing the 'do not disturb' button on his phone so Katy wouldn't walk in on him, he opened the tightly packed plastic package. Reaching into the Adidas holdall he took one of the cleaner notes, rolling it deftly into a neat tube. He could do with a hit if he was to remain remotely unfazed by this latest turn of events. Not to mention an evening at home with Felicity and her remorseless perfectionism.

Feeling considerably better about things, Michael left for the evening. His office, conveniently located in Clyde Road, was a brisk ten-minute walk from Grovesbury Road. By the time he reached his house, he had convinced himself that everything was under control. Stopping for a moment, he paused to admire the gracious proportions of his magnificent home. Built at the turn of the century, in the typical High Victorian Tudor style, the house was one of the few on the road to retain its original beauty. Felicity's impeccable taste had seen to that. The house had been in need of work when they had bought it ten years ago. A hideous extension had been removed, and with painstaking effort, and considerable expense, which involved bringing over specialised arts and crafts builders from England, the house had been lovingly and sympathetically restored and enlarged. Felicity had relished doing the interior herself, believing, as did generations of her family before her, that interior designers were for people who had neither taste nor breeding. And Michael's generous budget allowed her to demonstrate admirably the kind of understated elegance and luxury that other people had spent fortunes and lifetimes trying to emulate without success. Soon, numerous interiors magazines, who had heard on the grapevine about the house, were clamouring to do a 'spread'. Felicity declined them all politely.

A real log fire crackled in the huge square hall providing a cheerful and warming welcome as Michael let himself in. It was one of many. Felicity didn't believe in gas fires. A real home, she was fond of saying, has real fires or none at all.

Taking off his coat, Michael wandered into the sitting room, where Felicity was speaking into the phone in what sounded like rapid German.

'Hi, darling,' Michael kissed her lightly on the cheek before heading to the drinks cabinet.

'You're early!' she mouthed at him, looking mildly irritated. Felicity didn't welcome disruptions to the daily routine. Finishing her phone call, she sat down on the sofa and stretched her elegantly clad ten-denier legs.

'Drink, darling?' Michael asked as he poured himself a large whiskey.

'Yah, please, seeing as it's Friday I will.' Felicity was rigorous about not drinking during the week; it was part of her policy of self-restraint.

Handing her a generous gin and tonic, Michael collapsed on the sofa beside her gratefully.

'Bad day?' Felicity ran a practised eye over her husband.

'Oh, I've had worse.' Michael was careful to avoid her penetrating gaze. He hoped desperately his pupils hadn't shrunk to pinpoints – she'd be bound to notice. Swigging his whiskey, he willed the alcohol to reverse the process as quickly as possible. He changed the subject quickly. 'We're not doing anything on Thursday, are we?'

'I don't think so,' Felicity ran a hand through her perfectly blow-dried hair. 'I've got bridge with the girls but I'm sure they can get another fourth if necessary. Why?'

'Oh, it's Simon. He's roped us into some bloody dinner party he's been going on non-stop about. I couldn't get out of it.'

'Ghastly Simon who works for you?' Felicity said, making a disdainful face.

'I'm afraid so. He's bent on impressing his latest girlfriend. The Lemass girl – you know her.'

'Not Lornagh Lemass, surely?' Felicity was incredulous. 'I can't believe it!'

'The Sheehans are going, too.' Michael thought he'd better offload the full implications of the evening.

'Oh, great! That's supposed to be a consolation is it?' Although Felicity was fond of Pascal, she couldn't bear Melissa, whom she constantly referred to as 'that vulgar woman'. If only she knew, Michael thought wryly; even Felicity couldn't imagine how Melissa somehow turned vulgarity into an art form. Particularly when sex was involved. Michael cleared his throat quickly. He'd better not follow that train of thought!

'It's hardly my idea of a great night out either, darling, but duty calls and all that. He does work for me, after all.'

'Oh, all right. But only if you promise I don't have to talk to that frightful Melissa woman. If she comes over to monopolise me like she did at lunch the other day, I shall feign a headache and leave immediately.'

'That's my girl,' Michael chuckled. He knew Melissa took a sadistic pleasure in fraternising with her lover's spouse, and Michael rather enjoyed the nervous thrill he derived from it. 'Look on the bright side. We can listen to Simon talk about himself all evening.'

Felicity groaned. 'Will you ever forget that dinner here when he actually started to discuss what our furniture might be worth? I thought I was going to die! Do you know, I honestly think he thought he was impressing everybody.' Felicity began to laugh. 'The sheer arrogance of the man knows no bounds. Every time I've met him he's either talking about who owns what or how much their house is worth. I've never come across anyone so gauche.'

'Poor Simon.' Michael shook his head, laughing. 'He just doesn't get it. Now knock back that drink, Mrs Moriarty, and let's find out what that scintillating smell is wafting from the kitchen.'

After an excellent dinner of pheasant washed down

with a particularly pleasing burgundy – Felicity counted a cordon bleu diploma among her many accomplishments – Felicity and Michael retired to watch a movie. Their children were, for once, all out, making for an unusually peaceful evening. Sipping a port, Michael sneaked a look at Felicity as she watched the screen intently. After 16 years of marriage and four children, she still held a fascination for him. She had always been good-looking in a classical sense, but it was more than just her looks that attracted him. There was an unusual aloofness about her. Even in bed, Felicity was remote. There were no gushing compliments, no whispered endearments. Michael had to admit he found it strangely compelling. He felt himself stiffen just thinking about it. He risked trailing a finger from the nape of her elegant neck slowly down to her collar-bone. 'I was contemplating an early night,' he said huskily. 'Do you think you could be enticed?'

Felicity shuddered. Michael couldn't tell if it was with pleasure or otherwise. 'Go ahead, I'll be up shortly,' she said curtly.

Michael did as he was told, heading upstairs to their bedroom. He undressed quickly and lay on the bed.

When Felicity finally came to join him, clad in thigh-high boots, a black leather corset and very little else, he groaned in anticipation.

Brandishing the riding crop that she claimed had been in her family for generations, she turned him over, trailing the battered leather strap tantalisingly along his spine, producing, not surprisingly, a far more effective response than any ever achieved on the hunting field.

'Michael, Michael,' she murmured, 'you've been a very, *very* bad boy.'

CHAPTER FOUR

Lornagh snuggled up to Simon on his velvet-covered sofa and sighed. It had been a lovely evening. Staying in for a change, they had opened a bottle of wine and ordered a takeaway from their local Chinese. Watching Simon as he fiddled with the remote control, Lornagh was feeling pleasantly sleepy and looking forward to falling into bed. Earlier, she had thanked him for the flowers and apologised if she had been unnecessarily snappy. She had a lot on her plate right now, she had admitted, but that was no reason to take it out on him. Now everything was perfect again; as usual she had been too hasty in her judgement.

'Si? Sorry, Simon?' Simon hated anyone abbreviating his name.

'Hmm?'

'What about a Bailey's?'

'I was just about to suggest one,' Simon lied. Trying not to appear irritated, he got up to produce two glasses and poured in the creamy liqueur, adding a generous helping of brandy to his own. Sitting down beside

Lornagh, Simon put his feet up. The evening movie was just about to start, the announcer informed them. Sipping her drink, Lornagh watched as *Parenthood*, starring Steve Martin, appeared on screen. She'd seen it before, on a plane somewhere, but was quite happy to sit through it again.

'Lornagh?'

'Mmm?'

'I know about your famous mother, Angela, obviously.' Simon was probing. 'But you don't say much about your father, Maxwell Lemass; he was a very well-respected man, I believe?' Simon had researched Lornagh's pedigree thoroughly and was dying to find out everything he could.

Lornagh took a deep breath. She'd expected this, sooner or later. 'Maxwell *was* a wonderful man and the best father any girl could have wanted; but he wasn't my father.'

'What do you mean, not your father?'

'He was married to my mother, sure, but he took me on as well. I think I was about three years old at the time. He was wonderful to me, and as far as having a father, well, he was as close as I got.'

'But, then, who *is* your father? You must know, surely?'

'Actually, I don't. And at this stage, I have no wish to find out, even if I could.'

'B-but your mother, she must have *told* you?'

'My mother doesn't know either. She has a ... a *suspicion*, but the parties involved are all dead now, so I believe, and anyway, it was all so long ago ...' Lornagh trailed off, watching Simon's reaction. 'Maxwell was the father I needed, and he loved me as if, no *better* than if, I were his own daughter. I can't tell you how I miss him.'

Simon swallowed hard. He couldn't believe what he was hearing. Lornagh Lemass, the most beautiful girl in Dublin, daughter of a famous movie star, didn't even know who her own father was? Why, she was illegitimate. It was unthinkable. What was he going to tell his mother? How would he introduce his prospective bride? 'Hello, Mother, Father, this is Lornagh, only daughter of Angela Lemass, movie star – father unknown.'

'But haven't you tried to find out? I mean, it's possible to track down almost *anyone* these days, through the internet or ...'

'I told you, Simon, I don't want to. I don't *need* to. It doesn't matter to me, Simon, not at this stage of my life, so I hope it doesn't matter to you?'

'No, no, of course not,' Simon lied. 'I was just trying to be helpful, that's all.'

They watched the rest of the movie in relative silence, and when it was over, Lornagh got up and stretched, holding out a hand to Simon. 'I'm exhausted; come on, let's go to bed.'

'Er, Lornagh, would you mind if you didn't stay tonight?' Apart from the latest startling revelation, Simon still hadn't forgiven Lornagh for seeing her girlfriends the other night instead of him. 'I have an early start in the morning and there's the dinner party and everything … you do understand?'

'What?' Lornagh recovered herself quickly, although the intended stab hurt. 'Oh, sure, I had almost forgotten. No, of course I don't mind. I'll see you tomorrow, then.'

Simon hid a triumphant smile as he got up to call a cab for her. That would teach her. No one, not even Lornagh Lemass, was going to take him for granted.

When the cab arrived, within minutes, Simon followed her to the door and kissed her. 'Drive carefully, won't you?' he said to the driver, and then to Lornagh, 'I want you all in one beautiful piece beside me at the table tomorrow.' He smiled indulgently at her. 'Sleep tight, and dream nice dreams of me.'

After she had left, Simon poured himself another brandy and sat down. Lornagh didn't have a father! He couldn't believe it. She hadn't even the remotest clue who the man was. This put a totally different perspective on things. This wouldn't go down at all well with Mater. Well, there was only one thing for it. There was no need for her to know. Lornagh would just have to keep the unsavoury knowledge to herself. As far as Simon's parents were concerned, Maxwell Lemass had been her father. And that was all there was to it.

'Hello, poppet. I wasn't expecting you back tonight. However, you're just in time to join me for a nightcap. I assumed you were staying at Simon's.'

'I thought so too, but apparently not.'

'Trouble in paradise?' Lawrence looked hopeful.

'Not exactly, more a case of shock, I'd say.'

'Excellent, do tell.'

'Well, I told Simon about my, er, parental situation, or rather, lack of ...'

'Ah, I see. Was he suitably appalled?'

'I think that might be an understatement; although he tried hard not to be.'

'Now why does that not surprise me?'

'Come on, Lawrence, that's not fair.'

'Who said anything about being fair? You know perfectly well I think Simon is a self-righteous, judgemental prick. It's written all over his pursed-up, disapproving, bourgeois face. He's not for you, Lornagh, and what's more, you know it. I'm amazed you've lasted this long, to be honest. When are you going to get real?'

'I beg your pardon?'

'Oh, come off it, Lornagh. Ever since you've come back from the States you've been trying to turn yourself into Little Miss Prissy. It won't wash. Not with me, not with your real friends. It's not you. Not the you we know and love anyhow.'

'I just want a normal life! Is that so much to ask for?'

'In your case, yes. You're a lot of things Lornagh: funny, interesting, complex, yes, even bossy sometimes. But you're far from ordinary. That's what makes you intriguing. And that is why having a boring, ordinary life with a man who wants you to be something you are not will make you unutterably miserable. There's no escaping it, poppet, origins will out. You are not your run-of-the-mill Dublin 4 girl and I for one am thankful. You should be, too.'

Lornagh was, unusually, at a loss for a retort. She suddenly felt terribly tired, as if all the air had been sucked out of her. 'I'm not going to turn into her, Lawrence; I don't care what you say, what any of you think, I am not,' she protested, 'under any circumstances, going to turn into my mother.'

'Of course you're not. You're going to become Lornagh. That's what this whole thing is about. You've got to own up to being you, whatever that is, and Simon, for one, isn't going to help you do that. How is darling Angela, by the way?'

'Ebullient as ever.' Lornagh scowled. 'Answer me this: how does one person create such havoc for everyone else around her and continually emerge unscathed?'

'No idea, but I'm working on acquiring just such an entertaining talent myself. I don't know why you make her such hard work, Lornagh. You don't have to, you know; she's really an old dear. I adore her.'

'I know, the feeling's mutual – you're the daughter she's always wanted.'

Lawrence chuckled. 'That's more like it. Now come along, poppet, drink up! There's a lot of the world left to put to rights yet, and I want to tell you about a certain

Italian chef I've met recently called Mauricio, whose talents, I'm happy to confirm, are not remotely confined to the culinary.'

Despite the soporific effects of the nightcap, Lornagh was unable to sleep. Tossing and turning for what remained of the night, she wrestled with conflicting emotions. It was no use. However she tried to silence her doubts, Lawrence was right. Simon was not for her. She supposed, deep down, she had always known it, but she had so wanted this relationship to work. She dragged herself out of bed and padded downstairs to the kitchen, where she made a cup of tea and sat down to try and think. Everything had seemed so right in the beginning. When she had finally made the decision to come home, a relationship had been the last thing on her mind. But Simon had come into her life and, truth be told, she had found him attractive and desperately wanted him to be 'the one'.

She wanted to settle down, she wanted stability in her life, and she wanted it here: in Dublin, with her friends and family around her. She was so tired of starting over. And here she was, facing it all over again. What was it she had read somewhere? Something about the universe sending you the same challenge time and time again until you finally met it? Well, the Powers That Be were having a field day with her!

She would talk to Simon tomorrow, she resolved; she

wouldn't think about it now. Tomorrow – or rather, today, she thought wearily, looking at the kitchen clock that cheerfully informed her it was now four o'clock in the morning. She'd better get back to bed to have any chance of coping with the sizeable hangover that was threatening to complicate her immediate future even further.

In her cool bed, sleep toyed with her infuriatingly, competing with a nagging thought that refused to take proper shape in her fuzzy head. What the hell was it? With a blinding flash of realisation it came to her, banishing whatever hopes she had of catching a few hours' kip. Tomorrow! Tomorrow was Simon's dinner party.

The murmur of lively conversation interspersed with bursts of laughter filled the room. So far, the evening had surpassed even Simon's expectations.

Everything was perfect. But then, he wouldn't have settled for anything less. This, he had made sure, would be a night for people to remember. The apartment looked stunning: a miniature Victorian palace. Dark red and green flock-covered walls were reflected in majestic gilt-framed mirrors, and rich velvets and damasks adorned graceful chairs and sofas. Looking around the room, Simon was pleased to see the light of countless candles, flickering softly, created a truly magical effect.

The caterers had provided a superb feast and the dining-room table was a work of art, laid out with his carefully chosen antique china and crystal, and two magnificent silver candelabra holding court majestically at either end. Champagne was flowing and so was the conversation. Simon sat at the head of the table with Lornagh on his right-hand side. For some reason, Simon noted, she wasn't looking her best. In fact, she looked downright shaken. No doubt it was nerves. She would understand how important it was to him that she made a good impression tonight. He smiled and sipped his red wine slowly, basking in the glory of what was without doubt a superb evening. Well, the best was yet to come.

Melissa was deep in discussion with Gerald Steven's fiancée, Candice, about the pros and cons of plastic surgery. 'Ay was watching a fascinatin' programme last night about penile enlargement.' She reached under the table where Michael had conveniently been seated next to her and began to caress his thigh. 'It's amazin' what they can do nowadays, although I'm happy to say I've never come across anyone who needed it!'

'Well, I'm all for it!' Candice gave a throaty laugh, flashing alarmingly large white teeth. 'I'm from Texas, and *everything* is bigger there!'

Crikey! I'll bet those teeth could do some damage, thought Michael, finding himself immediately aroused. He made a mental note to get her number later.

After a magnificent pudding of feather-light chocolate soufflé, coffee and liqueurs were now being served. A comfortable mellowness had settled around the table and Simon knew the perfect moment had arrived to end a perfect evening. Tapping his glass for silence, he rose to his feet. 'Ladies and gentlemen! Your attention, please! And may I say how happy I am that you're all here to share this special moment with me.' Immediately he had the attention of seven curious, expectant faces. Simon reached inside his breast pocket, and turning to Lornagh, who looked as puzzled as everyone else, he proudly opened a small box where a large square-cut diamond sparkled invitingly. 'Lornagh,' he began, dropping his ponderous voice an octave lower, 'from the moment I met you, I knew we would make the perfect couple.' He paused dramatically, sneaking a quick glance at the mesmerised faces around the table. 'Marry me, Lornagh! And let tonight be the first of all our tomorrows!' There was a collective gasp around the table and all eyes swivelled towards Lornagh, who had turned as white as a sheet.

'Simon. I, I ...'

'You're overwhelmed?' Simon's chest puffed out as he relished the dramatic twist he had given to the evening. Patting his carefully gelled waves, he smiled around the table.

'I can't believe you'd do this to me!' Lornagh gasped. 'How *could* you?'

'Wha-what?' stammered Simon. 'What do you mean?'

'I mean,' cried Lornagh, pushing herself up so quickly from the table that her chair fell backwards, 'that it's utterly unforgivable! It's over, Simon! I never want to see you again!' Sobbing, she fled from the room.

After that, everything was a bit of a blur for Simon as he stood there with his mouth opening and closing like a fish. People hurriedly made their excuses and embarrassed farewells and left quietly.

'Bad luck, old chap.' He vaguely heard Michael's commiserations as he was patted on the shoulder. 'Take it on the chin. She may feel differently in the morning.'

Three hours later, Simon sat at the table nursing his third tumbler of brandy. A recurring chant played in his increasingly unfocused mind. *The stupid, stuck up, vicious bitch! How dare she? How dare she humiliate him like that in front of all those people? How dare she?*

Melissa was floating around Whitakers, Dublin's newest designer store, on a high. Life had taken on new meaning since The Interview. She had finally won the recognition she deserved and now considered herself a fully fledged celebrity. She had even begun to think quite kindly of that sly little reporter, Carol. After all, it was thanks to her that she had discovered she was such a natural on TV. Three society magazines had already called her for interviews, one of which wanted to do a spread on the house. And she had been asked to appear on a popular TV quiz show. As she perused the latest collections, Melissa wondered idly if she should get herself an agent. A deep voice interrupted her reverie.

'Melissa! Lovely to see you!' It was Basil, the debonair managing director of the store. 'I really enjoyed your TV interview the other night, you were great. That Versace evening dress looked stunning on you.'

'Oh, Basil,' Melissa purred, 'how naice of you to say so! Ay've just popped in to do a little shoppin' while I still have the time. My schedule is so busy these days.'

'I'm not surprised.' Basil was as charming as ever. 'Remember, Melissa, we'll be happy to send any of the new collections out to you if you can't get into the store.'

'That's so *kaind* of you.' Melissa gave him her best smile.

'Look, when you've finished, why don't you join me in the bar for a quick glass of champagne? I'd love to tell you some of my plans for our new designers.'

'Give me half an hour, Basil. Ay'd love to!' Melissa was thrilled.

'Great! 12.30, then.' Basil strode away smiling. It would be time well invested. When a customer spent as much as Melissa did in any one session, it was really the least he could do.

Melissa finally settled on a brown silk-and-lace trouser suit which would be perfect for the occasion she had in mind. She and Pascal were off to a wedding in Ashford Castle that weekend and, as they were travelling by helicopter, she didn't want to risk a dress that might fly up around her waist because of the wind generated by the blades. Not that she minded showing off her legs.

They were almost perfect; just another liposculpture session or two would do the trick. She made a mental note to check in with her surgeon later that week.

The assistant wrapped the suit for Melissa carefully, discreetly handing her the credit-card slip which read a healthy £2,800. Melissa barely glanced at it, signing with a flourish. Parcels in hand, she made for the escalator, stopping off at ground level for a quick recce at the accessories. She was just past the jewellery counter when a beautiful brown-and-gold hand-painted scarf caught her attention. Melissa fingered the delicate material thoughtfully. It would set off her new trouser suit perfectly. Looking around carefully, she deftly slipped the scarf into the bag with her previous purchase. No point in keeping Basil waiting for a matter of a mere £225. Immediately she felt the familiar rush of adrenaline. Security tags were such a bore these days, but nothing she couldn't handle. Why, in her day, she'd been the best of the best. Anyway, they'd never dare arrest her, and if they did she'd just say it was a silly mistake.

Flushed with success, Melissa tripped lightly down the plush caramel carpeted stairs to the downstairs bar, where Basil was waiting with a chilled bottle of champagne. She waved gaily as she made her way over to join him. Shopping really was such fun!

Pascal was worried. It wasn't anything in particular, just a vague feeling that something wasn't quite right. Mind you, since his escapade the other night when he had woken up the whole road, Melissa had made it clear in no uncertain terms just how very wrong he had got it. He had been in the dog house ever since. In fact, Pascal thought ruefully, he would have been happier in a dog house (if they'd had one) than in his ridiculous excuse of a home, where Melissa's pugs, Dolce and Gabbana, reigned in more luxury than most mortals he had ever known.

'What's the matter, Paccy? You haven't been yourself lately.' Eva was concerned about him.

Pascal counted the moments until he could be with her these days.

'Ah, it's nothing,' Pascal said, brushing it off. 'At least I'm the better for seeing you.'

Eva smiled. 'I've got your favourite! Steak and kidney pie. Sit down there now and tell me what you've been up to.'

Tucking into a delicious dinner, Pascal told Eva all about his day out with Charlie and his subsequent fall from grace. He had brought the video from the security camera with him, and they fell about laughing as they watched the replay of Pascal grappling helplessly with the new constructions in his front garden before finally falling in a drunken stupor through his own front door.

'Oh, stop! I can't watch any more!' Eva was gasping for breath between gales of laughter.

'Ha, ha, ha, will you look at that eejit Jesus sending

his poor wife out in front of him to protect him against the "intruder"?' Pascal was enjoying it more every time he watched it.

'What's that he's waving about like a madman?' Eva peered at the screen wiping tears of mirth from her eyes.

'Ha, ha, that's the new Big Bertha Melissa bought me when she wanted me to take up golf,' Pascal wheezed. 'At least it's put to better use as a self-defence weapon. Sure it's never been out of its wrapper.'

'You? Play golf?' shrieked Eva. 'Ho, ho, oh that's a good one!' And they had collapsed all over again.

Eva adored the time she spent with him. He was so kind to her, and they got on so well together. When they had finally watched all they could take of the security video, Pascal told her about the extraordinary dinner party he had been to at Simon Sullivan's. When he came to the bit about Simon proposing to Lornagh out of the blue, Eva's mouth fell open in astonishment.

'What? In front of all those people? I don't believe it! The poor girl! What kind of an eejit is he, this Simon fella?' Eva was indignant.

'You may well ask,' Pascal chortled. 'He's Michael's lackey, really. I don't know where he found him, but he seems to think he's running the office for us now.'

'And Michael, was he at the party too?' Eva loved hearing everything.

'Oh yes, and Felicity, his wife.'

'I think I've seen pictures of her in the magazines.'

Eva nodded knowingly. 'She seems a lovely, elegant woman.' Eva kept up to date with the society pages, always eager for a glimpse of Pascal and his famous friends.

'She is a nice woman,' agreed Pascal. 'And a smart one, and she keeps a tight rein on Michael. He has a lot to thank her for.' Pascal liked Felicity; she was always pleasant to him and never made him feel stupid or inadequate. A lot of people didn't like her – they considered her stuck up. But Pascal understood her natural reserve and thought her a real lady.

'Well, I hope Michael appreciates her.'

'To be fair, I think he does, in his own way.'

'I'd say Michael wouldn't be the easiest to live with.'

'What makes you say that?' Pascal was interested in Eva's opinions. She was a great judge of character.

'Oh, I don't know really, he strikes me as being a bit driven, and all that schmoozing with his celebrity clients, it can't be easy for his wife.'

'Mmm, I hadn't thought of that.' Pascal was thoughtful. 'Now that you mention it, he has seemed under a bit of strain these days. I hope it's not domestic trouble.'

'How d'you mean?' Eva was curious.

'Well, he's seemed sort of jumpy lately. Usually he's so laid back, he's horizontal. And he's lost a good bit of weight, not that he needed to. The other night, at the dinner party, he looked sort of pale and sweaty, and he kept slipping out to go to the loo.' Now that Pascal thought about it, Michael definitely hadn't been himself lately. He tried to remember where else it was he had recently heard something along those lines. He had a vague memory of someone saying something interesting about Michael that he had meant to follow up but, try as he could, he couldn't for the life of him think what it was. He would take Michael out to lunch next week and find out what was going on.

'Eva?'

'What, love?' Eva looked up from stacking the dishwasher. Something in Pascal's voice caught her attention.

'I'm going to leave Melissa.' Pascal had thought long and hard about it. He really couldn't take any more.

'Oh Pascal!' Eva was torn between dismay and guilty delight. 'You mustn't rush into anything serious. You know how she is. This phase will pass; it always does. Besides, this arrangement is good for both of us, we've always said so, and nobody gets hurt.'

Much as she adored Pascal, Eva had grown to enjoy her independent lifestyle. And recently, she had met a very nice widower at the golf club, who had three grown up daughters. Although at this stage they were just very good friends, Eva suspected he had feelings for her and, as she told herself, she wasn't getting any younger. It was time, she felt, to expand her horizons a little. Whether Pascal was aware of it or not, Eva knew he would never get Melissa out of his system. There was no point in him even trying. 'Please, Pascal,' she cautioned, 'promise me you won't rush into anything silly?' Eva looked so worried that Pascal smiled. 'Well, maybe not today, but I can't take much more, Eva, really I can't.' And Eva knew from his tone that he meant it. She silently cursed Melissa's stupidity. Pascal asked for so little and was so generous himself. It should have been so easy for her to keep him happy. It wasn't fair. Now it looked as if Melissa was going to ruin everything. Something would have to be done, Eva vowed. And done quickly. But what?

Pulling into Fitzwilliam Square at 12.15, Carol had allowed plenty of time to avoid any mishaps. She was rewarded by a parking space magically materialising exactly opposite the ornately decorated Georgian door that led to the home and consulting rooms of Dr Gerald Stevens. She had 15 minutes to spare. Manoeuvring into the space, she switched off the ignition and checked her make-up in the rearview mirror. It was flawless: she looked every inch the slick reporter and a very far cry from the desolate young girl he had left behind all those years ago. She would have to keep a tight rein on her emotions here, she reminded herself firmly. No chink in the armour was going to upset her carefully laid plans. She had been robbed of much more than her innocence, and now it was payback time. Just a few more months, if that, and Dr Goldfinger Stevens was going to rue the day he had ever been born.

'Carol!' The tap on her shoulder had made her jump clean out of her skin. She had arrived in Dublin early by bus, having bunked off her morning's classes, and was not due to arrive at her aunt's house, where she was staying, until evening. She planned to spend the afternoon looking around the bewildering array of shops that seemed so infinitely sophisticated compared to the few local boutiques in her home town. 'Dr Stevens!' A deep flush had suffused her face as she turned to find him standing behind her in the newsagent's where she had been looking through a magazine. Mortified to have been caught in her school uniform, she had stuttered and stammered an embarrassed hello.

'What are you doing in the big metropolis?' He had smiled warmly, seeming pleased to bump into her. He looked every bit as gorgeous as she had remembered, with his dark blue eyes and black curls that reminded her of David Essex. 'Shouldn't you be at school, young lady?' The twinkling eyes had seemed friendly and conspiratorial. She explained falteringly that she had come up to town to spend a few days with her aunt and was just about to buy a sandwich and a coke for her lunch, blushing even more deeply as she cursed herself for sounding so gauche.

'Isn't your mother meeting you?' He had seemed concerned for her.

'No, no, I'm on my own. I'm getting the bus to my aunt's this evening,' Carol had explained.

'In that case, you must allow me buy you lunch. I wouldn't hear of you having a sandwich on your own for *your first trip to Dublin. I was just heading to my favourite Italian restaurant around the corner. Now you can keep me company. Do you like Italian food?' Carol wished the ground would open up and swallow her, but he seemed so nice and friendly, and the thought of going to a real restaurant was something she had often dreamed of. If only she wasn't wearing her horrible school uniform. She said as much to him and he had laughed it off, telling her she looked absolutely fine. She had nearly fainted with pleasure. He had walked her to the restaurant, talking all the while and telling her funny stories about his morning at the hospital.*

The restaurant was a cosy little place, with red checked table cloths and pretty wooden chairs. Carol had never seen anything as stylish and continental at home. The friendly Italian waiters greeted Dr Stevens warmly and made a big fuss of them, seating them at a lovely table for two against a brightly painted wall hung with photographs of famous clients. Carol recognized Gay Byrne, Eamonn Andrews and even Jack Lynch. Wait until she told her friends back home: they'd be green with envy.

She had felt awkward and silly when the menu arrived: all the strange sounding names meant nothing to her, and she hadn't a clue what to order, but Dr Stevens – or Gerald as he had insisted she call him – had made it easy by ordering for her. He had insisted she have a glass of red wine too, which Carol had thought very grown up. She didn't like the taste very much at first, but she didn't want to seem a complete country bumpkin. Soon she found herself chatting away happily to him.

He was so easy to talk to, and he seemed genuinely interested in everything about school and the sports she played. When she told him she was on the school hockey team he had seemed impressed, and he even said she must tell him if they ever had a match in Dublin and he would come and cheer her on.

Carol wanted the lunch to last forever. She had never dreamed of having such a good time. By the time they had finished dessert and ordered frothy coffees – or cappuccinos as Gerald had called them – she was finally beginning to feel really at ease, confident even. Maybe even she could turn into one of those sophisticated girls whom she had seen strolling nonchalantly down Grafton Street. Life had suddenly seemed full of expectation and possibilities.

Finally, it was time to go. Carol thanked Gerald coyly and told him she'd a wonderful time. Sadly, she said she would have to catch the bus to Milltown where her aunt lived.

'Milltown?' he had said sounding surprised. 'Why, I'm just on my way there to play a round of golf. I'll be able to give you a lift.' Although she protested, saying he had been far too kind already, secretly she was thrilled at the thought of even the tiniest bit of extra time she could spend with him. Carol looked at him shyly as he drove confidently through the traffic. She tried to work out what age he was: much older than her, maybe 25 or 26 she thought, but he was so good-looking she realised he must have loads of girlfriends. Trying to sound casual, she couldn't resist asking him. He had looked at her and laughed kindly, his beautiful mouth turning up at the corners and making creases around his lovely eyes.

'Girlfriend? Me? Not right now, Carol, I'm much too busy. Why, is that an offer?' He had winked, and she had blushed crimson with embarrassment and delight. She couldn't dream he would ever be interested in anyone like her, but she was still glad he didn't have someone special. She sighed. No one would be good enough for him in her eyes, no one.

'Penny for them?' he said, as he pulled the car up at the road where her aunt lived. She had just smiled and told him to stop a little way before her aunt's house so she could simply say she had got the bus over. She just wanted to keep this dreamy day to herself. She said goodbye and thanked him again for the lovely time she had had with him. And as he leaned over to open the car door for her, his hand had accidentally brushed her thigh, sending a shiver of goose bumps all along her leg. The unfamiliar feeling almost paralysed her.

'G-goodbye!' she had stammered, torn at the thought of ending this magical moment.

'As they say in Italian, "A presto, bella!"' He had winked at her again, before the powerful engine revved up and the car sped away. Carol could barely walk into the house. As soon as she could she looked up an old Italian phrase book she had seen in her aunt's study. When she saw the words and their English translation, 'See you soon', she nearly fainted. She took the book up to bed with her that night and *read them over and over again. Whatever this feeling was, she never wanted it to end. She stayed awake as long as she could, just to go over every delicious minute, determined not to give in to the sleep which might deprive her of a moment's thought of him.*

Carol was, for the first time in her life, utterly and completely in love. She could never, ever possibly feel this way about anyone else again.

She little knew how accurate her teenage predictions would prove.

Carol willed herself back to the present. Out of the corner of her eye, a movement across the road caught her attention. The door of Dr Steven's office was opening. As Carol watched, she saw two young Asian girls come down the steps and head towards Leeson Street.

Getting out of her car, she locked it and walked carefully across the road. Standing on the steps outside the elegant building, she rang the bell, announcing herself over the intercom. There was a loud buzz and the door opened. Immediately she was greeted by a glamorous receptionist who showed her to a beautifully decorated waiting room. Sitting down on one of the plush, comfortable sofas, she listened to the softly playing music, noticing the hundreds of photos on the walls of besotted mothers proudly showing off their offspring, expertly delivered by Dr Gerald Stevens. Naturally, many of them were well-known celebrities. Carol recognised politicians, rock chicks and a general selection of showbiz faces among them. It was a triumph of public relations.

'Dr Stevens will see you now,' said the receptionist, popping her head around the door. 'Follow me, I'll show you up.'

Carol ascended the stairs behind her, taking a few slow, deep breaths. Now that the actual face-to-face meeting was imminent, she could feel her confidence rapidly deserting her. Tapping into the steely determination that had got her through the last 18 years, she rapidly regained her composure. She was damned if she was going to crack now!

'Ms Dalton! What a pleasure! I've heard so much about you.' And finally he stood before her, holding out his hand in greeting, his warm blue eyes crinkling as he smiled and looked her over with interest.

'Dr Stevens.' Carol shook his hand confidently, meeting his gaze squarely. For a split second, she was afraid. The merest flicker of curiosity crossed his face, and she knew he was wondering if there was something familiar about her – but he had so many hundreds, no, thousands of patients he couldn't possibly place her. Then the moment had passed and she knew she was safe.

'Have I treated you before, Ms Dalton?' he asked as he showed her into his office and Carol sat down on a magnificent velvet-covered sofa. 'There's something familiar about you, but I'm sure I'd remember if we'd met before.' The easy charm was employed as disarmingly as ever.

'No.' Carol smiled broadly at him, giving him the full benefit of her straightened, shiny white teeth. Wearing the braces had been agonising – especially as she had been in her twenties – but she had persevered; when the steel wires had been removed followed by a few bleaching sessions with her dentist, she had been rewarded with a smile a starlet would have been proud of. 'I've never been a patient of yours, Dr Stevens,' she continued, crossing her shapely legs, 'but plenty of my friends have, and you come very highly recommended.' She dimpled prettily at him, watching the slow smile of satisfaction cross his face.

'Yes, I do treat an awful lot of, er, high-profile people. I like to think I understand, particularly in my line of work, that women, even celebrities, can feel rather vulnerable.'

Oh I'll bet you do, you bastard. Carol's fixed smile hid her increasingly angry thoughts.

'I'm sure you do, Dr Stevens. Your reputation precedes you. Now, let's get down to business, shall we?' Carol had her notepad and digital recorder at the ready.

Dr Stevens leaned back and stretched an arm along the back of the sofa. 'Please, call me Gerald. Dr Stevens sounds a little clinical for an interview, don't you think?'

He went on to tell her how he had always longed to become a doctor. And how, in his third year of study, the decision to become a gynaecologist took shape. After qualifying from the College of Surgeons he took a year to do some relief work in Thailand and was so appalled by the conditions that the women lived in, preyed on by the lucrative sex industry, he became even more resolute in his vocation.

It made riveting listening, Carol thought, the profile already taking shape in her mind. Boy, but he was good! A virtuoso self-publicist! His media skills were also perfectly honed, probably from his years in America; he would come across dramatically well on television. Age, thought Carol, had if anything improved him. It just wasn't fair. She reckoned he must be about 45 by now. No doubt his attractive youthfulness had been carefully maintained by discreet plastic surgery over the years. After all, it was *de rigeur* in LA where he had been based. They'd both come a long way since that time 18 years ago when she had been a naïve 16, and he an ambitious 27.

'I hope you don't think it presumptuous of me,' Gerald checked his watch, smiling. 'But I took the liberty of organising a little lunch for us. If it's all right with you, I'll have the girls bring it in to us now.' He really had thought of everything, Carol thought wryly to herself. She agreed that a spot of lunch would be nice and they could continue working on the interview.

Gerald buzzed through to his secretary. A minute or two later, the door opened, and the two young Asian girls that Carol had earlier seen descending the steps outside came in with two large trays. As they set the trays down on the table, Carol couldn't help noticing how exceptionally pretty the girls were.

'It's a little selection from a Thai restaurant on Leeson Street that's just opened,' Gerald explained. 'They do marvellous food to order. I hope you'll agree when you've tried some of this?' He smiled warmly at her and thanked the two girls who had brought it in for them. After they had left the room, Carol asked him about them.

Gerald shook his head, looking serious. 'Their mother works for me. She looks after the house for my fiancée, Candice, and me. She asked if she could bring her girls over here to live with her. Let's face it, they had no chance whatsoever of a decent life back home in Thailand. Of course I said yes,' he smiled reassuringly, 'and they help their mother out here, and go to classes in the evening. They both want to pursue a career in nursing, and I'm helping them in any way I can.' Something in his voice – or was it his expression? – alerted Carol's razor-sharp instincts. There was more to this than met the eye. A penchant for young girls didn't go away. She looked at him as he ate his food meticulously. He was so damned attractive; they wouldn't stand a chance. Just as she hadn't. And he would ruin their lives just as he had ruined hers, or tried to. Carol felt the familiar rage boiling up inside her. Not now, she willed herself, not now! She would ruin everything if she wasn't careful. The only slight grain of comfort was the fact that now she was finally safe from his attentions. After all, at thirty-four, she must be at least 18, no, probably 20 years too old for him.

Michael sat in the bar of the Anglesea sipping a mineral water. The sophisticated new hotel had become the latest local for the Grovesbury set. He was meeting Pascal for lunch and he had to get his head together. Pascal might come across as an affable, harmless and decidedly jovial individual, but Michael knew better than most than to risk messing with him. You didn't get to be one of the richest men in Ireland by being soft. Pascal had a heart of gold, for sure, but he didn't take kindly to being crossed. An uncomfortable feeling ran down Michael's spine. He couldn't possibly suspect anything, could he? No, it was impossible; he had covered his tracks meticulously. And besides, Pascal had been so wrapped up in the prospective new St Rita's building he hardly had eyes or ears for anything else. Lately, the name Sean O'Rourke had become Pascal's mantra. It was Sean this, Sean that, Sean the other, and Michael was getting heartily fed up with it. Okay, so the guy was an architectural genius, but he could
be an awkward sonofabitch too. Talk about temperamental! Still, he had to admit he was doing a fantastic job for them – and he certainly had a way with the builders, who practically fawned over him. Michael checked his watch. Pascal would be here in five minutes. He would just pop into the gents' for a quick top up;

after all, he had to make sure he had a clear head. He couldn't afford to let anything slip. Not now.

When Michael came back, he saw that Pascal had already been shown to his favourite table in the restaurant. Strolling over to join him, he ordered another mineral water from the waiter.

'Hey, Pascal!' Michael patted him on the back. 'We finally get to catch up!'

As Michael sat down, Pascal thought he looked even worse than usual. A pallid greyness masked his usual healthy colour, and the lines around his eyes seemed ever more deeply etched.

Pascal ordered a sirloin steak, while Michael went for the grilled sole, both of which were excellent. But Pascal noticed that Michael was fidgety throughout the meal and only toyed with his food. By the time he had excused himself from the table to go to the loo, Pascal was downright worried about him. It was true! There was something wrong with him. He definitely wasn't himself; in fact, he looked positively ill. He wondered if he should say anything. Or maybe he should have a quiet word with Felicity. Surely she'd have noticed – you couldn't fail to. And the amount of weight he had lost, why his suit was practically hanging off him. When Michael came back to the table, Pascal was looking thoroughly miserable. Poor Michael, he thought to himself, he can't be well, it could even be cancer or something, God forbid!

Maybe he was in denial, or just trying to be brave about it.

'Jesus, Pascal! When's the funeral?' Michael's voice sounded oddly robust in contrast to his increasingly shrunken frame.

'Wha– what?' Pascal stammered, appalled at having his thoughts read so accurately.

Michael laughed. 'You look about as happy as a turkey at Christmas! Now tell me all about the latest on the St Rita's building. I could do with hearing a bit of good news myself, and by all accounts that architect of ours is doing us proud.'

As usual, Michael had said the right thing. Pascal was only too happy to launch into the latest accounts of what was happening on site. And they passed the remainder of the meal in happy discussions about planning projections and, most of all, profits.

By the time they had ordered coffees and Michael had called for the bill, Pascal had almost forgotten his worries. Perhaps he was imagining things. After all, Eva was always laughing at him and telling him what a hypochondriac he was. Maybe Michael was just a bit stressed. Comforted by this reassuring thought, Pascal turned to chat to the manager who had come over to their table to pay his respects, happily unaware of the distinct tremor in Michael's hand as he reached for his pen.

CHAPTER FIVE

'I don't believe it. A public proposal, that's so *cool*.'

'Presumptuous should be the word that springs to mind.' Lawrence looked pityingly at Wendy.

'You must have given him *some* encouragement, Lornagh, I mean he'd hardly have risked it otherwise.' Avril was feeling slightly envious.

'I bloody didn't. I was more gobsmacked than anyone.'

'Tell us again. Right from the beginning,' Wendy demanded.

'No way. It's bad enough that it actually happened without having to retell it a thousand times.' Lornagh was beginning to feel uncomfortable.

'I bet he's seething with rage.' Avril grinned.

'That's not fair. How do you know he isn't incredibly wounded? Scarred for life by the woman who scorned him. In public,' Wendy added gleefully.

'Bit late for that,' said Lawrence.

'I didn't scorn him. I got a shock, that's all.'

'Not as big a one as he did,' said Lawrence, grinning.

''Ow I would love to 'ave been there. A flea on the wall as you say,' Mauricio said enviously.

'Fly, Mauricio. We say fly, not flea.' Lawrence took a bowl of steaming pasta from him and put it on the table.

'Anyway,' Wendy asked, 'what are you going to do now? You have to talk to him sooner or later.'

'I know,' Lornagh said glumly. 'That's the problem.'

'Meet him for a drink on neutral territory, so you can make a quick escape if things turn nasty,' suggested Avril.

'Yeah,' said Wendy, 'and be sure to say you want to stay friends. That's what the bastards always say to me.'

Friends! Pah!

Simon practically spat at the very mention of the word.

After careful consideration, he had decided to ring Lornagh to arrange a meeting where he would demand to know the reason for her outrageous behaviour at the dinner party. He still hadn't recovered from it. The nerve of her! In front of all those people he had been trying to impress! After the first red tidal wave of anger had subsided, Simon had conceded that perhaps his proposal might have come as a shock to Lornagh. Still, it was no excuse for her ridiculous reaction. Why, she had practically flung the ring in his face! But he had to keep his eye on the ball here, he reminded himself, and not lose sight of the main objective. Lornagh was a prize, a trophy, and one he was willing to make exceptions for. After all, when she eventually became his wife (and he had no doubts on that score whatsoever) then *he* would be calling the shots. And things would be different. Very different. He could be patient, he resolved, for a little bit longer.

They had met in the bar of the Berkeley Court. Simon had arrived first and sat at a quiet corner table where they could talk in relative privacy. He would be magnanimous, he would be willing to forgive her outburst, and, after a definite cooling on his part, they would work things out. It was just a little hitch in the plan.

He checked his watch. At the very stroke of five o'clock, Lornagh walked into the bar, looking pale and tired. So far, so good, thought Simon: she seemed to appear suitably chastened. They ordered their drinks and Simon waited imperiously for the abject apologies to begin.

'I hope you've had sufficient time to contemplate your behaviour,' he said coldly.

Lornagh sighed. 'Look, Simon, what happened the other night was unfortunate to say the least, but since it happened, yes, I have done a lot of thinking, and I need you to understand why I acted as I did.'

Simon sat back and waited, his full lips curving in a supercilious sneer. 'Well?'

Lornagh began to tell him, as carefully as she could, how she had been feeling about the relationship for the last few weeks. How she had begun to feel uncomfortable around him, how she felt that they wanted different things from life, and that she felt sure he would agree that lately they had drifted further and further apart. She went on to say that the last thing on earth she had expected from him was a proposal of marriage, particularly as they had never even discussed the subject. She added that she could have done without a riveted audience at the time. She finished by saying that it was clear their relationship had no future and she hoped they could remain friends. And then, seeing the look of outrage on his face, she had said she was truly sorry things hadn't worked out for them, that she wished him all the best. Then she had calmly got up and walked away without so much as a backward glance.

Friends! The word reverberated around his brain like a particularly nasty virus. As he sat scowling into his drink, Simon groped for words vindictive enough to give vent to the ugly emotions churning inside him.

Anger was much too small a word for what he was feeling.

Pascal was not the only one to notice the change in Michael's appearance. Melissa was not at all happy about his apparently increasing dependency. Apart from the obvious physical deterioration, the little gifts and surprises he used to spring on her had dried up, and, with it, his sex appeal as far as she was concerned. She used to find him amusing; now he was tetchy and jumpy all the time. It was no fun.

She said as much to him as they shared a bottle of Cristal champagne after a particularly uneventful lovemaking session in her black and gold bedroom.

'What the fuck's the matter with you?' she said, her eyes narrowing as she reclined cat-like against lurid leopard-print cushions. 'You can't even get it up properly! I warned you about that stuff!'

'Oh, leave it out, will you? So I'm a little stressed right now. Doesn't a guy get any time off with you? You're bloody insatiable!' Michael was feeling under increasing pressure to perform from all fronts; he sure as hell didn't need it from a spoiled mistress.

'I expect my lovers to be proficient in the bedroom, darling. I can't really see the point otherwise, can you?' Melissa was spoiling for a fight.

'Oh, for Christ's sake! Give me a break. I'm tired, that's all.'

'But that's *not* all, Michael, and you know it.' Melissa was like a dog with a bone. 'You've got a problem, I've seen it coming for weeks now. I told you not to keep stuffing that shit up your nose. Look at you, you can hardly function without it! And where are you getting it from anyway. Who's your dealer?'

'None of your damned business!'

'Oh, I see. It's like that, is it?'

Something inside Michael finally snapped. 'You

wouldn't know what anything was like unless it came bloody gift-wrapped.' Michael had had enough. A chink had appeared in his armour, and all the pent-up stress and fear that had been piling up inside him like a cancer came pouring out. 'Look at yourself, why don't you? You're just a spoiled, pathetic little social climber, bleeding that poor husband of yours to death, and anyone else who happens to come across you. You're a bloody laughing stock. You think you're so clever, don't you? You think you're fooling everyone with your ridiculous accent and your airs and graces. Well, you don't fool anyone. You're just a scrubber, Melissa! It's written all over you in full, glorious technicolour. And you'll never be anything else. No matter how much money you get your grubby little paws on. A million designer outfits wouldn't make you halfway decent. And no amount of elocution lessons will teach you anything about knowing how to behave.' Michael was so worked up now, he couldn't stop himself. 'Grow up and accept it, Melissa! You'll never be one of us, never. It's about time you started to appreciate Pascal. God knows, he's the only poor fool I know who'd put up with you.'

Melissa shrank back in the pillows as if she'd been hit. He was like a madman. She couldn't, she wouldn't hear any more of this vicious bile. She put her hands over her ears but he wouldn't stop.

'You're all the bloody same!' He was shouting now. 'I should have remembered what my mother said,' he paused to draw a shuddering breath, 'if you lie down with dogs, you get up with fleas!' And with that, he flung on his clothes and, feeling strangely elated, headed out into what was left of the cold, unwelcoming February evening.

Melissa listened to the door slam. She lay there for a long time, not moving. It wasn't happening. It would go away. It wasn't real. She hadn't heard all those terrible, horrible things he'd said about her. He *had* found her attractive, irresistible, she *knew* he had. It wasn't true, any of it. But the words kept whispering in her head. *You're just an ugly little scrubber.* That's what they said, what they all thought of her, what they'd always thought of her, for as long ago as she could remember. Her father had said it to her, her brothers had said it to her. Only her mother had believed in her, and she had died when Melissa had been twelve. Nobody gave a damn about her. They never had, unless she had come up with the goods. Not until, a little voice reminded her, she had met Pascal. That was the only truth in any of the vitriolic outburst that bollix had spewed. Pascal had been kind to her. From day one, he had told her she was the princess she had always believed deep down inside she could be. And look where it had got him.

Still she lay there, a million memories shouting at her, demons, all of them, demanding their voice after so long in exile. We know who you are, they screamed. You can never get away! Never!

She didn't know how long she had lain there, all her

energy draining away from her as if she was bleeding to death. Who was she kidding? She was just Mary Pat O'Malley from the back streets. Glamorous Melissa Sheehan didn't exist, except in her own stupid imagination. She was a nobody. She was nothing. She reached for the bottle of champagne, and, downing what was left with a couple of Valium, passed out.

Sometime later she became vaguely aware of someone gently licking her face. That, and a great pain biting into her belly. 'Michael,' she whispered, her tongue moving in the arid desert that was her mouth. She fought to open her eyes. It was dark, and she felt like hell. The licking continued on her face, and someone was gently nibbling her right hand. Melissa struggled to find the bedside lamp and managed to turn it on, the blinding light both terrible and welcoming. Beside her a worried little face gradually took shape, little pop eyes peering at her, and a little nose snuffling into her, nudging her to wake up. Melissa, half laughing, half sobbing, gathered Dolce and Gabbana to her and, gasping with pain, realised the new leopard-skin corset she had donned in honour of Michael's visit was threatening to asphyxiate her slowly and painfully. Staggering into an upright position, she ripped it off, along with the stockings and the six-inch Manolo Blahniks that she had stupidly thought would serve her so well. Pulling on her favourite satin dressing gown, she headed for her shower and turned the water on full, before stepping in and succumbing to its almost unbearable force.

Climbing back into bed with her dogs settled happily

beside her, she called Maria to bring her up a snack of cheese on toast. Gradually the fuzziness cleared from her head, and a slow, deliberate evaluation of events played over piece by piece in her bruised mind. She remembered every harsh word, every cruel insult, and viewed them as if they were dismembered pieces of a long-dead corpse. All the while, she cuddled her little dogs, soothing them with gentle stroking. It was all beginning to make sense. She wouldn't think about it now, though; she was too tired to be focused. She would deal with it tomorrow. Melissa Sheehan may have taken a battering, but she was slowly and very definitely coming back to life.

Overcome with fatigue and emotion, she wondered where Pascal could be: it was well past midnight. Probably with that architect he never stopped talking about these days. Well, she would make it up to him when he got home. If she could stay awake that was. Everything would be different from now on. Drifting off to sleep, she was rudely awakened by the phone ringing. She picked it up to hear a voice asking to speak to Pascal. It was a woman's voice, low and sultry. When Melissa said that Pascal wasn't at home, there was a pause and then the phone went dead. Exhausted though she was, something niggled her about it. She looked at the bedside clock and saw it was a quarter to one. Who on earth would call at that time of night?

Pascal inhaled deeply. It was a good day. There was nothing like a sausage and bacon buttie to get a man off to the right start of a morning. He had stopped off at his favourite café down at the docks on his way to the St Rita's site, and he was now regarding the magnificent sandwich in his car with the kind of reverence other people reserved for *haute cuisine*. He bit into it with relish, savouring every complex flavour of what was affectionately referred to on the menu as the Triple Bypass Special. Washing it down with a scalding mug of tea you could trot a mouse on, he reflected that life wasn't so bad after all. He switched on the ignition in his powerful Mercedes, sticking the plastic mug into the handy holder designed for that very purpose, and gave the Germans full credit for the practicality of their design skills along with their faultless engineering. They must be a great bunch of people if they understood that sometimes a man had to drive and eat at the same time.

He had a meeting on site with Sean O'Rourke and he didn't want to be late.

It was 8.30 exactly when he arrived, and Sean was already there, talking animatedly to the foreman. Pascal donned the hard hat that was given to him and joined them.

'How's she cuttin', Sean?'

'Like a blue Gillette!' Sean was quick to retort in familiar 'Dublinese'. He smiled as he looked up from the plans. He liked Pascal immensely and appreciated his genuine interest in the progress of the building. Pascal had put his heart into this project and it showed. He wasn't like the others, always wanting to know about figures and projections and schedules. Pascal just wanted it to be right. It wasn't often an architect had the luxury of dealing with an investor who shared his dream for the eventual development, and Pascal was one of the few people Sean had any time for on the site. Apart from that, he could relate to Pascal; they were both genuine Dubs. Pascal didn't have any of the airs and graces that usually went hand in hand with the kind of money he had made. He and Sean had a lot in common. Sean couldn't stand bullshitters. He had come up the hard way himself and fought long and hard for every small success that had brought him slowly but surely to the pinnacle of his career. And he was now widely acknowledged as one of the most brilliant architects in Europe.

They walked the site with the foreman, Mike, and went over details of what had been done and what was proposed for the following week. Everything was going to plan. Pascal marvelled at their ability to see how anything as complex as the buildings he had been shown on plan could ever materialise from what appeared to him to be a sea of concrete and mud. But everyone seemed happy with the progress and the builders were working away.

'Michael was here yesterday,' Sean mentioned to Pascal as they made their way over the rough terrain back towards his car. 'He's taken a very sudden interest in construction, seemed agitated about a few things. Any idea why?' Sean didn't need any more distractions on site than he could avoid. He didn't mind Michael, but he didn't understand the complexities of the project and, no matter how much reassurance Sean gave him, he seemed uneasy. Sean was only too well aware how that kind of behaviour became contagious, and the last thing he needed was anxious investors dancing about on his site. It always caused trouble.

'Michael?' Pascal seemed surprised. 'I saw him yesterday and he didn't mention it to me. What exactly was he on about?'

'Oh, the usual, timing, costings, weekly averages, that sort of thing. I thought we had agreed to discuss all that stuff at the office. I really don't need people turning up demanding figures on site. It just wastes time, you know.' Sean took off the hard hat and ran a hand through his hair. 'We've a difficult enough job to get finished on schedule as it is. I'd appreciate it if you could have a quiet word with him.'

'Consider it done. I'll talk to him today.' Pascal spoke lightly, but he was concerned. It wasn't like Michael to be interfering. All he had to do was look after the financial end, and everything in that respect was right on target. He'd have to keep a closer eye on things. Find out what was making Michael so twitchy these days.

'Good luck!' Sean thumped the roof of his car good-humouredly as Pascal started to reverse out of the site.

As he turned the car around, a movement in the rearview mirror caught his eye. He just made out two bulky figures slipping behind the construction office. He looked around for Sean, but he had disappeared back to the site. It was probably nothing, Pascal thought; all the same, he must remember to check the security arrangements on the site. The last thing they needed was valuable machinery going missing. There were some very strange people around these days, and you couldn't be too careful.

Carol was enjoying that rarest of things for her, a weekday lie-in. If you could call seven o'clock in the morning a lie-in. Usually she was up and on the road with her personal trainer at six. But today she had an appointment with the private investigator she had hired, and by all accounts he had some interesting information for her.

She was due to meet with him at half-past nine, so she decided to take the time off and go into work later. The 'profile' she was working on for Dr Gerald Stevens was coming along nicely and, with a bit of luck, what she was about to find out today might make it even better.

She stretched luxuriously and sipped her coffee, listening mindlessly to the morning bantering of the DJ on the radio. A song began to play, and suddenly she was transported, its melody such a vivid memory that if she closed her eyes she could smell the sea and feel the damp sand beneath her toes.

'You were brilliant!' he had said, as she came off the pitch

glowing with triumph, her short games skirt flapping around her long skinny legs.

She had written to the hospital to thank him for taking her to lunch when she had been up in Dublin. To her wild amazement, he had written back to her. They had continued to correspond on a weekly basis, and Carol lived for the moment the letters arrived, rushing to her room, or taking them with her into school so she could go over them time and time again until she knew them by heart. She had kept them tied with a pink ribbon and hidden under a floorboard in her bedroom, just as she had seen done in a romantic old movie.

No one had ever taken such interest in her and she fell more and more under his spell with every passing day. Soon he had said he wanted to meet her again and asked her when would she be up in Dublin. She had thought long and hard about it. She couldn't possibly risk her parents or aunt finding out, so she told him she would be playing a hockey match in Wicklow the next week. He had said he would come down especially to see her play and that maybe afterwards they could go for a picnic on the beach.

It had all been too perfect. As soon as their minibus had arrived at the school, she saw him standing by the field and her heart contracted. He looked so handsome in his jeans and denim shirt and cool leather jacket. She had said he was a cousin, and the other girls were green with envy. They had won their match: she had scored the winning goal, and he had cheered her on the whole way. Afterwards they had gone to Brittas Bay, and he had brought a picnic as he had promised.

He had told the minibus driver that he would personally see to it that Carol was dropped back to school, so they didn't have to rush back. It had been the best day of her life. It was a bright September day and the weather was unusually warm. They had sat in a sheltered sand dune and eaten their picnic and shared a bottle of wine. She had felt woozy with love and longing and could hardly eat for excitement. Afterwards, they had walked along the deserted beach, their feet making footprints in the sand. He told her that she was special, that he had never met anyone like her before, who could understand so much about him. Her letters, he had said, were proof of how mature she was for her age, and then he looked into her eyes and told her he thought he was falling in love with her. Taking her into his arms he had kissed her, slowly and with infinite tenderness. From that moment on, she was lost.

Carol flung the clothes off her bed in exasperation. Bloody radio! Why now, of all times, did they have to play that stupid song? She headed for the bathroom and turned the taps on full blast. She always felt the need to wash herself from head to toe after remembering those days. Well, she had come a long way since then, and she was going to go a whole lot further before it was all over. 'I'm on your case, Dr Gerald Stevens,' she said out loud. 'And bit by bit, I'm going to hunt you down and see you put behind bars like the dangerous animal you are.'

The gas fire was turned up full blast in Michael's office. Even so, he couldn't stop shivering. He had come in especially early this morning, partly to escape Felicity's astute observations, partly because he needed to go over some urgent figures.

He was expecting a call from Eddie and he had to make sure everything was up to scratch. Christ, but he was cold! He wondered was he still in shock. After his appalling verbal attack on Melissa yesterday, he hadn't been able to think straight. Talk about paranoia! What had got into him? He, of all people, who was usually so calm and controlled under pressure. He was used to watching other people lose their composure. He used to sit back and smile while they all dug their own pathetic little graves, plot by plot, and here he was going at it hell for leather himself!

He could still hardly believe the awful things he had said to her. Sure, she had been on his case lately, but she hadn't deserved that outburst of vitriol. For the first time in his life, Michael Moriarty felt truly ashamed of himself, and he didn't like it.

He had tried ringing her mobile phone but to no avai;, it was switched off, and he daren't ring her at home. He would send flowers immediately, he decided, and a note of apology. But all the same, he knew deep down that she would never forgive him. The hurtful things he had said were far too close to home.

He shivered again just thinking about it. Melissa Sheehan was not the kind of person you wanted as an enemy.

The sound of his desk phone ringing made him jump.

It was his secretary, Katy, informing him that a Mr Hartigan of Hartigan Holdings was on the line for him.

'Put him through, Katy,' Michael said wearily. He was a big client and, whatever else, business had to continue as usual; the show had to go on.

'Michael?' The voice sounded hesitant on the end of the line.

'Frank! Good to hear from you, what can I do you for?' Michael tried to inject his usual enthusiasm into the exchange although he felt as if a lead weight was sitting on his shoulders.

They exchanged the usual pleasantries and then Frank Hartigan came straight to the point.

'Er, there's no easy way to say this Michael, but our, em, accountants have been going through the books and, well, they've noticed a few discrepancies and, well, we've had a board meeting about it and, um, well, in view of the fact that we've had a good longstanding working relationship, we, uh, I – well, let's just say we're withdrawing our account from Romany Investments. We'll be putting it in writing, of course, but I just wanted you to hear from me first. I'm sorry, old boy, but business is business and all that.'

'Now Frank, just back up a minute there!' Michael clutched the receiver more tightly. 'I'm sure there's been some mistake. Look, can't we meet and talk about this? Please?'

There was a brief pause. 'I'm afraid that's out of the

question, Michael. And, before you say anything else, consider yourself lucky we're only taking it this far. We've always understood each other. Don't push your luck, eh?' The line went dead.

Shit! This was the second big client he had lost in as many weeks! He leant back in his chair and tried to breathe, but somehow it was becoming more and more of an effort. He could feel himself breaking out in a cold, clammy sweat. The stupid pricks! Who the hell did they think they were? He, Michael, had made them their fortunes! He got up and began to pace the floor. This wouldn't do, it wouldn't do at all. Pascal was going to have a fit when he heard, and it was only a matter of time! A day or two if he was lucky. He had to think, had to get back on track, had to turn things around and fast. He fumbled quickly for the key he kept to his private drawer and frantically rummaged for what he needed. He didn't like doing it at the office, but panic was threatening to get the better of him. He took a long slow breath, and let the white powder work its magic.

By the time Eddie's call came through, Michael was feeling better. He was back in control. Sure it had been a blow, but nothing he couldn't handle. Frank Hartigan and his poxy company could go screw themselves.

'Michael.' The gravelly voice cut into his brain.

'Eddie! Good to hear you!'

'How's tricks?'

'Fine, great! I've got those figures for you, hang on one sec and I'll just ...'

'No need, Michael, no need. I'll be in the neighbourhood this afternoon, I thought I'd drop by the office and see for myself.'

That was all Michael needed. 'Look, Eddie, that's not a good idea, what about ...'

'What's the matter, Michael? No welcome for your most important client?'

'No, it's not like that Eddie. I just think ...'

'How does four o'clock suit?' It was a demand, not a question. Followed by a chuckle. 'And don't worry, I clean up nice!'

Whatever feelings of recovery Michael had been enjoying rapidly began to fade. He put his head in his hands and tried to remember when he had begun to feel like a prisoner in his own life.

CHAPTER SIX

'So he took it well, then.' Avril listened as Lornagh recounted her meeting with Simon, while driving the girls into town. They were all on a day off, heading into Brown Thomas's to do some damage. Lornagh had borrowed Lawrence's jeep in anticipation of accommodating all the prospective purchases. Then they planned on lunch in Fitzers Café and adjourning to Blue Eriu for the afternoon.

'Let's just say he didn't seem keen to remain friends.'

'He wouldn't know the meaning of the word!' Wendy was getting into the swing of things.

'Wendy!'

'Well, I never liked him anyway. He always hated us being around, never mind Lawrence.'

'Still, it's a pity. I hate things ending on a bad note.' Hugely relieved the whole episode was over, Lornagh felt she could indulge in a little remorse.

'You were grown up about it. Now it's his problem,

or, should I say, one of his many problems, according to Lawrence.'

'What has Lawrence been saying now?' Lornagh sounded alarmed.

'Let's just say he's glad you're shot of him,' Avril confirmed. The girls had agreed it was unnecessary to reveal to Lornagh the fascinating results of Lawrence's discreet, but thorough, research into Simon's secret life.

'Look on it as a *brief* but educational experience in the many shortcomings of the male species,' said Wendy, winking at Avril.

'Yeah, I'll put it down to experience, it's all I can do,' said Lornagh, the double entendre going right over her head.

'*Corset* is!' said Avril, biting her lip.

'Oh shit! I've just remembered,' Lornagh changed lanes just in time. 'I left my new credit card in the office. Sorry girls, but a quick detour is required before retail therapy can commence.'

'This is where you work?' Avril sounded incredulous, as Lornagh pulled into the obstacle course that was the St Rita's building site. 'I thought PR was supposed to be a *glamorous* career.' The whole place had been turned upside down since the building started. The site office had taken over the general parking area, which had now become a row of prefabs. Lornagh winced as the jeep bravely tackled mountains of mud and debris to finally reach what remained of any free space.

Turning to manoeuvre around a JCB, Lornagh began to reverse between it and a large pile of rubble. Suddenly the JCB started to move: it was coming towards them and it didn't show any sign of stopping.

'Watch out, Lornagh!' yelled Avril.

Lornagh frantically swung around and, blaring her horn at the driver, managed to miss him by inches. Her sigh of relief was cut short by the sickening crunch of metal and she found herself being flung forcibly into the steering wheel. When she had caught her breath, Lornagh got out of the car on trembling legs. Avril and Wendy hopped out quickly; they were both fine despite the near miss.

'Whoops,' said Wendy, 'that was a bit close for comfort. Are you okay, Lornagh?'

'Yeah, I'm fine, considering the alternative.' She rubbed her arm, which was starting to throb.

'Me too,' said Avril. 'Uh oh, look, here comes the cavalry.'

Lornagh looked up to see two of the builders running towards her.

'Are y'all righ' girls?'

'Grand bit of reversing that, wha'? Michael Schumacher or wha'? Pity about the car though!'

Still slightly dazed, Lornagh looked around and realised that, in her panic to avoid the JCB, she had reversed at speed into a brand new Saab that now sported a startling dent in its right wing. Lawrence's jeep, on the other hand, was remarkably unblemished.

'Is that your car? I'm so sorry,' she gasped, taking in the spectacular damage.

'Nothing to me, love, it's the boss you'll be apologising to!'

'Who?' Lornagh was getting more confused by the minute.

'Look! Here he comes now,' the builder chuckled.

Lornagh followed their gaze, to see the tall figure of Sean O'Rourke striding towards them, his face like thunder. 'What the hell is going on?' he shouted, as the builders melted away, chuckling. As he turned to the girls in absolute fury, Lornagh suddenly found the explanation about the JCB drying up in her mouth.

'What's the matter with you?' he yelled. 'Can't you dizzy blondes read?' He pointed to the big red-and-white sign that had somehow escaped Lornagh's notice. It read NO VEHICLES ON SITE UNTIL FURTHER NOTICE. 'You could have bloody killed yourself! Or one of my men!'

'It was an accident!' Lornagh yelled back at him. 'I'm sorry!'

A supercilious smile hovered at the corners of his mouth. 'You should be: sorry Daddy didn't teach you to drive before letting you on the road in a four-wheel drive. Typical,' he snorted, 'I bet the only off-road diversion you take is to Brown Thomas's car park. Why take up one space when two will do nicely?'

Lornagh flinched inwardly at the accuracy of his comment. 'Oh, I see,' she said, flashing him a cynical smile, 'you're one of those.'

'One of what?'

'The perfectly balanced types: chips on *both* shoulders.'

Sean's eyes narrowed. 'You'd better be insured,' he said, nodding curtly at his injured Saab. 'That's going to take quite a bit of fixing.'

'Oh, you needn't worry on that account,' Lornagh said sweetly, 'I'm sure *Daddy* will take care of it. Won't he, girls?' She turned to Avril and Wendy who had taken several steps back and seemed to have entirely disassociated themselves from the whole incident.

'Well, you can get your car out of here for starters. Parking's on the road until further notice.' He looked down at her, his dark eyes glinting with anger. 'And in case you didn't get the memo, no one's allowed on site without official authorisation.'

Lornagh walked back to the jeep, shaking with anger. Who the hell did he think he was?

'Who,' asked Wendy, in a strangely breathless voice, 'was *that*?'

'That overbearing, ignorant pig is the architect.'

'He can rock *my* foundations anytime,' said Avril.

Simon was feeling decidedly better about things. A package he had been waiting for had arrived that morning and it had cheered him up immensely. It had taken quite a bit of discreet research on his part – after all, he had an image to maintain in Dublin – but a few careful inquiries and research on the net had been well worth the time spent.

He had gone to the post office to pick it up. He would never have risked having it sent to his apartment; God knows who might have got wind of it. Although, as a rule, his neighbours kept themselves to themselves, and Simon certainly didn't encourage anyone to drop by unannounced.

The anonymity of living in an apartment complex was exactly what appealed to him. That, and the fact that he had seen no reason whatsoever to splash out ridiculous amounts of money on a house when he was going to marry someone due to inherit a magnificent home at arguably the best address in Dublin 4.

The parcel had sat in his car, silently disrupting his concentration all morning. He had nipped home at lunchtime, unable for a minute longer to resist its lure. He set it carefully on his bed, admiring the bland, official nature of the packaging. He opened it carefully, lifting the lid off and folding back the crisp tissue paper. It was all there, along with the latest catalogue, every carefully chosen item. There was a whole weekend's enjoyment in it. Simon shivered. One by one he gently lifted out the bikini briefs (large), the matching lace trimmed bras (46A) and the silk and fishnet stockings (extra large).

He checked his watch. It was a pity he had to go back

to the office this afternoon, but the whole weekend stretched before him, full of fantastical possibilities. He changed quickly and deftly. And five minutes later he was on his way back to Clyde Road and Romany Investments.

As he sat imperiously at his desk that afternoon, carefully preparing the figures Michael had asked him for earlier, no one would ever have guessed that underneath his conservative navy suit a pair of sheer black silk stockings clung comfortingly to his legs, hidden by his finest black wool socks.

As he worked away, the irritations of recent events receded, and when they threatened to intrude, he just reached down to stroke the unseen bumps of his synthetic suspenders. He sighed happily. Did Lornagh Lemass really think for a moment she could discard him like an out-of-season accessory?

By the time he'd finished with her, she'd be begging him to take her back.

Melissa was back, firing on all cylinders. If anything, she felt even stronger than before. The events of the last few days had woken her up with a bang, and she had a lot of work to do.

Her first port of call had been to her psychic Reiki healer. She had booked in for an emergency session and had taken Dolce and Gabbana with her. After all, her babies had been seriously traumatised by the whole incident. They must have thought 'Mummy' was about to abandon them. *As if!* Whatever else Melissa contemplated doing in her journey through this lifetime, leaving it before she'd fulfilled every single one of her ambitions wasn't part of the plan. And there was a lot left for her to accomplish. The demise of Michael Moriarty being just one item on the agenda that sprang to mind.

The Reiki session had been both healing and revealing. Inga, her Swedish Reiki healer, had understood perfectly. Melissa had lain gratefully on the table, cocooned in soft fluffy blankets while Inga had moved her special crystals over Melissa's various chakras, murmuring the soothing chant of cleansing rituals. Afterwards, she had recommended a spiritual cleansing and assessing of the situation. She had gone into her 'higher spirit' and, contacting Michael's higher spirit, had come up with a few revelations. As Melissa watched spellbound, Inga's head dropped dramatically to her chest, and she began to chant. Then she paused and, nodding to herself, chuckled knowingly.

'What?' Melissa could hardly contain herself. 'What is it? What are they telling you?'

Inga came back to the present and smiled broadly at Melissa. 'It's so obvious. Poor Melissa, you have been through the battles!'

She went on to explain that Michael and Melissa had been tied together in past lifetimes, in the eternal dance of reincarnation. But Michael's spirit was being pulled towards the darkness, while Melissa's was headed for the 'light'. Melissa nodded fervently.

In their most recent lifetime, Inga went on to say, Melissa and another man had been monks in the same order. But Michael had been the evil archbishop who was trying to undo all their good works. Until the pattern was broken, Inga warned her, this 'Michael' would continue trying to sabotage whatever she and the other man were trying to build. 'This man I see, he is a good man. I can't tell you who he is, but he is someone close to you and,' she smiled, 'he seems to scratch his head a lot.'

'That's Pascal! My husband.' Melissa beamed.

'Be careful, Melissa,' warned Inga. 'More than your marriage is at stake here. Watch out for this Michael, he is not the friend you think he is!'

Melissa didn't need telling twice. After Dolce and Gabbana had had a special animal healing and cleansing, Melissa headed home, thoroughly reinvigorated. She would stop that little bollix in his tracks if it was the last thing she ever did. But how? He had been ringing her everyday and sending obscene amounts of flowers, no doubt shivering in his boots now that he had realised how reckless his behavior had been. By rights, she should have nothing to do with him, but then, she thought shrewdly, that was exactly what he would expect. No, she was far too clever for that. She would pretend to forgive him, pretend to understand that his vicious outburst had been nothing more than the stress and pressure he kept going on about these days. Stress, pah! Michael Moriarty would discover exactly what stress was, now that he had crossed her. He would rue the day he had ever mentioned the word.

Melissa turned into Grovesbury Road, waving cheerfully at the French ambassador's wife who was taking her two elegant French poodles for a walk.

She must give one of her little soirées one of these days: she had been so caught up in her stupid affair with Michael, she had been neglecting her social life. It wouldn't do. You were only as good as your last party in this neighbourhood.

She hummed happily as she let herself into the house. There was no sign of Maria or that lazy husband of hers, Jesus. Maria was probably doing the shopping at the Merrion Centre. The house, as usual, was immaculate. But she would conduct a quick inspection all the same. Melissa liked to keep on top of things.

Settling Dolce and Gabbana for a little rest on their favourite sofa, she had a quick look around. She popped her head into Pascal's study: everything seemed to be in order. She plumped up a few cushions for good measure, tested the rims of a few frames for dust and, satisfied, was turning to leave when her eagle eye was drawn to the lid of the mahogany coal bucket, which appeared slightly askew. Pouncing on it, she whipped it up and, sure enough, found a stack of *Caravan Connoisseur* magazines, neatly rolled in their latest hiding place. She sighed. She really for the life of her couldn't see what Pascal's fatal attraction for the feckin' things were! Pornography would be more normal. Flicking idly through the latest issue, she remembered the early days, when caravans had been all they had. She allowed herself a whimsical smile: they had been fun, those times. She would leave him to it, she supposed. She had been horrible to him these last few months; he really didn't deserve it. But she would start making it up to him, right from today. She was just about to put the magazine back when a little piece of paper slipped out of it and fluttered to the ground. Picking it up casually, Melissa glanced at it, and then looked again, sharply. It was a receipt, but not from a newsagent's. The little piece of paper staring her in the face was from Boudoir, Dublin's most exclusive lingerie shop. The amount for that particular purchase came to £500.

Melissa sat down, her legs suddenly weak. Pascal had always been generous, to be sure, but she couldn't for the life of her remember the last time he had bought her lingerie. She put the offensive piece of paper quickly in her pocket and went to pour herself a large vodka.

This wasn't good. It wasn't good at all.

Pascal left the bank after a brief but informative meeting with the manager who looked after the St Rita's project account. He was deeply perturbed as he got into his car and drove back to the office. Things weren't adding up, and that was putting it mildly.

Sitting down at his desk in Romany Investments, he rang Katy, Michael's secretary, and asked her when Michael was due in. She informed him that Michael wouldn't be in until Monday. He had meetings out of the office all day and wasn't likely to be back. Would she get Michael to ring him?

'No, no, that's all right, Katy, I'll talk to him on Monday.' Pascal put the phone down thoughtfully. He realised Michael hadn't been himself these last few days, but there was no excuse for what he had just heard. Nor for the fact that he had only just discovered they had lost two of their biggest clients and Michael hadn't even thought to tell him. He'd had to find out about it when the formal letters of resignation arrived on his desk. Naturally, he had gone straight to the bank, where he had learned to his distress that funds in the account appeared to be insufficient.

When Michael and he had set up the company account called Tiger Holdings Ltd. (after Michael's cat) to finance the St Rita's development, Pascal had immediately transferred all of the fifty million he had personally put up for the development. Michael's other investors were supposed to have made up the balance, and as yet there was little sign of it. To say Pascal was worried was an understatement. The whole thing could go belly up. What the hell was Michael doing? A nasty feeling began to crawl down Pascal's spine. He trusted Michael implicitly – after all they had been friends and business partners for years – but something was wrong. Very wrong.

He wondered could Michael possibly be in some sort of trouble, and then dismissed it as absurd. Why, he was one of the most brilliant business brains in the country! He was happily married, as far as Pascal knew, and his wife Felicity was a capable woman, running that successful au pair agency of hers and not prone to mad spending sprees like some people he could mention.

He thought about calling Michael at home over the weekend and then thought better of it. He would talk to him first thing on Monday. Perhaps he was overreacting; perhaps there was some plausible explanation for it all.

He very much hoped there was.

Carol made her way down the narrow staircase holding tightly on to the banister. She didn't realise it, but she was shaking with anger. What the private investigator had come up with had confirmed every one of her suspicions.

The daylight in Temple Bar assaulted her as she emerged from the dimly lit building that housed the discreet offices of 'Trailer and Son'. Pausing for breath, she looked around and found the coffee shop she remembered from the last time she was in the area.

Having ordered a large latte, she sat back and lit a

cigarette, taking out her calculator to do some quick arithmetic. It would be expensive, yes, but there was no way she was letting up now. She sipped her coffee slowly and wondered had he used the same subtly persuasive manner, whispered the same endearments, that she had listened to all those years ago.

'God Carol, I want you!' he had groaned, pulling her closer to him and pressing himself into her as they lay on the sofa in his small apartment. She had been breathless with desire heightened by fear, and he was driven with urgency to conclude the painstakingly careful plan of her seduction, so tantalisingly within his reach.

She had been staying with her aunt in Dublin and had concocted a story about staying over with a friend for the night, thus engineering a whole day and night together with him. At first, she had been terrified. Arriving at his flat in her school uniform, she had suddenly felt gauche and inexperienced. All they had ever done so far was kiss. He had been delighted to see her and had gone out of his way to make her feel comfortable, pouring her a drink while she sat down awkwardly in the sitting room. As usual, he had put her gently at ease, teasing her and making her laugh with his funny stories and comments, until gradually she began to relax. They had watched Dr Zhivago on television, which immediately became her favourite movie of all time.

Then he had ordered a take-away and they had talked and laughed the evening away. She had never felt so secure, so adult and sophisticated. It was already eight o'clock when she realised she was still in her uniform and hadn't changed into the new jeans she had brought with her especially. But when she mentioned changing, he had laughed softly and told her she looked gorgeous just the way she was. 'Gorgeous!' No one had ever told Carol she had looked anything other than 'all right' or 'respectable'. He had sat next to her on the sofa, and before long he was stroking her hair and face and telling her how much he loved her, how much she turned him on.

They never made it to the bedroom. Bit by bit he had peeled off her clothes, covering her with feather-light kisses, until she was left with only her plaid school skirt and white socks crumpling around her ankles. All the while, he whispered soothing words and murmured in her ear how beautiful she was and how much he loved her. Trembling, she let him guide her hand to hold him, let him show her how to arouse him and please him, and eventually guide him into her, the sharp pang of pain made all the more pleasurable by the infinite knowledge that now she was a real woman. Now he could be hers, not just in her dreams, but here in his flat, where they would live happily, tucked away from the rest of the world.

Angrily, Carol stubbed out her cigarette.

Boise, Idaho, small town America, the detective had said. Carol had only the vaguest idea of where it was, but she had a pretty good idea of what to expect. A pale, innocent, trusting young girl. By all accounts 15 or maybe even younger. Too terrified to even comprehend what was happening to her. And unable to understand that the tall, handsome God of a doctor she worshipped could ever have been capable of putting her in this situation.

Carol would just have to send the detective over there to follow up the story. If she could have, she would have gone herself; but that was out of the question. She had a show to run. And she had absolutely no intention of handing over to any of the other presenters who were always hovering around her slot like vultures.

Carol was not under any illusions. It had taken her years to get this show up and on the road, and she was damned if she was going to let anyone else get their greedy little clutches on it, even for one episode.

She just hoped against hope the girl would co-operate. If she could be persuaded, then everything would have been worthwhile.

'Mr McEntee to see you.' Katy had shown Eddie into Michael's office, smiling approvingly at the lean, perfectly honed physique in the expensively tailored suit. The look wasn't lost on Eddie, who flashed her a crooked smile before making himself comfortable in one of the large leather chairs in front of Michael's desk.

'Tea? Coffee?' Katy offered hopefully.

'No thanks, Katy,' Michael said crisply, hardly believing his ears. Normally Katy thought it beneath her to offer refreshments, usually sending in her junior assistant to deal with such duties.

'Tea'd be great, pet! Two sugars!' Eddie showed his white, even teeth appreciatively.

'So, to what do I owe this unexpected pleasure?' Michael smiled thinly, unable to disguise the sarcasm. He had made it clear to Eddie that he didn't want any 'business' conducted at the office, it was far too dangerous. Obviously, Eddie had other ideas.

'Like I said, Michael, I was in the neighbourhood.' He regarded Michael with amusement. 'I like to keep in touch with my business interests.'

'I've got the figures you wanted.' Michael pushed over the sheaf of papers Simon had prepared for him earlier.

'Good, Michael, that's very good. I'm impressed.'

'Everything's going according to plan, you've nothing to worry about.' Michael fervently wished he sounded more confident than he felt, now that this man was sitting in front of him.

'You're looking a little peaky, Michael. You should take better care of yourself.'

'I'm just a little stressed at the moment, nothing I can't handle.'

'I hope so, Michael, I hope so.' Eddie's voice was dangerously low. 'The trouble is, I don't think you *can* handle it.'

'Sorry?'

'I've been hearing things, Michael, things I don't like the sound of.'

'Such as?' Michael felt cold, although beads of sweat started to trickle down his spine.

'Such as losing two of your biggest clients, Michael. Word's getting out about your habit. You're letting things slip, Michael. I don't like that. It makes me nervous, y'know.'

'That's business, these things run in cycles. You lose some, you gain some new ones,' Michael bluffed.

'How, Michael? By dipping into client accounts? That's not very clever, is it?' The words hung in the air like a dog fart.

'I'm an accountant, remember? It's my job to move money around. Not that it's any of your business!'

Eddie laughed softly. 'You're right Michael, it's none of my business. Not unless it's my money, and you wouldn't think of messing with that, would you? If you're in trouble, you should have come to me, we could have worked something out, y'know. I could have helped you.'

'I don't need your help. We just need to get the money through and everyone's happy.'

'That's just it, Michael, everyone's not happy. I had a call from one of my suppliers, the fella handling the drainage systems. He said his cheque bounced. Now how could that be, Michael? I've kept my end of the deal; the money's been coming through nice and regular, just as we arranged.'

'Look, it's just the usual red tape, that's all. You know what banks are like! Pascal's a slow mover, but he always comes through. It just takes a while. I'll talk to him on Monday, get him to talk to the bank, move things along a little bit.' Michael's heart was hammering beneath his shirt.

'You do that, Michael. I don't like my friends being messed around, y'know?'

Just then, Katy came in with the tea. Eddie sat back and watched her with interest as she poured two cups and placed one carefully in front of him, adding two spoons of sugar.

'Thanks, pet.' Eddie smiled at her, and Michael watched in disbelief as the normally cool, aloof Katy turned pink with pleasure. It was usually *he* who had that kind of effect on people!

After she had left the room, Eddie concluded the conversation.

'Get it sorted, Michael.'

'It'll take a phone call, that's all. I'll do it first thing Monday morning.'

'Just as long as we understand each other.' And with that Eddie got up. 'I'll see myself out.'

When the door closed softly behind him, Michael noticed Eddie hadn't so much as touched his tea.

Michael sat there for a long time, the events of the last few days playing over and over in his mind. He heard various members of staff leaving for the weekend, and finally Katy, who popped her head around to see if there was anything else he needed before she left. *A new life maybe,* Michael thought bitterly to himself.

He had the office to himself now. It was only 6.30, but no one hung around on a Friday evening. He got up and wandered over to the drinks cabinet and poured himself a large whiskey. He didn't feel like going home just yet. He had to think, and he couldn't do that in the grip of Felicity's watchful gaze or the inevitable noise of four lively teenagers.

He sipped his drink slowly, anger starting to burn inside him like a well-stoked furnace. God, but they were arrogant! All of them! Arrogant, ungrateful idiots! He had worked his guts out, and for what? So he could dance to their stupid little tunes for the rest of his life? *I don't think so!* He thought about them all. Pascal, always asking him questions, always watching him lately. And his ridiculous wife, Melissa. It had been fun in the beginning; he had thought she was different, but in the end they all wanted the same thing. Attention, attention, attention. And more money, of course. And as for Eddie! He was only a goddam gangster! Michael shivered, throwing back the last of his drink. What did Eddie know about anything besides peddling his grubby and decidedly unsavoury wares? They would regret the day they had tangled with him, all of them. Didn't they realise they were dealing with the financial genius of their generation? At least Felicity understood him. Knew when to leave him in peace. She wasn't always trying to bleed him dry. She went about her business just as he did, and he had to admit she ran a fabulous home for them all. She deserved better. *He* deserved better. When had he turned into a puppet who jumped every time someone pulled his strings? Well, that was about to come to an abrupt end. He would show them all who was boss, who was really in charge of the game. And then they could all whistle! But it would be too late. He smiled. Did they really think they could get the better of him?

Slowly he went over the plan that was beginning to take shape in his head. It was sheer brilliance. Why settle for ten million when he could have fifty? It was all so clear, so simple. He could stall Pascal and Eddie for a while longer, and then it would be too late. Too late for anyone to try and stop him. Fifty million would set him up nicely in a new life.

Setting up the private Swiss bank account had been surprisingly easy. And he had been filling it steadily. It was perfect. So what if a few cheques had bounced? He would just be more careful about suppliers, put a completion date on any more money going out and they'd just have to wait. And if Pascal asked questions, he'd blame the other 'investors'. Pascal wouldn't push it; he trusted Michael with his life. And if Eddie got antsy again, he'd blame Pascal. Eddie wouldn't dare mess with him; after all, he was one of Ireland's biggest property developers. That had to count for something.

And by the time any of them cottoned on to the fact that fifty million had never turned up in the account, he'd be well out of it, on his way to a new life. He pulled on his coat and locked up the office, before going home to his perfect house. He was sorry in a way Felicity wouldn't be coming with him, but there was no point asking her. She wouldn't understand and she would never leave the children. It was a pity, they made a good team in so many ways. But maybe he could send for her later. He was surprised to find he didn't worry about Felicity. After all, she was a remarkably resilient woman. Felicity could take care of herself. And he would make sure the family was looked after financially, once he was settled, and it was safe.

It was time to move on. He needed a bigger stage to play on. Ireland was too small a place for someone of his talents. Timing was everything in this life. And his was just about to begin.

CHAPTER SEVEN

Despite the rather unpredictable start to their shopping expedition, the girls had continued the day as planned. After a light lunch in Fitzers, they had adjourned to Blue Eriu, succumbing to a variety of wonderfully pampering treatments. A relaxing aromatherapy massage had restored Lornagh's equlibrium and she was feeling decidedly more human. By the time she had dropped the girls off and headed back to Lawrence's, she had almost forgotten about the whole unnerving incident.

Lawrence and Mauricio were in the kitchen when she came in.

'Ah,' said Lawrence, casting an approving eye over Lornagh's parcels, 'I see considerable damage was done. Come on, let's have a look.'

'Speaking of damage,' Lornagh sat down, looking sheepish, 'I may have inflicted some on your jeep.'

'What happened?' Lawrence asked, with concern. 'You're not hurt, are you?'

'It's only a scratch, but the other car didn't fare so well.'

Lawrence and Mauricio listened as Lornagh recounted the earlier collision at St Rita's.

'Anyhow,' said Lornagh indignantly, taking a gulp of the wine that Mauricio had poured for her, 'he *so* overreacted.'

'Who?'

'The ignorant gobshite of an architect.'

'Who is?'

'Oh, someone O'Rourke, or something.' Lornagh got up to tear off a chunk of tomato-and-basil focaccia fresh from the oven.

'Not *Sean* O'Rourke!' Lawrence's eyes opened wide.

'Yeah, I think that's it.'

'*The* Sean O'Rourke! You never told me he was involved in the St Rita's building!' Lawrence said accusingly.

'You never asked. Don't tell me he's a friend of yours.'

'I wish. I'd give my right hand to work with him! In a strictly professional capacity of course.'

'I can't possibly imagine why.'

'He's only one of the finest architects in the world, quite apart from being sex on legs. You do know who we mean, don't you?' Lawrence turned to Mauricio.

'Yes, yes, he trained in Florence, no? With the famous Serlupi? I remember he was a great favourite with the ladies. My family's restaurant is in Florence,' Mauricio explained to Lornagh. 'He was dating the great Serlupi's daughter a few years ago. It was in all the gossip magazines in Italy. Such a handsome couple!'

'That's right, I'd forgotten he studied in Florence,' Lawrence said thoughtfully. 'How interesting. He was always attractive, but I bet a few years in Italy knocked the rough spots off him.'

'Not so's you'd notice,' Lornagh said drily.

'I'm sure you'd think differently if you'd met under different circumstances,' Lawrence interjected, looking slyly at Lornagh.

'No, I would not. He's rude, arrogant and obviously a complete chauvinist pig.'

'Bossier than you? Impossible.'

'Well, I can see it's no use expecting you to take my side; you're obviously smitten.'

'Me and most of the female population in general, I should imagine.'

'As far as I'm concerned, they're welcome to him. Anyway, I'm having an early night, I'm shagged,' Lornagh said, yawning.

'Chance would be a fine thing!'

'What?'

'Nothing,' Lawrence said innocently. 'I was just thinking you looked as if you could do with getting a … good night's sleep.'

'That's exactly what I intend to do.' Lornagh shot him a withering look. 'Sex is not the answer to everything, you know.'

'Of course it isn't. Not unless you're talking about *great* sex, that is.'

'I won't dignify that remark with a reply. I'm off to bed. 'Night, all.'

As Lornagh went upstairs, Lawrence turned to Mauricio and poured another glass of wine. 'How interesting. Don't you think?'

A throbbing headache that two Nurofen had done little to improve hovered behind Simon's eyes. He was feeling rather shaken, to put it mildly. The previous evening, he had invited a few of his select gathering of friends around and they had had themselves quite a night of it. He didn't often 'break out', but lately he had felt the need to escape the pressures that bore down upon him so relentlessly.

They had arrived one by one, all sober-suited and respectable, bringing the obligatory bottle of wine and their briefcases. Simon smiled to himself. Most of them were married and in long-term relationships. If their wives and significant others could have *seen* them!

They had swapped gossip and business information and speculated on the state of the economy. It had all been very enjoyable. Very soothing. The fact that they liked to do so clad from head to toe in women's clothes really had very little to do with anything. Simon had been able to show off his latest array of lingerie and swimwear, which had gone down very well indeed. They had all been very impressed. It was hard to come up with anything vaguely tasteful in *larger* sizes, and the little Asian man he had discovered with his wonderful catalogues had opened up a whole new channel of fantasies. His range of lingerie and swimwear was called La Pearlesque and was a blatant rip off of a well-known upmarket women's brand. Simon had to admit the attention to detail was most accurate. Mr Singh had even offered him commission if Simon could sell some of his creations at his 'evenings' and pass on his catalogue discreetly to prospective customers. The whole range had gone down like a bomb. Simon had taken orders for at least twenty sets. This could become quite a nice little earner, he thought to himself.

Lornagh's make-up had come in handy too. She had left quite a bit behind in his apartment and Simon had put it to very good use. It was amazing, his friends had agreed, how the more expensive brands really did feel better against the skin. After all, there was only so much you could buy in your local Boots. One product, aptly named 'After Hours Secrets', promised to eradicate any evidence of late-night partying effects on the complexion, and Simon had to admit it really did work. Why, his skin was glowing, yet he hadn't got to bed until three o'clock that morning! That and the eye pack had done the trick: he looked positively brimming with health.

He checked his watch: it was time to hit the gym. After all, a chap had to keep in shape. He had to find himself another girlfriend, and quickly. It was a bore, but he had to stick to The Plan.

He knew exactly upon whom he would bestow his attentions and he was confident she would be bowled over. Being an au pair, she wouldn't have any money, but as she would only be a decoy, it wouldn't matter. She was good-looking, which was of paramount importance. He had only seen her a few times, walking along the road to Michael's house, or once or twice when she had come by the office. And she didn't even speak very good English, which was a definite bonus. She was one of Felicity's many 'girls', and Simon thought he had heard Michael mention that she was from the Czech Republic. Wherever she was from, she was a knockout, and her halting, hesitant accent was extremely charming. She was bound to have good manners too, so she wouldn't embarrass him in the restaurants to which he planned to bring her. Felicity liked to train all her girls herself, before sending them out to their exclusive 'homes'. Simon envied Michael. Imagine finding a wife who was well-bred, good-looking *and* ran her own business. He really was a very clever man.

He would make his first move this afternoon, Simon decided. There was no time to lose.

Melissa searched the house like a madwoman. No insignificant paper, no innocent ornament was left unturned. Maria and Jesus were on their day off and

Pascal was at the office, so she had the privacy she needed to conduct her investigation.

Already she had turned up three more receipts, a set of La Perla underwear (her favourite) and, to her dismay, a set of tickets for two to Venice! Mr and Mrs Sheehan: the printed names plunged a sickening knife through her heart. She had always wanted to go to Venice: Pascal had always protested, saying it was too hot and smelly, and didn't they have a Grand Canal right here in Dublin?

She could hardly take it all in. Pascal, *her* Pascal, having an affair. It couldn't be true, but it was. Wasn't the evidence staring her straight in the face?

Whoever the little hoor was, she was a skinny bitch. Melissa regarded the underwear as if it was contagious. 34C bra and 'small' thong briefs in delicate hand-stitched lace. Shite! This woman must have the figure of a supermodel. This was no ordinary affair. This was competition. Packaged in a young, silky-skinned, flawless nymph of a creature. Melissa's imagination ran riot. Images of Eva Herzegova and Helena Christensen in their glorious abandon floated before her eyes. What did she look like? Who was she, this harlot? This nameless, shameless hussy of a woman? How could she? More to the point, how could *he*? In her abject terror, Melissa conveniently forgot her own dalliances over the years, preferring now to plunge herself into self-pitying martyrdom.

She replaced the set of underwear carefully, folding it

back into its perfect box and putting it in the drawer of Pascal's desk with her special set of keys. She would have to keep calm; she would have to think very carefully.

As always, she confronted the worst scenario first: that Pascal would leave her and run off with this exotic, skinny supermodel. But the thought sucked the very breath from her lungs. It was unthinkable! It couldn't happen! She would be the laughing stock of Dublin society. There she is, they would whisper, sniggering behind their designer handbags: Melissa Sheehan – she used to be married to Pascal Sheehan, you know, Ireland's biggest property developer, but he dumped her for a newer, younger, skinnier model! He's much happier now, they would all say knowingly. This girl is much better for him – why he's like a new man, looking ten years younger. The imagined conversations bit into her confidence like savage dogs. She imagined herself as a cast-off. The former Mrs Pascal Sheehan. She would lose her home, her carefully cultivated lifestyle. She would be a nobody again. Who would want the ex-Mrs Sheehan? With a shudder, Melissa admitted to herself, painful though it was, that she would be nothing without Pascal. She would be plain Mary Pat again, just with a lot more money. And a lot fewer friends.

Melissa sat down feeling weak and clutched the arm of the old leather chair. Okay, so that was the worst scenario. And the best? Melissa took a deep breath. She would win him back. No matter what it took, she would make Pascal love her again. She knew she had been a complete bitch to him. But he had loved her once, he could love her again. He had to. The alternative was just too awful to contemplate. She, Melissa, was not afraid of a fight. She had spent her whole life fighting. Clawing and climbing her way to get where she wanted to be. What was it they said? 'Keep your eye on the ball and not on the cup!' Well, she had nobody but herself to blame for losing sight of the ball. In her stupid quest to become one of Dublin's so-called 'charity queens', she had very nearly sacrificed the most important thing of all, her marriage to a kind, good (and extremely rich) man, whom, she realized with a pang, she very much loved. Melissa considered the emotion with unease. She didn't like feeling vulnerable. And loving someone always made you vulnerable, to all sorts of things. She would win. She had to win, and she would get into training right away. This would be the Mother of all Battles. Pascal was *her* husband, and, if she had anything to do with it, he was going to *stay* her husband.

As Dolce and Gabbana hopped up on the sofa beside her, Melissa cried tears of remorse that fell bitterly onto their concerned little faces.

Pascal snored soundly, blissfully unaware of the consternation that was going on in his own home. He had slipped away to the caravan, and Eva had surprised him with a slap-up meal of liver and onions. They had watched Ireland beat Holland and Pascal had fallen into a sound and happy sleep in front of the TV.

Eva regarded him affectionately as he slept. She should feel guilty, she supposed. What she was doing was wrong; but in a way, she consoled herself, it was only for the good of everyone concerned.

The idea had come to her suddenly, out of the blue. It had been staring her in the face the whole time. It was so obvious!

If only Melissa *knew* she had a rival for Pascal's attentions, Eva felt sure she would put up a fight, and a good one. Not even a stupid fool like Melissa would want to lose a good husband.

The trouble was, Eva considered shrewdly, that Melissa would never regard *her*, plump, motherly Eva, as serious competition. Why, she would have laughed at the very idea! No, Melissa needed to believe a young, lithe, gorgeous creature was her opponent. A young girl, without dependants, complications or cellulite. And Eva had been absolutely right.

But how to set it up? For a few days, Eva had been stymied. And then the solution had presented itself, handed to her on a plate by none other than Pascal himself. He had been talking about the couple who kept house for him and Melissa and had been telling Eva about some of Jesus's funnier exploits, not least of which was his fondness for siphoning off Pascal's supply of alcohol.

Setting it up had been easy. She had waited discreetly

in her car outside Pascal's house when she knew the coast was clear and had seen Jesus come out with the rubbish. She had called him over to the car, pulled twenty quid from her handbag and in slow, careful English put the proposition to him. He would have to be careful, she warned him, a lot was riding on the correct handling of the 'situation'. His very job could be at stake. But the rewards were greater! A generous payment and a regular supply of tequila, his and Maria's favourite tipple. What a welcome respite from the whiskey, gin and wine that was all he could get his hands on at the Sheehans'! Jesus had gotten into the car and listened carefully, nodding earnestly as the intricate plan was laid before him.

All he had to do was make a few purchases in such and such an underwear shop, and such and such a travel agent, and leave evidence of the purchases carefully 'hidden' around the house, where they would eventually be found by Melissa. Jesus was thrilled! It was exactly the kind of sly, subversive activity he thrived on! Almost as good as being back in the secret police in the old days, before the Sandanistas had forced him to flee his native Nicaragua.

He had immediately told his wife Maria about it. He wouldn't dare act without her blessing and risk her wrath. Surprisingly, she had agreed with the plan. It was important for them, too, that the Sheehans stayed together. Maria was fond of Pascal and thought that it was high time his uppity wife got a wake-up call.

So far, things had gone without a hitch. After a few timely telephone calls when she knew Pascal would be out of the house, Eva had been answered by Melissa, and promptly hung up. Now, according to the latest report from Jesus, Melissa had begun to unearth the 'evidence'. With any luck, there should be a distinct change of tack in the atmosphere at the Sheehan residence.

Eva stroked Pascal's face lovingly as he snored contentedly beside her. It was true, she thought, you never knew what you were capable of doing until the time came and you were faced with a challenging situation.

The arrangement suited everyone just as it was; she was damned if she was going to let Melissa mess things up again.

Carol was covered in clay from head to toe. As she lay back on the reclining table, tightly bound in bandages, she reflected that this was probably as close as she was ever going to get to feeling like a mummy. Not that her biological clock was ticking: she checked routinely, just out of interest, but at thirty-four years of age it was still gratifyingly silent.

Anyway, there was still plenty of time for all *that*.

Right now, she had more immediate priorities. The detoxifying body wrap promised an overall loss of at least five inches; and, since she was going to wear her littlest black dress to the film premiere she would be attending in New York, extreme means were called for. Carol found long-haul flights always made her retain fluid, and this should counteract the effects nicely in advance.

'Okay there, Carol?' the therapist asked, checking on her.

'Fine, thanks.'

They were fussing over her as usual; eager for a favourable report on the forthcoming show that she would be doing on emergency beauty treatments. 'Last Minute Life Savers', Carol thought she would call it. Well, time would tell: if the end result lived up to its promise, she'd oblige; if not, they'd be history.

She went to his flat at every available opportunity when she could get up to Dublin. Her elderly parents were far too wrapped up in her two older brothers and running their local grocery store to bother about Carol, the only girl. They were relieved when she went up to Dublin to stay with her widowed aunt, who was a big noise at the golf club, spending her days either playing golf or organising competitions. It suited Carol perfectly; all she had to do was get a few friends to back her up and explain her whereabouts when she escaped to meet him. She always made sure to ring her aunt and let her know she was all right, and no one was any the wiser.

When she couldn't get up to Dublin, he would drive down to meet her at her various hockey matches, and afterwards they would go for drives in his car and walks along deserted forest tracks, or to the beach.

Carol was giddy with love. She thought about him every waking moment and lived for his letters whenever they were apart. She had even learned to cook a few simple things so she could impress him with her homemaking skills when they were together in his flat. Scrambled eggs on toast, spaghetti bolognese and, his favourite, roast chicken. He would tease her about how she distracted him from his studies – he always seemed to working on some paper or other – and then, after she had tidied up, they would make love, sometimes for hours, and she had nearly died of happiness. Lately, he had been encouraging her to go on the pill. He didn't like using protection. He explained that, for a man, it took away from the pleasure of getting really close to her. At first she had been afraid of the idea: suppose someone found out? But she adored him and wanted to do everything possible to please him. There would be no problem, he had said, he could write her the prescription and pick it up for her at his own pharmacy. No one need know anything, as long as she kept them well hidden and remembered to take them every day, at the same time. Was that so difficult? he had asked her, smiling at her worried little face. And, of course, she had said she would. She would have done anything to please him, to stop the frown of displeasure that sometimes crossed his face, threatening to spoil what little time they had together.

At first, the pill hadn't agreed with her. She had felt bloated and had the occasional dizzy spell, but she hadn't said anything to him. She was too afraid of upsetting him, making him angry. She had persevered, even though she had *begun to put on weight and found herself slowing down on the hockey field.*

He had told her she looked incredible, sexy and womanly, her new curves testimony to the mature woman that she was becoming.

During her end-of-year exams, she suddenly realised she had forgotten to take her pills for a few days, but she just went straight back to taking them and guiltily kept her secret to herself. After all, three or four days couldn't possibly matter, could they?

And then she had forgotten all about it, consumed with excitement at the thought of meeting him again and celebrating her school holidays.

'There we are,' the therapist pronounced happily, measuring Carol after the bandages had been unwrapped, 'six and half inches. And one whole inch off your waist.'

Carol surveyed the results with satisfaction; she felt lighter already and her skin was unbelievably smooth to the touch. She dressed quickly and left, promising to be in touch about the show.

Hopping into her black Audi TT Roadster, she decided to stop by the office before heading home, to check her e-mails. Once she was home, there would be plenty of time to look over her research on the Irish actor she would be interviewing in New York; then it would be an early night.

It was true, Carol thought smiling: hard work certainly brought its own rewards.

Felicity regarded Alexi, her latest recruit, astutely. With a little bit of finessing, she would be perfect. They were sitting in the dining room at Felicity's magnificent table, and Alexi was learning the intricacies of finding her way around the bewildering array of cutlery set out before her.

'Rule number one?' Felicity asked expectantly.

'Vork your vay from the outside in!' Alexi said proudly in her charming accent.

'Very good!' Felicity said smiling. She would have liked to add that, if in doubt, watch the other people at the table and follow their lead, but with the appalling state of table manners in Ireland today, she felt this piece of advice was no longer acceptable. Eat and run, or rather, shovel and run, seemed to be the sum total of people's interaction with food these days, and it was such a shame. Food and its appreciation was one of life's great sensual pleasures, and one that set a person apart from the rest of the herd.

Today they were progressing to soup and the correct way to hold a knife and fork.

'Remember Alexi, we *eat* soup, we don't drink it. I know it's confusing, but it's important to remember these little things.'

Alexi listened attentively, making careful notes in her journal. Really, thought Felicity, these middle-European girls were glorious. Not only did they look like supermodels with their carved-out cheekbones and wonderful bodies, but, more importantly, they were bright and eager to learn.

Next, Felicity showed her how to hold a knife. 'This is where you'll find quite a bit of conflicting advice, but there is only one correct way.' Felicity took the knife, and holding it with her index finger placed firmly on top, proceeded to cut into a piece of bread she used for the 'dummy run'. 'Never, ever, hold it like this,' she twisted the knife until it sat between her index finger and thumb like a pen. 'This is absolutely incorrect; we call it "writing home to mother", and it's how you hold a pen, not a knife.'

Alexi nodded earnestly, taking everything in.

'Perfect!' Felicity said, watching the girl use the cutlery faultlessly. 'That's enough for today. It's your afternoon off, isn't it?'

Alexi nodded happily. She enjoyed these lessons greatly and had enormous respect for Mrs Moriarty who was such an elegant woman, and who was taking such trouble to teach her everything she knew about how to behave impeccably. It was the passport to the life she fully intended to acquire for herself.

'Do try and fit in a trip to a museum or the National Gallery this afternoon, Alexi. I'll give you directions before you set off. And tomorrow the Belgian ambassador and his wife will be joining us for dinner. They're charming people, and you can put everything you've learnt this week into practice.'

Alexi beamed. When you were invited to join the

Moriartys' elegant dinner parties, it was the ultimate sign of approval from Felicity for her girls. It was better than any graduation ceremony. 'Thank you so much, Mrs Moriarty, I vould be delighted.'

Felicity smiled. She had done well with this girl; why, she could pass for an aristocrat. 'You'll find a leaflet with a little map on the hall table, it has all the galleries on it. Run along now, and enjoy your afternoon.'

CHAPTER EIGHT

Hearing a light knock on the open door of her office, Lornagh looked up from the press release she was writing to see Sean O'Rourke standing in the doorway. 'Is this a bad time?'

'Depends what for,' Lornagh retorted crisply.

'I just came by to get your insurance details, but if you're too busy …'

'Nope, come on in, it's as good a time as any. I could do with the distraction.' Lornagh pulled out her telephone book and scribbled the name and number of her insurance company.

'So, what do you do in this place?' he regarded her with curiosity.

'Public relations.' Lornagh didn't feel the need to elaborate, although she had to bite her lip to refrain from saying *you could do with a few lessons*. She pushed the number over to him without looking up. 'I've already given them all the details, just call them up and ask for Paula. She'll sort you out.'

'Thanks.' He paused uncertainly. 'Look, I'm, er, sorry,

I was a bit hot-headed yesterday. What I said, well, I was out of order.'

'You shouldn't make assumptions about people.' Lornagh looked up at him properly. Without his hard hat, and dressed in black jeans and a black polo shirt, she hardly recognised him. He looked disturbingly attractive.

He brushed a hand through his dark-blond hair. 'Yeah, well, we had an accident on site a couple of years ago. When I hear a noise and see people running, it always makes me imagine the worst.' He frowned. 'People don't realise what dangerous places building sites can be.'

'You needn't worry, I think I got the message. And I'm sorry about your car, really.'

He grinned suddenly, a lopsided smile creasing his face. 'It's almost one o'clock; I was just going to grab a sandwich in Grogan's. Why don't you let me buy you a drink and we'll call it quits, okay?'

Lornagh opened her mouth to politely decline and instead found herself saying, 'Thanks, that'd be nice. Just let me grab my coat.'

Alexi, her name was. And she was even more gorgeous close up.

Simon had circled round the block a few times in his car, and sure enough, at half-past two, she had come out of the Moriartys' house and proceeded to walk towards the bus stop on the Merrion Road. He had tooted the horn, pulled up beside her and offered her a lift. After peering cautiously into the car, she had immediately recognised him as a colleague of Michael's and accepted the lift graciously.

They were now on their way to the National Gallery. Simon was impressed. When she had said where she was going, he had asked her if she minded if he accompanied her. He would consider it a privilege, he had said, to show her around. As it was, it suited him perfectly; he could do with brushing up on his art, and he needed to look over the various Le Souquets on view, just to remind himself how expensive they were. Soon, the undiscovered Le Souquet that he was about to buy in the charity auction for a snip would be hanging among them.

'Mrs Moriarty likes us to educate ourselves in the arts venever possible on our days off,' explained Alexi in her lilting English.

Clever old Felicity, thought Simon, no wonder her au pairs were in such demand: not just in Ireland, but in all the top-notch homes in England, Europe and especially America.

'It's your day off? In that case,' said Simon, 'you must allow me to take you to afternoon tea in the Shelbourne afterwards.'

'That vould be very nice!' Alexi smiled warmly at him.

This was getting better and better, Simon thought. The sooner he was seen in public with this gorgeous creature, the sooner Lornagh Lemass would get to hear about it. There was nothing like a bit of continental glamour to put the wind up the local girls.

'Your wife is on the line, Pascal,' Lucy, his PA, informed him. 'Will I put her through?'

'Go ahead, Lucy,' Pascal sighed. Melissa ringing him at the office was a bad sign. He held the phone a safe three inches from his ear and braced himself.

'Sweetheart?'

'Melissa?'

'I'm just doing a little shopping in town, sweetie, and I, er, was wondering if you could get away from the office? I thought we could have a little lunch in Cooke's. That's if you're not too busy?' Melissa held her breath. 'Pascal? Are you there?'

'Yes, yes, love, er, that sounds nice.' He checked his diary briefly. 'I could get in for ten to one, that suit you?'

'See you there! I'll be the blonde with all the bags!' Melissa tittered, relief making her nervous.

'Ten to one in Cooke's, then.' Pascal repeated the words disbelievingly as he put down the phone. This must be worse than he thought. He racked his brains frantically. What could he have possibly done, or rather *not* done, to warrant an appointment with Melissa in the middle of the day? He scratched his head in bewilderment. He was either in deep shite, or Melissa wanted something very, very badly.

He opened his desk drawer. Clearly he was going to need his chequebook.

Jesus fingered the beautiful silky underwear in wonderment.

Melissa was out, and Maria had taken Dolce and Gabbana to the dog parlour in Donnybrook for their weekly shampoo, so he had the house to himself.

It was a pity, he thought, that Eva had told him to buy the underwear in such a ridiculous size. What kind of a woman would fit into these tiny things? Why, they would hardly cover a doll! Where he came from, a woman like this would be considered malnourished. He would have bought some larger sizes too if he thought he could persuade Maria to wear them, but somehow he was pretty sure she wouldn't react favourably to the suggestion. She would only send him to confession.

He shook his head. Imagine buying all this expensive underwear for a fictitious woman! Who would believe it?

These Irish people were strange, very strange indeed.

The big airbus sat on the runway.

Carol settled herself into her comfortable seat in premier and flicked through the in-flight magazine while the remaining passengers boarded. Finally, the doors were locked, and the cabin crew went through the safety procedures as they began to taxi slowly down the runway. Carol was only half listening. She looked around her. The usual mix of business people and a healthy sprinkling of serious shoppers were on board, all off to sample the delights of the Big Apple. The safety video came to an end, and the big plane swung around, lumbering awkwardly along the tarmac before pausing to gather strength for takeoff. The captain's voice came across, warm and welcoming, thanking them for flying Aer Lingus and telling them the approximate flight time and weather to expect on route. The huge engines revved into life, and the airbus surged forward, hurtling down the runway until, gracefully, it lifted off, and they were airborne. Carol watched the green fields beneath her grow smaller and smaller as they headed through the clouds.

She couldn't remember exactly when she had begun to feel sick. At the time, she had put it down to 'flu. Thankfully it didn't last for long, and soon she was feeling perfectly well again. She had been sick once more in his flat, after a particularly spicy curry, and he had been concerned and understanding, even though she had been embarrassed about it. 'You have been taking your pills, Carol?' he had asked, smiling, although she heard something else in his tone that she couldn't quite place. Then she had told him. It had been a relief to tell him how the pills never really agreed with her and how she had missed three days, no more, about a month ago. It was probably the pill that was making her so sick. He had been wonderful, told her not to worry her head about it, but just to be sure he could do a test for her right then and there.

Suddenly she had been very afraid. He had become the doctor again, and she the nervous patient. He had given her a small jar and told her to go into the bathroom. Afterwards, she had handed it to him with a trembling hand. He had told her to make a cup of tea and sit down, while he went into the bedroom and closed the door. It had been the longest five minutes of her life. She couldn't be pregnant, she couldn't be! He was a doctor. He knew what to do. And she had taken her horrible pills just as he had told her to, except for those three stupid days. And then the door had opened, and he had come out smiling. The test had been negative; she had absolutely nothing to worry about. She had nearly fainted with relief. Afterwards, they had made love again, and he had been especially tender and gentle with her. Lying there in his arms, she had thought about how she would love to have his baby one day; it would be a boy and look just like him, and she would be the happiest girl alive. She drifted off to sleep happy in her fantasy, unaware of him slipping from the room, closing the door softly. He poured himself a drink and sat on the small sofa, staring resolutely ahead. Then, he got up and, flicking through his address book, dialled the number.

'More champagne, Miss Dalton?' The air hostess smiled as she refilled Carol's glass. 'We're just about to serve lunch; we'll be along with it in a moment.'

Carol sat back as the tasty food was put in front of her. She had chosen the Lemon Sole from the menu, accompanied by her favourite Chardonnay. They were two hours into the flight, and the various movies were about to begin. She flicked channels, just out of curiosity, pausing to watch a convincing actress huffing and puffing in labour while her demented husband drove like a lunatic to get her to the hospital. Was there no let up? Carol tuned out impatiently. Resorting instead to her latest book, she took it out and began to read.

'How long is it since I've seen you? Professionally speaking, that is?' he was smiling at her.

'What? You mean since my examination?' Carol blushed crimson, hating to remember the day when her mother had brought her to his rooms and she had been so embarrassed. It felt like a whole lifetime ago, although it could hardly have been a year.

'About a year, why?'

'It's probably time you had a check up, just to make sure. Cysts can be painful little beggars if they're not caught in time.' He looked serious. 'If you like, I can see you after I finish with my outpatients today. Why don't you call by at about six o'clock? And don't look so worried, Carol, I'm a doctor, remember?' He had tweaked her hair playfully. 'And you're my most important patient! We wouldn't want anything like a cyst to get in the way of our fun, now would we?' his teasing tone had cajoled her.

She had gone along obediently, just as she always had, and showed up at the clinic at six o'clock. It had been quiet, and the receptionist was finishing up to leave for the evening.

Sure enough, he had popped his head around the door

*and told her to come in. She remembered thinking how
handsome he had looked in his white coat, how the
twinkling blue of his eyes had seemed brighter than ever.*

*'Who's that?' She had asked hesitantly, seeing the young
dark-skinned woman also wearing a white coat standing in
the room.*

*'This is Walecha, she's doing her internship, hoping to
pick up a few tricks from us, right, Walecha?' He had
winked. 'Don't worry Carol, it's all perfectly routine.'*

*He had helped her on to the chair and she had leaned
back, her face burning as her legs were opened and
positioned in the stirrups.*

*'This won't hurt a bit. You'll just feel a little sting.' Walecha
slipped the needle into her hand and rubbed it gently.*

*'It's just a dye we use to show the area up more clearly,'
Gerald had explained. 'Means we can get a more accurate
look at things. That's it, Carol, you're doing fine!' And that
had been the last thing she had remembered.*

Carol pushed the meal away from her. Jumping up
from her seat she almost collided with a surprised air
hostess in her anxiety to get the toilets. She was going to
be horribly, violently ill.

Felicity sat at a window table in Café Noir, sipping a
mineral water while she waited for her companion. The
restaurant was as yet reasonably quiet; in a few minutes,
it would be packed with the most fashionable of the
Ballsbridge set, all keen to see and be seen.

Its stylish proprietor, Jasmine, kept a watchful eye on proceedings. Her success as a restaurateur was legendary. It was a particular favourite of Felicity's for lunch.

A few minutes later, a stunning, dark-haired young woman of about 25 walked through the door. She was about five feet ten in height and could have passed for a young Yasmin Le Bon. She saw Felicity, smiled and made her way over to the table.

Over delicious chicken vinaigrette salads, they got straight down to business. Felicity listened intently as the girl relayed her information in scrupulous detail. Felicity frowned occasionally and nodded knowingly. To all intents and purposes, they could have been discussing the merits of the latest Lainey Keogh collection, and not the vitally important state of Michael's finances.

The girl had done a sterling job, Felicity admitted. She had known she would come in useful in the scheme of things. An accountant by profession, she had left her native Poland in search of a more glamorous life, and hopefully an extremely wealthy husband. In the meantime, she was working as one of Felicity's 'girls', which would undoubtedly help her acquire both.

Felicity had known Michael had needed an extra pair of hands in the office to deal with the extra workload a while back. What he had got, in the shapely form of Ivanka, was an extra pair of eyes and ears as well as an extremely astute financial brain, used to working quickly under pressure. Ivanka had access to almost all the information she needed to report to Felicity, and what she didn't have access to she very cleverly obtained.

Of course Michael had slept with her. He slept with all of them. Felicity had long since given up caring. She had known it was only a matter of time when she had married him. Felicity understood her husband better than he understood himself. She knew his boredom threshold, his insatiable hunger for success at any cost and his willingness to pursue it at any level. All this she could accept. But she knew instinctively that, like all brilliant people, Michael had a fatal flaw. One that would eventually bring about his downfall. Underneath it all – the easy charm, the quick mind, the entertaining personality – Michael was desperately insecure. It was what drove him. And Felicity guessed correctly that, one day, the very complex nature of that insecurity could bring about his downfall.

Listening to Ivanka, Felicity was thoughtful. It seemed that things were even worse than she had suspected. Michael was losing control. Losing vitally important perspective. Thank God she had kept an eye on things, had seen the warning signs. It was still not too late to take action.

As they finished lunch and ordered coffees, Felicity congratulated Ivanka on a job well done. She had trained her well; trained all her girls well. Thanks to them, and her own particular brand of intuitive professionalism, there was no information in Dublin that escaped her. It had served her very well over the years, particularly in her dealings with the stock market, which by any standards were spectacularly successful. She smiled thinking about it. She couldn't understand why women always thought men were so difficult to understand. A little artful flattery, and a lot of artful sex, and even the most unlikely candidates succumbed eventually. That knowledge alone had made her a very rich woman in her own right.

She thought, fleetingly, of her own, very different education on the streets in London. When she had run away from her lush of a mother, and her mother's latest violent, abusive boyfriend, she had been just 12 years old – going on 35. By the time she was a streetwise 14, a particularly smitten 'client' had brought her to Paris, where she had quickly ditched him. Starving and vulnerable, she had been lucky enough to be taken in by the notorious Madame Bouvier, who had taught her everything she knew. Felicity had become her star pupil. She had been particularly popular with the phenomenally wealthy Arabs, who found her aristocratic good looks so appealing. And, after years of hard work on various yachts and parties in the most sophisticated of European resorts, she had finally made enough money to go out on her own. Reinventing herself had been easy, recreating her aristocratic and wealthy background less so; but she had done a meticulous job.

Now her beautiful, hand-picked girls did the hard

work for her. And the rewards were spectacular. After completing Felicity's careful training course, there was nothing a girl couldn't accomplish. No doors were left unopened, no *entrée* into elegant society was denied them. Why, several of her girls had already married into European aristocracy.

Felicity called for the bill and sent the beautiful Ivanka on her way, thanking her for her valuable information.

After chatting to Jasmine for a few moments, Felicity made her exit, nodding to the various faces who smiled in recognition at the much-admired, aloof woman who was considered the very epitome of elegance. It was true, she often reminded her girls: appearances were absolutely everything.

Clad in an immaculately cut Chanel suit, Felicity disappeared gracefully into the interior of her dark-green Range Rover. Nobody watching her would ever have dreamed they were looking at the *madame* who ran one of the slickest brothels in Europe. Felicity Moriarty provided Ireland, Europe, America and the Middle East with the legendarily beautiful hand-picked prostitutes whose looks could compete with those of any supermodel.

And her brilliant husband had absolutely no idea.

She made a mental note to ring Alexi when she got home. Now that Simon Sullivan was taking Alexi out, Felicity could gather even more important information about Michael. There were only one or two missing pieces of the jigsaw left to find. And time was of the essence.

CHAPTER NINE

Sean and Lornagh made their way into the small pub across the road just in time to claim the last available table. Sitting down, they ordered sandwiches, a mineral water for Sean and a glass of white wine for Lornagh.

'Mind if I smoke?' he asked.

'No, go ahead.'

Sean stretched out his long legs, lit a cigarette and inhaled. Watching him, Lornagh suddenly wished she'd never given them up.

'I assume you don't,' he said offering her one.

'I used to. I gave up when I lived in New York. It was just easier in the end.'

'No vices, huh?'

'I didn't say that.' Lornagh suddenly felt uncomfortable as he looked at her. Why did she feel she should defend herself to him?

'You're a Dublin 4 girl, aren't you?' He looked at her speculatively.

'I grew up there, yes. Is it that obvious?' Lornagh was immediately furious for sounding as if she cared.

'Me, too.' Sean replied, ignoring her question.

'Oh, really, where?'

'Ringsend.' He was watching her again with that amused look.

'Oh, I see. It's, er, very trendy these days.' Lornagh could feel herself blushing. The bastard was deliberately trying to make her squirm. Ringsend, although now ludicrously expensive because of its central address, would, until recent years, have been considered very much the *wrong* side of the tracks as far as Dublin 4 was concerned.

'Tell me about New York.'

'It was fun, I lived there for five years, and then I decided to come home.'

'Why?'

'I was fired.'

Sean raised an amused eyebrow. 'What for?'

Over lunch, Lornagh found herself telling him the whole story. About the disastrous romance; the phone call to her mother; Angela's subsequent arrival in New York; and finally, how she had flipped at work under the pressure of it all.

'She must be quite a woman, your mother. Ireland's answer to Sophia Loren, isn't that what they say?

'In her day, yeah, I suppose.'

'You look like her.'

'No, I don't.'

'Sure you do, same lines. You're blonde, but there's no

mistaking the resemblance,' Sean said, then, watching Lornagh's face, 'I wouldn't have thought that was a problem.'

'It isn't. We're just very different, that's all.'

'Right.'

'What about you?' Lornagh found all the questions disconcerting. 'How did you become the golden boy of Irish architecture?'

'I wanted to be an architect ever since I was a nipper. I got a scholarship to Bolton Street, and then I got lucky, I won a place at the Instituto dell Oratorio in Florence. The great Serlupi took me under his wing: he was like a father to me, and he taught me a lot. I owe him everything, really.'

And what about his daughter? Lornagh suddenly wanted to ask. *What did she teach you?*

'It must have been fantastic, living in Florence.'

'It was. I very nearly stayed.'

'Why didn't you?'

The serious look vanished, replaced by deliberate lightness. 'Ah, you know what they say: you can take the boy out of Dublin, but you can't take Dublin out of the boy. Anyway, it's a great time to be here; things are happening in this city we've waited a long time for. It's good to be part of that.' His dark blue eyes were intense as they held hers. 'Look, I've got to go,' he said suddenly. 'I've got a 2.30 meeting with a client in Temple Bar. I'd better get a move on.'

'Oh sure, well, thanks for lunch.' Lornagh stood up

feeling unusually dwarfed by his immense height. 'And I'm sorry again, about your car.'

'No worries. No real damage done.' Outside, he looked down at her and grinned. 'Well, see you around,' and he turned to head in towards town.

'Yeah, see you,' Lornagh said, noticing several women's heads swivel in his direction as he walked away with easy grace.

Lawrence, as usual, had been right.

Sean O'Rourke oozed sex appeal from every pore.

Just as well, Lornagh reassured herself, that he wasn't remotely her type.

A bitingly cold winter had given way to the first burgeoning signs of spring, and Simon was feeling remarkably upbeat about things. He and Alexi had been out and about for almost a month now, and he felt sure they were cutting a suitable dash. She certainly turned heads wherever they went, with her fabulous figure and her long, dark-blonde hair. And, as far as he could tell, she spoke at least three languages.

He had run into an old friend of his who wrote a gossip column for a well-known Sunday newspaper, and he had promised to give Simon and his current 'squeeze' a mention. Simon couldn't wait. He was going to invite her to the St Rita's ball, which was only a month or so away now. That would show Lornagh Lemass just what she was up against! He must make sure Alexi had a suitable evening dress, he reminded himself: he would take her shopping at the weekend if necessary. He didn't like the thought of her choosing a dress herself; it was vital she made the right impression. After all, this was a strategically important part of the plan. He strolled into the newsagent's, and, along with his paper, bought a hefty selection of the latest fashion magazines: *Vogue, Elle, Image* and *In Style*. He would study them carefully this evening. He had a good idea of the kind of 'look' he had in mind for her, but he would go over the latest collections, just to make sure.

Melissa shrieked with delight as she stood on her scales. She had lost five whole pounds! And she hadn't even been dieting. It must be all this worrying she had been doing since she had found out about Pascal's affair with the X-ray Woman. Well, if she kept going at this rate, soon she herself would fit into the wretched underwear. It was an ill wind and all that, she thought to herself happily.

So far, her tactics were working well. She had to be careful not to overdo it. She didn't want Pascal to suspect she knew anything. That would be disastrous. It nearly killed her not to ask leading questions when he went out for an evening, or to make scathing, sarcastic innuendoes upon his return, but she had kept her mouth valiantly shut and worked instead on revitalising her shaky marriage.

To her immense surprise, she even found herself

enjoying it. She had forgotten what fun they used to have together. And it was a relief to let herself go, to have a few drinks and be her old uproarious self, not worrying about her accent or her manners or whether she was going to put her foot in it if she made an inappropriate remark.

Her mobile phone rang as she was doing her make-up, and she checked the number that flashed on screen before answering it. It was Michael's. She flicked her phone off instantly. Hah! She had that gobshite exactly where she wanted him. Grovelling as if his life depended on it. She had met him a few times after that horrible afternoon and had let him apologise profusely. She had even, eventually, allowed him make love to her again, just to show she didn't have any hard feelings towards him. He had been pathetically grateful and was now showering her with compliments and gifts to beat the band.

In a way, she supposed she should be grateful to him. He had woken her up to just how lazy she'd allowed herself to become. She'd taken her eye off the ball, but it wouldn't happen again.

Yesterday, they had met for what was to be their last rendezvous, although *he* didn't know that. Melissa had turned up at one of the many apartments that Michael owned in the city, and he had put on quite a show for her.

They had had a wonderful lunch, cooked at the Coq Hardi restaurant, delivered to the apartment and served by two of the restaurant's waiters.

Afterwards they had drunk copious quantities of her

favourite Cristal champagne and had made very satisfactory, if insincere, love.

Then, while Michael was showering, Melissa had deftly slipped his Palm Pilot computer out of his jacket pocket and into her handbag. She knew he never travelled anywhere without it and, as he often said, it contained all the vital information he needed if he was ever out of the office.

Melissa's sister, Phil, was a computer programmer, and Phil would easily be able to copy everything onto a disk for her and print it out, so Melissa could peruse it at leisure.

She would return it to him afterwards, of course. It wasn't that she wanted to *inconvenience* him, she just wanted to have a little look at some of the names and addresses that would undoubtedly be on it. You could never have too much information where people like Michael Moriarty were concerned.

He had shown her his true colours that day in her bedroom, and they weren't pretty.

Melissa got dressed quickly. She had more important things to think about than an ex-lover. St Rita's ball was only a matter of weeks away, and she had her eye on a spectacular Versace number she had seen on her last foray into town.

She was determined to look a million dollars that night, and the competition was going to be tough.

Pascal was sitting in Michael's office going over the figures with him and was feeling much happier. Michael had everything under control, there was just the usual red tape holding things up. The discrepancies in the accounts had been nothing more than an oversight. Funds appeared to have been suitably restored.

'Hey, you know what these guys are like, Pascal.' Michael seemed relaxed and energetic, almost back to his old self. 'They take forever to get approval from their boards. Everything has to be gone over by solicitors, accountants and then more solicitors. It's a miracle we can ever get a deal up and running in this country.'

'Tell me about it.' Pascal was used to moving vast amounts of finance into place for his property deals, but he left the details to Michael, who had never let him down yet.

Michael had got on to the bank first thing that morning, and he and Pascal had sat down with the manager for an emergency meeting, at the end of which they had been assured that the funds were being lodged as planned.

The apparent shortage had arisen because of a separate account set up by Michael for advances to suppliers. The bank, for some reason, had not realised this was part of the general finance deal. Once that had been cleared up, everything was back on track.

Pascal was hugely relieved. He had been overreacting as usual. It was just as well, he thought to himself. He had enough on his plate without having to worry about this deal.

Melissa was behaving very strangely. She had asked

him to come home early this afternoon because she had a 'little surprise' planned for him. Pascal felt rather dubious about it, although for the last week or so she had been positively charming to him.

He wondered what had got into her although, to be honest, he was enjoying it thoroughly. Melissa could be very entertaining company. She was a brilliant mimic, and her impressions of some of the people they knew had him in stitches.

Last night they had sat up for hours over a nightcap, talking and laughing. And afterwards she had made love to him with a passion he hadn't experienced since their early days together. He had to pinch himself to believe it. It was almost like old times. Oh well, he would enjoy it while he could. After all, it couldn't possibly last for long.

Carol made her way back to her seat and took a quick gulp of her champagne. She still felt queasy, but not nearly as bad as she had a few moments ago.

'Miss Dalton, are you all right? Can I get you anything?' The air hostess was concerned as she came to take the tray away.

'No thanks, I'm fine,' Carol smiled gratefully at her. 'I'll just settle down to watch the movie. A glass of water would be nice, then you can forget about me.' Whatever people said about Aer Lingus, the cabin crew, thought Carol, were out on their own. Carol had travelled extensively all over the world, and no other cabin crew ever came close.

She put on her headphones and tuned into the movie channel but found herself unable to concentrate. Hideous memories were churning around in her mind; it was all coming back.

She had woken up some time later in his apartment, groggy from the anaesthetic, aware of an insistent cramping in her pelvis.

'What happened?' She had desperately tried to focus, seeing his lovely concerned face hovering above her as she lay on the sofa in his flat.

'Shh, don't worry, sweetheart. You're fine, it's all over now. I'm just going to give you something to help you sleep.'

Later, she had woken again, ravenous hunger competing with the now subsiding cramps. He was at her side immediately.

'How are you feeling, sweetheart? Can I get you anything? A little tea and toast maybe?'

Carol had struggled to sit up. 'What happened at the clinic? Why am I like this?' She had been overcome with fatigue and confusion.

'You were lucky we caught it in time, Carol. There was another cyst there, and it was dangerously close to an important artery.' She could hardly take in what he was saying.

'But I got it out, all of it, it's all over now. You've nothing to worry about, except getting better.'

'But, why? How?' Carol struggled to comprehend.

'Wouldn't you rather it was this way? Think about it, Carol,' he had said. 'I'm your doctor, your gynaecologist. If I hadn't done the procedure, you'd have eventually discovered something was wrong. You would have gone to your GP, he would have referred you back to me anyhow, except he'd probably have had to involve your mother again, and you'd have had to wait for weeks, maybe with a lot of pain and unnecessary worry.' He stroked her face all the time. 'As it was, we were very lucky that Walecha is an anaesthetist. She was able to put you out there and then, so I could operate. Now it's all over, and nobody but you and I have to know a thing about it.'

The whole thing had come as such a shock, Carol could barely take it in.

'I'm going to make you some tea and toast now, and then you're going straight back to bed, young lady. And tomorrow, you'll be as right as rain, you'll see.'

The next day she had felt a lot better. She had slept off the anaesthetic, and was keen to get up.

'Take it easy, Carol!' he had warned her before he set off for the hospital. 'And call me immediately if you notice anything unusual.' He had told her to expect some mild cramping to continue for a day or so, and he had given her painkillers to take. They made her feel a bit queasy, but they got rid of the cramps almost immediately. The worst thing about the whole ordeal was these awful pads she had to wear until she healed up. 'No tampons, Carol,' he had said. 'And

I'm afraid no sex either, not for at least six weeks.' He had smiled at her distraught face. 'I know, it'll be hard for me too, although, in a way, it's good timing.'

'What do you mean?' she had asked.

'I'll be away for a couple of weeks, I have to leave on Tuesday. It's a lecture tour in the Middle East. So in a way, it's just as well all this came about the way it did.'

'When will you be back?' Carol was miserable at the thought of him being away.

'Two or three weeks at most. You'll hardly know I'm gone. Then, when I get back, we can escape for a few days, maybe to London. How about that?' And she had brightened up, the thought of having him to herself in a big city like London for a few days giving her hope again. She had never even been out of Ireland.

Michael sat in his convertible Aston Martin and pressed the button to release the electric roof. It was a spanking gorgeous day in May, and summer had announced itself without any warning. He was setting off to the exclusive K Club for a golf competition with several well-known celebrities in aid of charity, and the day stretched ahead full of pleasure and promise. Putting on his favourite Persol sunglasses, he pulled out of his driveway and headed onto Ailesbury Road and up towards Donnybrook church where a few early churchgoers were trickling into mass. Heads turned as the throaty engine of the Aston Martin cut into the early-morning ennui, and admiring glances followed the magnificent car and its handsome driver.

Traffic was light, and it wasn't long before he reached the motorway. He put his foot down lightly on the accelerator and the car responded instantly, eating up the miles to the encouraging pace of Van Morrison's 'Gloria'.

God, but it felt good! He was invincible again, back in the driving seat where he had always belonged. The last few months had taken their toll, and Michael had finally taken action. He didn't like not being in control, and lately he had felt himself slipping dangerously. With immense determination he had started cutting back on his little habit and, tough though it had been, he was managing it, day by day. He had come close, perilously close, to disaster. He had nearly blown everything. What with his vitriolic outburst towards Melissa, and his reckless handling of the transfer of funds, everything had very nearly come tumbling down around his ears. Luckily, he had been able to redress the situation without anyone being any the wiser. He had simply reinstated enough money back into the account to make up for what he had taken out. That, and he had made sure there was enough to pay all suppliers 25 percent of their fee, with the balance coming through on completion.

Of course that would never happen. By then he would have restocked his Swiss bank account and be on his way to a new, exciting life in South America. Sure, the shit would hit the fan, but that wouldn't be his problem. By then he would be far away from any annoying repercussions.

He had been lucky too with Melissa. Amazingly, she had forgiven him for his unwarranted personal attack. Michael wondered privately if she even remembered some of the vile things he had said to her. Perhaps she had had so much champagne by then she didn't remember word for word exactly what he had said. She certainly didn't give any indication of doing so. She seemed to think it had been more of a lover's tiff, and he had breathed a mighty sigh of relief.

Melissa was one woman you didn't want to mess with. It had come as a surprise to him when she had announced they should take a break for a while. She had told him in all seriousness that she wanted to work on her marriage. And while Michael tried to keep a straight face, he had to admit in a way it had been a huge relief to him. They had had an eventful afternoon saying their 'goodbyes', and had parted the best of friends.

Pascal, too, seemed in better form these days. Why, he was positively chirpy and had a very definite spring in his step. Michael was happy for him. Melissa must be a nightmare to live with, and an expensive one at that. The least she could do was make her husband happy.

All's well that ends well, he thought to himself as he turned into the K Club, pulling up outside the beautiful hotel. Getting out of the car, he took his green crested member's jacket out of the back seat and his clubs out of the boot. He would have a quick shower to freshen up and then head over to the clubhouse. He was looking forward to the competition, which was in aid of a very deserving childrens' hospital. A well-known buisnessman had organised a great bunch of people. Tiger Woods had even been flown in for the day. Michael hoped his swing would be up to scratch. He didn't play that often, although it was true that more money was made on the golf course in Ireland than around any boardroom table.

Last time he checked, his handicap had been a healthy four. With a bit of luck, he might knock it down to three this summer. He didn't know why people agonised over their game so much. Succeeding at golf was a lot like succeeding with women really, he mused. If you tried too hard, the rewards seemed to escape you.

It was no wonder he excelled at it.

CHAPTER TEN

There were only four weeks to go.

Lornagh had never been so busy in her entire life. She had a million things to organise for the ball, and they were all demanding her attention.

All going well, it was promising to be quite a night.

The venue was the newly finished Anglesea Hotel: a magnificently restored building in the heart of Ballsbridge, which just a few weeks ago had opened its doors to universal acclaim.

Right now, Lornagh was concentrating on putting together a short video which would show the typical workings of the charity and also provide a behind-the-scenes look at the building of the new offices, leisure centre and housing for the families. She had shot some particularly poignant and insightful footage of the mothers and children who had agreed to talk on the video, and some of the stories were both heart-rending and uplifting. Although it was a relatively new organisation, in the last five years St Rita's had gained quite a profile and Lornagh was confident that, after the ball, the public would be left in no doubt as to just how valuable their help and contributions to the cause would be.

Today, Sean was going to show her over the new buildings so she could capture the progress on camera.

It was a blisteringly hot day in June, and Lornagh was wearing her favourite jeans and a skimpy white T-shirt. Not that she had taken any particular trouble with her appearance for the occasion – why should she? – but all the same, she knew she looked good. Videocam in hand, she made her way over to the prefabs, where Sean was standing talking to the foreman and a few of the builders. She hadn't seen him much since their lunch, except on the few days when he waved at her from the site. Up close, she noticed, his skin had darkened considerably in the sun, especially his forearms, which revealed a distinct tanning mark when he rolled up his sleeves.

'Hi! Is this a good time for you?' Lornagh asked.

'Sure, I'm all yours. Here, put this on, will you?'

The builders whistled appreciatively as she donned the hard hat, and they made their way over to the almost finished building.

'It's unbelievable!' Lornagh shook her head. 'I would never have thought so much could be completed in just a few months. The new buildings are going to be fantastic, although I have to say I'll be sad to see the old place demolished.'

'I know,' Sean agreed. 'It's always a bit emotional

seeing an old building go, however outdated it is. But the old has to make way for the new.' He held Lornagh's eyes for a fraction. 'And I can safely assure you that the storage space, shelving in particular, will be greatly improved!'

Lornagh laughed, although she felt herself going pink remembering how she had thought him to be the handyman. Listening to him talking about the project as they walked along, she couldn't help being infected by the obvious passion he had for his work. She had to admit she found him intriguing, and she'd been doing a little research of her own courtesy of Sister Kay, who didn't need much prompting.

Apparently, Sean's family had had to struggle to survive after the untimely death of his father, whom he barely remembered. Sean's mother had raised him and his four sisters on her own and had made a wonderful job of it.

It was a far cry from Lornagh's own upbringing, growing up in the gilded surroundings of Grovesbury Road. But while Sean's family may have been short of money, there had been no shortage of love and, according to Sister Kay, they were a very closely knit bunch.

'Are you coming along for a drink on Friday?' Lornagh asked casually. It had been Sister Kay's idea to have a few drinks with the staff and committee in the old building to give it a 'good send off' before it was demolished.

'Oh, I've received my instructions! Apparently, I'm expected to say a few words.'

'Rather you than me!' Lornagh felt a spring in her step.

'What about yourself?' Sean pushed an unruly lock of hair out of his eyes as he looked at her expectantly.

'I'll be on duty, too.' Lornagh tried to sound casual but suddenly found herself blushing under the intensity of his gaze. He held her eyes for a second longer and seemed about to say something else, then thought better of it.

'Well, that's about it,' he said as they finished the tour. 'Have you got all you need, do you think?'

'Yeah, there's enough footage here to make a documentary! The tough part will be editing it all down to three minutes.' Turning back to head down the concrete steps Lornagh suddenly lost her footing and, clutching on to the videocam, found herself lurching dangerously forward. Sean caught her just in time to stop her and the camera hurtling to the ground.

'Hey! Careful! These steps are still wet. Are you okay?' His arm was around her and pulling her back towards him as she struggled to find her feet.

'Shit! I mean, thanks,' Lornagh babbled, mortified at her clumsiness.

'Here, let me have that,' he said, taking the camera as he let go of her. 'We've had enough collisions on this site already.'

Reaching the bottom of the steps, Lornagh heaved a sigh of relief. That had been far too close for comfort.

'Do you think you can make it back to the office in one piece?' he said, grinning as he handed the camera back to her.

'Er, sure, thanks!' Lornagh could feel her face flaming.

'No problem, just another near-miss.' He looked amused.

'Yeah. Bye.'

Heading back towards the office, Lornagh heard another round of appreciative wolf whistles. She tried not to look around but couldn't help wondering if Sean, too, was perhaps watching her walk away; in these jeans, she tended to have that effect on men. Sneaking a quick backward glance, she was just in time to see a startlingly beautiful dark-haired girl fling her arms about Sean to the cheers of the onlooking men.

'Darling!' she heard her cry, in heavily accented tones. 'It's been too long. I couldn't wait another moment.' And then she kissed him, long and lingeringly.

Simon was desperate to get another look at the painting, just to make absolutely sure. The trouble was, it was in Lornagh's mother's house for safekeeping until the night of the ball. He had thought about ringing Lornagh, but it didn't appeal to him. He hadn't seen her for a few weeks now even though he had desperately been trying to bump into her, preferably with Alexi on his arm, but so far she had eluded him. It was most irritating. She was probably keeping a low profile now that he was out and about with a gorgeous new girlfriend. So she should be.

He had been mentioned in the gossip column of the leading Sunday broadsheet and the write-up had been very gratifying. Simon had been described as one of

Ireland's most eligible bachelors, and he had made sure to mention that *he* had ended his previous relationship with Lornagh Lemass. That would give her something to think about. The article went on to say how he had found his new 'love', the exotic Alexi Provnovitch, while they were both in the National Gallery and had literally bumped into each other while admiring the Le Souquets. Simon came across in the piece as quite the Culture Vulture.

He sipped a drink as he pored over his collection of art books and brochures. There was absolutely no doubt the painting was genuine; all the same, he'd like to see it again.

Suddenly, he had an idea. He was free this evening, having extricated himself from a date with Alexi on the pretext of a late meeting with Michael Moriarty. The girl was wearing him out. She was even worse than Lornagh. What was it with women these days? They were positively sex mad. Hadn't they heard that it's much more attractive to let a man do the chasing? Simon had needed to take a night off. Why, if he took any more Viagra, he was in danger of walking around with a permanent erection. Anyhow, he now had a free evening and he knew just how he was going to spend it. He didn't need Lornagh Lemass's permission any more. He would drop by her mother's house unannounced. Once he had explained that he was on the committee for the ball and needed to see the painting before the auction, she would be bound to let him in. Then he could have a good look at the Le Souquet and indeed at the rest of the house, and not before time. Lornagh had never even bothered to introduce him to her mother. Well, he would introduce himself. They would have a nice little chat, and Mrs Lemass would see for herself what her daughter had turned down. Before long, she would say as much to Lornagh, if Simon knew what mothers were like. Then Lornagh would see the error of her ways. He checked the time: he would take a quick shower and freshen up. He had to look the part. He would probably wear his tweed jacket and waistcoat; he looked very much the country squire in it. That would be bound to impress her. Now that he had thought of the idea, he couldn't believe he hadn't come up with it before. He was dying to see the house, and indeed the famous Mrs Lemass. After all, she couldn't last forever, and then the house would be his. His chest swelled with pride at the thought. Simon Sullivan of Grovesbury Road.

Yes, it was high time he paid a visit to his prospective home.

Melissa breathed a deep sigh and surrendered to the skilful hands of her aromatherapist. She had the treatment in her own home at least once a week and always felt the better for it. Today, she was having an energising massage rather than her usual relaxing one, and heaven knows she needed it. She hadn't realised how much the last few weeks had drained her.

It was hard work being a seductress, especially when the man you were seducing was your own husband. It called for far more inventiveness and inspiration than your run-of-the-mill fling. She smiled as the revitalising oils went to work on her weary body. If she was feeling tired, Pascal must be completely worn out. He had left work early at least three times last week for their mid-afternoon rendezvous, and Melissa had made sure it was well worth his while.

Yesterday, she had answered the door herself dressed in a very fetching French maid's outfit. Wearing high heels and fishnet stockings with a teeny little white apron and matching frilly hat, she had let Pascal chase her up the stairs and all around the bedroom as Melissa shrieked, 'Oooh la la!' and 'Non! Non! Monsieur is very naughty!' And then they had collapsed onto the bed in helpless giggles while Dolce and Gabbana danced around the room, barking in excitement.

Later, she had heated up a lovely Beef Provençal that Maria had made earlier, and they had had a cosy dinner in the kitchen, and afterwards sat in Pascal's study listening to Edith Piaf and drinking several Irish coffees. Pascal had even suggested they must take a trip to Paris soon, and Melissa had almost burst into tears with relief and happiness. It was a breakthrough, and an important one. If he was taking her away with him, then it meant he must still love her, just a little bit anyway, and she would make sure he enjoyed every minute of the trip. She would even let him go in a feckin' caravan if he wanted. She didn't care. Just as long as he didn't leave her for that horrible, skinny supermodel woman.

Melissa scowled just thinking about it. She must be strong: she couldn't weaken now, not when things were going so well. For the last three days, she had not come across any further 'evidence', and she was beginning to hope there was light at the end of the tunnel. Still, it wouldn't do to get complacent. She wouldn't make that mistake again. She would remind Pascal about Paris tonight: the sooner they went, the better. If she was lucky, she might even fit in a bit of shopping. Now there was an idea. She had always fancied owning a French *haute couture* evening gown and, if St Rita's ball didn't warrant something show-stopping, what did?

Pascal put the phone down after talking to Eva and smiled. There was something special about that woman; she just seemed to bring the best out in everybody.

She had informed Pascal that she would be going away for a couple of weeks' holiday. What she neglected to tell him was that it was with the nice widower she had recently befriended. 'It's a last minute thing, Paccy. I really could do with a spot of sun, you understand, don't you?'

'Of course I do, Eva, how could I not? You go and enjoy yourself, love.'

Eva had smiled at her end of the line. 'I knew you

would, Paccy! I'll miss you, of course, but we'll see each other when I get back. Oh, and Paccy?'

'What, love?'

'You might consider spending a little quality time with Melissa, if you know what I mean.' Eva held her breath and was delighted to hear Pascal chuckle down the line.

'Oh, you needn't worry on that account.' He neglected to go into detail about just *how* thoroughly Melissa had been putting him through his paces.

'Good.' Eva was pleased. 'Well, bye for now love, I'll ring you soon.'

'Have a great time, Eva.'

As Pascal sat in his office smiling, he was surprised to notice that he did not feel a sense of despair threatening to overwhelm him as it usually did whenever Eva was away from him for any length of time. He felt genuinely happy for her, but he didn't dwell on it for long. He had a busy morning ahead of him. He must remind his secretary to get on to the Paris Ritz. A few days in Paris would do him and Melissa the world of good.

Let's face it, it wasn't every day you discovered your wife of 19 years was still the girl you married.

Pascal grinned and picked up the phone. He would see if Charlie was free for lunch and tell him the good news. Charlie would be very happy for him.

New York was hot on the blazing June day and starting to get humid. Carol was grateful to get into the cab and start on the slow journey to Manhattan. The driver was obviously Russian or Middle European and spoke hardly any English. But when she mentioned Fitzpatrick's Hotel on Lexington Avenue, it seemed to register with him. Although she was exhausted after the flight, she found she was greatly looking forward to spending two days in New York. She would hook up with a few old friends and maybe do a bit of retail therapy, and there was nowhere like Fitzpatrick's if you were Irish in New York. The hotel was as close as you could get to a home from home.

Carol looked out the window at the slow procession of small timber houses as they made their way through Queens and wondered at all the different lives that were going on in each one of them.

She had even tried to ring him a few times, hoping desperately to hear the sound of his voice, to hear some kind of explanation, some slim reed of a chance that would take this horrible, cold, clammy feeling away from her. But each time the answer was the same. 'Dr Stevens is out of the country. No, we don't expect him back. As far as we know he's in Saudi Arabia on a lecture tour. No, he's not planning to return to Dublin. He finished his term at the clinic before he left.' And that had been that.

He had known all along he would never have to see her again. He hadn't even said goodbye. It was that silly little thought, that inconsequential, stupid word that she had never even got to hear, that suddenly opened the floodgates.

Alone and bereft, in a little public phone box along a

country road in Ireland, Carol Dalton had collapsed to her knees wracked with sobs that tore through her still tender body and shattered her 16-year-old heart.

Eddie 'The Shark' McEntee was not a patient man.

Two of his men stood before him in the warehouse, where he sat with legs resting on the makeshift desk in front of him. A cigarette hung from the corner of his mouth where a slow curl of smoke now snaked upwards through the cold, damp air. Eddie didn't believe in heating. It made people far too comfortable.

'What's the story?' he asked.

'No change, boss. We've been hanging around like you said, keeping an eye on things, y'know.'

'So where's it at now?'

'They're demolishing the old building on Frida. The rest of the construction's going up all right. That architect fella's always around the place; it's not easy to be inconspicuous, y'know.'

'I didn't ask you to be inconspicuous, I asked you to be efficient.'

'That's it, really, boss.' The bigger of the men shifted uncomfortably. 'The builders can't tell us any more. It's going a bit slow, but it's happening.'

'Not fast enough!' Eddie's mouth tightened. 'This Pascal fella, have you seen him on site?'

'Yeah, sure, I seen him at least twice.'

'Could you recognise him?'

'Sure, you'd know him anywhere.'

'Good. He's the one who's holding me up. I think it's time we gave him a little incentive to close his part of the deal.'

The men waited obediently for their instructions.

CHAPTER ELEVEN

'And just *where* do you think you're going dressed like that?' Lawrence asked, as Mauricio whistled appreciatively at Lornagh from the kitchen, where he was rustling up a delicious pasta.

'Nowhere to get excited about, not that it's any of *your* business,' she added good-humouredly. 'We're just having a few drinks with the mothers and staff at the old building before it's demolished.'

'Ah, I see,' said Lawrence looking pointedly at Mauricio as Lornagh descended the three steps into the kitchen, dressed in a short chocolate leather skirt and white silk shirt. 'And who's the lucky man?'

'I don't know what you mean,' Lornagh said innocently, as she wandered over to sit down at the kitchen table and poured herself a glass of wine. 'What's that? It smells divine.'

'Don't try to change the subject. That's a man-trapping outfit if ever I saw one. Right, Mauricio?'

'Si, bellissimo!' Mauricio nodded vehemently.

Lawrence ran a critical eye over her. 'Let's see, short

leather skirt – not quite a belt, but close enough – to show off the long shapely legs. Chocolate suede knee-high boots with three, no, four-inch heels. Hmm, he must be tall, this chap, at least six three, wouldn't you say, Mauricio? After all you're … what? Five feet ten in bare feet, Lornagh?'

More nodding and a wide grin from Mauricio.

'And a white silk shirt, virginal yet tactile, and open just enough to be decidedly inviting. Hair freshly washed, but slightly dishevelled, and not too much make-up. And, if I'm not mistaken, you've had your highlights done this week. I'd say we're not sure of this chap yet, are we? We're playing safe, but interested. Casual, but definitely sexy. A hint of comehitherishness, but ready to retreat with dignity if the favoured reaction isn't forthcoming …'

'You're pathetic!' said Lornagh shaking her head, but she couldn't help grinning.

'So who exactly is attending this little soirée of yours?'

'I told you. Just the staff, Sister Kay of course, some of the mothers and their families, anyone from the committee who's interested.'

'What about our famous architect?'

'I've no idea.'

'Well, well, well. You don't fool me for a minute. I thought you'd lost that peaky look you had about you when you were seeing Slimy Si.' Lawrence shuddered.

'Don't be ridiculous!'

'Well, go and do your worst then. We won't wait up

for you, will we, Mauricio?' Lawrence was looking decidedly speculative as Mauricio put the finishing touches to the pasta. He and Lawrence had become an 'item' in the last few weeks and Lornagh was happy for her friend. Mauricio was hilarious company and his gourmet concoctions were only one of his many talents, according to his delighted boyfriend.

'I'd better go, see you later.' Lornagh made for the door, pulling on a light jacket. Although it was June, the evenings were still cool enough.

'Or possibly not, if you get lucky!' She closed the door behind her and left them to their dinner. Lawrence was always irrepressible, but egged on by Mauricio he could get way out of hand. She had left just in time, Lornagh decided.

At a quarter to eight, the roads were fairly clear, and Lornagh found herself outside St Rita's offices at eight o'clock exactly. She got out of the cab, paid the driver and proceeded to walk gingerly over the upturned ground and into the old building.

St Rita's had been a wing of an old convent in its previous life and had suited the charity's purposes perfectly, with its rabbit warrens of rooms and the hall, where children could play while their mothers talked to the social workers and staff about their problems.

Lornagh trailed her hand along the walls pensively. She would be sad to see the old place going, even though it was noisy, draughty and hopelessly outdated. It had always been a cheerful working environment, despite its rather woebegone appearance, and had a happy, purposeful atmosphere.

A good crowd had already gathered by the time she arrived, and Lornagh dumped her coat and bag in her office and went to join them.

Sister Kay was talking animatedly to a group of mothers, telling them all about the wonderful plans for the new buildings; and Lornagh noticed that the model of the housing and leisure centre, as well as the new apartments, was displayed prominently in the middle of the room. So far, so good.

'Lornagh!' Sister Kay called to her. 'You're just in time; here, take this tray of brownies from me before I demolish them all; they're going down a bomb! Mrs O'Connor baked them specially for us. Hand them round for me, would you?'

'Sure thing.' Lornagh took the tray and circulated for a bit, chatting to all the people she knew, eager to catch up with some familiar faces. She searched the room for Sean but he was nowhere to be seen.

The brownies smelt delicious and reminded her she was ravenous. Helping herself to a few, she headed over to Pascal and his wife Melissa – both looking extremely well – to say hello.

'Hi, I didn't think we'd see you here.' She had a very soft spot for Pascal, who, she noted, was looking very pleased with himself for some reason.

'Oh, we wouldn't miss it,' Pascal said warmly. 'I've great hopes for this venture of ours, and we're into the home stretch now.' He had to shout to be heard above the rapidly increasing noise level. 'How are you? We haven't seen you since the, er, dinner party!' Pascal winked.

Melissa tut-tutted disapprovingly. 'It was in very poor taste. I don't know what Simon can have been thinking of,' she said, although at the time she had enjoyed every minute of it.

Before Lornagh could reply, Sister Kay rang a bell and called for silence.

'Ladies and gentlemen! Your attention please!' She suddenly giggled. 'I'd just like to say … it's been an absolute pleasure … ha ha ha … oh dear me! What I mean to say is …'

'What's up?' Pascal asked, highly amused. 'Has she been at the gargle, or what?'

'No way, she doesn't drink,' Lornagh said, watching in amazement.

'Ooh, you're not off the hook yet,' Sister Kay continued, when she had composed herself. 'Before you put your dancing shoes on, I'd, ha, ha, like you to give a warm welcome to our, ha, ha, em, architect, Sean O'Rourke, who dedicated his renowned talents free of charge.'

'For God's sake, get her off, she's completely out of it!' one of the social workers said, looking alarmed.

A couple of the women went to rescue Sister Kay. Lornagh would have gone with them, but she suddenly found she was feeling strangely light-headed. Instead, she searched the room for Sean: at first there was no sign of him. And then she saw him, and her breath caught. He was lounging against the doorway, his tall frame and posture accentuating his obvious feeling of awkwardness. If anything, it made him even more attractive. He was wearing a white linen shirt over dark linen trousers and held a matching jacket casually over one shoulder. With his dark-blond hair brushing the collar of his shirt and his broad shoulders, he looked as if he'd walked straight out of an Armani ad. As his eyes met hers across the room, Lornagh was seized by an unbelievable rush of desire.

'He's quite something, that architect chap, isn't he?' Melissa purred, watching her closely.

'What? Oh, yes, I suppose so.' Lornagh was caught off guard. She had hoped to sound suitably disinterested but suddenly found herself catching Melissa's eye as they both chuckled. She wasn't sure quite what was so amusing, and she hurriedly composed herself as the room became quiet and Sean walked over and stood before the model buildings. He spoke slowly and deliberately about the project, explaining the tremendous implications it had for the charity and indeed the whole area.

As Sean stepped down to polite applause, Lornagh made the decision. Melissa was right: he *was* quite something. And tonight, he was going to be hers. It was time she enjoyed herself; let her hair down a bit. Time she showed Sean O'Rourke just what he was missing.

Soon the disco was in full swing, and Lornagh found herself swept on to the floor by Pascal who took off to the strains of 'Rock Around The Clock' with alarming enthusiasm: it was all Lornagh could do to keep up with him. Feeling quite out of breath, Lornagh excused herself and headed for the bar, helping herself to a large glass of punch. The brownies had made her incredibly thirsty and she needed a chance to track down Sean. She would have to move quickly if she was to put her plan into action; and luckily, the Italian girl she had seen him with the other day was not in evidence. *Carpe diem!* she thought to herself.

Pascal and Melissa were rocking away again on the floor and behaving, in general, like a couple of love-struck teenagers. Lornagh had never seen anyone dance quite like Pascal. With all his limbs thrashing around simultaneously, it was amazing he was able to stay upright at all, although Melissa seemed to have worked out a way of keeping up with him without sustaining a serious injury. That was one of the benefits of a long-term relationship, Lornagh mused: you could always tell the couples who went the distance; the series of well-negotiated moves became an unconscious dance over time. She looked around for Sean, but he was nowhere to be seen. Checking her watch, she saw that it was twenty to ten, and wondered if maybe he had left already.

After what Mauricio had said about him being such a hit with the Italian girls – and one in particular – Lornagh found herself experiencing a surprising stab of jealousy. Surely he wouldn't have gone without even talking to her? The thought made her heart plummet and the evening suddenly lost its earlier promise. She had hoped for at least *one* dance, she realised with a pang; watching him earlier on the floor, she had noticed his graceful ease and smooth natural rhythm. Before she could stop herself, she found herself wondering if he moved like that in bed. If that was the case, then no wonder the Italian women had found him so attractive. Sod it, she thought, feeling surprisingly giddy, I'm going to have a good time tonight, Sean O'Rourke or no Sean O'Rourke.

And then she caught sight of him, talking to Melissa, who was gazing at him with ill-disguised lust. This was Lornagh's chance. Feeling incredibly predatory and wonderfully uninhibited, Lornagh walked boldly over to him.

'I suppose a dance is out of the question?' She placed a hand on his shoulder and smiled seductively.

'Lornagh!' He seemed surprised, his dark eyes questioning, as he pushed a damp lock of hair back from his forehead and smiled down at her.

Lornagh gestured towards the floor, forgetting the glass of punch in her other hand, which obligingly shot straight onto her white silk shirt. She watched in dismay as it trickled slowly down her front, leaving a bright trail of colour in its wake, before disappearing into her carefully arranged cleavage.

'Ooops, silly me!'

Melissa cracked up. 'Oh, Ay'd better go and find Pascal – this party is such fun. Ay can't remember when Ay've enjoyed myself so much.'

Sean took the glass from Lornagh and, taking her hand, pulled her onto the floor. 'Come on, you'll dry out after a dance or two, and there's no way I'm going to attempt to mop that up.'

The DJ was still on a rock 'n' roll streak, and Lornagh laughed as Sean spun her around with ease. He was a fantastic dancer. Suddenly the tempo changed as a slow, smoochy number began to play. For a split second, Lornagh stood rooted to the spot, not sure if Sean would seize the moment to make a break for the bar.

Instead, he moved towards her and pulled her to him, holding her hand in his. She felt his arm slip comfortably around the small of her back. Relaxing against him, she closed her eyes and swayed to the music, hoping desperately he couldn't hear the ridiculous thumping of her heart.

'How's the shirt doing?' He looked down at her.

'What shirt?' Lornagh looked up at the lopsided grin and felt her heart do another slow turnover.

'Attagirl!' He laughed softly, pulling her just a little bit closer.

Lornagh sighed, resting her head against his shoulder and willed the slow set to continue.

The DJ obliged and, as the lights grew dimmer, Sean held her close as they moved in perfect unison to the music. And then, just as suddenly, it was over, the moment broken as the DJ announced that the karaoke competition was about to begin.

'I don't know about you, but karaoke isn't really my thing. How about getting out of here and grabbing something to eat?' Sean suggested, gently removing Lornagh's arms, which had sneaked up around his neck entirely of their own accord. Lornagh eagerly agreed.

'I've just got to get my jacket and bag from my office, I'll meet you outside.' She slipped out of the hall and into her office, feeling as giddy as a teenager on her first date. She hadn't eaten since breakfast, apart from the brownies; the thought of food was suddenly overwhelming. Pulling on her jacket, she reached for her bag, and took a last look around the little office, now bereft of furniture except for her old chair and desk in the corner. It was funny to think she would never sit here again, never walk along the narrow little corridors or make tea in the tiny old-fashioned kitchenette. She patted the wall sentimentally and whispered her goodbye.

She closed the door behind her, hurried down the three flights of stairs and out through the main entrance to where he was waiting, leaning pensively against the old brick wall.

'Okay?' His dark eyes flickered over her, making her shiver.

'Mmm, never better.' Lornagh turned to look behind her one last time.

'No looking back.' He took her hand and tugged gently. 'Come on, let's get something to eat. You live in Sandymount, right?'

'How did you know?'

'You told me. At least three times.'

'I did? Oh, yes, I share a house with my best friend, Lawrence. But he's gay, so you have nothing to worry about.'

'Is that so?' Sean hid a smile. This was a very different Lornagh from the one he'd seen to date. 'I know a great place not too far from there, the pasta's good and the music's not bad either.'

'Fine by me.' Lornagh felt a small stab of disappointment. The only restaurants she knew around Ballsbridge or Sandymount were all lively and bustling on a Friday night. She had hoped for something a little more intimate now that she finally admitted to herself how gorgeous he was.

They got into his car and were soon making their way along the canal and back towards Ringsend. Neither of them said a word, and Lornagh was painfully aware of the slow current of electricity building between them. Looking at his long, graceful fingers on the wheel, she wondered how on earth she hadn't realised before how attractive he was. She had been so caught up with Simon and his manipulative, controlling ways that she had been blind to everything that was going on around her.

She couldn't help thinking aloud. 'You have beautiful hands, do you know that?'

'Er, thank you.'

She was so busy sneaking surreptitious looks at him, she didn't notice they had made a left-hand turn and were heading down a narrow little road Lornagh had never noticed before. Pulling in to an entrance flagged by large timber gates, Sean turned to her. 'Well, this is it.'

Getting out of the car, Lornagh found herself in front of a beautifully converted old warehouse. It was located in a spectacular position overlooking the canal basin.

Sean unlocked the door. As she followed him in and the lights went on, Lornagh gasped. 'Wow! This is amazing!'

'Well, I like it.'

Lornagh took in the floor-to-ceiling glass wall that encased the front of the house, providing an uninterrupted view of the water. Across the way, the lights of Ringsend twinkled merrily.

The whole ground floor was open plan, dominated by a magnificent Italian stone fireplace that almost took up the entire wall. The expanse of natural wood and flagstone floor was empty except for one vast sofa and table in front of the fire. The whole effect was staggering.

'It's stunning!' Lornagh said shaking her head. 'The fireplace looks like something out of a medieval castle!'

'Close enough. Actually, it's from a Venetian palazzo. I found it in an old salvage yard, and I had it shipped home. I thought we'd stick with the red theme unless you'd prefer something else?' he said, smiling as he handed her a glass of red wine. His amused eyes followed the trail of red that her earlier spill had left on her white silk shirt and lingered for a second on her cleavage, causing Lornagh to be seized by another powerful tug of desire.

'Well, make yourself comfortable while I get the fire going.'

Sean bent down to light the fire and reached for the logs piled in the vast grate, throwing them on to fuel the leaping flames.

Lornagh sank into the huge sofa and slowly pulled off her boots, smiling to herself as she softly started singing, 'Come on baby, light my fire.'

'Are you sure you're all right?' Sean held his head to one side as he considered her. 'You, er, don't seem to be …'

'Hot? Sexy?' Lornagh was feeling provocative.

'I was going to say, you don't seem to be quite yourself.'

'Oh, and what would *you* know about that?'

'Not a lot, admittedly.' He hid a smile as he flicked on the music system, and the room was suddenly filled with the sound of a heart-rending aria Lornagh recognised from *La Bohème*.

'Well, maybe,' Lornagh got up and padded over to him, 'it's time you found out.'

Standing in front of her, his eyes flickered over her face. 'How hungry are you?' He smiled the lopsided grin and Lornagh felt her mouth become suddenly dry. It was a deliberately leading question and he knew it. She tried to answer but only managed to clear her throat as a strangulated squeak threatened to escape.

His eyes never left her face as he took the glass of wine from her hand and put it on the table. Gently, with his other hand, he slipped her shirt off one shoulder and brushed her collarbone lightly with his lips. 'This hungry?' he murmured, as Lornagh gasped with pleasure at the touch of his lips.

She felt his hair brush her shoulder as he continued slowly, his tongue tracing a burning pattern on her neck as he nibbled her throat. 'Or this hungry?' His voice was husky as he continued to kiss her neck and slowly work his way up to her mouth where his lips claimed hers softly at first, and then with increasing demand, his tongue deftly exploring her own soft, eagerly responsive lips.

As the kiss went on and on Lornagh thought she would faint. Moving his hands behind her, Sean pulled her to him, kneading the small of her back through the silk of her shirt. She moaned softly, feeling him hard against her. He pulled back and looked at her, shaking his head. 'Are you sure you want to do this, Lornagh?'

She gazed back at him giddily, trailing a finger along the open neck of his shirt. 'I'm sure I want to do *you*.' Another giggle escaped.

Sweeping her up in his arms, Sean carried her to the bedroom, depositing her gently on the vast bed that overlooked the dark water of the canal. He made love to her slowly, savouring every inch of her body, stroking her and kissing her until she was in a frenzy of lust. 'You're quite a revelation,' he murmured.

Much later, he looked at her thoughtfully while she slept, watching the artful shadows of the night play across her long, slender body.

She awoke with a start to light flooding into the bedroom. Her head was pounding and for a moment she had no idea where she was. Then it all came back to her and she struggled to sit up, feeling very much alone in the huge bed. The delicious aroma of freshly ground coffee drifted in from the kitchen and Lornagh got up gingerly, trying desperately not to aggravate her throbbing head. Grabbing a shirt of Sean's, she padded out into the living room, where he sat at the kitchen table dressed in jeans and a T-shirt, reading the morning paper.

'Hey!' He looked up as she walked in uncertainly, and gave her a big smile. 'I didn't want to wake you. Come and have a cup of coffee.'

Lornagh sat down at the table feeling very fragile as she watched him go over to the stainless steel counter and pour her a coffee. He seemed taller than ever, and she couldn't take her eyes off him as he moved with that easy grace that made every gesture seem like a caress. The carefree confidence she had acquired last night had just as suddenly deserted her. She blushed, remembering the abandon of their lovemaking the night before, every touch and sensation burning itself onto her imagination. Putting the coffee beside her, Sean bent down and kissed her slowly, and Lornagh felt her unease evaporate.

The room looked even more spectacular in daylight; the morning rays of sun slanted through the glass wall, casting a rosy glow over the flagstone floor. Lornagh had always assumed she would have felt awkward and uncomfortable, waking up in a strange house with someone new, but now she just felt happy. No, blissful, she corrected herself, as she sat there and smiled, watching him sip his coffee.

'Did you sleep okay?'

'Mmm.'

'Good. How's the head?' he asked, raising an amused eyebrow.

'It's been better.' Lornagh blushed. 'Was I that bad?'

'You were terrific.'

'I, um, don't usually do this kind of thing, and I didn't think I had that much to drink.'

'Well, I'm very glad you did.' He reached over and stroked her face, tracing a finger across her mouth. 'And I'm not sure it was anything to do with drink.'

'Oh? Women throw themselves at you on a regular basis, I suppose?'

He chuckled. 'Sister Kay has been on the blower already, offering profuse apologies. Apparently, Mrs O'Connor's boys added a liberal helping of hash to her recipe. I don't think you're the only one feeling the effects.'

'Hash cakes! Oh God! I had at least five of them. That would explain a lot.' Lornagh put her head in her hands.

'Does this mean I can't expect a repeat performance?'

'I don't know,' she said, feeling suddenly shy. 'What do you think?'

'I think you've had plenty of time to sleep it off, and I'm not planning on giving you much rest.' He smiled evilly. 'It's Saturday, and it's far too early to be thinking of going anywhere.'

And then he pulled her to her feet, kissing her hungrily all the way back to the bedroom. Lornagh dissolved in giggles, helpless to protest. Her only response was to the insistent touch of his hands and mouth, and as she fell breathlessly back on to the bed she gave herself up to the delightful discovery of erogenous zones she never dreamed existed.

It was midday when they finally surfaced, and Lornagh dragged herself to the walk-in shower room, surrendering gratefully to the pulsing jets of water. She had a meeting that afternoon with the banqueting manager of the Anglesea and Sean had said he'd drop her home whenever she wanted. *Like never!* she thought to herself as she hummed happily, wrapping herself in a huge fluffy white towel. She attempted to brush her hair, tousled and tangled into knots of friction from their amorous exertions, and pulled on her leather skirt, belting another shirt of Sean's over it. It would have to do.

He was waiting for her as she came out, and it was all she could do to stop him persuading her to join him in the shower all over again.

'Sure you want to go?' he asked, running his hand along her thigh and sending delicious shivers down her spine.

'No, but I have to. Really.'

In the car, they drove in comfortable silence, and Lornagh sat encased in a shimmering bubble of joy as Sean rested one hand on her knee, stroking it gently, making her wish desperately she could go straight back to bed with him.

She directed him to Lawrence's house and they pulled up outside.

'How about dinner tonight? A real restaurant this time, I promise!' He leaned in to kiss her lingeringly. 'Although I'm not sure I can wait that long.'

'Me neither.'

'Eight o'clock?'

'Great.' Lornagh struggled to leave the delicious embrace. But she knew if she didn't she had no hope of making her meeting. There was the small matter of organising a ball for 350 people.

Dragging herself away, she got out of the car and tried desperately to compose herself as she let herself quietly in the front door. Her skin was still tingling and she had to force herself to wipe the idiotic grin of happiness from her face.

She almost made it to the stairs before she heard Lawrence calling up from the kitchen.

'Lornagh, is that *yoohoo*? Not so fast, poppet, come down and tell Uncle Lawrence all the gory details.'

Lornagh steeled herself as she tottered down to the kitchen where Lawrence sat in splendour, a knowing expression on his triumphant face.

'I stayed the night with a friend. Don't even dare start,' she warned him.

Lawrence looked pained. 'Far be it from *me* to say, "there's a girl who's had a jolly good seeing-to!" But, my darling Lornagh, it's written all over your delighted little face.'

Simon drove slowly along Grovesbury Road until he came to 'Canterbury', Angela Lemass's house. There were no imposing electric gates, just the simple timber ones common on the road about 30 years ago, before the movers and shakers had swarmed in, erecting fortresses around their ever-expanding mansions. He had thought he would have to park on the road but, seeing as the gates were open, he changed his mind and drove in. He might as well show off his sleek new Jaguar XK8 while he was about it. After all, first impressions were all important.

Simon checked his appearance in the car mirror before getting out. It was perfect, not a wave out of place, and the new matt bronzer he'd discovered gave his skin just the right amount of sun-kissed glow.

He walked up the steps, rang the bell and waited expectantly. For a moment he thought no one was at home. Then there was a scurry of movement, a twitch of curtain and the door opened tentatively to reveal a tiny woman in a black dress and white apron complete with a white lacy hat sitting jauntily on a nest of alarmingly back-combed hair. She peered at Simon suspiciously and uttered a surprisingly deep 'Yes?'

Simon cleared his throat. 'I would like to speak to Mrs Lemass if it's convenient.' He used his most imperious voice.

'Who shall I say?' The apparition in the apron didn't look impressed.

'Simon Sullivan. I'm a member of the St Rita's committee and have an interest in purchasing a painting I believe Mrs Lemass is looking after.'

'You'd better come in. Wait here and I'll see if Mrs Lemass is receiving visitors.' She showed Simon in to a vast, dark hall and scurried off around the corner.

Simon took a good look at the place. The house shared the beautiful proportions of the others on the road, but that was where the similarities ended. To say it was run-down was an understatement. It was more like something out of Dickens's *Great Expectations*. He half-expected Miss Havisham to come floating out to greet him in a billowing gown.

The place would need an absolute *fortune* spent on it to bring it up to date. Still, it was the best address in Dublin 4 and that was what mattered.

A flurry of activity announced the return of the little woman.

'Mrs Lemass will see you in the drawing room. Follow me, please.'

Simon did as he was told and was ushered in to a huge, dimly lit room where, in the furthest corner, he just about made out a reclining figure. So this was the famous Angela Lemass. As Simon approached her, he saw a stunning woman of perhaps 65. It was easy to see where Lornagh had got her looks. Even in the strange outfit she was wearing, Angela looked spectacular. Simon hadn't come across turbans worn in the Princess Grace style before, and he was suitably impressed. He wasn't so sure about the kaftan, though.

Angela exhaled a cloud of smoke and regarded him with amused interest.

'And you are …?'

'Simon Sullivan.' Simon extended his hand, which

she shook lightly. 'And may I say what a very great pleasure it is to meet you at last, Mrs Lemass. Lornagh has told me so much about you.'

'A gentleman caller. We don't get too many of those nowadays, do we, Mary?'

'No indeed, Mrs L,' the little woman chuckled.

'Do sit down. Can we offer you a drink, Mr Sullivan?'

'Very kind of you. I'll have a gin and tonic please.'

Simon wasn't sure if this was appropriate, but he was feeling twitchy and the thought of a gin and tonic proved extremely comforting.

'Mary would you bring Mr Sullivan a gin and tonic, and freshen up my glass, there's a dear.'

'Right away, Mrs L.'

Angela turned to Simon and smiled disarmingly. 'You know my daughter Lornagh, you say? I don't believe she's mentioned you to me.'

'I, er, yes, we're very good friends.' Simon was put out. This wasn't quite the opening he had been hoping for. 'Of course, I'm a very busy man, I don't get to see my friends as often as I'd like to.' He took a quick look around the room. There were some seriously nice pieces of furniture nestling under a blanket of dust. Simon shivered involuntarily. He had never seen so much dust. He hoped it wouldn't get onto his precious clothes. And was that …? Yes, it *had* to be a genuine Yeats on the far wall. Why, the sale of that alone would refurbish the entire house, inside and out. Lornagh hadn't mentioned her mother's art collection to him, he thought crossly.

'You're sure she's never mentioned me?' Simon couldn't believe it. The silly old bat probably didn't even remember it. Now that he noticed, she seemed half-cut.

'Should she have?' Angela drawled dismissively, flicking her cigarette ash into a crystal ashtray. 'Mary mentioned something about a painting you wanted to see?'

'Yes, that's right. Lady Sheldon is donating it for the auction. I believe you have it here and I'm interested in having another look at it, if I may.'

'Of course. You'll find it over there, by the coal bucket. Are you a collector, Mr Sullivan?'

Simon was finding all these questions off-putting. There was something in the woman's tone he didn't like. She was being scrupulously polite, but there was something decidedly unnerving about her. He couldn't put his finger on it.

He went over to where the painting lay on the ground, face inwards to the wall. He turned it around carefully and took a few steps back to look at it critically. His heart leaped. There was no doubt about it. It was a genuine Le Souquet. *Sunrise over Pont Neuf,* as the old catalogue had informed him. Why, it must be priceless. He turned the painting back and replaced it. It wouldn't do to arouse suspicion.

'I'm thinking of bidding for it myself at the ball. I

rather like the style, although it looks as if it could do with a bit of restoration,' Simon pronounced knowledgeably.

'Couldn't we all?' Angela gave a throaty chuckle.

Simon sat down again and took a quick swig of his gin. He didn't know what to make of this woman. He had the distinct impression that she was laughing at him. Stuck up old trout. He tried again to impress her.

'If I'm not mistaken, that's a very nice Yeats you have there.' That would show her.

'Yes, indeed. How clever of you, Mr Sullivan. My late husband gave it to me for our first wedding anniversary. I keep the others in my bedroom. I do love Yeats – all that latent, repressed sexuality. So inspiring.'

Simon nearly choked on his drink. The woman was outrageous! He looked at her warily, but she seemed unperturbed and apparently unaware of the effect she was having on him. Was she deliberately trying to embarrass him? You could never tell with these upper-crust types.

But, more to the point, there were other Yeats paintings. She must be sitting on a bloody fortune. Why on earth was she living in this crumbling, decaying old pile when she could afford to do the house up several times over? Never mind, he thought, all the more for Lornagh to inherit.

'Er, how is Lornagh? I haven't been in touch with her for a while.' Simon hoped for the opportunity to innocently drop a hint or two about their relationship.

'Lornagh's very well.' There was the amused smile again. 'Of course, she's working far too hard in that awful refuge place.' Simon was thrown slightly until he twigged she must mean St Rita's. Well, that was one thing they agreed on. Before he could successfully pursue the thread of conversation, Angela continued.

'And you? What do *you* do, Mr Sullivan?' She waited with an indulgent smile.

Simon leaned back in his chair and stretched out his legs, relishing the chance to reveal just what a catch he was. 'I'm an accountant by profession. Currently I'm working for Romany Investments with my colleague, Michael Moriarty.' He smiled, waiting for the full implications of how successful he was to register with her.

'Really? How nice for you.' Angela's gaze sharpened.

'Yes, I must say it's been an enjoyable year or so for me.' Simon warmed to his theme. 'And, of course, a partnership in the firm is imminent,' he boasted. Let her think about that for a moment or two.

Suddenly, the corners of Angela's mouth began to twitch. Simon was caught off guard. What did the silly old trout find so amusing? He cleared his throat again and was about to ask her about her collection of Yeats's when she silenced him with a wave of her elegant hand.

'Of course! It's all coming back to me now. You're Lornagh's ex. Lawrence told us all about you. Didn't he, Mary?' Angela threw a meaningful look at Mary, who had suddenly busied herself rearranging the silver.

'Mary, this is the man who proposed to Lornagh at that, er, dinner party, in front of all those people!'

Simon froze.

Angela looked highly amused. 'Haven't you heard, Mr Sullivan, that it's customary to have been introduced to one's intended's parents *prior* to proposing marriage?'

Simon's breath was sucked straight out of him. How dare she? She was making deliberate fun of him. This couldn't be happening. And now the little crone of a woman was chuckling, doubled up with strangulated cackling. He tried to stand up but found his legs had become strangely heavy. He could only watch in helpless horror as these two mad creatures surveyed him with distinct amusement. He, Simon Sullivan. The most eligible bachelor in Dublin.

'Don't you know anything at *all* about how to behave?' Angela demanded. 'And now you're here to have a good old snoop around the house.' Angela's controlled humour suddenly dried up. 'Well, Mr Sullivan. It would appear my daughter is more desperate than even *I* had anticipated. But rest assured, as long as there's a breath of life left in *this* old dame, no snivelling little number-cruncher's going to get their hands on my daughter or anything that may or may not be coming to her. So add that into your mercenary little calculations and see what you come up with.'

Simon stood up, trying to think of a suitably cutting retort, but found his mouth was working so much he could barely control it. Before he could utter a word, the woman cut him short.

'Mary!' she said imperiously. 'Show Mr Sullivan out, would you? I believe he's just about to leave.'

Seething with anger, Simon managed to make it to the door, then fled to the sanctuary of his car and speedily made his escape. Good God, she was a complete madwoman! No wonder Lornagh hadn't introduced him to her. And, as for the other weird little creature who worked for her, she was another lunatic. Raving nutters. As mad as bloody brushes. How dare they laugh at him? How *dare* they? Well, he would have the last laugh. Oh yes. When he married Lornagh. As he surely would once he had explained that he had met her daft mother and understood her obvious embarrassment about her. Then Mrs Angela Lemass would be shoved straight into a home. If any would take her, that is. Yes, he would make allowances, Simon decided. It wasn't Lornagh's fault her mother was barking. And once she was out of the way, he would have that house and the Yeats collection to himself. Then he could start the long overdue work of bringing the house up to scratch.

He took a shuddering breath. He wasn't the better of the experience. He would go straight home and pour himself a large drink. In the morning, he could start investigating old people's homes in the city. Some of the better ones had notoriously long waiting lists. He shivered again. Nothing a large cash donation wouldn't fix. In Simon's opinion, it would be money *extremely* well spent.

Melissa donned a headscarf and dark glasses and hurried out to the waiting Bentley where the chauffeur was sitting at the wheel.

'Good morning, Mrs Sheehan! And where are we off to?' Matt held the door open as Melissa eased herself into the luxurious leather seat.

'Cadogan Clinic, Matt, please.' Melissa checked her watch. She would arrive at one minute to ten o'clock and not a second earlier. Then she would phone Dr O'Brien's secretary from the car so she could sweep in the moment her appointment became available. Melissa was damned if she was going to sit around in some waiting room while half of Dublin gawked at her trying to work out who she was. Those days were long behind her. Privately she was rather annoyed that the celebrated Dr O'Brien had refused to make a house call for her Botox injections, despite a most generous financial incentive from Melissa. It was out of the question, he had said. It was the clinic or nothing. Melissa had had to button her lip and quell the tart response that had been on the tip of her tongue.

She could have gone to London, of course, but Melissa preferred her non-invasive cosmetic people on her home ground, so to speak. After all, one never knew when one might need a quick top-up, so it was definitely better to stay local. All the same, it was irritating that Dr

O'Brien wouldn't come to the house. Very vexing. But there was absolutely nothing she could do about it. Melissa didn't want just *any* of the doctors that were all jumping on the Botox wagon and who would have been happy to make a house call. When it came to Botox, nothing less than an artist would do.

She arrived at the clinic bang on time and, after verifying that the way was clear, swept up the steps and into the waiting lift. After a darting glance left and right to make sure no one she knew was about, she dived into Dr O'Brien's rooms and straight past the waiting patients perusing magazines.

'Melissa! How nice to see you. Take a seat there and I'll do you in a moment.' Dr O'Brien looked carefully at Melissa's face and assessed the halted progress of time.

'Good. That's just the effect we were after. We'll go for the same again. How long is it since we last did you?'

'Three months to the day,' the nurse said, checking the records.

Melissa would have come in sooner if she could. She had begun to feel the effects wearing off for the last two weeks, but Dr O'Brien was rigorous about not overdoing it. If you did, he explained, your body built up antibodies to the Botox and it would cease to have any effect at all. Melissa gasped in horror at the thought.

Dr O'Brien wielded the syringe and Melissa steeled herself. It was never too bad, but it wasn't exactly comfortable either, particularly in her temples where she felt it acutely. Still, no pain, no gain. It was over in about two minutes, and Melissa peered at herself. 'Are you sure that's enough?' she asked anxiously.

'Quite sure, Melissa,' Dr O'Brien said smiling. He was used to the constant refrain. People were so thrilled with his results they always asked for more. 'Remember, it's no good if you look "frozen". We want to retain enough mobility in your face so you don't get that awful "plastic" look. Come back and see me in three months.'

Melissa left the consulting rooms with a buoyant spring in her step and tripped outside to the car, where Matt was waiting to ferry her home.

'I think we'll take a little detour, Matt,' Melissa said as they approached RTE studios to take the right-hand turn into Nutley Lane. 'Just go straight on to Donnybrook, would you? I'd like to pop into Babe.'

'Very good, Mrs Sheehan.' Matt changed lanes accordingly and headed for Donnybrook village where he pulled up outside the hottest boutique in Dublin 4.

Vanessa, Babe's stylish proprietor, had rung Melissa earlier in the week to let her know a select collection of evening gowns had arrived. Melissa thought she'd better go and check them out. She was planning on buying an *haute couture* original for the ball, now that she and Pascal were going to Paris for a few days to get reacquainted. But she'd been toying with the idea of a gorgeous Dolce and Gabbana outfit, featured in *Vogue*, that had just come in to Babe. Melissa decided that if she liked it she would buy it anyway. It wasn't as if she didn't get enough opportunities to parade her evening-wear collection. And anyway, she couldn't possibly be seen wearing the same dress twice. Well, not for at least six months.

With this happy thought in mind, she bounced into Babe, admiring her smooth, untroubled brow in the mirror before diving on a spun-silver gossamer creation which she held up in front of her, admiring the shimmering reflection that looked back at her.

'Can I help you, Mrs Sheehan?' one of the assistants asked.

'I think I'll try this on.' Melissa disappeared into the fitting room and wriggled into the dress, coming out to a chorus of 'oohs' and 'aahhs' from the staff. There was no doubt about it, it was made for her. The dress clung to every curve and fanned out in a beautiful fishtail at the back.

'I'll take it.' Melissa didn't hang about when it came to knowing what suited her.

She waited patiently as the assistant wrapped the dress for her and chatted about the latest collections, before slipping her the bill. As it was £3,500, Melissa supposed she should at least have frowned. And then she remembered she couldn't. Good old Botox. Well, she wasn't going to feel guilty. She was playing a vital part in the economy by spending. How else did people expect to keep their jobs, for heaven's sake?

Pascal had booked the Ritz and the flight to Paris for the week after next. He was surprised just how much he was looking forward to getting away for a few days with Melissa. He had been working like a dog since the St Rita's project had got underway, and, now that they had turned the corner, Pascal felt a few days off wouldn't hurt. His stomach gave a healthy grumble reminding him it was lunchtime and he was due to meet Charlie for a pint in Ashton's. Pascal smiled broadly. There was nothing like the thought of a cool pint on a hot summer's day. He left the office and got into his car, pausing to open the sunroof before setting off. On a day like this, he could understand the ever-increasing amount of convertibles on the road. Occasionally he was tempted to order one himself, but it never lasted for long. For the three good days they got on average each summer, Pascal was usually stuck in the office anyway. No, he would leave convertibles to Melissa. One in any family was enough.

Taking off his jacket and rolling up his shirtsleeves he set off for Ashton's, turning right into Anglesea Road and up towards Donnybrook, humming cheerfully as he thought longingly of the cool pint awaiting him. He crossed the lights at Donnybrook church and continued up through Beaver Row, blissfully unaware of the anonymous black Nissan that followed him.

Carol sat up in bed in Fitzpatrick's and opened her laptop. She was wide-awake at 4.30 in the morning so she thought she might as well put the time to good use. She always suffered badly with jet lag. No matter how late she stayed up the night before, she found herself awake and painfully aware of the time difference. She had stayed out late catching up with her friends in New York, with dinner at Balthazar and martinis at Bar 89 where the amazing clear-glass doors on the unisex loos were the main topic of conversation. Clear, that is, until you locked the door, when they obligingly frosted up.

Today, she had her interview with Mick Jameson, the hot young Irish actor whose career in the States had taken off. She was due to meet him at eight o'clock in the W hotel, and after that the day was hers to prepare for the première that she would cover for TV 2000. She would put in a few hours in Barney's and then hit Elizabeth Arden for a massage, full make-up and blow-dry. She wondered briefly about ringing the detective to find out how he was getting on, and then decided against it. Time enough for all that on her return.

Michael was back on top form. He had acquitted himself admirably at the golf tournament; for his efforts, he had a signed photo of himself with Tiger Woods to add to the collection on display in his office.

St Rita's ball was only a week away; then he would be off to start his new life in Buenos Aires. He couldn't believe how well everything was going. Simon was helping him move funds and tie up any annoyingly loose ends. Of course, Simon had no idea what he was effectively collaborating with. That was the trouble people risked when they took things at face value. And Simon was an accident waiting to happen in that respect. As long as someone spoke with a nice accent and lived at a suitably correct address, Simon didn't ask questions. He was much too busy being impressed.

He wondered briefly about Felicity again. She had been strangely occupied of late, which suited him in a way. He had worried for a while that she might have been on to something. But since he had cut back on the coke, she seemed to keep less of an eagle eye on him. He didn't need to worry about her anyway: Felicity was a survivor. He would send for them all when the dust settled. In the meantime, he had left suitable funds in an offshore account, which would tide them over for a while at least.

At the thought of funds, Michael smiled. Things were arranging themselves nicely. After the wake-up call he'd had when the cheques to suppliers had bounced, he had been scrupulously careful. He had restored the relevant monies until everyone had got their 25 percent up front. Of course, the balance was now being channelled into his offshore account and then on to Switzerland. Michael felt a shiver of anticipation run down his spine. It was brilliant! Absolutely brilliant. He'd have to make sure he got a copy of the Irish papers when the news broke. It would be the talk of the country. That would teach them to take him for granted.

And as for Eddie 'The Shark' McEntee, well, he would just have to take a taste of his own medicine. God knows, he must have dished out enough of it over the years. Well, it was payback time. Michael felt a surge of pride wash over him. Did Eddie really think he could mess with him? Did he really believe Michael was that easily bullied by a few miserable thugs? Michael grinned. He had taken on the most dangerous man in Ireland and won. They would make a movie about it for sure!

Now that he came to think of it, Eddie had bought the story about the delay in funds surprisingly easily. For a while, Michael had been worried Eddie might make trouble for him, but he was obviously lying low. Just as well. Michael knew he could tie any of them up in knots once he started on his financial jargon. They hadn't a clue, any of them. Not even the banks. He almost laughed out loud thinking about how easy it had been to dupe them. It was a pity he wouldn't be around to see the reactions. Particularly Melissa's. But he would have moved on to far more interesting things by then.

He picked up the phone and dialled Simon. He would ask him to order the tickets from the travel agency for him on the company account, just for a laugh. He would say he wanted to whisk Felicity away on a surprise trip. And, of course, Simon would swallow it. He would never think of creasing his Botoxed brow and actually putting two and two together. Michael was well aware of the amount of money Simon spent on his appearance. Well, Simon might as well enjoy his little beauty treats while he could! Once the shit hit the fan, it would be a lot more than his expression that would be frozen. All the funds and transactions of Romany Investments would be under investigation for a very, very long while.

CHAPTER TWELVE

The last two weeks had passed in soft-focused bliss. Lornagh floated through the days counting the minutes until she could be with Sean.

Since that first night together, they had barely spent a night apart; and, despite her best attempts not to get involved, she found herself falling completely and utterly in love with him. Not that the 'L' word had been mentioned yet, she reminded herself, feeling a pang of disappointment; but it was early days, and all the signs were promising.

Now that the old St Rita's building was demolished, she was free to concentrate on finalising the details for the ball, which was barely a week away; and, more importantly, free to indulge in savouring every minute of the delicious happiness she felt when she was with Sean.

She would never in her wildest dreams have believed that someone could be so right for her. And, so far, he appeared to share her feelings.

Lornagh lay back in the old roll-top bath, which was brimming over with bubbles, and smiled. She hardly dared to think about it. But, no matter how she warned herself to be careful, or chided herself about past mistakes, she knew instinctively this was IT. He was The One. She had never in her life felt anything like it. And nothing could puncture her bubble of joy.

Even the weird meeting she had had with Simon hadn't fazed her. He had rung her the day before yesterday and asked her to meet him, saying he had something important he wanted to discuss with her. Lornagh had agreed to meet him; after all, she thought, she owed him that much. She had suggested the Anglesea, since she was going over the seating arrangements for the ball with the banqueting team, and they had met there for lunch.

Simon had taken one look at her glowing, happy appearance and scowled. He had then related a most extraordinary account of having called on her mother to inspect the painting Lady Sheldon had donated for the auction which, he had said, he was mildly interested in bidding for. Lornagh had only half-listened, a dreamy expression on her face as she remembered the previous night of delicious sex she'd had with Sean.

'Are you listening to me, Lornagh?' Simon had snapped.

'Sorry? Yes, the painting. You were saying?' Lornagh toyed with her caesar salad and tried to look interested.

'What I am saying, Lornagh, is that I understand everything now.'

'Understand what?' She was completely bemused.

'I understand now why you never introduced me to your mother when we were together.' Simon cleared his throat and smiled magnanimously. 'You don't have to explain anything, Lornagh. I can understand *perfectly* how much of an embarrassment she must be for you. The woman's as daft as a brush.' Simon allowed himself a chuckle. 'Of *course* you wouldn't have wanted me to meet her. She's completely barking. Not to mention downright rude. And it was perfectly obvious she was as drunk as a skunk! I felt very sorry for you after meeting her. But it's all right.' Simon held up a hand to stop Lornagh interrupting. 'I can see you have miraculously escaped the dodgy gene pool. Obviously, you must take after your late father.' Simon had paused to draw a satisfied breath.

'I beg your pardon?' Lornagh fixed Simon with a frosty glare.

'Oh, er, yes, sorry, I almost forgot. I meant Maxwell, your, er, stepfather, must have had a very beneficial influence on you.' Simon recovered himself and smiled encouragingly. 'So, you see, you needn't have worried. I can cope with the situation. We all have to make allowances, don't we?' Simon had watched with satisfaction as Lornagh's jaw dropped. 'So, although you understandably thought it was best to end our relationship rather than risk my finding out about her and, er, your rather awkward parental situation, I'm willing to give it another go. I think that's fair of me, Lornagh. What do you say?' Simon had sat back and smiled expectantly. 'Let's take up where we left off and make a fresh start.'

Lornagh shook her head in disbelief as she lay in her hot bath remembering the surreal conversation. If it had been a few weeks earlier, she would have been incandescent with anger. As it was, she was so happy with her current romantic status that she found she almost felt sorry for Simon and his ridiculous and insulting behaviour. Almost, but not quite.

Once she had digested his insufferable implications, Lornagh had put him straight.

'I'm sorry you found my mother a little unsettling, Simon. You obviously caught her at a bad moment,' she had said coldly. 'But you had no right whatsoever to descend on her like that. And you needn't look outraged: I know exactly what you were up to.'

Simon had paled visibly. Surely she couldn't have guessed about the painting? His mouth tightened. 'And what, precisely, is that supposed to mean?'

'Come off it, Simon! You could have rung me at any time if you wanted to see the painting. As it was, you just wanted an excuse to snoop around and make trouble, which is exactly what I would expect from you at this stage. My mother is certainly a colourful character, and I won't deny she can be difficult, but what you did was despicable! Whatever you think about her, I happen to love her. And how she chooses to live is absolutely none of your goddamned business. Frankly, you're not fit to darken her door. And, for the record, the reason I didn't introduce you to her is that, even then, I knew on some level that we weren't going anywhere, so I didn't see the point. As for starting afresh, well, I'm afraid that's out of the question. I'm involved with someone else now, very happily I might add. So, if that's all, Simon, I hope you'll excuse me. I have a ball to organise!' And with that, Lornagh had left him to it, his mouth working in speechless fury as she smiled serenely and left the table.

Lornagh got out of the bath and patted herself dry. She had stayed at Lawrence's last night because Sean had a meeting in London and wasn't due back until this morning. It had been her first night away from him and, she reflected happily, her first night of sleep for about a fortnight. They weren't due to meet until this evening but, looking out at the gorgeous summer day, Lornagh decided she couldn't possibly wait that long. She would throw a few clothes together and stop by the deli to pick up a fresh baguette and some cheese and pâté, and they could have a lovely alfresco lunch overlooking the water. And then, if he wasn't too busy, they could go for a walk on Sandymount Strand.

Having slipped into a pair of well-worn Levi's and a skimpy white cut-off T-shirt, she looked at her glowing reflection in the mirror and grinned. It really was amazing what love did for a girl!

Outside, the sun shone relentlessly, and a few clouds scudded across the bright blue of the sky. Dublin shimmered in the heat haze and, everywhere she looked, people basked happily, sitting outside the pubs or lying in parks eagerly lapping up the welcome rays.

The trip to the deli was quick and successful and in a few minutes she was on her way. Pulling in to Sean's place, she noticed there was no sign of his car. Perhaps he wasn't back yet, but it didn't matter: she had her own key.

Humming happily, she opened the door and wandered across to the kitchen, where she put the food on the stainless-steel counter and checked the contents of the huge, American-style fridge. A few bottles of chilled white wine stood invitingly on the upper shelf, and she took one out and opened it, then poured herself a generous glass. She would sit outside on the deck for a while and sip her drink until Sean turned up. Putting the bottle back in the fridge, she was just about to close the door when she froze at the sound of an angry voice.

'What the 'ell do you theenk you're doing?' heavily accented tones accused her.

Lornagh wheeled around in shock to discover the incredibly beautiful girl she had seen on the site with Sean. The girl stood before her, completely naked except for a large fluffy white towel which she barely attempted to cover herself with. Damp, jet-black waves tumbled about her statuesque shoulders and framed her exquisite face. It was like looking at a particularly beautiful and haughty Renaissance portrait. Her disturbingly dark, almond-shaped eyes regarded Lornagh with disdain, as her full, sensual lips curled in a sneer.

'Wh-who are you? And where's Sean?' Lornagh bleated.

'Sean has gone to get some food for *us*.' Lornagh flinched at the deliberate implication of the 'us' as she stood helplessly rooted to the spot. 'I don't know who you are honey, but I theenk you'd better leave now, before you, how you say, create a scene.'

'But I ...' Lornagh groped for words.

'But you what?' The girl looked Lornagh up and down dismissively. 'You thought you were the only woman in hees life?' She laughed at Lornagh's stricken face. 'A man like Sean will always have more than one woman in his life, honey. He may have been amusing himself with you, but he always comes back to me sooner or later. You better go now; if he finds you here he will be embarrassed, and men *hate* to be embarrassed, no?'

'Are you, you must be Antonia?' Lornagh stammered, realisation dawning as the scene unfolded in front of her.

'Yes. I am Antonia. Of course Sean has told you about me,' she drawled, towelling her damp hair, oozing confidence in her splendid nudity.

Despite herself, Lornagh couldn't help staring at the girl's voluptuous curves and the tiny waist that flared into curvaceous hips and long, shapely legs; at the top of which she could see a landing strip of dark pubic hair shaped in an eye-wateringly perfect Brazilian wax.

Antonia smiled, enjoying Lornagh's obvious discomfort,

and continued the conversation in a disturbingly matter-of-fact manner. 'I thought I could live without Sean when he left Italy, but I found that life was so *dull* without heem, and I don' enjoy long distance romance.' She looked at Lornagh, defiantly shaking back her glossy curls. 'Whatever you had with heem is nothing! Sean belongs to me. We are *fabulous* together. So, like I said, honey, you'd better go. Eet will save Sean the trouble of asking you to leave.'

Lornagh tried to take it all in but couldn't. Her brain wasn't working properly. The sickening slug of fear she had felt settling into the pit of her stomach was giving way to something more primal. She held on to the counter top and steadied herself, fighting to catch her breath. Angela's genes were finally kicking in.

Huge tidal waves of repressed anger began to surge through her. Antonia was looking at her suspiciously now, and her air of self-assurance had changed to one of wariness. 'Are you all right?' she asked hesitantly.

All right! Lornagh tried not to scream with rage. 'No, I'm not all right!' she yelled, looking wildly round the kitchen. 'But I will be in a minute!' Grabbing the bag from the deli, Lornagh reached inside in a trice and, ripping open the carton of olive tapenade, she flung it at an astounded Antonia. 'Welcome to Dublin, Antonia! This should make you feel at home, you oily Italian tart! And for your information, Sean and I are crazy about each other, so you needn't think I'm going anywhere!'

'You beeetch!' screamed Antonia, dripping black

rivulets of oil onto the white towel, which she now clutched to herself. Then darting to the table beside her, where the architectural plans Sean had been working on were now drenched in oil, she rushed to gather them up. 'You stupid beetch! Look what you've done! You've ruined these! Get out now! Sean will be incredibly angry.' Antonia shoved the papers in the bin.

'Good!' shouted Lornagh, feeling strangely liberated.

'Lornagh! Antonia! What the hell is going on?'

Lornagh wheeled around to find Sean, his face white with anger, looking at her incredulously.

''Elp! 'Elp!' screeched Antonia, running over to cower beside him. 'She's a madwoman! She attack me from nowhere!'

'And I haven't finished yet.' Adrenaline was pumping through Lornagh now as she regarded them with utter contempt. Picking up the baguette, she swiped Sean on the head as he watched her in amazement. 'That's for you, you lily livered, two-timing bastard!' she hissed. 'All I can say is, as far as I'm concerned, you and your fat Italian tart deserve each other!' Then she fled, stumbling through the door and out into her little car.

'Lornagh! Wait! Lornagh!' She was vaguely aware of Sean shouting her name as he ran after her but she couldn't get away fast enough. Her stomach was churning and she felt violently sick.

Revving up the engine and leaving skid marks on the

gravel, she willed her car to somehow make it home, fighting to see through the blur of unshed tears burning her eyes.

Involved with someone else! And very happily! Who the hell did Lornagh Lemass think she was? Simon sat at his desk at Romany Investments and seethed. Who could it be? He had to find out immediately. This could ruin everything. Well, he was damned if he was going to be beaten to the post at this late stage in the game. Perhaps she was making it up? That was it. She couldn't possibly be seeing anyone else seriously. The fact that he was dating Alexi didn't count. She was only a decoy. Just someone to tide him over until his real relationship was back on track.

Simon picked up the phone and demanded to be put straight through to his chief contact on the gossip columns. If anyone could find out, he could.

After the call, satisfied he had done all he could for the present, he turned his thoughts to the work in hand. Michael Moriarty had asked him to organise two first-class tickets to Buenos Aires out of London Heathrow. Apparently he was whisking Felicity off on a surprise holiday, right after the ball on Saturday. How glamorous. Simon shook his head in admiration. Buenos Aires had such an exotic ring to it. He allowed himself a five-minute daydream where he was running in slow motion along a golden beach, his bronzed, toned body honed to perfection. Behind him, a bevy of Brazilian beauties in teeny-weeny thong bikinis ran after him, calling his name beseechingly. But – and this was the best part – they never caught up with him.

Melissa slipped behind the wheel of her Mercedes Sports and waited for the electric roof to slide gracefully back before she set off. It had been an exhausting day at the Anglesea, where she and the other ladies on the committee had been wrapping all the items due to be featured in the auction and raffles. Inside, the air conditioning had helped keep everyone cool despite the soaring temperatures. But now, in her car, Melissa felt beads of sweat begin to trickle down her spine. The thought of a long leisurely swim in her Romanesque-style swimming pool seemed incredibly inviting. She popped on her dark glasses and drove out of the hotel gates, enjoying the breeze as it whipped her hair playfully around her face.

Five minutes later, she was outside her house. Pausing to turn in, she noticed the electric gates were open. Typical! Jesus and Maria usually did the weekly shop in the Merrion Centre at this time and, as usual, they'd neglected to close the gates behind them. She would speak to them about it as soon as they got back. It was ridiculous how careless they had become. Letting herself in the front door, Melissa dropped her handbag and glasses on the hall table and wandered down to the kitchen to pour herself a glass of water. She wondered briefly where Dolce and Gabanna were. Usually they raced down to greet her with a chorus of snuffling – perhaps Jesus had taken them for their walk. Melissa smiled just thinking about them. They found the hot weather particularly hard to take and favoured the cool tiles of the kitchen where they would lie panting extravagantly.

Melissa looked out at the magnificent pool shimmering in the sunlight. What a pity there was no one here to share it with. She fancied a skinny dip but it wasn't nearly so much fun on her own. Oh well, she could go for a dip with Pascal later when he came home from work. In the meantime, the azure water shimmered alluringly.

Heading back up to the hall, she retrieved her handbag and paused outside Pascal's study. The door was closed but she was sure she had heard a noise. It had better not be Jesus snooping around: she wouldn't put it past him! Grabbing the handle, she flung open the door to find the room in disarray. She froze as a figure dressed in black wheeled round in surprise.

'What the fuck do you think you're doing?' Melissa screeched.

'What the f …' The man reached for an iron bar on the desk beside him and Melissa fled upstairs three at a time, screaming at the top of her lungs as he followed in hot pursuit.

Oh God! A burglar! And she was on her own in the

house! Melissa reached the landing and flung her handbag at him. It hit him full in the face as he cursed and stumbled. Frantically grabbing the banisters, she scrambled up the next flight, flinging her six-inch red stiletto behind her blindly and hitting him bang on the nose. Screaming as he reached out to grab her ankle, she managed to fling herself into her bedroom and lock the door behind her. Oh God, oh God, where was her mobile? She was shaking so much she could hardly think. The panic button, where was it? Beside the bed. She pressed her trembling hand against it and lifted the phone beside the bed. Nothing. They must have cut the wires.

Hearing the sinister sound of the handle on the door being turned, she screamed again. Suddenly, she heard frantic, muffled barking coming from somewhere. She stumbled into the bathroom where the sound grew distinctly louder, but she could see nothing. What was happening? Where was everybody when she needed them? The strangulated sounds seemed to be coming from somewhere in the ground. Her babies! Where were they? Had the bastard buried them alive somewhere? Getting down on her hands and knees she called to them hysterically: 'Dolce, sweetie? Gabby, darling, where are you?'

A volley of strangulated barking followed. Following the sound, Melissa tore at cupboards and presses, until finally, pulling out the drawer of the specially fitted laundry press, she found them. Jumping out gratefully, Dolce appeared first, sporting a pair of silk knickers on his head, followed swiftly by Gabbana who was tangled in a pair of pink suspenders. They covered her in a frenzy of licking as she gathered them to her, still trembling with fear as she was. 'My poor, poor babies! What have they done to you?' Melissa sobbed.

Outside, the handle of her bedroom door was still being rattled; the terrifying sound was now accompanied by another voice and the thud, thud of a body throwing itself against the door. Melissa huddled against the cool sandstone of her sunken bath and screamed louder, frantically looking around for a weapon to defend herself with.

Suddenly, she heard the door give. Preparing herself for the worst, she clung on to her growling dogs with one hand, and with the other awkwardly held her one remaining stiletto and a swiftly grabbed can of hairspray.

She smelled them before they appeared: two bulky figures dressed in black, their faces eerily distorted by stockings.

'Stay away from me!' screeched Melissa. 'I'm warning you! You'll regret it!'

'Well, well, look what we've got here!' The first one sniggered. 'A tigress and her two rottweilers, wha'? You'd better shut your mouth, love, if you know what's good for you.' He advanced towards her as Melissa gave another piercing scream.

Insulted beyond belief at being compared to something as ungainly as a Rottweiler, and ferociously determined to protect his beloved mistress, Dolce wriggled out of Melissa's grip and hurled himself with unerring accuracy at the intruder's crotch where he latched on with startling effect.

'Aaarrrgh,' the man howled in agony, staggering back as Dolce dangled between his legs, jaws locked and growling fiercely. 'Get this fuckin' muppet off me!'

Not to be outdone, Gabbana yapped excitedly and dived on the ankle of the second thug, gnawing viciously as Melissa watched in disbelief. Grabbing her chance, she aimed the hairspray at the man as he lurched sideways and sprayed it liberally into his eyes, then stabbed him as hard as she could with the six-inch stiletto.

'Aaahh! You fuckin' bitch! You'll pay for this!' he screamed, frantically clawing at his eyes and ripping the stocking off his face, where an angry slash exposed the flesh over one eye.

'Ya silly bastard!' the other one yelled at him, gasping with pain as his hands twisted around the neck of Dolce, who was still attached to his most vital weapon. 'She's only gone an' seen your face now hasn't she? We'll have to fuckin' take her!'

Melissa's blood ran cold. They were going to kill her. She tried desperately to keep calm.

'Look, take whatever you want,' she begged. 'Just don't hurt me or the dogs, please! I'll give you anything you want!' Melissa was abject with terror as she watched Dolce struggling for breath as the thug strangled him.

Gabbana, sensing Dolce was in danger, now began to whimper in fright.

The second man had now recovered himself and, like a flash, whipped up a wildly protesting Gabbana and held a knife to her indignant little throat.

'Get the dog offa him, missus, or they'll both get a taste of their own blood!'

'Dolce!' Melissa's voice was like a whip crack. 'Enough! Leave him! Come to Mummy at once!'

Whether Dolce obeyed her, or the final wrench that was administered to his neck was too much for him, Melissa never knew. But he fell to the floor with a sickening thud and lay there, horribly still.

'You fucking bastard! You've killed him,' Melissa screamed, struggling helplessly in the grip of the other man who had her arms pinned behind her back.

'You've got a mouth on you that'll get you into trouble, d'ya know that?' he hissed in her ear, his foul breath making her want to retch.

'Come on, we'd better get out of here. This has got way outta hand,' the bigger one said angrily. 'An' now we'll have to take her with us, thanks to you showing your ugly mug off! Nice goin', Jimbo.'

'She nearly fuckin' blinded me! Wha' was I supposed to do?' Jimbo wiped his face which was now streaming with blood. 'She's fuckin' vicious, this one!'

'Come on, let's move!'

'Why aren't you taking anything?' Melissa bleated.

'We've got what we came for. Now shut your face and let's go!' They hustled her out of the room but Melissa screamed again in protest.

'Not without my dogs. I'm not leaving poor Dolce like that! You'll have to kill me first!' she sobbed.

'Take the bleedin' muppets then!' the big one said, taking Gabbana from Jimbo. 'But so much as a feckin' whimper outta you an' they're history! Righ'?'

'Oh, yes, yes, I'll do anything you say, I promise. I'll go quietly, just please, please don't hurt Gabby.' As Jimbo released his grip, Melissa fell on her knees beside Dolce and picked him up as gently as she could. He lay limp in her arms but she could just about make out a faint heartbeat.

For the first time in a long while, Melissa prayed to the God she had cheerfully ignored and promised him anything if he would only keep her precious Dolce alive.

Drowsy from heat and several pints he had shared with Charlie, Pascal headed home with a happy smile on his face. It was only half-past four but he had no intention of going back to the office. Judging by the amount of bare flesh on view around him, half of Dublin had the same idea.

If he thought about it, he could even work up to going for a swim. God knows, they hardly ever used the damn pool. Melissa had insisted on putting it in when they moved into Grovesbury Road. Then, once it had been finished at vast expense, she had promptly abandoned it in favour of the built-in gym. Pascal sighed. He wasn't a great one for swimming, but he could certainly do with cooling off. His new hair was particularly irritating in this oppressive heat.

Pulling into Sudbury, he saw Melissa's car in the drive with the roof down. Good! She was home – maybe he could persuade her to join him. He got out of his car and quickly turned down his shirtsleeves. Normally he wouldn't have bothered, but Melissa couldn't stand him rolling them up, and she had been in such brilliantly good form for the last few weeks there was no point in upsetting her.

Once inside, Pascal was enveloped by the cool air of the hall. It was only when he paused to check the post on the hall table that he became aware of the terrible sobbing coming from his study and the volley of curses from an incensed Jesus. Walking slowly into his study, Pascal took in the ransacked room and was vaguely aware of Maria wringing her hands in despair while Jesus looked helplessly on.

'Oh, Mr Sheehan!' she sobbed. 'We've had a break out. Look! Look what these bad people do!'

Pascal tried to focus, but his instincts were screaming that there was something very wrong about the scene. The place was in utter chaos; yet, looking around, nothing valuable appeared to be missing. It was then that a sinister thought occurred to him.

'Where's Melissa? Where's my wife?' he shouted.

The shrill sound of the ringing phone intruded before Maria or Jesus could answer him and, with a growing sense of foreboding, Pascal guessed the terrible answer to his question.

'Uh oh, look sharp, here she comes,' muttered Pat, Carol's PA, as she spotted Carol arriving at the outer doors of the building.

Things had been nicely relaxed in the office during her absence. Not that things weren't ticking over as usual – there was no opportunity for slacking in a young, cutting-edge TV station. All the same, when Carol came into a room, everyone felt the need to sit up straighter and look busy. It was just the effect she had on people. She expected the ruthless discipline she demanded of herself from the rest of the staff, including her boss.

'Let's hope she's in better form than before she left,' one of the junior producers said darkly.

'Hi, Carol,' Pat greeted her brightly. 'How was New York?'

'Hot and sticky, but fun.'

'How did the interview with Mick go? Is he as sexy as he looks, up close?'

'He would be, if he didn't bore for Ireland. Up his own arse in a major way. Thanks,' she added as Pat placed a cup of steaming espresso in front of her.

'Mind you, it'll be fun to see his reaction when the

interview airs. His cousin in County Mayo has been more than happy to dish the dirt. He also bears a strong physical resemblance to him.' Carol had tracked down Mick's unsuccessful and extremely jealous cousin who was barely a year older than him. Mick, of course, had no idea. Carol planned to intercut Mick's account of his early years with the very different version his cousin had provided. 'Should make good viewing. Anything I should know about – while I was away?'

'Nope, just the usual.' Pat ran through some messages. 'Oh, and a Mr Trailer rang. He says he has the information you need, and he wants you to ring him a.s.a.p.'

'Thanks,' Carol said, affecting studied disinterest, although her heart beat slightly faster. 'Take these down to production, would you?' she asked, handing Pat her tapes of the interview, 'and close the door after you, please.'

'Sure.' Pat seemed glad to escape.

Once she was alone, Carol dialled the number, holding her breath as she waited for a response. Tightening her hold on the receiver, she noted with vague surprise the sudden trembling of her hand.

Eddie completed his daily fifty laps of the pool and hauled himself out of the water. Reaching for the thick white towel thrown on the sun lounger, he headed in towards the changing rooms, smiling at two twenty-something babes who were checking him out with barely concealed interest. If he'd had time he might have chatted them up. Eddie enjoyed the effect he had on women and, if his record so far was anything to go by, it would appear the feeling was mutual.

He would have liked to have had an extra three inches in height, but he kept his five feet ten physique in such incredible shape, always taking care to dress in monochromatic shades, that he achieved the desired effect of appearing taller than he actually was. That, and his uncanny similarity to Gabriel Byrne, the actor, ensured he was a big hit with the girls. Today, though, he had other fish to fry. Dressing quickly, he left the club and got into his car. The late afternoon sun slanted through the windscreen, casting a warm glow on the soft leather upholstery. Having put on his shades, Eddie lit a cigarette and flicked open his mobile. Hearing the recorded message again, his mouth set in a hard line. What was going on? They should be well finished and out of there by now. He drummed his fingers on the wheel impatiently. They were due to report back 20 minutes ago, and there was no message, nothing! They'd better have done a good job. God knows it was easy enough, but he wouldn't put anything past those eejits. He had to watch them like a hawk.

Eddie shook his head and smiled. This would put the wind up Michael Moriarty. Stuck up little fucker. He'd show him just how far you could push 'The Shark'! He grinned. So Michael thought he could palm him off with his smarmy spiel about red tape and investors having to be 'coaxed' and not hurried? Yeah, *right!*

Well, he'd have to get his ass in gear now. If Michael couldn't keep Pascal Sheehan's money rolling in on time, then he, Eddie, would make sure it did. A bit of gentle pressure always did the trick. Nothing too intimidating, just a gentle ransacking of a room or two, preferably Pascal's home office or study. Nothing would be taken, naturally. He didn't want it to look like a burglary. It was just a way of leaving his calling card, so to speak. A nice way of saying, get a move on, or next time we won't come calling for fun.

Of course, he could have tackled Michael's house instead, but that would have been far too obvious and predictable. No, much more effective to target Sheehan. Michael would be terrified of his business partner and next-door neighbour finding out about his little 'laundering' arrangement with Eddie. If anything could get things moving, this would.

The ringing of his mobile interrupted Eddie's thoughts and he picked it up quickly.

'Yeah?'

For a moment, fury overtook him, and he had to brake suddenly, narrowly avoiding slamming the jeep into the back of a small car.

He mustn't have heard correctly. Not even *his* goons could be so fuckin' stupid.

'You've done what?' He roared into the phone so viciously that a woman in the next lane felt compelled to ring in to her local radio station and complain vehemently about the increased incidence of road rage in the city.

CHAPTER THIRTEEN

How could the world change in the space of a few seconds?

For the life of her, Lornagh couldn't understand. It had been the longest week of her life and by far the most miserable.

Since that fateful day, she had heard nothing from Sean. Not a phone call, not a note, not even an e-mail. She tried to feel angry, to tap into the rage that had overtaken her, but found she felt even more wretched when she replayed the disastrous scene in her head.

If she was honest, she was utterly shattered by the whole ordeal. How could she have been so stupid? How could she have fallen for it all? Why had she thought Sean was any different from the others? And worst of all, how could she possibly have behaved so appallingly? So she had a right to be angry: but to shriek and fling food at a girl she didn't even know as if she was a raving lunatic? She really didn't know what had got into her. No matter how much Lawrence and the girls tried to make light of it all and tell her that her reaction, in their opinion, had been perfectly restrained, she knew they were just being nice.

Sean and Antonia were probably having a good laugh at her now. Lornagh put her head in her hands and felt her face burn with shame. Oh well, there was no going back. What was done, was done, and she'd just have to pick herself up and get on with it. Starting right now.

She had promised her mother she would bring her into town to take some of her silver into Weir & Sons of Grafton Street to be valued and cleaned. Lornagh's heart sank. She really didn't think she was up to it. But cancelling her appointment with Angela at this late stage just wasn't an option. Life was difficult enough. And anyway, if nothing else it would be a distraction.

Dragging herself out of bed, she took a quick shower, willing the steaming water to invigorate her. Doing the best she could with the pale, wan face that looked back at her from the mirror, and putting eye gel on the lids puffy from crying all night, Lornagh dragged her heavy limbs into a simple denim skirt and white cotton shirt. Her mother would say she looked a fright but she didn't care. She just had to get through today, and then the next day, and the one after that.

Reaching her mother's house on Grovesbury Road, Lornagh found Mary the housekeeper dusting down the inside of the 1972 Mercedes SLK that Maxwell Lemass had bought for Angela as a birthday surprise years ago.

Lornagh smiled, remembering how he had wrapped the keys in a small box and handed them to her mother, who of course assumed it was a trinket of jewellery. When she opened the box, she had squealed with delight and ran outside to find the car sitting in the driveway, gleaming in the sunshine and tied up in a bright red bow. It sat there now, looking just as inviting, its hood down and the soft red leather warming in the sun. Over the years, it had become a classic.

'I see the old girl's getting an outing, then?' Lornagh smiled at Mary, who was polishing the walnut dashboard lovingly.

'And about time too! I told your mother it's a sin to have a beautiful motor car like that sitting inside in a garage. And on a day like this!' Mary emerged from the car looking pleased with herself and patted her beehive. 'We're ready to go, Lornagh. I'll just call your mother.' She scurried inside.

'Hello, darling! I won't be a minute.' Lornagh caught sight of a pink chiffon sleeve as Angela waved merrily from the front door before dashing back inside again. When she emerged, she was the epitome of '50s glamour. 'I almost forgot my sunglasses! There we are!' Angela stepped gaily onto the gravel driveway, dressed in a bright pink flotilla of chiffon complete with matching floppy hat and shades. On anyone else the outfit would have closely resembled a pantomime dame's get-up, but Angela managed to make it look elegant. She kissed Lornagh warmly and slipped gracefully into the front seat. 'You'll drive, won't you, Lornagh? Mary and I just want to enjoy the scenery, don't we? Goodness, it's ages since we've been into town, I'm quite excited. Of course, since Brown Thomas and Switzers have gone it's not the same at all.'

'Brown Thomas hasn't gone, Mum, you know it's just across the road,' Lornagh reminded her wearily.

'Poof! It's not the *same,* Lornagh. You wouldn't understand. You know what I mean, Mary, don't you?'

'Indeed I do!' Mary shouted from the back, where she sat on three cushions carefully placed one on top of the other so she could see over the door. 'Why, Grafton Street is like a foreign country now, Mrs L. I can hardly tell which way's up anymore.'

Lornagh smiled despite herself as they prattled on. Angela could be very amusing company when she was of a mind to be.

Reaching Stephen's Green, Lornagh drove around towards Grafton Street and wondered where to park. 'What about the Brown Thomas car park, Mum?'

'What? Don't be silly Lornagh. Just drive around to Weir's and park outside. We'll only be half an hour or so.' Angela hadn't grasped the concept of clamping yet and would have flagrantly ignored it even if she had.

'We can't, Mum. I'll have to find a parking space or go to a car park.'

'Oh, for heaven's sake, Lornagh, don't be such a *scaredy* cat. Anyway, we'll have to stop outside or we'll never get all the silver into the shop. The boot's full of it. I telephoned the manager and he said if we parked outside and rang him, he'd send one of the young men down to collect it.'

Realising she was outnumbered, Lornagh drove down Dawson Street and turned left into Nassau Street, pulling up at the end of Grafton Street. Taking out her mobile, she called Weir's and asked for the manager who was as good as his word and sent someone down to ferry the boot-load of silver to the shop. The man himself then appeared and, with great aplomb, ushered in Angela and Mary, leaving Lornagh to park the car. There was no doubt about it: Angela Lemass had an incredible effect on the male population even if she was over 65.

Making her way back up to Wicklow Street and into Brown Thomas's new car park, she found a space and hurried back to Weir's to catch up with her mother.

True to form, Angela was sitting in splendour, surrounded by at least four senior members of staff – all men, of course – fawning over her.

'Mrs Lemass! What a pleasure to have you in the store again.'

'Mrs Lemass, can we get you a little refreshment?'

'Mrs Lemass, could I be so bold as to ask for your autograph?'

Angela crossed her famous legs and inhaled languorously through her cigarette holder, flirting outrageously with them all.

After suitable deliberations were given as to the collective worth of the silver, it was duly taken off for professional cleaning. Then Angela amused herself by sending off at least six members of staff to find various diamond rings, emerald earrings and ruby bracelets, none of which she had any intention of buying. But both staff and revered customer knew the drill by now and enjoyed the exchange thoroughly. Lornagh could never get over it. Anyone else would have been given short shrift long ago. But when Angela turned on the charm, everyone wanted to bask in the warm glow. Even if it meant emptying counters of goods that would be affectionately considered, but found ultimately lacking,

It was in the midst of one of these exchanges, with Angela debating the clarity of a vast four-carat diamond, that she intuitively sensed that less than one hundred percent of the staff's attention was being devoted to her. Sensitive to her audience at all times, she looked up to discover the distraction.

Across the counter, an extremely attractive young couple was deep in conversation over the rings. The girl, who was darkly voluptuous, was exquisite in a buttermilk suede wrap dress that clung to every curve and set off her jet-black eyes and long tumbling hair to perfection. Although she was wearing high heels, the man stood a good six inches taller than her, dressed in black jeans and a tan suede jacket. His dark-blond looks and pensive expression contrasted beautifully with her

Mediterranean exuberance, and they made an astonishingly good-looking couple.

'What a handsome couple!' Angela looked over appraisingly. 'Now *that's* what I call an attractive man. It's not often you see such a striking pair nowadays. And so nicely turned out, too.' She smiled indulgently. Then, turning to Lornagh, whom she neglected to notice had turned a sickly white, she said: 'Why can't *you* find yourself a man like that Lornagh? Hmm?'

If she could have trusted her voice, Lornagh would have readily retorted that she *had* found him, and he had turned out to be a lying, cheating, two-timing bastard like the rest of them.

As it was, it was all she could do to stay upright when Sean O'Rourke's eyes met hers across the counter and he nodded with cold politeness before turning away and taking Antonia by the arm.

'Are they friends of yours, Lornagh?' Angela was intrigued. 'Lornagh? What? Oh, for heaven's sake, what have I said now?'

Simon couldn't believe what he was hearing. Lornagh and Sean O'Rourke! It couldn't be possible. He tried to sound casual as his contact from the gossip column passed on this information, but inside he was seething.

He had immediately gone onto the net to discover everything he could about Dublin's architect *du jour*. And what he read didn't make him feel any better. Simon had certainly heard the name once or twice, but nothing prepared him for the string of adjectives peppering the sycophantic articles he found. 'An architectural genius!', 'A natural visionary'. A gushing article in a women's magazine went on to describe him: 'What David Ginola is to football, Sean O'Rourke is to architecture, and happily the similarities don't end there!' Simon clicked on a newspaper article accompanied by a fairly recent shot of Sean leaning out of one of the buildings he had designed in Temple Bar. It was true! The bastard did bear an uncanny resemblance to David Ginola. This wasn't good. Simon's jaw tightened and a small muscle began to twitch in his temple.

'Are you all right, Simon?' asked a concerned Katy as she passed his desk.

'I'm fine,' snapped Simon. 'Why shouldn't I be?'

'Oh, excuse *me* for breathing! It's just that you've been scratching your leg for the last ten minutes. I thought maybe you have fleas!'

'Very funny.' Simon snatched his hand back at once, livid at being caught on the hop. 'It's this material,' he looked down at the perfectly pressed crease in his new pinstripe trousers. 'I think I must be allergic to it.' He'd have to be more careful about the new 'Stay Up' lacy-topped stockings he had discovered. They were a pleasant change from suspenders, but far too distracting. Neither could he afford to get sidetracked by this latest spanner in the works in the shape of Sean O'Rourke.

Lornagh was on the rebound, that was all. Anyone could see that. She was just playing hard to get. Well, he would allow her her little fantasies, Simon thought spitefully. She'd soon find out who would be pulling the strings from now on.

He forced himself to concentrate. He had a lot to get through this afternoon. For the last week or so, Michael seemed to be transferring more and more client funds into various offshore accounts. It was all Simon could do to keep up with the workload. He sighed. He should be flattered, he supposed. It wasn't everybody who got to work with a financial wizard like Michael Moriarty or indeed was trusted with such *huge* amounts of money.

The cold smell of fear mingled with the sour stench of body odour seemed to penetrate Melissa's very pores as she lay helpless in the back of the van. She had been gagged and bound, and a blindfold spared her the pitiful sight of Dolce and Gabbana, still and quiet as they lay tied in a sack. Only the occasional whimper let her know one of them, at any rate, was still alive. Thinking about Dolce, tears began to stream down her face. Her brave little puppy! Who would have thought he could be so fierce? The bastards! She would make them pay for this! But how? The question loomed ominously in her mind. *You've been kidnapped!* Strange how the thought still took her by surprise. It wasn't so unusual at all. But somehow she never thought it would happen to her. It was always

Pascal who was being tipped off by the Special Branch. As one of Ireland's richest men, he was used to threats. She wondered who was behind it. Extremists? Gangsters?

How much did they want? *How much was she worth?* That was the question. Well, that depends on whom they were asking. And Pascal? What would he do? How would he cope? He would go out of his mind with worry. Unless – Melissa's blood ran cold at the thought – he didn't want her back? What if he ran off with his skinny underwear woman? The thought was enough to make her feel faint.

At least she was still alive. She had to remain positive, it was her only chance of survival. She breathed deeply and tried to relax, tried to imagine she was having an aromatherapy session to blobk out the vile smell of those lumbering great thugs. One thing at a time, she reminded herself. She had come through tough times before and she could do it again. She just had to remain calm and focused. After what felt like hours, the van suddenly turned to the left, jolted down a series of bumps and came to a stop.

Melissa waited, holding her breath as the front doors opened and shut and footsteps hastened to the back of the truck. Then the back doors were opened and Melissa felt herself being lifted out none too gently. 'Arrmmm … errrmm …' She tried to shout to Dolce and Gabbana, but only a strangulated squeak escaped. Hoisted over a hefty shoulder, Melissa was taken up steps somewhere inside a damp building and dumped unceremoniously on the cold, hard floor.

'Untie her,' a gravelly voice ordered. 'And lose the gag and blindfold.'

'Are ya sure, boss? She's dangerous, she nearly – '

'Do as I say.'

As the tape was roughly removed from her mouth and the ropes cut, a hand pulled the blindfold from her eyes. Disoriented and dizzy, Melissa shook her head, waiting until her eyes adjusted to the gloom before looking in the general direction of the voice.

At the end of the long room, which appeared to be some kind of warehouse, a figure of about six feet in height stood with his back to her. As he turned slowly round to face her, Melissa was just about to scream abuse at him when her throat went dry. It wasn't the gun he cradled idly in his hands that silenced her, or the grisly looking pitbull terrier at his feet. Even from 40 feet away, the man exuded such raw sex appeal he simply took her breath away. Watching him as he walked slowly towards her, Melissa felt a chill run down her spine. She was about to scream when she saw his lips part in an amused smile.

'We weren't expecting you, Mrs Sheehan.' Raking over her body, his dark eyes made her squirm. But it was the smile that unlocked something deep in Melissa's subconscious. For above it, just to the upper left of the sensual mouth, curled a scar that was as distinctive as it was attractive. And only one man could have worn it.

'Eddie!' Melissa gasped, pushing herself back against the damp wall as she reeled from the shock of sudden recognition.

Suddenly his bearing changed from amused onlooker to assessing predator. Every muscle in his body seemed to tense, ready and poised for action. He leaned in to Melissa as his hand went about her throat. 'How the fuck do you know my name, Mrs Sheehan?' The rasping tones demanded an answer. 'Did you blab, you goons?' He turned to the men who shuffled back from him.

'No, boss! No names, honest!' Things looked as if they were getting ugly, and the men shifted uncomfortably.

'Then how do you know my name, lady?' The hand tightened perceptibly around her throat.

'It's me, Eddie! Don't you recognise me?' She whispered: 'It's me, Melissa.'

'I know who the fuck *you* are! You haven't answered my question.'

Melissa came to her senses; of course he wouldn't know. 'It's *me*, Eddie! Mary Pat! Mary Pat O'Malley! Don't you see? I changed my name. I've changed a lot. It's been a long time,' she whimpered, terrified she had blown her cover and said the wrong thing. 'Eddie! For God's sake! It's *me!* I haven't seen you since we were 14 years old and you were carted off to reform school.' It all came out in a rush and Melissa waited for the response.

Eddie's eyes narrowed and seemed to bore right through her. Melissa stayed stock still, afraid to move a hair. She thought she saw a muscle tense in his jaw, and she said a quick Hail Mary. This could be it. It could all be over because she couldn't keep her big, ignorant mouth shut, as usual. She closed her eyes tight, waiting to feel the cool head of the pistol resting against her temple. Nothing happened. Turning her head away from him, she risked a quick glance from under her eyelashes. The mouth was still set in a grim line, and the muscle in the jaw was working, and then suddenly the hand loosened its grip around her neck and he took a step back, looking hard at every inch of her carefully cultivated appearance. His mouth began to twitch. The twitch creased into a smile, and the smile opened to reveal the perfectly even white teeth, from which escaped a shout of laughter so loud that the heavies looked at each other in alarm, and the pitbull at his feet began to bark excitedly.

It was the sound of the barking that brought Melissa to her senses. She had to strike while the iron was hot. At least if he recognised her there must be some hope of good feeling left between them. She tried frantically to remember: it was so long ago, another lifetime, but she was pretty sure she had always stood by him.

'My dogs!' she begged, beseeching him. 'Eddie, they took my dogs! That big fucker has nearly killed one of them.' She pointed at Jimbo's partner in crime who was looking warily at her. 'He was only trying to protect me. Please, you've got to help him – them – they're in the van. Oh Eddie, please! I don't care about myself. But if you've a shred of the Eddie I remember in you, you won't let my little dogs come to any harm. Please. I'm begging you.' Melissa started to cry, partly out of terror and partly out of exhausted relief that she could finally be honest with someone for the first time in years.

There was no hiding from Eddie; he knew her and her skeletons far too well.

Eddie shot an incredulous glance at Jimbo. 'Am I hearing right? We have *dogs* as well? What d'you think this is? A bleedin' animal rescue centre? I asked ya to leave a calling card! Not take the whole bleedin' household with you!' Eddie sucked in his breath and raised his eyes to the ceiling. 'You,' he said to Dolce's assailant. 'Bring them in.'

'But, boss …'

'Bring them in, d'ya hear me? We might as well have the whole feckin' menagerie in here while we're at it.' Eddie's roar instigated appropriate action from Jimbo and his sidekick. Seconds later, they reappeared with the sack, which they placed on the floor and opened as Melissa covered her face, afraid to confront her worst fears.

There was a shuffle, and then Gabby poked her nose out, panting with thirst. Locating her mistress's scent she rushed over to her, whining pathetically, before racing back to the sack to sniff and paw at the shape that lay unmoving inside it.

'Oh, oh,' sobbed Melissa. 'My darling little Dolce.

He's dead. You've killed him! You and your vicious, ignorant thugs have killed him!' She tried to go over to Gabby, to comfort her, but she was hysterical now and could hardly see for tears. Lurching towards Eddie, she fell against him, pummelling him with her fists and clawing at his face like a tigress as his men looked on in amazement.

'Hold on a minute! Jesus, woman! Will you get a hold of yourself?' Eddie struggled until he extricated himself from the assault. Pinning her arms behind her with one hand, his other stroked her face with unexpected tenderness as Melissa collapsed, sobbing helplessly.

'Just hold on, Mary P.' Melissa felt absurdly relieved to be called her by her old name even though she had hated it. 'Just cool it, okay? We're gonna look at your dog, okay?' Gradually Melissa calmed down, and Eddie let her go. Shivering uncontrollably, she watched, unable to move, as he knelt down beside the bulging sack; pulling it open, he reached inside and gently lifted out little Dolce, limp and unmoving. Holding him in his arms, he bent down to listen for breath and feel for a heartbeat as his own dog lay in respectful silence at his feet, watching intently.

'It wasn't my fault, boss,' Deke blubbered. 'He went for me. Right between the legs. He done me a serious injury.' Deke winced visibly as Gabby growled in his direction.

'Shut up.' Eddie's face was like stone. 'I can still feel

a pulse. Jimbo.' It was a command. 'Take him down to Mick, now. Take my car and say I sent you and it's an emergency. And don't leave until you've got news, all right?'

'Yes, boss, right away, boss.' Jimbo took Dolce from Eddie and made for the door.

'Oh, please! Let me go with him. He'll be so afraid on his own, he's never been away from me or Gabby,' Melissa pleaded.

'No way, pet.' Eddie's arm went around her as she began to sob again, utterly overcome with fright and exhaustion. 'We need to keep you here for a while.' And then he put a hand under her chin and lifted it to him. 'Look at me, Mary P. If anyone can save your dog, Mick can. I'd trust him with my life.'

'He … he's a good vet, then?' Melissa looked up at him tearfully.

'No, pet.' Eddie smiled. 'He's the best fuckin' general surgeon in the country. But he loves dogs and he owes me, right? So don't worry. Your little mutt is in skilled hands. Now come and have a drink with me – we've got a lot of catching up to do.'

'Answer it, Maria!' Pascal sounded sterner than intended, but he had to keep control of things.

Maria sniffed reproachfully and did as she was told. 'Good afternoon. The Sheehan residence,' she managed, sounding strangely subdued. 'One moment please,' she handed the phone to Pascal, who was watching intently, and mouthed: 'It's for you.'

Taking the phone, Pascal motioned for them to leave the room, sat down behind his desk and took a deep breath.

'This is Pascal Sheehan,' he said.

'We've got your wife,' said a raw, gravelly voice.

Pascal sucked in his breath. 'Who is this?'

'She's all right. There's no need for anyone to get hurt as long as you do as I say.'

'How do I know that?' Pascal felt the blood drain from his face. 'Put her on! Now!'

'Not so fast. You're taking the orders now.'

'Put my wife on or I'll call the cops now.'

'That wouldn't be very clever, Sheehan. Not very clever at all.'

'Pascal?' It was Melissa's voice.

'Melissa! Are you all right, love?'

'I'm okay, Pascal. Just please do as they say. They … they've got Dolce and Gabbana as well, and Dolce –'

The phone was snatched away from her and the gravelly voice was back on the line.

'Just stay put, Sheehan. No funny stuff. No cops. You won't be doing yourself any favours, right?'

'Who are you? What do you want?'

'We'll let you know. Stand by, Sheehan, we'll be in touch.' And the line went dead.

Pascal put his head in his hands. They had the dogs too! Melissa had said 'they' so there must be a few of them. They must be raving psychopaths! He got up and poured himself a large whiskey. He had to keep calm. He needed to think. And fast.

It was better than she could possibly have imagined.

If 'better' was the word one could use to describe the litany of misery he must have left in his wake. He had been careful, to be sure, covering his tracks by preying on young, inarticulate, impressionable girls, mostly from the backwaters of middle America, but the trail was there nonetheless. The private investigator had done a good job. And the latest victim from small-town America had been extremely co-operative. Particularly when she had been prompted by the generous cash incentive provided.

Carol finished her glass of wine and looked out over the balcony of her penthouse apartment at the gently lapping water. She closed the sliding door behind her as she went inside.

Sitting at her lap-top, she began to write. She worked long into the night, pausing occasionally to stretch her legs and pour a cup of coffee.

By 3.30 a.m., she had finished. Although the piece had practically written itself, she felt completely wrung out.

Falling into bed, she set her alarm for six. There was no need: she didn't sleep a wink.

Michael was just about to leave the office when the call came through.

'Yes, Katy? I'm just about to finish up here, so unless it's important …'

'It's Mr Sheehan on the line, Mr Moriarty. He says it's extremely urgent.'

'Pascal?' Michael braced himself, picking up the call. 'What's up?'

'Michael! It's Melissa. She's been kidnapped!' The urgency was palpable in Pascal's distraught voice.

'What? Are you sure? Couldn't there be some mistake?' Michael couldn't believe what he was hearing.

'Of course I'm sure. The place has been roughed up and they've taken her and the dogs.'

'Have you got on to the guards?'

'Don't be stupid, man! They warned me not to … Michael, think! Think hard. Is there anyone, a client or someone, we could have pissed off? If anything, I mean *anything,* comes to mind, call me. This is serious, Michael. Melissa's life is at stake. These guys mean business, whoever they are.'

'Wait there. I'm coming round now.'

'No. No, don't. Just call me if anything out of the ordinary happens. They might get on to you at the office. Who knows what they'll do? I need you to be ready to get the cash if we need it.'

'You're not going to pay them off, are you?'

'What do you expect me to do? Wait for Melissa to be sent in little pieces through the letterbox?'

'Okay, okay. Look, I'm sorry, I didn't mean … I just

don't want you to do anything rash. You shouldn't be dealing with this on your own.'

'I won't be.'

'What do you mean?'

'Never mind. Just keep your mobile on you and get ready to move some cash, okay?'

'Of course. And … Pascal? Good luck.'

'Thanks, I'll need it.'

Michael put the phone down with a trembling hand. Shit! What the fuck was going on? There was only one person who could be behind a stunt like this and that was Eddie McEntee. The bastard. What the hell did he think he was doing? More to the point, what did he know? Michael felt a cold hand clutch at his heart. He couldn't possibly have got wind of anything, could he? No. Michael took a deep breath. He'd checked all the transfers this morning and gone over all the payments to suppliers. Everything was up to scratch. There was no way Eddie, or anyone else for that matter, could have the slightest idea what was being planned.

All the same, he'd need to get a move on. The ball was in three days' time. He thought briefly of Melissa. Well, if anyone could hold their own in a kidnap situation, it would be her. He felt confident her captors would release her with huge relief once things had been sorted out. Anyway, he had enough on his plate without worrying about the stupid bitch. Whatever trouble she had gotten herself into, she could get herself out of it. What was he, her minder?

He picked up the phone and dialled Simon's mobile. 'Hi, Simon, Michael here. Those tickets I asked you to organise for Buenos Aires? Good, good. I'll pick them up at the office tomorrow.'

CHAPTER FOURTEEN

Lornagh felt sick. Things were going from bad to worse. Seeing Sean and Antonia in Weir's looking so comfortable together as they looked at jewellery and rings had all but unhinged her. He hadn't even had the grace to look bashful when he'd been caught red-handed. God, what a *bastard* he was. Well, she had had another lucky escape. She steeled herself to read about their engagement in all the papers any day now.

The thought made her heart twist. However hard she tried, she just couldn't stop thinking about him and how wonderful she had felt when they were together. Had it meant nothing to him? She couldn't believe it; unless he was a superlative actor among other things. And she had asked him to this stupid ball that was only three days away. Now he'd probably bring Antonia and she, Lornagh, would have no one. She'd have to ask Lawrence to be her partner, and everyone knew he was gay. Oh God! Why couldn't things have worked out, just this once? Wandering down to the kitchen, she flicked on the TV and made herself a cup of tea. She was still sitting there an hour later staring into space when Lawrence arrived home.

'Uh oh.' He took one look at her face, dumped the shopping on the counter, and went over and put his arms around her.

The sobs came from the very tips of her toes. If she hadn't felt so miserable, she would have been embarrassed by her howls of sorrow, but she was too sad and too wounded to care.

'Come on, poppet.' Lawrence handed her an immaculate handkerchief and made her blow her nose. 'I'm going to barbecue some steaks, then we're going to open a nice bottle of wine and sort out this awful mess.'

'There's nothing to sort out. That's the problem. It's over,' Lornagh said miserably. 'I threw myself at him and now he's thrown me over – in favour of a bloody Italian cow.'

'Are you sure there's no hope?' Looking at Lornagh's cynically raised eyebrow, he hastily continued: 'I mean, you didn't really let him explain, did you?'

'He didn't even try, Lawrence. And anyway, a naked Italian girl in your apartment doesn't require an explanation. It's pretty obvious.'

'Not necessarily. I've had plenty of beautiful, naked girls in my apartment – including you, I might add – and I never touched one of them.'

'That's different and you know it. I was just taken in

by him. I'm obviously just a Dublin 4 notch on his belt.' Lornagh sniffed.

'You haven't heard from him then, I take it?'

'Nothing.'

'Don't you think it's worth a phone call?'

'What?' Lornagh shrieked. 'Me? Ring him? Lawrence, I saw them in Weir's looking at rings, for God's sake! With my *mother* of all people.'

'I know, I heard about that bit.' Lawrence allowed himself a smile.

'It's not funny.'

'It is the way Angela tells it.'

'I thought you were on my side!'

'I am, poppet, truly I am. But I just think you might have been a little, well, *hasty*. If he means this much to you, surely it's worth hearing his side of the story?'

'He froze me out in Weir's. You should have seen the look on his face when he saw me.'

'Maybe he was caught off guard.'

'Huh! He obviously makes a habit of that.'

'Look.' Lawrence tried to be rational. 'He walks in on you and this girl, and she's dripping with olive tapenade which you have thrown over her. Then you hit him with a baguette and do a runner. It's not exactly civilised behaviour, is it? The word *puerile* even springs to mind …'

'You don't understand, she –'

'I don't care what she said. I want to hear what *he* has

to say. Give the guy a chance, Lornagh. If you don't, I know plenty of women who will.'

'What if he doesn't want to talk to me?' Lornagh's voice sounded very small.

'That, my darling, is a risk you'll have to take.'

Just then, Mauricio arrived with Avril and Wendy, who had picked him up, laden down with Italian delicacies, from the airport.

'How was Florence, darling boy?' Lawrence asked, beaming with pleasure to have him back. A week of dealing with a depressed Lornagh on his own had taken its toll.

'Magnificent!' Mauricio said, kissing Lornagh's hand and the top of Lawrence's darkly waved head.

Over barbecued steak and several bottles of red wine, they listened intently to Mauricio's hilarious account of meeting up with his eccentric extended family. Lornagh was slightly miffed that the subject of her traumatic break-up wasn't a riveting topic of conversation anymore. She picked up the copy of *Sensacional,* one of Italy's more scandalous gossip magazines, that Mauricio had brought from the airport, and began to flick through it mindlessly. She was just about to finish her glass of wine and call it a night when she saw the picture. Peering again at the vaguely familiar face, she searched frantically for the appropriate caption to the shot. There it was! 'Antonia Serlupi' in bold type underneath the grainy black-and-white, long lens *paparazzo* shot.

Looking more closely, Lornagh made out the distinctive chiselled features, the full sensual mouth turned down in a scowl, the dark glasses and the hair tied back under a dark scarf, the hand outstretched to fend off the photographer. Beside her name, Lornagh read the words 'Sanatorium della Delusionales'. Gibbering with excitement, she grabbed Mauricio and asked him to translate.

'Look! It's her! Lawrence! Mauricio! It's Antonia. That's her! That's the girl I saw in Sean's house. Read it. Tell me what it says.'

Grabbing the magazine from her, Mauricio read through the short paragraph, nodding knowingly.

'Aha, yes, it doesn't surprise me at all …'

'What?' exclaimed Lornagh, frantic to hear. 'What does it say, for heaven's sake?'

'Basically, it says, 'Glamorous aristocratic beauty, Antonia Serlupi, daughter of Italy's most famous architect, leaves the Santa Maria Clinic. It's for alcohol- and drug-related problems,' he explained to Lornagh. 'Umm, uh huh, yes, it says this was her third stay in the clinic this year and she was sent in by her bodyguard boyfriend after she tried to poison him. Of course, that's not the whole story,' Mauricio confided. 'The girl is extremely unbalanced, especially when it comes to men, kind of like in the movie *Fatal Attraction*, you know? I heard she threatened the mother of her last boyfriend with a knife because she heard the woman didn't approve of her.' Mauricio shook his head. 'Such a pity. So beautiful, and so mixed up. Apparently her father is at his wits' end about her. Your Sean had a lucky escape.'

'Ah,' said Lawrence, tactfully, 'you haven't heard the latest instalment. There's been a development or two since you were on hols.'

Mauricio was brought up to date on recent developments in the romance department as Lornagh sat looking sheepish. Mauricio clapped his hands theatrically. 'Bravo, Lornagh! Such passion! Your reaction is a cry from the heart.'

'Shame it bypassed the head,' Lawrence couldn't resist adding. 'It's all very well, Mauricio, for you Italians to go around in high drama, but the rest of us Irish, *men in particular*, aren't keen on histrionics. Believe me, I know. And now our Lornagh here is in a bit of a pickle.'

'What peekle?' Mauricio beamed. 'Don't you see? You must talk to him, Lornagh! Antonia is a, how you say, a nutcake.'

'Fruitcake.'

'Whatever. No one knows what she was planning to do. Poor Sean, he come back to find not one, but two angry women in his apartment. He has injured pride, no? You must go to him – find out his story, make everything all right. Yes?'

'Exactly what I've been trying to tell her for the last two weeks,' Lawrence sighed.

'Go now!' Mauricio banged his fist on the table for effect. 'Strike while the poker is hot.'

'Iron, you mean.' Lawrence grinned.

'Under the circumstances,' quipped Avril, 'I quite like poker.'

Half an hour later, she was outside Sean's house.

Taking a deep breath, she drove in the gates and parked her car. He was at home, or at least his car was. Smoothing down her creased linen skirt she pressed a trembling finger against the intercom system.

'Yeah?' Lornagh nearly turned and ran at the sound of his voice.

'It's me, Lornagh.' Her voice sounded small and tinny as if it came from a million miles away.

There was an agonising pause, and then the door opened. Sean stood there in jeans and a T-shirt, his face impassive, eyes dark and brooding. Lornagh nearly choked. His feet were bare, and the dark golden skin with a scattering of blond hairs brought back such erotic memories that she began to feel weak.

'May I come in please?'

He looked at her for a moment, then stood back to allow her through.

'Go ahead,' he said darkly, 'you know the way.'

Clearly, Lornagh thought, he wasn't going to make this easy.

'Drink?' he asked, as Lornagh noticed the opened bottle of white wine on the table.

'Er, yes please.' Having handed her a glass of white wine, he stood leaning against the wall.

Lornagh took a deep breath. 'I … um, I want to apologise, for my, er, behaviour that day. I had no right to, er, to behave like that.'

'No, you didn't.'

Lornagh was momentarily thrown. 'Well, it's big of you to be so understanding. I walk in and find a naked girl in your house who accosts me and tells me you and she are lovers and –'

'I don't care what she said.' Sean's voice was chilling. 'You didn't exactly wait for an explanation.' He regarded her coldly.

'Well, what *was* your explanation?'

'I don't know that you deserve one.' He walked over to the table and topped up his glass.

Lornagh took a deep breath. 'I meant I would *appreciate* an explanation. Please?'

Sean sat down. 'Antonia, as you know, was an old girlfriend of mine. We went out for a while when I first went to Italy and eventually moved in together. Her father became my mentor and great friend. To put it bluntly, Antonia's got a few problems, but she's been a big part of my life.'

'And?'

'Two weeks ago, she rang me from the airport. That was the day you saw her on the site with me. She stayed for a couple of days and she seemed much better, more like her old self. Well, one thing led to another and she said she wanted to give "us" another try.'

'I see,' said Lornagh, feeling suddenly sick. 'And what did you say to this? Or is that a stupid question?'

'Are you going to shut up and listen?'

'Sorry.'

'I said I'd think about it. And then, well, then you happened.'

'How inconvenient for you.'

Sean ignored the sarcasm. 'Antonia arrived back on my doorstep the day I got back from London, the day you and she …'

'I remember.'

'I wasn't expecting her.'

'Clearly.'

'She wanted an answer – and I gave her one.' He paused; and Lornagh bit her lip.

'I told her I had met someone new and that I thought we had something really special.' Sean looked directly into her eyes. 'Now I'm not so sure.'

'Wh-what do you mean?'

'I've already had one hysterical woman in my life, Lornagh – I sure as hell don't need another.'

'But I'm not hysterical.'

'You certainly gave a good impression of it.'

'But that day in Weir's … you were looking at rings together …'

Sean raised an eyebrow. 'It was her father's seventieth

birthday; she wanted to go into town to get him something nice. She bought him a bronze sculpture, and then we went home. I drove her to the airport and put her on a plane.' He looked tired. 'The rest, as they say, is history.'

'I see.' Lornagh suddenly felt very small.

'I'm not at all sure you do.' He picked up the copy of *Sensacional* that Lornagh had brought with her – and now wished fervently she hadn't.

'I can't believe you read that trash,' he said, flicking through it.

Lornagh squirmed. 'I don't, usually. A friend brought it back from Italy.'

'Those rags generate the kind of pressure that gives people breakdowns,' he said, throwing it aside.

'I'm sorry. Look, I just came around to apologise for ruining your plans and, and …' A big tear rolled down her face.

'Lornagh, for God's sake, none of this was planned!'

'Not those plans! Your work plans on the table that Antonia was so upset about. The ones that got covered in oil.'

Sean looked at her as if she was mad. 'What plans on the table? What are you talking about?'

'The plans that were on the table when I threw the olive tapenade at Antonia; they were ruined … she put them in the bin …' Lornagh trailed off, knowing how ridiculous she must sound.

'There were no plans on the table. I never leave my work out.'

It was true; Lornagh had never seen so much as a piece of paper lying around his house. 'Well, they were ruined anyway.' Lornagh sniffed. 'What are you doing?' she asked as Sean sat at his computer, running through a couple of programmes.

'Oh fuck,' he said quietly.

He was so riveted by whatever he had discovered, he didn't hear Lornagh slip quietly from the room, and from there to her car. She had a horrible feeling something had gone very wrong; and it was very likely all her fault.

Simon was sitting in an elegant boutique off Grafton Street while Alexi was having the final alterations made to the dress he was buying her to wear to the ball.

Emerging from the private fitting room, she did a twirl and looked at herself in the full-length mirror to ooohs and ahhs from the shop assistants. 'Vat do you think?' she asked coquettishly.

'Very nice! Yes, very nice indeed,' Simon said, puffing up with self-importance, enjoying the stir she was creating. The dress, which clung to her in all the right places, was a riot of bright-red sequins with a daring slit up one side. It was costing him a small fortune but he didn't care. It was vital he made an instant impression when he entered the room, and there was nothing like a decorative piece of arm-candy to turn heads.

'Couldn't it be a bit tighter there, er, at the back?' Simon pointed to Alexi's shapely bottom which was already clearly outlined.

'Oh, it's perfect as it is.' The seamstress smiled.

'I don't think so!' Simon was determined to get his pound of flesh. He was bloody well paying enough for it.

'Darlink!' Alexi demurred. 'I can hardly valk in it as it is!'

'I think it should be tighter there. Please take it in again.' Simon's mouth was pursed.

'Vatever.' Alexi was getting bored. She had never in her life worn such an expensive gown, and if making it tighter meant Simon was happier footing the bill, then tighter it would be.

'Very well!' The seamstress went to work pinning again, disapproval written all over her face.

Finally satisfied, Simon settled the bill and tried not to wince. It would all be worth it, he reminded himself, when he saw Lornagh Lemass's face drop.

It was just a pity Alexi was a size eight. He would have liked to see how the dress looked on him when he got it home. And there was no way he would ever get into it.

Never mind – once the ball was over, he would have it dry cleaned and bring it back to the shop. He had no intention of allowing Alexi to keep it. They would have to give him a credit note, and then he could put the money to much better use.

Concentrating instead on the painting he was about

to acquire, he immediately basked in a warm glow of satisfaction. Only one more day to go. And then he would own a priceless masterpiece. He quivered in anticipation. He would be worth a fortune.

Melissa was shivering uncontrollably. Despite wearing three of Eddie's jackets, she was chilled to the bone. She sat glaring at him as he worked at his computer. From time to time, he looked over at her and laughed softly. 'Sorry, pet! But we have to keep you here for a day or two, it's for your own good.'

'Nothing you did was ever any good for me,' Melissa snapped.

In the corner beside her, Gabby lay sound asleep, exhausted by the trauma, and Eddie's pitbull snored contentedly with his head resting on hers.

'Can't you keep that horrible mongrel away from my Gabby? He'll give her fleas or some horrible disease.'

'They look perfectly happy to me.' Eddie glanced over. 'The company'll do Tyson good – he can be a bit unsociable.'

Melissa shivered again. Coming face to face with Eddie had unnerved her. It was bringing back too many memories she would rather forget. After the initial shock of recognition, Melissa had learned a lot. The last time she had seen him was when they had been going steady. He had been her first real boyfriend back in the old days, when she had been Mary Pat O'Malley and Eddie had been head of the local gang. Even then he had been trouble, and it wasn't long before he had been picked up for a string of break-ins and theft and carted off to reform school. They had been just 14. At the time, she had been devastated, she remembered, but it had been a wake-up call to her and she had vowed to move on and claw her way out of the tough, inner-city neighbourhood.

'You did well for yourself, Mary P. I always knew you would.' He looked over, reading her thoughts.

'What if I have?'

He grinned. 'You and little Paccy Sheehan! Who'd have thought it?'

'I met Pascal when we had both made a life for ourselves.' Melissa scowled. 'We didn't even realise we had known each other. We were kids back then, for God's sake. Anyway, you haven't told me why I'm here. If it's money you want, why don't you just say so? Pascal will pay anything you want to get me back,' she boasted, although privately she wasn't so sure.

'He oughta be more careful about the company he keeps.'

'What do you mean?'

'His partner, Michael Moriarty, needs watching.'

'What about him?' Melissa's antennae were up instantly.

'Oh, I forgot, you were cosy with him an' all, weren't you?'

Melissa gasped in horror. 'I don't know what you mean!'

'Don't worry, pet! Your sordid little secrets are safe

with me – for now. There's a lot more to our Michael than meets the eye.'

As Melissa listened in growing disbelief, Eddie outlined the business arrangement he and Michael had. 'But your darlin' husband is holding us up. I don't like delays. They make me nervous. We just wanted him to get his act together. But then you walked in on things, and the boys, well, they didn't want to leave any loose ends lying around.' Eddie wasn't going to let on for a moment how livid he was that his heavies had bungled things by panicking and taking Melissa with them.

A terrifying thought was struggling to form itself at the back of Melissa's mind. 'But Pascal couldn't be holding things up. I know for a fact he put up his share of the money weeks ago.'

Eddie's eyes narrowed. 'What do you mean?'

'Just what I said. Sure, Pascal's been talking about nothing else for the last year. It's St Rita's this and St Rita's that and Tiger Investments the other. I know he tied up his end of things because he said so. Apart from that, Michael, er, confirmed it to me – we were celebrating things finally going ahead. He was placating Pascal because his other investors hadn't come through. Meaning, presumably, *you!* A nervous note had crept into Melissa's voice. She didn't like the look on Eddie's face as he listened to her. It had turned to stone. It was all very well them knowing each other from the past. But she couldn't forget for a minute that he was now 'The

Shark', arguably the most dangerous man in the country. Men like Eddie didn't like being swindled, and God knows what would become of her, caught up in the middle of this sinister mess. Fucking Michael Moriarty. The lying, swindling, two-faced hoor! Whatever was going on, he was behind it. She just knew it. Hadn't her Reiki healer, Inga, warned her to be careful of him? She could be killed! Cut up in tiny pieces and sent fingers and toes through Michael's letterbox. She imagined the look on Felicity's snooty face when she opened an envelope to find one of Melissa's immaculately manicured fingers, and would have laughed if she hadn't suddenly felt faint with fear.

'What else do you know, Mary P?' Eddie was advancing towards her, his mouth set in a cruel line.

'N-nothing, I swear. That's all.'

'You better think hard. I'm not going to be made a fool of by some nancy-boy number cruncher. You an' he had a thing goin'. He must have talked to you. Think, woman, *think!*'

Melissa's mind immediately went blank. 'I don't know. I'd tell you if I did.' She was gibbering with terror now, realising the full implications of her situation. 'Eddie, please. I swear I don't know!' Gabby had woken up now and was growling fiercely at Eddie, while his own dog, Tyson, looked simultaneously impressed and besotted.

'There's too much at stake here for me to get sentimental, pet.' His hand went around her throat and grasped it gently while his other stroked her face. 'Such a pretty face,' he whispered, and then she saw the flick knife. 'Shame to have to mess it up, seeing as you've spent so much on it,' he added nastily.

That did it. The only knife Melissa had any intention of letting near her face wasn't going to be wielded by a butcher like him. In a flash, she remembered her handbag. Thank God she had brought it with her: never had she been so ecstatic to see a Prada label in all her life.

'Wait! There is something.'

'What?'

'My handbag! Over there.' Eddie looked to where his men had thrown it on the floor and picked it up. 'Go on. This better be good.'

'There's an envelope, I'd forgotten. I had his palm computer downloaded just in case. He said he kept his whole life on the thing. My sister did it for me. There's a disk there as well.'

Eddie suddenly grinned. 'That's more like it.' Taking the envelope out, he grabbed the disk and shoved it into his own computer.

'Well, well, well!'

'What?' Melissa cringed at his tone, praying she hadn't just made things worse for herself and Pascal.

'This is very interesting. Very interesting indeed. You've done well, Mary P. I couldn't have done better myself. Look's like we've got to Mr Moriarty in the nick of time.'

Before she could inquire further, the door opened,

and in came Jimbo carrying a very indignant Dolce in a cat basket. He opened the door, and Dolce immediately poked his nose out and, to Melissa's delight, ran across to greet her, barking ecstatically.

'Dolce!' she screamed. 'My darling little puppy!' A cacophony of yelping and barking ensued as Gabby hurled herself at him in delight and even Tyson began to dance around excitedly, not wanting to be excluded from the wonderful doggie exchanges that were flying back and forth.

'Mick fixed him, then?' Eddie couldn't help smiling at the carry-on.

'Yeah,' muttered Jimbo, not looking at all happy about the outcome. 'Shot of adrenaline did the trick. Said he'd be grand. More than I can say for meself.' He shot Melissa a venomous glance. 'He nearly bleedin' put me out of action, that muppet.'

Dolce looked around and, satisfied his beloved mistress was out of danger, busied himself in sniffing Tyson's bottom. Tyson at least had the grace to look embarrassed. He wasn't used to meeting other dogs, and these wonderfully exotic creatures with their pop eyes, little black faces, smooth minky coats and curly tails fascinated him.

'It's time I made another call to your husband,' Eddie said. 'Let's hope for your sake he hasn't done anything stupid.'

Pascal was frantic.

He had sat up all night waiting for another call, but

there had been nothing. Terrified Melissa would come to harm, he had refrained from calling the guards. These situations had to be handled with kid gloves, and right now he felt safer if he were wearing them. His hand shook as he took another gulp of whiskey. He couldn't help remembering the John O'Grady kidnap a few years back when the poor chap had two fingers hacked off; it was only because he was a dentist with basic medical training that he knew to cauterize the wound with a flame and managed to save the hand at all. Pascal shuddered. There was no knowing what these people would do. And the dogs. What was that about? Poor Melissa. She worshipped Dolce and Gabbana as if the dogs were the children she and Pascal never had, and spoilt them accordingly. She wouldn't be able to cope if the kidnappers did anything to them. They were clever bastards, whoever they were. Sick, but clever. Thinking about children, Pascal felt the familiar sadness sneak up. He would have given anything to have a family, but seemingly it wasn't to be. Both he and Melissa had had interminable tests and absolutely nothing seemed to be wrong. They were told they would just have to let nature take its course and keep trying. So far nature hadn't obliged, and after years of repeated disappointments – not to mention the deterioration of the marriage in general – they had each given up hope and thrown themselves into other, more attainable pursuits: Pascal his work, Melissa a shopping career and insatiable cosmetic reconstruction. Pascal smiled ruefully. He had always thought her gorgeous, but Melissa was never satisfied with herself. She had turned self-improvement into an art form. And lately, she had managed to surprise him all over again. Out of nowhere, she had suddenly become affectionate and interested in him. And the flame of their marriage had reignited. She had even gone with him to a caravan show in Toulouse. They had had a whale of a time and even managed a quickie by locking themselves in the 'Roving Roger' that was the star attraction. Pascal could hardly believe it. He didn't bother trying to analyse why things had changed, he was too busy enjoying this new Melissa, or rather the old Melissa who had miraculously reappeared. And now this. He couldn't bear to think of her tied up in some hole of a place, maybe being raped or tortured. Pascal banged the table in frustration. He couldn't just sit there, letting the bastards control him! He had to do something. But what? He didn't for the life of him know. But he knew a man who did. Picking up the phone, he dialled Charlie's number and prayed he was in town.

The impossibly slender, toned models strolled down the catwalk, parading the latest summer collections at a private viewing to women who could afford the designer clothes but, generally, lacked the bodies to show them off.

From her front-row seat, Carol made notes, watching

the women watch each other; whispering behind their catalogues, warily assessing the competition.

The show was being recorded, and Carol had already met with the models as they were coiffed and made up for the 'behind the scenes' footage. After the show, she would be having dinner with the exceptionally talented designer in Patrick Guilbaud's. She spotted Felicity Moriarty across the way, looking as resolutely elegant as ever, in sharp black and white linen; her long titian hair was pulled back from her face in a youthful ponytail. The usual faces were in evidence; except, Carol noticed, Melissa, who was conspicuous by her absence. It wasn't like her to miss a photo opportunity like this. Beside Felicity sat a tall, blonde, all-American-type girl, who had pointed excitedly at the magnificent wedding gown which triumphantly concluded the show. Carol immediately recognised the girl, with her big teeth and gravity-defying breasts, as Candice Stetner, Dr Gerald Stevens's heiress fiancée. Not long now, she thought gleefully, before both of them were brought resoundingly down to earth.

'All set for tomorrow evening?'

'Sorry, darling?' Michael jumped behind his morning paper as Felicity poured his orange juice.

'The Anglesea. The St Rita's ball, Michael, or had you forgotten?' Felicity's voice was crisp.

'Chance would be a fine thing.' Relief swept over him.

'Come on. It'll be fun! It's ages since I've been to a

decent ball, and to be fair this one sounds fantastic. I was talking to Lornagh Lemass the other day and she was telling me about the auction. They're hoping to raise over a hundred thousand on the night. And the raffle prizes are spectacular.'

'What are you wearing, Flick?' Michael changed the subject deftly. He would have to act normally. The slightest little slip-up now could be disastrous.

'Oh, I thought I'd wear my black Yves St Laurent. What do you think?'

Michael knew the dress. It was elegant with a severity of line most women would have shied away from, but Felicity could carry it off and looked wonderful in it.

'Mmm, it's fabulous on you, but you could always treat yourself to a new one. It's been a while, hasn't it?' He could afford to be generous, Michael thought. Felicity was a marvellous wife and he would miss her. The least he could do was buy her a new evening dress before he made his exit.

'Yes, I suppose I could.' Felicity smiled. 'But you know me, I'm happier with what suits me. The devil you know and all that …'

'Well, whatever you wear you'll be the most stylish woman there, darling,' Michael said warmly.

'Let's hope so.' Felicity smiled enigmatically. 'I have to keep up with you, don't I?'

CHAPTER FIFTEEN

Lornagh looked around the pristine white walls of her apartment and tried to feel enthused. It was another new beginning. The painters had finished the day before, and at lunchtime the enormous bed she had ordered had finally been delivered. So far, it was the only piece of furniture in the place.

'You can't possibly move in yet, not until you get organised anyhow,' Lawrence had ordered.

Well, there wasn't much more she had to do. The apartment was pretty, and Lornagh wanted to keep it simple and uncluttered. It was part of a newly built block on the seafront at Sandymount and had a large wraparound balcony and wonderful views over the sea. She planned on moving in next week. By then the ball would be over, and life would be back to normal – such as it could be. She was just about to leave when the bell rang.

'Yes?' Lornagh picked up the intercom system, thinking the delivery men must have forgotten something.

'Lornagh?' The voice was disturbingly familiar. 'It's Sean, can I come up for a sec?'

'Sure. Top floor.' Lornagh suddenly felt jittery. She hadn't heard from him since the day before yesterday, when she had tiptoed out of his house.

She jumped when there was a loud knock on the door and, taking a deep breath, went to open it.

'Hi.' He was carrying a bottle. 'Moving-in present.' He handed it to her.

'Oh, thanks.' Lornagh stood awkwardly. 'Em, come on in. How did you know I was here?'

'Lawrence. You left your mobile behind; he picked up the call and told me you were here.'

'Oh.' Lornagh was at a loss for words. 'I'd ask you to sit down, but as you can see I'm bereft of furniture.'

'It's okay, I'm sorry I didn't call, but there were a few things I had to sort out.' He ran a hand through his hair in the familiar gesture Lornagh found so unsettling. 'I owe you an apology.'

'What for?' Lornagh had been expecting an outburst. This latest development was disconcerting.

'Saving my bacon, to put it bluntly.' Sean leant against the window.

'What?'

'Let's just say Antonia's intentions weren't entirely honourable.' Sean touched his eye tentatively, which Lornagh now noticed was ringed with purple. 'Those plans you saw on the table were for an incredibly important project in Milan. It's a hugely prestigious job – a new modern wing for the municipal art gallery. Architects from all over the world are pitching for it. Antonia's father was among them. I guess they didn't like having competition from the Irish quarter. Anyhow, that's what she was after. That's what you saw on the kitchen table.'

'Your plans?'

'Yup, and she very nearly got away with them. I had to go over to Florence and … Well, it wasn't pleasant.'

Lornagh felt relief sweep through her, although she could hardly take it all in.

'Oh,' she said again. 'I'm sorry, really. That must have been difficult.'

'Let's stop apologising to each other, shall we?'

'But I am sorry, you've no idea how sorry I am for shouting at you and saying all those awful things …'

'Forget it. I should have guessed … well anyway …' he trailed off.

'But she was so – so gorgeous-looking, so perfect. Even down to her Brazilian bikini wax.'

Sean raised an amused eyebrow.

'I couldn't help it! I just couldn't bear the thought of you with another woman. I know I lost it, but she was so horrible to me. And I … I have a problem with repressed anger! And it all came out! I'm sorry I hit you with the baguette. Really I am.'

'Repressed anger, huh?' The first flicker of a smile played around his mouth.

'I know.' Lornagh felt incredibly sheepish. 'I thought I had it under control.'

'Have you any other repressed feelings?' He walked over to her and trailed a finger along her jaw.

'I, um, don't know,' she said, shivering at his touch. Things were suddenly starting to look up.

'How about this?' He brushed his lips along her collarbone.

'Mmm. Just the faintest flicker …'

'And this?' He was nuzzling her ear.

'Ooooh, yes,' she gasped, 'definitely repressed.'

'What about here?' His hand had slipped underneath her shirt and he was rubbing a nipple between his finger and thumb.

'I can definitely feel something. Mmm.'

'And here?' His fingers slipped under the thin linen skirt and up the inside of her thighs. Lornagh shuddered.

'I think we're getting somewhere now, Miss Lemass.' Carrying her into the bedroom, he threw her onto the huge bed and began to kiss her hungrily. 'How's your repressed anger now?' he mumbled.

'Oh, much, much better!' Lornagh's lips were being crushed deliciously. Suddenly a thought occurred to her and she pulled away. 'I know this is a really stupid question, but does this mean you'll come to the ball with me?'

'Oh, I think I can safely promise you I'll come,' he said, entering her quickly.

'I've got nothing to wear!' wailed Lornagh later that day, trawling through the haphazard contents of her transient wardrobe.

The last few weeks had been such a whirlwind of frenzied activity she had neglected to attend to the one vital task she had left until last.

Several times, she had meant to go into town but, what with overseeing the finished details of her apartment and dealing with her unpredictable personal life, she had never got around to it.

She now regarded her one reasonably respectable evening dress without enthusiasm. Oh well, there was nothing for it: she would just have to make do.

After a hectic day organising the gifts and donations for the charity auction and raffle at the hotel, it was finally time to leave the last details to the banqueting team. Everyone had had a well-earned glass of champagne and flown off to have their last minute blow-dries and beauty treatments.

It was now half past four, and Lornagh remembered she had promised to call into her mother, who had suddenly announced the week before that she would like to go to the ball. Lawrence had encouraged her wildly, saying that he and Mauricio would be delighted to escort her, and insisting that she joined their table. It was all Lornagh needed, she thought wryly, to finally unnerve her: as she hauled herself up onto the podium to make her speech, Angela was quite likely to shriek at her to speak up from wherever she was sitting.

Arriving at 'Canterbury' exhausted and frazzled, Lornagh was greeted by a state of high excitement.

'Come on up, Lornagh!' Mary shouted down to her. 'We're having the dress rehearsal.' Lornagh trailed up the stairs wearily to her mother's vast, heavily draped bedroom.

'Well, what do you think, Lornagh?' Angela emerged from her dressing room in a full-length dress of magnificently draped grey chiffon banded at the wrist and neck with silver sequins. The high collar framed her elegant neck perfectly and the softly draped chiffon sleeves emphasised her still graceful arms. As she did a slow twirl, the cloud-grey chiffon floated delicately, settling in tiered layers that fell gracefully to the floor. With her hair softly arranged in a French pleat, she looked startlingly beautiful. Lornagh gasped. 'It's amazing, Mum. You look gorgeous.'

'Thank you, darling. It was wildly expensive, but I owe it to my fans to look my best. What are *you* wearing, Lornagh?'

Lornagh flopped down on the bed and stretched. 'Oh, my black strapless number. It's all I've got. I meant to get something new but I just didn't have time.'

'That old thing! You can't possibly.' Angela looked horrified.

'It's an old reliable, and I feel comfortable in it,' she lied.

Angela was gazing at herself in the full-length mirror when suddenly her fact lit up. 'Mary! In the attic: the old Molyneux box! You know the one I mean? Have we still got it, do you think?'

'As if I could forget it! I'll check right away, Mrs L.'

Scurrying back a few minutes later, Mary laid a large box on the bed and opened it excitedly. 'There you are, Mrs L. That's the one.'

Lifting it out carefully from the faded tissue paper, Angela held up what looked like a simple column of white silk. 'Try this on, Lornagh, quickly. Take it into my dressing room.'

Tired as Lornagh was, it was no use arguing with Angela and Mary once they'd got the bit between their teeth. In the dressing room, she shrugged off her jeans and top, took off her bra and slipped into the deceptively simple dress. Looking in the mirror, she gasped with pleasure. The cool, white *crêpe de chine* gown glistened against her golden skin, its Grecian neckline plunging almost to her navel and rising to drape over her shoulders in beautifully arranged pleats. Gathered softly from a high waist, it fell to the floor in soft folds which arranged themselves perfectly around her feet. It was, quite simply, stunning.

'Well? Come out, Lornagh, for heaven's sake!' Angela's voice was impatient.

Walking out uncertainly into the bedroom, Lornagh was greeted by a triumphant smile from Angela and a gasp from Mary, who promptly burst into tears. 'Oh, Mrs L, it's beautiful. Why, that takes me back, so it does. She's just like a – a *film star* in it.'

Angela smiled, arranging the straps on Lornagh's shoulders meticulously. 'I wore that dress the evening

Maxwell proposed to me. He informed me later he had no choice in the matter once he had set eyes on me wearing it. It's perfect on you, darling, absolutely perfect.' Angela stood back to admire her handiwork.

'Are you sure, Mum?' Lornagh could hardly believe the transformation.

'Of course I'm sure. I know I haven't been the best mother in the world, Lornagh, but at least you can thank me for your looks and figure. The Delacey genes were always kind to the girls in our family.' Angela turned away quickly to hide suspiciously bright eyes.

Lornagh hugged her mother. 'I love it! Are you sure you don't mind me wearing it?'

'Don't be silly. I only hope it's as effective for you as it was for me. Anyway, this is your night, Lornagh, and you can't possibly be upstaged by your own mother! Now go home and get ready. Your hair's a fright.'

Dancing down the stairs and out into her car a horrible thought suddenly struck Lornagh. The speech! She had left it in the temporary office at St Rita's. She would have to race back and get it.

Simon sat in his Victorian drawing room and willed himself not to get up and pace the room. Inside, Alexi was putting the final touches to her make-up and he had to admit she looked the business. Taking a sip of brandy, he thought gratifyingly of the night ahead. This was it – the night that would change his life. He patted his breast pocket for the hundredth time, making sure he had his chequebook. Tonight, the prized Le Souquet painting would be his, and then everybody had better sit back and fasten their seat belts. He checked his watch and sighed. The minutes ticked by agonisingly slowly, but he was determined not to arrive too early. It was crucial he made a suitably late, dramatic entrance with Alexi, his exotically beautiful arm accessory, clinging to him. He smiled, savouring the exquisite *frisson* of expectation. He couldn't wait to see their gobsmacked faces. Lornagh's in particular. He wriggled in his chair with excitement. The pink silk La Perla panties he had treated himself to were having the desired effect. He would have to remember to go into the closed cubicles in the gents' during the night, or it would be all too easy to expose himself accidentally.

They'd made it through the lobby.

It was six o'clock. In just an hour, if everything went to plan, Pascal should be arriving with her outfit. She hoped desperately he'd bring the right dress. It was a shame she couldn't ring him to make sure, but Eddie had taken her mobile and there was no chance of escaping from him.

Eddie had dispatched his thugs around the various entrances to the hotel and he walked beside her now, holding on to her arm in a way she found most unnerving, not least because of the proprietorial sneer on his lean, hungry face. Shoving her into the lift, he pressed the third-floor button and grinned. 'Room 303, that's us!'

When they arrived at the room, he promptly put up the 'do not disturb' sign. 'Go and do your stuff, pet. The bathroom's all yours.'

'Pascal?'

'Jacko! What have you got for me?' Pascal gripped the phone. Jacko was an old informer of Charlie's. If anyone knew what was going down he would.

'You're not going to like it.' Jacko's voice was disturbingly tense.

Pascal braced himself. 'Go on.'

'It's "The Shark". He's behind this. He's got Melissa. Pascal? Are you there?'

Pascal's throat constricted. The Shark was the most ruthless man in the country.

'Are you sure, Jacko?'

''Fraid so. Pascal, there's no way you can deal with this on your own, you realise that, don't you? These people are dangerous.'

'I don't have any choice, Jacko. I won't risk any harm coming to Melissa. I have to do as they say.'

There was a pause. 'Well, I'm here if you need me. I'll have a few of the boys on standby; there's no need to give them any details. And ... Pascal?'

'Yes?'

'Don't do anything stupid, okay?'

It was the third time today someone had told him that. Pascal was getting heartily fed up with it.

'I'm not going to risk Melissa's life. Whatever the bastard wants he can have! I'm doing it his way, it's all I can do.'

'Good luck. You've got my number.'

Pascal looked at the designer dress hanging in the hall and almost cried. He just prayed fervently he'd get to see Melissa in it. Whatever it cost him.

He had ten minutes to get there. Ten minutes that would dictate the rest of his life.

Now the end was in sight. The long, agonising wait of 18 years would be over, and she would finally see the look on Gerald Stevens's handsome, arrogant face when she confronted him.

Better still, this would be no ordinary, run-of-the-mill confrontation that he could wriggle and squirm his way out of. Oh, no. That would be far too good for him.

This would be front-page stuff. Her old colleague Jimmy, from her trade-journal days, now edited the leading Sunday tabloid, and Carol had approached him with her scoop. Initially Jimmy had shied away from her proposition. The paper, he had pointed out, didn't need a lengthy and expensive litigation case on its hands; but, after thorough checks of Carol's meticulous evidence by the paper's legal department, and a bit of old-style investigation of his own, he had been persuaded that the riveting story was libel-proof and had been only too keen to print it.

Tonight Carol was covering St Rita's ball for the society slot in her regular programme. Since Dr Gerald Stevens, as St Rita's medical representative, was on the organising committee, he would be attending the ball with his fiancée, Candice, and the usual group of sycophantic cronies.

It would be the perfect opportunity!

She had already proved herself as an entertainment programme presenter, but this would be the big time. It would be the media event of the decade. And she, Carol, would have nailed the 'exclusive'. She would be hailed as a brilliant reporter as well as attracting sympathy as one of his victims.

Dr Gerald Stevens could kiss his career goodbye and, more than likely, his freedom. He had been lured to his destruction with a similar skill and finesse to that he had himself employed when he had preyed on all those helpless, vulnerable young girls.

And there was absolutely nothing he could do about it. The early edition of the paper was being sent to her at the hotel by courier. And, when the time presented itself, Carol planned on handing it to Gerald personally.

Checking her appearance one last time, Carol left the room and headed for the lift. It was going to be quite a night! Turning the corner, she looked back at the sound of whispered voices. She must be imagining things: she could have sworn she saw Melissa Sheehan darting into a room with an extremely attractive stranger. It must be the light playing tricks with her eyes.

'Ready, darling?' Michael called up to Felicity, who was now making her way downstairs, a vision in black, her titian hair beautifully piled on top of her elegant head. 'Phew! You look stunning. I'm a lucky man. Shall we go, Mrs Moriarty? Your carriage awaits.'

'Ready when you are. Oh just a sec, I almost forgot my mobile.' Felicity popped the sleek phone into her antique evening bag.

'I've got mine, darling! Why bother with yours?'

'Just habit.' Felicity glided to the front door ahead of him. 'A girl can't afford to be out of touch these days. Don't forget I have a business to run, too. I never know when one of my girls will need me.'

'You're too conscientious, Flick.'

'Let's just say I like to be prepared.'

'We'll take the Aston, shall we?' Michael said, walking towards his most cherished possession. It was the one thing that would really hurt to leave behind.

He must remember to order a new one, just a soon as it was humanly possible.

CHAPTER SIXTEEN

The lobby of the Anglesea was humming.

At a quarter past seven, guests were beginning to arrive in throngs and drift in their finery into the Blue Room, where the champagne reception was in full swing. A busy hum of conversation filled the room as people pounced on friends they hadn't seen for at least a week; and beautiful women craned graceful necks to make sure they hadn't been outdone or, worse, copied in their gorgeous evening wear.

Lornagh circulated happily, chatting to people and making sure everyone was prompted towards the items on view for the silent auction. Sean had arrived a few minutes earlier and had joined her, and she was now shyly introducing him as her boyfriend. They made an incredibly handsome couple with their tall, blond good looks: all around the room people whispered to one another and sneaked admiring glances in their direction. Sean could hardly take his eyes off her and had a proudly possessive arm around her waist at every available opportunity.

'Lornagh! You're looking fabulous.' Carol Dalton of TV 2000 swooped on her. 'Come and say a few words to camera and introduce me to this gorgeous man of yours. Sean O'Rourke, if I'm not mistaken?'

Happy to oblige, and feeling relaxed now that all the hard work was over, Lornagh said a few words about the night ahead and the marvellous cause it was all in aid of.

'And what about this latest romance of yours, Lornagh? Could this be it? You make a simply divine couple.' Carol was eyeing Sean with interest. 'And Sean, tell us about your latest designs.'

Sean grinned broadly giving Lornagh a squeeze. 'I couldn't possibly Carol, they involve a certain young lady here and they're not repeatable on live TV.'

'Well, viewers, don't forget!' Carol said coquettishly to camera. 'You heard it from me first. I'm putting my money on *that* pair cementing their foundations.'

As Lornagh and Sean moved away, Carol turned around to find Simon Sullivan and his latest glamorous escort standing behind her. Simon was absolutely livid to have just witnessed Lornagh and Sean interviewed on television, and he was determined to follow suit. He held out his hand confidently. 'Carol! You remember me? Simon Sullivan. And this is –'

'Sorry, excuse me.' Carol was curt. 'I have a lot of ground to cover tonight.' And she brushed straight past them.

Simon was furious. He looked around frantically for a photographer. If it was the last thing he did, he was going to get a shot taken of him and Alexi. He was just about to commandeer one when the man turned around and gasped. 'Crikey, that's Angela Lemass over there! She hasn't been seen in public for ages. I've got to get a shot of her,' he muttered and made his way over to where Angela was holding court surrounded by a group of elderly love-struck admirers.

Simon took a few slow, deep breaths and tried to lower his escalating blood pressure. Just wait, he thought, just wait until word gets out that I discovered and purchased the most important painting to come on the market in this decade: *then* you'll be sorry.

The resounding clang of the gong, signalling to guests that they should make their way to the ballroom and take their seats, cut short his private rant; and Simon took Alexi firmly by the arm to restrain her: 'What's your rush?' he hissed. 'Wait until I tell you, and *then* we'll walk in – slowly, okay?'

'Vatever,' said Alexi, giving a rather prosperous-looking man a fluttering of her impressive eyelashes. He returned the eye contact longingly, until his wife poked him in the back and steered him very definitely towards the ballroom.

It was like walking onto a film set of fairyland.

Crystal chandeliers shone dimly, and hundreds of candles adorned the elegant walls, diffusing their magical, flickering light across the room. The tables were dressed in shell-pink linen, and magnificent floral arrangements (designed by Lawrence) of palest pink roses, entwined with silver-sprayed branches, wove in graceful intricacy towards the ceiling. To the side of the magnificent room, three sets of French doors were thrown open and led into a vast striped marquee lined in pale-pink chiffon.

Guests gasped at the elaborate decorations reflected in shimmering detail in the mirrored walls, murmuring they had never seen anything like it. The whole effect was absolutely mesmeric.

Lornagh kept an eagle eye on proceedings, helping people find their respective tables and urging latecomers to take their places. Looking around, she saw her mother and Lady Sheldon deep in conversation, while Lawrence and Mauricio merrily poured what appeared to be an unceasing flow of champagne into the glasses on their table.

A little to the left of them was Pascal and Melissa's table, where Gerald Stevens and his fiancée Candice were also seated. An attractive man Lornagh hadn't seen before sat on Melissa's right, his dark, sensual looks drawing interested glances from nearby women. Melissa, Lornagh thought, didn't seem her usual exuberant self, although she looked terrific in a drop-dead gorgeous dress, consisting of little more than intricately woven silver lace. Pascal too, she thought, seemed subdued, appearing to be miles away and fiddling obsessively with his table napkin.

To their right, at another table, sat Michael and

Felicity Moriarty, both looking as elegant as ever. Simon had been asked to join the exclusive table, to his immense relief, and sat with his extremely attractive girlfriend, Alexi, beside him. It looked like a fun table, Lornagh thought. A lot of the Grovesbury Road set were there, some of them clients of Michael's; and judging by the noise level, everyone was warming up to make a good night of it.

Lornagh waited until everyone was settled and made her way to the podium. 'Ladies and gentlemen! If I could just have your attention for a few moments – I won't keep you long.' She was greeted by eager applause and a round of appreciative wolf whistles.

Speaking briefly about the importance of the cause, and thanking the committee for all their hard work, Lornagh gave the signal for the short video to be shown on the huge screen. It was just three minutes long but the effect was profound. The short film portrayed more about the charity and its workings than any speech. By the time it came to an end, many women in the room were wiping away a surreptitious tear.

'I'd like to finish,' Lornagh concluded, 'by thanking all of you for joining us this evening in aid of such an important cause, and I hope you all have a wonderful night.' She stepped down to polite clapping and an escalating noise level, as people got stuck into the delicious first course. Relieved that her speech was over, Lornagh slipped back to her seat beside Sean and threw herself into enjoying the rest of what promised to be a fabulous night.

Dinner was superb. The lobster and prawn mousse with chilli, coriander and lemongrass was followed by a choice of either rack of lamb or wild Irish salmon and rounded off by a mouth-watering summer-berries roulade or chocolate tart with *crème fraîche*.

Across the room, Lornagh saw her mother enjoying herself thoroughly with Lawrence and Mauricio, shrieks of laughter coming from their table.

Catching her eye, Simon shot her a venomous look from his table, but Lornagh was far too happy to care. She was pleased to see he had a new companion and hoped they would be happy, although somehow she doubted it.

It seemed no time at all before coffee was being served and members of the committee began doing the rounds of the tables, selling raffle tickets which, happily, were in great demand.

It was time for the auction. Martin O'Kelly, the debonair auctioneer, was ushered up to the podium. Martin was a pro and swiftly commanded everybody's attention as they settled down to the real business at hand.

'Lot number one!' began Martin. 'Your very own Beetle! Money won't buy you love. But it will go to a very good cause if you'd like to have this little beauty sitting outside your front door.' The bright blue Volkswagen

Beetle had been donated by a well-known philanthropic property developer whose consummate generosity was legendary.

Bidding opened swiftly at £5,000 and went up rapidly to £25,000 amidst gasps of delight from the excited audience. In the end the car went to a high-profile solicitor to howls of excitement from her table.

Next to be auctioned was a holiday consisting of two first-class tickets to the Caribbean island of Aruba and a week's stay at a fabulous villa to sleep four. After frenzied bidding, the holiday went to the extremely sexy-looking man sitting in between Pascal and Melissa Sheehan. Although he looked disturbingly familiar, no one could put a name to the face. As he sauntered up to collect the voucher for his prize, more than one woman noted the lean, carefully honed physique and took in the raw sensuality of his smile.

'Who *is* that?' muttered Angela to Lawrence. 'He reminds me of Gabriel Byrne.'

'No idea, Angela. But I wouldn't mind finding out.'

'And now, ladies and gentlemen!' Martin O'Kelly continued. 'Lot number three, a very fine landscape generously donated by Lady Sheldon, from her late husband's collection.'

Oh, just get *on* with it would you, Simon thought as his mouth twitched nervously.

'Who will open the bidding at £500? £500 please? Yes, from the gentleman at the back! £500. Thank you!'

Simon looked on with horror as a well-known financier opened the bidding. Christ! If he was interested, Simon wouldn't stand a chance. He began to break out in a cold sweat. Quickly he nodded in the auctioneer's direction. A girl on the floor picked up his bid and raised a flag. '£1,000! From the gentleman on my right. Thank you, sir!

'£2,000! £2,500!' Simon quailed. He had never expected such competition. But people were getting into the swing of things and the bidding was hotting up.

'£3,000!' Simon twisted in his chair to see a glamorous business woman put up her hand confidently.

'£3,500 on my right! Thank you, madam.' Simon nearly hit Alexi as she put her bid in, drawing appreciative titters from the table.

'Put your hand down, you silly bitch!' he hissed. 'You're raising the price.'

'Isn't zat vat ve're supposed to be doing? This is charity, no?' Alexi was indignant.

'Yes, but *I'm* buying. Just shut up! You're only a bloody skivvy.' Simon was livid.

'£4,000? £4,000, anyone? For this fine example of Impressionism.'

Interest finally seemed to have peaked as bidders paused, waiting with bated breath.

Simon's hand went up again.

'£4,000! To the gentleman on my right. Any other bids? £4,000 on my right, going, going ...' Bang went the gavel. 'Gone! For £4,000 to the gentleman on my right. Well done, sir!'

As Simon signed the purchase docket he breathed a sigh of relief. For a moment or two there he thought he was in trouble. There was no way he could have afforded to go up against the serious money that sat around the room. He had taken a chance and he had won. The Le Souquet was his. Relief swept over him in tides. He would be a millionaire now, for sure. Once the word was out about the origin of the great work of art, galleries would be clamouring for it. Alexi was kissing him in a frenzy of excitement.

'Oh, for God's sake stop slobbering all over me!' Simon snapped, confident again now he had his acquisition. He didn't need the Alexis of this world anymore. From now on it would be 'top drawer' or nothing at all. He sneaked a glance over in Lornagh's direction, only to find her canoodling with Sean O'Rourke. Simon almost threw up.

'Good evening! Mr Sullivan, I believe?' Simon was caught unawares by the croaky, aristocratic voice. Looking up, he saw the wrinkled face of Lady Sheldon leaning over him. 'I'm on Angela Lemass's table tonight, such fun!'

'Oh, er, yes! How do you do?' Simon stood up.

'I must say, young man, I *am* impressed by your generosity!'

'Not at all,' Simon demurred, gratified by the acknowledgement of his spending spree.

'My late husband would have been delighted!' she boomed.

'He, er, must have had quite an eye.'

'Couldn't get him away from his wretched paintings! Used to drive me mad, bless him, with his "masterpieces" as he called them; always said he was wasted in the House of Lords. Just leave me to my forgeries, he used to laugh!'

'I beg your pardon?' Simon wasn't following her.

'It was his pastime d'you see?' she wheezed. 'Copying famous paintings, like Le Souquet's *Sunrise over Pont Neuf*. He had hundreds of them! Impressionists were his favourite. He could sit for hours painting them. I'd never have believed it would go for so much! Damned generous of you, young man. All in a good cause though, what?' And, having slapped him heartily on the back, Lady Sheldon strode back across the floor to Angela's table, where she proceeded to get well and truly stuck in to the *crème de menthe frappés* that were circulating.

Simon felt sick. It wasn't possible. The old bat must be off her trolley. Perhaps she had dreamed it, or her husband hadn't wanted to tell her the truth? Didn't want her to know how much his paintings were *really* worth. His stomach clenched in fright. But she said he had hundreds of them …

'Are you all right, darlink?' Alexi was unaware of the complexities of the situation.

'Oh, just shut up, will you?' Simon threw back his chair and headed for the gents'. When he pushed the door open, the place was quiet, apart from two burly figures who stood talking to each other at the back. Simon didn't like the way they looked at him. Well, fuck them! He didn't care now. Slapping some ice-cold water on his face, he sucked in a shuddering breath. He would keep calm. There must be something he could do. He would demand his money back. Simon groaned at the thought of spending £4,000 on a copy. He would say he'd been drunk, that was it! And that Alexi had shoved his hand up by mistake and the auctioneer must have taken it as a bid. But then his heart sank. This was a charity do, for heaven's sake. It would go down like a cup of cold sick if he asked for his money back. And all those stuck-up, wealthy, Dublin 4 types would turn up their supercilious noses at him and laugh behind their Turnbull & Asser shirtsleeves. He might as well take out an ad in *The Irish Times* saying, 'Simon Sullivan is a stingy fucker.' And as for Lornagh! Well, she and that boyfriend of hers would have a field day. No, there was only one thing to do and that was grin and bear it. Walking weakly back to his table, where Alexi turned her back on him to talk to a media millionaire, Simon proceeded to get well and truly smashed.

People were beginning to table hop when the salsa dancers, the supporting act for the first 15 minutes or so, hit the floor. Accompanied by their own musicians, the three Brazilian girls and one man took to the floor to giddy applause. Scantily clad in their shimmering outfits, they writhed and wriggled around the floor before the raptly attentive crowd. When they invited various guests around the room to join in with them, there were shrieks of excitement. Rowena O'Neill, a gorgeous model, waved at Lornagh as she was whisked on to the floor by Romaldo, the lead male dancer, and hooted with laughter as her good-looking husband, Charlie, executed a mean shimmy with one of the Brazilian girls.

Sean, who had been chatting to a fellow eminent architect, caught Lornagh by the hand as she passed by and pulled her onto the floor for a twirl.

As the sexy tempo filled the room, one of the dancers, a gorgeous coffee-skinned creature, shimmered over to Simon and tried to entice him from the table and onto the floor to yells of encouragement from his table. In his cantankerous state of mind, Simon imagined they were sniggering at him and that this girl was trying to make an even bigger fool of him. 'Leave me alone, you stupid nigger!' he snapped, snatching his hand back.

The girl promptly slapped his face and let rip with a stream of Portuguese invective. Before he could stop himself, Simon promptly slapped her back. By now, the people at other nearby tables were looking his way, although no one yet realised quite what had happened. The leading salsa dancer, Romaldo, who was a little snake-hipped fellow with mean, darting eyes, heard the commotion and came over to see what was going on.

When his indignant dancer explained and pointed at Simon, Romaldo socked him on the nose. Unhinged with anger, Simon went for him. Suddenly, he felt his arms pinned behind him. 'Where I come from,' said a resoundingly Dublin accent, 'we pick on people our own size!' Eddie's men felt it was time to get involved.

Simon looked into the face of the man he had seen in the gents', while his companion held him back. 'Oh yeah?' Simon spat. 'Well, you should know! No one could get tired of kicking a face like that!' It was the last thing he said for quite a while, because the second blow that landed on his nose smashed it up against the side of his face. Simon collapsed, but not before he stuck a fork into the other oaf's bulging thigh.

'Hey, hey, that's enough,' called someone, as Alexi screamed, ''Elp, 'elp!'

The band took to the stage just in time.

The dance floor became a mass of writhing bodies, as people eagerly claimed their partners and proceeded to dance the night away.

Glancing around the room, Carol Dalton noticed Dr Gerald Stevens sitting alone: his fiancée, Candice, had persuaded Pascal to take to the floor. Carol spotted her opportunity. It was now or never. Walking purposefully towards his table, she tapped him on the shoulder.

'Why, Carol! What a pleasure to see you,' he exclaimed, standing up to greet her, 'and looking so well, if I may say.' His eyes roamed over her appreciatively. 'How about a dance?'

'Not right now, Gerald,' she looked at him playfully. 'I'd much rather join you for a drink, if that's all right?'

'I'd be delighted. Allow me.' Gerald gestured for her to sit down and filled a glass with champagne.

'Cheers!' he said jovially, clinking his glass with hers. 'Is tonight all business, or can you indulge in a little pleasure?' He looked at her speculatively.

'Well, *this* certainly isn't business, is it?' Carol countered, flirtatiously.

'I hope not,' Gerald replied, flattered. 'Er, that TV interview with me you're working on: any idea of when the actual programme is planned to go ahead?'

'Won't be long now, I should think. Call me on Monday and we'll set up a date.'

'Great.' Gerald sat back in his chair, anticipating the unparalleled publicity for his ever-expanding practice.

'There is one thing,' Carol paused meaningfully, 'you might find even more interesting to consider …'

'Oh?' Gerald looked hopeful. 'What's that?'

'This.' Carol smacked the early edition of the following day's Sunday tabloid in front of him. 'Why don't you take a look? It's hard to miss.'

Gerald looked bemused as he picked up the paper, then paled visibly as the lurid headline accosted him: 'Goldfinger Stevens: the slimy gynae who preys on young girls – an exclusive exposé by Carol Dalton.'

'I think you'll find it makes riveting reading, Gerald.'

'You vicious bitch,' he sputtered. 'This is utter libel! I'll sue the pants off you.'

'I don't *think* so, Gerald. It's only libel if it's fabricated. Every word in that article is true. I should know. Me, Carol Doherty; one of your earlier victims, I imagine. Whose pregnancy you so conveniently terminated without my knowledge. You must be some sick bastard to dispose of your own baby.' Carol rose to leave. 'Don't worry though, it should generate plenty of publicity – but not the kind you were expecting.' Leaving him speechless with horror, she walked calmly away.

Michael had spotted his chance. A little distraction was just what was needed. While Alexi was attending to Simon, Michael picked up a glass of red wine and tipped it neatly over the thug who was rubbing his leg where Simon had jabbed him with the fork. The man looked up in rage. 'Hey! Who the fuck did that?'

'It was him!' Michael pointed deftly to Mauricio, who had come to see what the commotion was about.

'Why you …' Livid with anger, Jimbo picked up a crystal jug of chocolate sauce and poured it slowly over Mauricio's immaculate white Armani evening suit.

'My suit!' Mauricio howled. 'You animal! This is an Armani original!'

'What on earth is going on?' Lawrence caught up with Mauricio.

'Eet was heem!' Mauricio wailed. 'That animal 'as destroyed me!'

'Bloody bully!' Lawrence, joining in the fun, grabbed one of the long branches from his intricately designed floral arrangements. Suitably attired in an eighteenth-century style ruffled white shirt, he jumped gracefully onto the table from where he wielded the branch like a sword, striking an impressive fencing pose and yelling '*En garde!*' He took a swipe at Jimbo, who immediately ducked, causing Lawrence to inadvertently lift the carefully arranged toupé of an unsuspecting passerby. The unfortunate man patted his bald head in disbelief and immediately whirled around and tackled the chap behind him, whom he assumed to be the perpetrator of the crime.

It was time to go.

The band were bravely playing on, despite dwindling interest as more and more people hurried to see what all the hullaballoo was about. Michael was afforded the perfect opportunity to slip away unnoticed. He looked around for Felicity: she was nowhere to be seen. It was too late to get sentimental now. He had a ticket to Heathrow and then it was on to Buenos Aires – and there would be plenty of time to practise his salsa routine then.

Slipping out the French doors, Michael walked through to the marquee and, lifting a flap, slipped through it like a shadow. Making his way onto the gravel path lit by a full moon, he checked his pockets for the keys to the Aston. They were gone! He checked again. No, definitely not there. Had he possibly given them to the doorman? No, of course not. He paused for a split second. Well, he would just have to get a cab, but it wasn't part of the plan. Head down, he kept close to the wall. When he rounded the corner, he just had to walk slowly onto the road. So far, so good.

'Going somewhere, darling?' Michael was prodded with something cold against his back; it felt uncannily like a gun.

'Flick! I was just getting a breath of air. I –'

'Save it, sweetheart! Just keep walking, or, believe me, I won't hesitate to use this.' She poked the pistol angrily into his back.

'Flick! Wait, what's going on?'

'The very question I would have liked to ask you – you bastard. If Ivanka and Alexi hadn't kept me informed, I don't like to think of the mess you'd be dragging us into. Very tacky, Michael. You disappoint me.'

Just then there was the sound of running feet behind them and a shout.

'There he is! Quick! Don't let him get away!' It was two of Eddie's henchmen, Jimbo and Deke. Having escaped from the fray, they were now terrified of facing the consequences if they let Eddie's prey escape.

'Oh fuck!' Michael whispered. 'Run, Flick! Hurry! Or

they'll come after you!' Realising he was done for, Michael felt he could play the caring husband in defeat.

'Shut up!' hissed Felicity, as a screech of tyres sent gravel spraying in front of them, and to his amazement Michael saw his dark-blue convertible Aston pull up and the passenger door being flung open.

'Get in! Move!' As Felicity shoved him into the back seat and jumped in after him, Alexi took off like a rocket, scattering bewildered doormen and tourists like scared chickens.

'Where are we going?' Michael was incredulous.

'I hardly think you're in a position to ask questions,' Felicity said, chillingly.

Inside, the ballroom resembled the great fight scene from *The Quiet Man*.

Chairs were thrown, tables turned over and one bright spark had even managed to climb up the curtains where he proceeded to holler like Tarzan before jumping onto the crowd below.

Angela, a veteran of some of the most notorious night-club punch-ups in Europe in her heyday, landed a well-aimed kick to the backside of a man tackling Lawrence. Not to be outdone, Lady Sheldon charged into the middle of the fray 'hallooing' loudly, and Mauricio's opponent found himself pinned back by a pair of iron forearms that, in days gone by, had brought tears to the eyes of many a male member of the Ward Union Hunt.

Pascal, who had been in the gents' trying to put an urgent call through to Jacko, arrived back at the *mêlée*; frantically searching for Melissa, he saw her being held back by Eddie. Pascal dived under whatever tables remained unturned and proceeded to crawl through the heaving mass of bodies in a vain attempt to reach her.

Suddenly an earth-shattering crack ripped through the air.

The shot that rang out stunned the room to silence. A gravelly voice was clearly heard to say, 'Let's go, lads!'

Melissa never heard it. Escaping from Eddie's clutches, she had immediately jumped onto one of the remaining tables, fork poised to stick into the hand of one of the thugs who appeared to be trying to tear off Pascal's new hair. The ricocheting bullet bounced off the wall before finding her neck. Unnoticed, she fell to the ground, where she lay quietly, blood collecting in a pool around her head.

EPILOGUE

Lornagh sat on the balcony of the beautiful Hotel Santa Caterina which overlooked the spectacular Amalfi coastline, and gazed out at the azure sea.

Sean had whisked her away immediately after the unbelievable turn of events at the ball that had left everybody reeling. Despite the uproar on the night, they had managed to raise over £100,000 for the charity and, as Carol Dalton of TV 2000 had been there to cover the evening, the cameras had got more than they bargained for.

The subsequent publicity was proving even more beneficial for St Rita's, and already people were clamouring for tickets to next year's event. Overnight, it seemed, St Rita's had become the most fashionable charity in the country.

Lornagh smiled as Sean wandered out to join her, settling a bottle of champagne and two glasses on the old wrought-iron table. 'I thought a little aperitif before dinner might go down well,' he said, sitting down opposite her and filling the glasses.

Lornagh looked at him as he stretched out his long, tanned legs and ran a hand through his hair. They had had an amazing week here just relaxing and exploring the surrounding coast, and Lornagh would have been happy never to go home, but it was their last night and they would just have to make the most of it.

'Here, you might need this.' Sean pushed a folded paper napkin over to her.

'What for?'

'Open it and see.'

Lornagh unfolded the napkin slowly.

'Darling Lornagh,' she read. 'Please let me take you off the shelf. I promise to love and cherish you for the rest of your life. Sean.'

When she had finished crying, of course she said yes.

Simon sat shivering in his apartment despite the still balmy weather Dublin was enjoying. He was afraid to budge. The Special Branch had called to interview him on three separate occasions and he had never been so terrified in his entire life.

They seemed to be under the impression that he had masterminded some sort of bizarre money-laundering operation and, despite their gruelling interrogations, he had been able to tell them nothing. Going over the company accounts, they had uncovered some suspicious movement of funds to and from various offshore accounts but, strangely, any discrepancies appeared to have been rectified; and the figures, despite some round-about routes, all balanced perfectly. He genuinely couldn't explain anything. Eventually they had finished questioning him but had warned that he would be under constant surveillance. Simon shivered again. Not even his 40-denier Wolford opaques could keep him warm.

Melissa was in deep shock.

Having made a full and suitably dramatic recovery, she now sat in Dr Edwards's surgery to have her postoperative stitches removed. She tried to digest the astounding news. 'You're quite, quite sure?'

'Absolutely! They ran a battery of tests on you when you were taken in; it's routine. You were unconscious for most of them.'

'How, um, how far along am I?' she attempted, feeling faint already. This could be disastrous.

'Oh, early days yet, I'd say about four or five weeks according to these results.'

Melissa blanched, and clutched the arm of her chair. A disturbing thought was surfacing in her mind.

'Are you all right, Melissa?' Dr Edwards was concerned.

'Oh, er, yes! It's just, Ay've had quite a shock, that's all.'

'Of course you have. Here, have a drink of water. I'll

bet you can't wait to get back to Pascal to tell him the news.' Dr Edwards smiled warmly.

Regaining her composure, Melissa thought quickly. She simply wouldn't tell him. Or her, if it was a little girl. No, as long as she lived, Melissa vowed, she would never tell her firstborn he or she had been conceived at a caravan show, never mind in an actual caravan. It simply wasn't the right start one needed in life!

Pascal Sheehan was not only one of the richest men in Ireland, he was now also one of the happiest.

After three days in intensive care, where Melissa had been critical, and he had been warned to prepare for the worst, she had miraculously turned the corner. Pascal, who had been desperate with worry, nearly passed out with relief when they had told him.

'She's incredibly lucky,' the nice general surgeon had told him. 'Another half a millimetre and the artery would have been severed. As it was, it was touch and go. But she's going to pull through.'

Pascal had wept with relief; and the surgeon, who was used to overcome relatives, patted him on the back and suggested he had a stiff drink to celebrate.

Two days later, the same man had nearly fainted himself, when an anonymous bank draft landed on his desk in favour of the hospital board. It covered, amongst other things, the expense of the new research wing that the hospital trustees had projected would require funds taking, at the very least, five years to raise.

Two weeks later, Melissa was released from hospital. She was as good as new: apart from a tiny scar on her neck, which she had decided would prove the perfect opportunity for a quick trip to her plastic surgeon – she had felt a neck lift coming on for a few months now and this would provide the perfect excuse.

Pascal heard her key in the door and leapt up to greet her. She still looked a little pale, and her frailty made her even more precious to him.

'Sweetheart! How did the doctor say you were doing?' Pascal hugged her to him.

'Pascal,' she said firmly. 'I think you'd better sit down. There's something I have to tell you.'

Melissa wasn't the only one in a state of shock.

Michael Moriarty could hardly take in what was happening to him. Somehow, Felicity had known all along what he had been planning. The result was something he would never in his wildest dreams have envisaged. After Alexi had driven them to a secret location deep in the west of Ireland, Michael had listened in rapidly growing disbelief as his wife had told him in no uncertain terms just what he was going to do.

The misappropriated funds, she said, were to be immediately reinstated. When Michael had spluttered denial and feigned innocence, Felicity had produced the evidence gathered so efficiently by Ivanka. When he had finally admitted to his plans, and told Felicity of the ten million he now owed which had driven him to this wild plan of escape, she had merely snorted.

'You think I didn't know that, Michael?' She had leaned in towards him, still wielding the gun, as he shrank back petrified. 'Ten million's the least of your problems. I can sort that out.'

'But what about Eddie? He'll come after me!' He was frantic now. 'For God's sake, Felicity, he'll kill me! He'll kill all of us – you don't know what he's like!'

'Oh, don't I?' Felicity had sneered. 'Right now, his chumps are probably chasing two of my girls, who have very obligingly taken that flight to Buenos Aires you so thoughtfully booked.'

'I don't understand,' Michael bleated.

'You never have, darling. We're staying put here for a few days until all the fuss dies down. Then, my little man, you have a lot of making up to do.'

'Anything, Flick. I promise you. Anything you want.'

Michael's marriage had somehow undergone a seismic power shift.

He was disturbed to discover he found it quite a turn on.

The next day, Felicity phoned a number procured with great difficulty by her girls.

'Yeah.' The gravelly voice was unmistakable.

'Eddie, this is Felicity Moriarty. No doubt you're familiar with a few of my girls. The Grovesbury Club ring any bells? Good. Here's the deal. I've sorted that little matter my husband allowed to get so out of hand. You'll find all the money's exactly where it should be. *Of course* I can prove it. You can check the accounts now. Yes, Monday would be fine. It's best you deal with me from now on. I look forward to doing business with you.'

Gabbana had been behaving strangely. She had taken to rearranging the cushions from the couch in Melissa's bedroom and bringing them into the wardrobe where she would sit for hours and refuse to come out. She allowed nobody near her and Dolce was beginning to pine. Melissa took her straight to the vet where, after a brief examination, it was pronounced that she was about to give birth any minute.

'That's impossible!' shrieked Melissa.

'Well, you didn't have her spayed, Melissa. I warned you.'

'But Dolce had his vasectomy! Gabby is *never* exposed to other dogs.'

'Well, someone's got at her.' The vet tried to hide his amusement.

'Oh, no!' Melissa paled, a horrible thought coming to her. 'This is *terrible*. This is a catastrophe. It'll kill her. It's that vile pitbull creature. He was always sniffing around her.'

Twenty minutes later, after a successful canine

caesarean section, Gabby came around from the anaesthetic and sniffed her new offspring eagerly, licking them thoroughly from top to toe. Dolce stood by wagging his tail, paternal instinct happily overcoming the unusual appearance of the pups, who squirmed and nuzzled up to their proud mother.

'Congratulations, Melissa,' said the vet, smiling. 'I can't say I've ever come across a pug/pitbull crossbreed before.' He was just in time to catch her as she fainted.

The wedding was in November and was hailed as the most beautiful of the decade.

The bride, radiant in a figure-hugging, white satin creation trimmed with white fur, carried a bouquet of white winter roses trailing with ivy. Gliding to the altar of Donnybrook church on the arm of a ridiculously proud Lawrence, she was given away with feigned regret to the handsome groom.

The church was crowded to overflowing; besides the guests, plenty of curious onlookers had huddled in the back, anxious for a glance at Dublin's most glamorous young couple.

A succession of candles lined the aisle, and every pew had an exquisite floral arrangement.

Melissa was there, heavily pregnant in a Versace maternity outfit, and Pascal stood at her side, bursting with pride.

Angela, who had taken to her role as 'mother of the

bride' with relish, looked magnificent in ankle-length chiffon and dabbed her eyes theatrically whenever anyone was looking.

After the ceremony was over, the guests followed an ecstatic Mr and Mrs O'Rourke outside where eager photographers jostled for shots.

Jesus and Maria congratulated themselves on a job well done as Pascal and Melissa rushed over to where they had been minding the dogs. Dolce and Gabbana were sporting white fluffy dog coats and were accompanied by their extraordinary looking puppies, who had big white ribbons tied around their necks. Lornagh and Sean were taking one of the puppies just as soon as they got back from their honeymoon. Pascal had insisted on keeping the other one for himself. He had fallen totally in love with him and called him Lucky, as a reminder of all they had come through in the terrifying kidnap ordeal. Lucky now accompanied Pascal everywhere he went, growling protectively at anyone who came near his adored master.

To the delight of the crowd, Sean scooped Lornagh into his arms and carried her off to the waiting car that would take them back to the reception in Angela's house on Grovesbury Road.

Eva looked at the spread of the wedding in her favourite society magazine and felt quite sentimental. She and her nice widower Frank had, along with the rest of the country, watched the spectacle at the ball on television in amazement. Later, she had followed the unfolding sequence of events in the papers with disbelief, feeling horribly concerned for Pascal. It was, therefore, with genuine happiness that she greeted Pascal's news that all was well, and he was finally to become a father.

It made it easier for her to tell him her own bit of good news.

'You're what?' he had asked, incredulously.

'I'm getting married. In Rome, next week.'

'But ...'

'Don't you dare say it ... I'm only 44! His name's Frank and he's a rather, ahem, handsome widower and, well, he loves me and I love him. You know you'll always be special to me, don't you, Paccy?'

'And you to me, love. Nobody deserves happiness more than you do, Eva. Frank's a lucky man.'

'That's what I told him.'

Carol was doing what she did best.

Sitting at her lap-top, she was gleaning whatever information she could about that devastatingly attractive criminal Eddie 'the Shark' McEntee.

Since the infamous night of the ball, her career had orbited and several high-profile TV networks had approached her with very alluring offers.

For the moment she was sitting tight. Her flawless instincts told her she was on to something very exciting.

She had achieved her life's ambition of exposing Dr

Gerald Stevens, who had been suspended from practising medicine and was under investigation from the authorities. Now, she had more important fish to fry.

Carol had caught the whole spectacle on camera. The event had subsequently been syndicated worldwide. Rumour had it that Eddie was behind the startling kidnap and attempted murder (albeit accidental) of Melissa Sheehan. Not only that, but Carol had *danced* with him on the night. He had bought an exotic holiday to the Caribbean Island of Aruba in the charity auction, and Carol had actually managed to interview him on camera, not realising for a moment who he was.

Holding her close on the floor later as they danced, he had invited her to join him on the island. Handing her a mobile number, he had told her to call him if she was interested.

Interested! Carol had never been so intrigued in all her life. What a story that would make. She could envisage the film rights already.

Sitting at her desk, she knew she should be cautious. This was no time for frivolity. But every instinct in her was telling her to go for it.

It had, she reminded herself, absolutely nothing to do with the way her insides had melted when he whispered in that gravelly voice how attractive he found her.

This would be the mother of all reporting coups if she could pull it off. She was young and attractive, for heaven's sake! She had wasted enough of her life on that monster Gerald Stevens. If she could handle that, she could handle anything.

Reaching for Eddie's number she flicked open her mobile phone and, taking a deep breath, punched in the digits.

'Yeah?' The raw sensuality of the voice that answered sent shivers down her spine. Eddie was definitely her kind of prey. But who exactly, asked a tiny voice inside her, would be hunting whom?

ACKNOWLEDGEMENTS

This book would not have been written without the help, encouragement (and when necessary, brute force!) of the following people. Heartfelt thanks to you all:

To Sharon Barnes, who introduced herself as the 'Wicked Witch of the South West', for making editing *Charity* an enlightening, challenging and always rewarding experience. It's good to know I can still make people curse!

To Edwin Higel, for an unerring instinct to provide encouragement, humour and lunch, when a needy 'first timer' is about to stall. And to everyone at New Island, particularly Ciara Considine, Joseph Hoban and Fidelma Slattery, for making my introduction to publishing so painless. Working with you all has been a pleasure and a privilege.

To my sister Mary McGrath, thankfully just around the corner for constant support, hilarity and liquid refreshment!

To my brothers, Dermot and Donogh O'Brien, whose transatlantic emails were always a welcome reinforcement.

To my aunts, Sisters Mary and Nora O'Brien of the Sacred Heart Order – no thanks can ever be adequate for your unceasing prayers on my behalf. Grateful thanks also for prayers to Sister Mary Joseph of St Joseph's Carmelite Convent, and to the Sisters of the Convent of St Clare.

To my niece, Caroline McGrath, for house-sitting, dog-sitting and generally being wonderful!

To my cousin Dr Anne 'Dentist to the Stars' MacGregor of London, who makes sure the smile stays in place in more ways than one!

To my former colleagues at DDFH&B advertising for 'the most fun you can have with your clothes on'. Old copywriters never die, they just disappear to lunch ...

To Carmelo Vadala, for creative Italian translation!

To the dearest and most delightful of friends any girl could be blessed with: Ansy McDevitt, Mary Kavanagh, Dickie Jeffares (never was there a more rewarding reason to attend boarding school), and Caroline Bergin. It's been a roller-coaster ride of highs, lows and unceasing laughter – but that's another story ...

To Orla O'Kelly, who effortlessly combines inimitable sound-engineering skills with equally inspiring counselling talents – all in the one session! The laughs will never be edited out!

To Kate Thompson, most generous of spirits, who selflessly provided encouragement, support and inspiration while turning out her own sublimely addictive novels.

To Eileen Colquhoun for wisdom, encouragement and resounding common sense. The visits are nothing if not entertaining!

To solicitors David and Mark Bergin of O'Connor

Bergin, for invaluable advice and support throughout the good times and the not so good. Your sensitivity, humour and kindness are appreciated more than you can know.

To my adorable 'rescued dogs' Bonnie and Harvey, for insisting on my daily exercise and reminding me to stop and smell the roses, the rocks, the lamp posts and things unmentionable! Who, I wonder, really rescued whom?

And, of course, to Sean – who made it all possible in the first place.

I am hopelessly indebted to you all, and if, in my frazzled state of mind, I have omitted anyone – lunch is on me!